Copyright © 2025 by Torie Gaylord

Cover Design by Miblart

www.miblart.com

First edition August 2025

ISBN 9798992238938 (Paperback)

ISBN 9798992238921 (E-Book)

Also by Torie Gaylord

Three Seconds
Three Seconds and Gone
Blink and You Miss It

Watch for more at toriegwriting.com.

To my biggest supporter - you have given me the courage to hold true to the ideas for this series, told me to push aside my doubts, and helped me embrace my weirdness.

BLINK
AND
YOU
MISS IT

TORIE GAYLORD

Chapter 1

Looking out the sliding glass doors from my couch with a warm cup of tea in hand, I still couldn't get used to the new surroundings. There was lush, green grass swaying in the breeze for as far as the eye could see with plenty of flowers joining the grass in its dance. Rolling hills extended for miles. Lou let out a content sigh as he joined me with his mug, taking a sip.

It had maybe been a week since we've been in this new world and we still had no idea where we were at. We knew for sure we were in the countryside given there weren't too many other houses around and there were quite a few places that looked like a farm, based on the various structures on the properties. Whenever we ventured on a walk or a drive, we didn't encounter too many people, but we also hadn't made it into the city yet. On those times outside, we came across quite a few castle ruins with their grey stones being overrun by leafy vines. It rained often enough to keep us inside my house more days than not, but I won't complain about that. *This house has traveled more than most people do*, I chuckled to myself listening to the soft patter of rain against the windows. Rainy days are just what we need to recover from the craziness we left behind.

The device Lou and I created to transport us here was sitting out in the open on the coffee table in front of us. There was no threat of Warrick here to steal it away from us, and since we haven't made too many friends (or any at all), it wasn't like we had to worry about visitors asking us too many questions. Given that we weren't facing any threats, Lou and I decided we wanted to hang low to let our wounds heal. We weren't just spending all this time lazing around the couch or going for leisurely strolls in the countryside. We started adding notes around the code we used to get us to this new world to the file my dad had to help us keep track of the worlds we jumped to. On top of that, we've decided to look into whether or not this little device of ours needs time to recharge before it can be used again.

"What's the plan for date night, Val? Staying couped up in the humble abode some more or are we actually going to make it into the city?"

I finished swallowing my mouthful of tea, taking some extra time just to mess with Lou a little bit more because I could tell he was getting antsy. "I was thinking we could have this one last evening in the house before we take our date nights out on the town. By the way, it's your turn to put something together."

I got a kiss on my forehead signaling his agreement as he got up to head into the kitchen. Not only has this time been good for us to heal from Warrick's wounds, but it's also helped us move at a slower pace in our relationship free from any outside pressure, namely Warrick (clearly he's left a big impression on us as that's the main reason we're staying holed up in these four walls).

I looked over at Lou who was digging through the fridge, admiring my view when his head popped up, "We're going to have to leave sooner rather than later, we don't have a whole lot left in here."

"I was afraid of that, but we should have enough to put together something for us to eat tonight," I left my cozy spot on the couch to join him.

He took a step back so I could get a full view of the fridge's contents, "I'm starting to think you want to stay in this house forever."

I ignored his comment while I took in what was in front of me – a whole lot of nothing. There were a few sauce jars scattered in the fridge amongst a couple of beer bottles. I took a look in the freezer to find it about as full as the fridge. Sighing, I faced Lou, "Looks like you get to take me out on the town after all."

He gave me a lazy grin, "Guess you'll finally have to get out of those sweats."

I rolled my eyes, holding back laughter, "What time are we leaving?"

"Soon? I'm honestly starving and we could use the time to go check this place out."

I nodded my head and went upstairs to get dressed. Even though we had basically been living together this entire time in the new world, I still wanted to look good on this date. Plus, it wouldn't hurt to make a good impression on the locals either.

I put on some music then got to work getting myself ready. This was the first time in a long time I had actually been excited for a date. I could tell by seeing the giddiness reflected in my green eyes while I swiped the finishing touches of mascara on my eyelashes. I took a step back to admire myself in the mirror: the natural makeup bringing out the color in my eyes, loose beach waves, a leather jacket, classic white v-neck, darker jeans, and some black booties to round out the look. I made my way back downstairs to find Lou not too far off from matching my outfit, except his white shirt was replaced with a dark grey one, his hair messy, and he was in a pair of casual, worn brown boots.

I crossed my arms and jokingly said, "Didn't realize there was a specific dress code for this date."

Humor danced in his grey eyes, "No? Glad you got it figured out anyway. Let's go."

He led the way to his car so he could open the passenger door for me. Once we were both settled, Lou drove us the only way we hadn't gone yet – towards the city. It was still the afternoon judging by the sun's position on the horizon, but evening would be upon us soon.

As buildings started taking form around us, I marveled at how almost every one was made of red bricks. There were buildings of vibrant colors sprinkled in between or stacked on top of the red of the bricks – blues, yellows, pinks, greens, you name it. Many places had flowerpots overflowing with various types of flowers around the outside adding even more color. Apartments topped the line of businesses down what looked like the main street, their balconies lined with even more of the overflowing flowerpots. While we hadn't seen very many people around the countryside, the opposite was true for here. Restaurants, stores, and apartment balconies were teeming with smiling faces, laughter, and loud voices. I rolled down my window taking in the smell of fresh grass mingling with the fragrant perfume from the flowers. I was surprised at being happy to see other people, but it did help that I no longer had to look over my shoulder.

As Lou was turning into a small parking garage situated under more residences, a huge gothic cathedral came into view, looming over the rest of the buildings on the street. There were many pinnacles reaching towards the sky with gargoyles looking out over the city. It was hauntingly beautiful with something drawing me in while pushing me away at the same time. I didn't have long to look at it before Lou got us in the confines of the parking garage, but the beauty of us staying in this world for a while is that I'll have plenty of time to explore it.

"Ready?" Lou asked as he shifted the car into park.

I smiled, "Let's go."

We got out of the car and joined hands to head into the streets in search of food. I didn't realize how hungry I was until the smell of something delicious wafted out from the various restaurants and bars.

Lou led us into the nearest bar, and also the most packed. As we walked up, I took in the building – it was situated on a corner, curving around the bend so half of it was situated on the main street. It had a mix of red and black paint coating its outside with the name of the place hiding behind a mini jungle of ferns and vines. There was a spattering of outdoor seating lining the side of the bar situated on the main street marked by a simple wrought-iron fence. Once inside, I was surprised at how packed this space was. It was bigger than it looked on the outside, people filling almost every inch of space. There were a lot of bar-height tables and chairs scattered throughout the middle of the room, booths lining the edges. You would think there was some big event going on, but there was nothing. No sports on the TV, no live music (the only music coming from speakers scattered throughout the space), just lots of alcohol and food. The walls were covered with pictures and artwork, not leaving much room for anything else to be added. An empty stage stood on the far opposite wall and looked forgotten judging by the layer of dust coating its surfaces. From what I could tell, the walls were wood paneling, giving the space a more cozy, rustic vibe. My head slowly turned towards the main bar area, a towering wall covered in various liquor bottles of all shapes and sizes. There was one bartender hustling around to fill the onslaught of orders being yelled at him.

I was so caught up taking in my surroundings, I hadn't noticed Lou leaving my side until he came back with two beers on the verge of overflowing, "Let's find a way outside. There's no way we're getting seats in here."

I nodded my head, following behind him as he made his way to the outdoor seating. My voice still wasn't up to trying to yell thanks to the damage Warrick did and I didn't feel like testing the waters quite yet.

Once we got settled, I reached across the table to rest my hand on his arm, "I thought you wanted food."

"I won't let you starve. Food's on the way."

I raised my eyebrows, "You're the starving one."

He laughed, "Don't think I couldn't hear your stomach growling."

Our banter went back and forth for a little while longer until a server brought out a large pizza. Seeing the familiar dish brought a pang of nostalgia thinking back to Lou's restaurant. It also brought another wave of hunger, but despite that, I couldn't resist calling him out, "Didn't have enough pizza back home, had to keep it coming here?"

"You might be thinking of this as an easy way out, but I wanted our first real date to be sentimental. The first time you walked into my life we shared a pizza. Figured that would be a good way to celebrate our first time out of the house in this new place. Call me a sap, but it's the way I roll."

He got me there. While it's just pizza, the significance was not lost on me.

We dove in enjoying each other's company and the ambiance. It was a perfect night – not too hot, not too cold. Other people were in a good mood judging by the laughter around us. We watched as people walked up and down the street, arms loaded with shopping bags as they wove their way in and out of the various stores. When we finished, we ventured our way back inside to get more beers finally finding an open table tucked away in a corner offering privacy. While we were sitting there, the sun started to set which acted almost like a signal for people to head home. There was a mass exodus leaving about 20 of us in the bar. Lou and I thought this was a little odd since we're used to more people piling in these types of places at night, so we made our way to the bar to pay our tab and see if we could figure anything out.

The bartender made his way over to us, "Ready to close out your tab?"

I noticed he asked this question in an Irish accent. *Damn accents are following me everywhere now.*

Lou responded before I could dig myself out of my thoughts, "Yeah." He fished some cash out of his wallet asking, "What's up with everyone leaving?"

"Ah, I could tell you're not from around here. Not too many people like to stay out after dark. They like the safety of their homes opposed to the ruckus that happens out here."

"Interesting," Lou said not succumbing to his want of asking more questions. "Thanks for helping us out."

Before I got a chance to interject, Lou grabbed my hand to lead me out. I gave a quick wave to the bartender then turned my head so I could at least watch where I was walking. I noted the once-open apartment doors and windows were now shut tight. The sounds from earlier in the day were practically non-existent now. The stark contrast made me feel like we were transported to an entirely different place.

Lou wasted no time with getting us back to our car. I took one last glance towards the cathedral, that unsettling feeling from earlier creeping back into me. Next thing I knew, I was in the car and we were halfway back to the house.

"What's the rush? That bad of a date?" I asked, looking over at Lou.

"No. I didn't want to waste too much time hanging around there to stand out more than we already do. Something about the way that bartender talked unsettled me. I didn't care to find out why, at least not yet," he tightened his grip on the steering wheel.

"I was surprised you didn't try to get more out of him, what with the cryptic talk and all."

I didn't want to quite reveal the strange feeling I was getting from the cathedral to Lou yet. No reason to add to the tension he was already feeling that was starting to seep into what was supposed to be a romantic evening. The rest of the journey home was in silence. *What a way to end a date.*

By the time we got settled in for the night in the house, Lou was still tense. He was twirling a glass of whiskey around in his hand staring towards the blinds covering the backdoor. I poured myself a glass of wine and made my way over to join him. I put my hand on his arm, "Is this really how we're going to end our date night?"

He didn't look at me as he replied, "I can't figure it out."

It was like he didn't hear my question. I set my glass down, angling myself more towards him, "Earth to Lou? Anyone home?"

He finally snapped out of whatever daze he was in, "Sorry, Val. What were you saying?"

"Are you okay?"

Lou ran his hand through his hair, "Yeah, I just don't like the feeling that's sitting with me."

"Can you describe it?"

He looked over at me, "I feel like I'm being watched, and when that bartender mentioned that people don't like to stay out too long after dark, it made that feeling pop back up. It's just weird, doesn't sit right with me." Lou trailed off then let out a little laugh, "Here I thought we finally landed somewhere peaceful to help you find your friends."

"Hey," I said, rubbing his arm. "Let's continue to lay low to keep an eye on things to see if we can figure out what that's all about. Meanwhile, want to get back to our date or are we calling it for the night?"

Lou draped his arm around my shoulders fixing a lazy grin on his face, "Let's continue. Don't let me ruin the fun."

I grabbed my wine glass, settling in against him, "Considering we need food and don't have the most money, I think we'll need to find some jobs."

"That's what you want to talk about on our date?" he asked, laughing. "I thought I was bad."

"Hey, it worked to change the topic, didn't it?"

"I guess so."

We continued going back and forth for a little while before jumping back into the game of getting to learn more about each other's past. The effects of the wine started to set in making me tired, so I moved to take my glass into the kitchen, "Thank you for taking me out tonight. I had a good time and enjoyed your company."

Lou joined me in the kitchen holding my face in between both of his hands, "Now that has to be one of the most cliché things you've said to me in a while."

He didn't give me a chance to reply as he planted a soft kiss on my lips. We kissed each other a couple more times before separating.

"I'm going to head to bed and wouldn't mind having your company tonight."

"Don't mind if I do," Lou said not missing a beat. I raised my eyebrows at him causing him to throw his hands up in mock surrender, "You said you wanted to take this slow, so I've been respecting that. It's been a while since we've been able to share a bed."

I rolled my eyes and made my way upstairs to start getting ready for bed. Ever since we've jumped to this world, Lou's been staying in one of the guest rooms to try not to suffocate me since we suddenly went from starting our relationship to living with each other.

It's been nice having the space in my bed, but given I was feeling a little off since our journey into the city, I figured it wouldn't be a bad idea to at least be in the same room tonight. I also wanted to try and find the right time to let Lou know I noticed something was off when we were in the pub too, but now didn't quite feel like the right time. One thing I knew for sure was that I couldn't figure out what I was feeling either. There was nothing out of place, no one was acting shifty, and it wasn't like we felt a constant threat while we were there. Sometimes there were moments when I felt unsettled, yet Lou seemed fine until the last interaction with the bartender.

I jumped when I heard voices coming from the TV. I poked my head out of my bathroom to find Lou relaxing with his arms behind his head, watching a movie we've seen hundreds of times at this point. He looked over at me and smiled, "I'll get your spot warmed up, just take your time."

"Good timing. I just finished up."

I made my way over to join him and snuggled right in. Between being comfortable with Lou and having a movie on that we can quote, it didn't take me long to nod off.

"*Here you go!*" *I said cheerfully as I slid the beer down the bar to meet the hands of the customer. He reached over and placed a generous tip in the cup I kept tucked away then left. I was wiping down the wet rings left behind from the pint glasses when a familiar voice spoke softly, "I'll have whatever he just got, love, except I'll take the bottle."*

I froze trying to convince myself he wasn't here. I slowly lifted my eyes to meet the ice blue eyes that haunted me more than I cared to admit. There was no way he could be here ... out of all the places, how did he end up here? I looked around to see if the other bartender was anywhere in sight only to be disappointed. I was on my own.

I reminded myself to take deep breaths to slow my heart rate. The last thing I wanted to do was to show Warrick he had a hold over me. I made quick work of the bottle cap and placed the beer right in front of him taking special care to stay out of reach. Couldn't let him get his hands on me ... the last time I did, I ended up flirting with death.

He gave me a wink then disappeared in the crowd.

Not too long after that, Lou sauntered up to the bar ready to spend the last moments of my workday with me as I started to work on cleaning things up. I was on the closing shift, but you would never know by the number of people who are still here.

I kept my head down, talking in a low whisper just loud enough for only Lou to hear me, "He's here."

"Where?" he asked, all muscles flexing with tension.

"I don't know exactly, but somewhere in here. I can still feel it."

Lou didn't say anything else as he went into surveillance mode. He kept scanning the place trying to get a quick glimpse of Warrick. I'm sure we were going to make it back to the house and dive into this problem headfirst. Of course we would, it changes things. We would need to speed up our search, try to figure out our next stop, determine when it's time to leave. My mind was spinning at this point with everything we suddenly needed to do. I didn't even realize Lou had left his usual spot at the bar.

A blood-curdling scream rang throughout the pub derailing my train of thought. Every part of me was saying it was something Warrick did. When I looked over to where Lou should've been and didn't see him, I was worried he chose to pick a fight with Warrick and someone got caught in the cross-fire.

The next thing I know I was moving out from behind the bar with my trusty baseball bat heading towards the source of the sound. The crowd parted making it easier for me which only added to the feeling of dread pooling in my gut. By the time I reached the corner of the bar where the scream came from, I didn't find Lou or

Warrick. Instead, I found an unconscious young woman with blood
pouring out from a neck wound. The familiar unsettled feeling I
associated with the cathedral washed over me while I was looking at
her.

I crouched down trying to ask her if she was okay only to be
met with no response and a slowing pulse. I yelled out for someone
to call for help as I looked around for anyone who had signs of her
blood on their hands, literally and figuratively. Just as I was about
to turn my attention back towards the woman convinced Warrick
was the culprit, I caught sight of a man smirking at me from the
shadows with blood coating his lips. I was frozen to my spot once
again confronted with the idea of something that had been a legend
to be real. Something I very much did not want to be real.

"Val!"

I startled awake to find Lou leaning over me
concern etched in his features. When I finally opened my eyes,
Lou gave me some more space. I was breathing hard and covered
in sweat. I propped myself up into a sitting position, "What the
hell, Lou?!"

"You were screaming and thrashing around. I didn't know
what was going on," he said with the concern still written all over
his face. "Everything okay?"

I held my head in my hands trying to push away the
grogginess, "Yeah, just a nightmare."

"Care to share?"

I sighed, lifting my head to meet his gaze, "I was working in the pub we went to yesterday and everything was going just fine until Warrick showed up."

I paused to see if Lou was going to say anything. When he didn't, I continued, "You were there to meet me at the end of my shift like always and I mentioned something about Warrick being there. You decided you were going to track him down, but when you left, one of the customers screamed. I found a woman unconscious, covered in blood from a neck wound. I thought it was something Warrick did, but I didn't see him or you there, so I scanned the faces around me to see if there were any signs that gave away the attacker."

"And?" Lou asked, encouraging me to go on this time.

I looked off in the distance vividly remembering the face I found in the crowd. A young guy, probably in his early twenties with brown, curly hair and brown eyes to match staring back at me with a sinister smirk covered in blood. I let out a sigh and explained this to Lou who looked more concerned by the time I ended the story than when I had started.

"So, not only was Warrick in the pub, but so was this new villain?"

"Yeah," I shook my head to quell the nerves. "It was just a nightmare though ... nothing more than that."

I moved to get out of bed to go splash some water on my face. I needed to do something to combat the feeling of dread that carried over from my nightmare. As I was doing so, I steadied myself, placing both of my hands on either side of the sink letting the water drip down my face as I raised my gaze to meet my green eyes in the mirror. Whatever peace Lou and I had felt when we first arrived is now slowly drifting away.

"Lou?" I called out.

"What's up?"

I dried my face off and moved out of the bathroom, "There was something I forgot to mention yesterday."

That brought Lou's full attention to me, "You sure you forgot, or did you just omit?"

"You got me there."

"Care to explain or are you just going to leave me sitting on the edge of my seat?" he asked sarcastically.

"Well, did you notice the cathedral when we went into town yesterday?"

"I didn't pay too much attention, but I did notice it."

I started twisting my hands together, directing my attention down at the ground, "It didn't sit right with me."

"What do you mean? How can a building not sit right with you when you weren't anywhere near it?" Lou asked while shifting into more of a sitting position.

I looked back up at him, "I mean that just by looking at it, I got the heebie jeebies. The hairs on the back of my neck stood up and everything in my gut was telling me to get as far away from that building as possible. I felt those same feelings again when we were leaving and I looked back over at it. I don't know if I've ever had that strong of a response from a building I was technically nowhere near."

"Why didn't you tell me right away? We could've grabbed something to-go and gotten out of there."

I shrugged my shoulders responding, "I thought I was being paranoid since it was the first time we were going out. And it was honestly really nice to be out of the house for a while, I didn't want to ruin it."

"You wouldn't have ruined anything, Val. You know I appreciate honesty and I would've understood."

"I get that. It just didn't get through to me in the moment."

"Do you think your nightmare is related to whatever was affecting you?"

I made my way back to the bed, settling in before I said, "I'm not sure. I don't know how the two things can be related, but I don't think we can rule that out given we're in a new space we don't know much about."

Lou glanced over at me, "Probably a safe bet to not rule it out. What do you think the likelihood is of that bartender working again today?"

I met his stare, "We won't know for sure unless we head back over there."

"You up for that?"

"Yeah, nothing serious happened so I don't know why I wouldn't be. You don't always need to worry about me, Lou. I can take care of myself."

He rolled his eyes as he climbed out of the bed, "Let's not waste too much time. I'd like to get things rolling sooner rather than later so we have time for a longer conversation. Maybe they serve breakfast too."

I nodded my head getting out of bed to get ready.

On our way out the door, Lou made a pit stop, grabbing the device. He waved it at me before heading upstairs, "Given your nightmare, I'm going to take a few precautions and lock this bad boy up. No need to risk it falling in the wrong hands."

It wasn't a bad idea to play it safe, especially in a new area with new people. Plus, if Warrick somehow magically appeared here, we don't want to give him the chance to get his hands on the technology he's so desperately after. Lou came back downstairs and told me where to find it.

It wasn't long before we were back on the road heading into the city in the hopes of trying to figure out what's going on with that cathedral and why people don't like to stay out after the sun goes down. As we pulled into the parking garage, I found myself staring at the vibrant buildings. Everyone had their windows and doors open again, happiness oozing from every corner. *Weird ... everything changes so much once the sun goes down.* While I was lost in thought, Lou grabbed my hand guiding us over to the pub.

"I see ya came back for more," the familiar voice of the bartender called out. The accent I had heard before was definitely present again. *Good to know I wasn't imagining that.* "What can I get you two lovebirds this fine morning?"

Lou took a seat at the bar with me following his lead, "Have any breakfast offerings?"

"I'll see what I can do. Anything else?" the bartender asked while wiping down the bar top. Since there was no one else here, I assumed that motion to be habit for him. *How very stereotypical behavior.*

"I was curious about the cathedral down the street. This a pretty religious city?" Lou asked, starting to get into the real reason why we came back here as early as we did.

The bartender held up a finger signaling us to wait a moment while he went back to the kitchen to see what food they could cook up. When he returned, he was shaking his head, "You've come in before we're technically open, so the kitchen isn't too happy with me. They're making an exception, though, just this once. As for your question, nothing out of the ordinary in terms of how many people around here believe, except we don't go to that cathedral. That's more for show to draw in tourists like yourselves. I see it still has its charm."

"Any reason why it leaves us feeling unsettled?" Lou casually asked, wasting no time to get to the point.

The bartender frowned, hesitating before he responded, choosing his words very carefully, "Not many people pick up on that feeling. Let's head to that table over there."

We followed his lead. Lou and I exchanged glances as we moved over into a corner of the pub that was further away from the kitchen, windows, and anything else that might lead outside or to where other people are at. *Very reminiscent of how Lou laid everything out to me on that first day in his world.*

When we were all settled, Lou gestured for the bartender to continue.

"Explain to me what exactly you mean by feeling unsettled with the cathedral."

It was my turn to jump into the conversation, "Yesterday when we were making our way over here, I looked at the cathedral. That action alone caused all the hairs on the back of my neck to stand up and had my gut telling me to get the hell out of here." I repeated almost the same thing I told Lou, but the reactions between Lou and the bartender were very different.

"Shite, people don't usually say that about that place. Where'd you say you two were from again?"

"We didn't," Lou grumbled, jumping back into the conversation. "Yesterday you also mentioned that people don't like to stay out after dark, why is that?"

We all paused while one of the cooks brought out a couple of plates filled with eggs, steak, and potatoes. The cook shot a glare over to the bartender but didn't say anything as he headed back towards the kitchen. The bartender kept his eyes on the cook and waited until the kitchen door stopped swinging before answering Lou.

"Look, this place is practically run by a group of people who don't have the most ethical way of handling things."

"What does this have to do with night and people tucking themselves in early?" I asked.

"Have you not heard the rumors?" the bartender asked incredulously.

"To be honest with you, we haven't gotten out much since we've arrived. So, no, we haven't heard the rumors. Please, enlighten us," I said, sass filling my response.

He held up his hands, "People around here don't like to stay out too late at night because things happen. People get hurt, go missing, or wind up dead. My shift pretty much ends with enough time for me to get back home before it's too late, so I can't confirm these things. I, myself, try to not ask too many questions around here because that can get you hurt."

Getting the hint in that last sentence, I didn't urge him to explain anymore. Instead, I took this moment to start diving into my food. Yet, Lou didn't seem to get the same message.

"Is there a connection between those who rule and the cathedral?" Lou asked.

"You really don't know how to take a hint, do you?"

I felt Lou bristle a little bit, but any annoyance or anger didn't come out in his answer, "I'm a little thick-headed, so I think that one escaped me. Back to the question – is there any correlation between the two?"

The bartender sighed then lowered his voice, "All I'm going to give you is a yes. Don't ask any more questions about that."

Silence fell over us for a few moments before I chimed back in, the words falling out of my mouth before I could consider what I was asking, "You guys hiring?"

"Now, that's a question I can answer," the bartender said, smiling. "As a matter of fact, we do need someone to work behind the bar. Got any experience?"

I nodded my head towards Lou, "Sure do and my reference is sitting right here."

Lou chuckled, "If there's one thing she's good at, it's bringing in customers."

The bartender looked back and forth between Lou and I then said, "How about her other skills? Think she can keep up here?"

"Oh yeah. She worked in my restaurant for a little while. After she started, the number of customers I saw increased, so needless to say, profits went up, too."

"One last question for this interview ... you're not just doting on this lass because she's your gal, are you?"

I let out a bark of laughter, "If he is, it's getting him bonus points."

Lou rolled his eyes, "No, while we are together and our relationship grew as a result of working together, she was about the best employee I've had. Quick on her feet, handled difficult customers well, and was good at keeping track of orders during the busy times. You won't be disappointed."

The bartender looked back over at me, sticking out his hand, "That settles it. Welcome to the team. When can you start?"

I shook his hand as I said, "Well, that was about the easiest and quickest interview I've ever gone through. I can start tomorrow."

"Works for me," the bartender responded. "The name's Conor. Yours?"

"I'm Val, this is Lou," I answered, jerking my thumb in Lou's direction. "Nice to meet you."

"Likewise. Now, plan on being here about an hour earlier than you were today and we'll start walking through everything you need to know. Just remember," he said as he made his way out of the booth. "Don't go around asking too many questions, or any at all if you can help it. Food's on the house this morning since you were kind enough to help me with my staffing problem."

We both gave him a little salute saying our thanks as Conor walked away. When he was finally out of earshot, Lou leaned closer to me, "You sure you want to start working?"

"I'll be fine, Lou. Plus, we got to get money coming in so we can get some fresh food in the house."

"If you say so. Did that conversation remind you of anything?"

I let a soft grin form, "Yeah, the first day we met."

Instead of being all sweet like I thought Lou was going to be, he came back with, "Do you make it a habit to have serious conversations about a new world in a secluded booth?"

I swatted at him, letting sarcasm ooze from my words, "Why yes, I love being sucked into an intense conversation about the things that go bump in the night when I arrive in a new world. What better way to get adjusted to a new space then discussing all the serious things first."

"Finish eating. We get to play tourist a little bit," Lou said with a smile. *At least someone appreciated my humor.*

I did as I was told and we headed out, giving Conor a little wave as we left. Instead of heading towards the cathedral like I thought we would, we went in the opposite direction to look at some of the little shops. There were a lot of touristy type places filled with the classic trinkets you would find at any popular destination: corny t-shirts, magnets with names on them, books filled with facts about the place, candy, stuffed bears with four-leaf clovers printed on the shirts they were wearing, small fake pint glasses, you name it. We eventually stumbled our way into a grocery store which thankfully wasn't too far from the pub, so I could stop there after work if needed.

We wandered our way back to the parking garage, both pausing a second to get a glimpse of the cathedral. It still filled me with the same unease as the previous day and I could tell it bugged Lou, too, judging by the way he tightened his grip on my hand.

We got back in the car and rode home in silence, both of us not wanting to spend too much time and energy on what we just felt.

Once we were back in the house, it was like a safety blanket was put over our shoulders. All tension from moments ago was lifted away and we eased back into our familiar routines. Lou was starting to make dinner when I said, "I'll plan on getting food tomorrow after I'm done with work."

"Speaking of work," Lou said. "Want me to pick you up when you're done?"

"Do we even know if our phones work here?" I asked.

Without saying anything else, Lou pulled out his phone and shot me a quick text. When nothing appeared after a couple of minutes, I looked at Lou, "What do we do now?"

"I'll drop you off at work and grab us a couple of phones. I'll take care of grabbing some food, too, since we're running low."

"How do you know when I'll be off?" I asked.

"I'll take a shot in the dark here and assume shift durations are the same here as they are in my world. Do you think Conor will let you off a little earlier?"

I shrugged, "Who knows? It's the first day. I could end it a little earlier or depending on how business is doing, or I could work the full shift."

Lou looked at me momentarily before focusing back on what he was cooking, "Either way, I'll be there for you."

I paused for a second, debating whether I should ask the question that's now starting to get louder. *Why not?*

"Lou? You wouldn't happen to have any idea as to why my phone worked in your world, but neither of ours are working here, would you?"

Lou chuckled a little bit, "I had a feeling you were going to ask that. My hunch is that Warrick has something to do with this. There was a little while where his company was making updates to the network in our world saying they were making improvements to the speed, but nothing changed. It would only make sense he was establishing a connection with your world to be able to communicate with your dad trying to get his hands on whatever he could to replicate the technology he so desperately wants."

"It always goes back to Warrick, doesn't it?" I sighed.

We arrived at the pub the next day, Lou leaning over to kiss my cheek, "I'll be back before you know it. Have to hold up my end and get us some phones so we can actually communicate in this place without being around each other all the time."

I felt some heat rush to my face in response to his kiss, "What are you going to spend your day doing?"

"Brushing up on all things Batman," he said with a smirk.

I gave him a playful shove suddenly feeling like a giddy high school girl, "Seriously Lou."

"After I drop your new phone off, I'll be looking into our device some more to see if I can figure out recharge time. I'll also take a look through your dad's files in case there's anything in there. Now, get out of here before you're late."

I leaned over the center console taking my turn to give him a quick kiss then made my way out the car and into the pub. Conor beamed over at me, "I knew I could rely on you. Not a minute late."

"Hey Conor," I said, returning the smile. "Where can I get started?"

"Start by taking a look through the drink menu to see if there's anything you don't know how to make. We'll go through a quick lesson on the things you don't know, then we'll have you take inventory and help with getting everything ready to go for the day."

I shot him a thumb's up and wasted no time starting on the task list he gave me. There were a few cocktails I wasn't sure how to make, so Conor took some time walking me through the steps. After that, I jumped into inventory like he asked and moved on to the final item. By the time I was done, there was only five minutes before opening and a line was forming outside the doors. I scanned the crowd to see if any of the faces belonged to Lou, but I guess it doesn't make sense to have him come back so soon if he's trying to find a place to grab us some phones.

After confirming Lou wasn't among the eager faces in line, I turned my attention back to the bar taking advantage of a quick moment to ask Conor about the line outside, "Is this typical? People line up for a drink in the middle of the day?"

Conor threw his towel over his shoulder then rested his hand on a hip, "Aye, you seem to forget we pull in a lot of tourists. Plus, it makes the rest of the workday go faster when you're feeling good."

Before I could say anything else, he went over to the door, opening it and greeting customers as they came in. It was non-stop as people flooded in. It didn't take me long to get into an easy rhythm, though: pour beer, serve, take food orders and pass those along to the kitchen, serve food orders, and grab empty glasses and dishes. Every now and then, I'd be able to slip away for a quick five-minute break, and during one of those breaks, Lou ran in holding out a small phone, "It's nothing fancy, but it's activated and good to go. I already have my number in there, so feel free to text when your shift is winding down. By the looks of it, you might be here the whole night."

I gave him a smile, accepting the phone, "Thanks, and yeah, safe to say I'm not getting out of here anytime soon. Want anything while you're here?"

He held up his hands, shaking his head, "I'm good. I'll head back so I can start checking out the device." Lou turned to leave, but came back to give me a quick kiss on the cheek, "Text me when things wind down, okay?"

"You got it," I flashed him another smile and watched as he left. I tucked the phone into my back pocket. I'll have time to figure it out on my next break, if I ever got one. The crowd in here had grown and I was having to move double-time.

Several more hours passed. I looked at the clock then out one of the windows to see the sun getting low in the sky which meant I didn't have too long before closing time. I shot Lou a text letting him know he could head my way. I was still looking at the screen when a guy asked me for a standard pint. I shoved my phone back in my pocket getting back to work, and when I put the glass in front of the man who asked for it, I felt chills run all throughout my body. The hairs on my neck stood straight up, which seems to be their new default, and I paused. The man holding his newly filled pint had a familiar sinister smirk plastered on his face. It was the man from my nightmare minus the blood on his face.

Chapter 2

Humor was dancing in his brown eyes, curly brown hair poking out from under his beanie. He was wearing the same sweater he had been in my dreams, again, minus the blood.

"Glad to see Conor finally getting some help. It's nice to not have to wait ages for a beer," he said with a thick Irish accent while lifting the glass I just gave him. He held out some money for a tip, trying to continue the conversation, "You look like you've seen a ghost. Lighten up, join me in a drink. I'm sure you're near the end of your shift."

As I reached for the money, he brushed his fingers against the back of my hand, sending a new round of shivers down my spine. I regained enough composure to respond, "I would, but you're a little behind the curve on drinking with me tonight. I've reached the max number Conor allows, so I guess you'll have to try again another day."

I didn't give him the chance to respond before I was moving on to the next customer who was flagging me down, thankfully at the other end of the bar. I found Conor after helping a few more people out, "What's next boss? Anything you need me to do to help get this place ready to close down for the night?"

He nodded his head towards the breakroom and I led the way. We took a seat, taking a moment to relax before jumping into conversation. He looked at me with a serious expression on his face, "I hate to do this on your first day, but would you be okay staying a little later? It's been a while since the pub has been this crowded."

I was a little confused by this ask since just the day before Conor reminded us that people tend to end their nights early around here.

He picked up on my confusion saying, "I know it wasn't too long ago I was saying people don't stay out too late. Occasionally, exceptions are made."

"What's the exception tonight?"

"We're getting close to a holiday. Business picks up and it's a little harder to close down on time," Conor stood, getting ready to go back out there. "Let your boyfriend know you're going to be a little later tonight."

He left and I took this moment to rub my hands over my face. I was starting to feel the effects of being here all day and not really stopping until now. I pulled my phone back out to let Lou know the change in plans only to get a response that he was already there. *Great, now Lou had to be in the same building as the guy who's creeping me out. Really taking me back to the early days.*

I took another deep breath to steady myself then headed back out to the chaos. It was so much more crowded than it was just minutes ago. I looked over to Conor who was hurrying through the onslaught of orders he just received when he noticed I was back out here, "Hey, Val, get your arse back out here! I could use an extra set of hands."

I wasted no time getting back to work to help get the crowd at the bar back down to a manageable level. I almost forgot Lou was here until I came face-to-face with him. I glanced back over at Conor to see if he was still rushing through everything to find that he was back to moving at a more relaxed pace. *Thank goodness.*

"What does it take to get a beer around here?" Lou asked, holding back a grin.

I started pouring him a pint, smiling and shaking my head, "A kind word. Some money. What else can I get out of you?"

"Just keep those beers coming and we'll see what you get," he said, nodding his head towards the glass in my hand.

I gave him a wink then went back to checking if the other customers needed anything else. I made my way out to the tables to start clearing some empty glasses, bottles, and plates noting the creepy guy was nowhere to be found, yet I couldn't shake the feeling like I was being watched. I headed back over to Lou appreciative that we survived the rush.

Lou didn't look up from his beer glass as he asked, "So, what's up with having to work late? Kind of goes against what we were told earlier."

I leaned against the bar top getting closer to him so I could keep my voice lower, "Apparently a holiday is coming up, so there's more people in town which makes it hard to close on time and lose out on all that money."

"Sounds like something Conor failed to mention," Lou responded, now looking at me. "I'm good with hanging out until closing time."

"Speaking of, where is Conor? I need to figure out my schedule and when we're actually shutting things down."

I turned around to find Conor ringing a bell announcing last call. He yelled out, "One more hour, then the lot of you find somewhere else to drink."

I turned back to Lou, "There you go. Would you like another one?"

"I'll take two."

I filled his order then made my way over to Conor to help with the last rush of the evening. As we were pouring drinks, I asked, "What's the schedule for the rest of the week?"

Without missing a beat, he answered, "More of the same, except you'll be staying here later and later as we get closer to the weekend. I assume that won't be a problem?"

"Nope. What do you need from me to start closing down the place?"

"Right now? Just help out with these drinks and picking up dishes. When the hour's up, I'll give you a list."

And that's what we did for the next hour. We filled everyone's drink order then made our rounds to start cleaning up. People slowly started to filter out until there was just a handful left. Since the pub cleared out pretty quickly, I got to work on the list Conor just handed me to make our lives a little easier. I noticed Lou and him chatting it up sharing a drink, so I just continued checking things off without taking a second to join them. When I turned back around, I almost ran into one of the few remaining customers, "Sorry about that. Let me move out of your way."

"Ah, no worries. I'm just happy I managed to bump into ya. What would you say the chances of me getting your number are?"

I slowly looked up, silently wishing the voice I was hearing didn't actually belong to the guy who creeped me out so much earlier. Turns out I'm not that lucky.

"Zero. I'm taken," I answered, curtly. "Excuse me, I have to get back to taking care of some things."

I tried to make a move around him, but was stopped when he placed a hand on my arm, "Don't make such a fuss, I only mean it as a compliment."

He was staring at me so intently I felt like I couldn't look away. "Thanks, I guess," I mumbled, trying to move away.

He only tightened his grip on my arm. I don't think I had ever felt hands as cold as his. I looked at his hand then back to his eyes hoping the panic I was starting to feel wasn't showing. His sinister grin from earlier was back, making the hairs on the back of my neck raise.

"Now, what's the rush? I just want to get to know you better, that's all. Join me," he said with a little bit of a threat laced in his words. This mystery man led me to his table in the farthest corner. I glanced over my shoulder at Lou to find him watching me closely with Conor doing the same, but they made no move towards me. *Thanks guys, I guess I can handle this myself.*

I sat across from this guy, waiting for him to continue the conversation. He was taking his time with finishing his drink almost as if he was savoring the moment.

I crossed my arms, starting to get impatient, "What do you want to know?"

"I know most people around here, but you're new. Plus, that accent of yours is a dead giveaway," he chuckled. "What's your name?"

"All good guesses," I said, squirming in my seat a little bit. "I'm Val. You are?"

Conor took this moment to chime in, "Liam! You dog, it's been a while. Thanks for stopping in, but I need to steal my new employee back. She's got some work to do and you're making the poor lass stay here longer than she needs to."

"My apologies, Conor," Liam said with some frustration. "Val, it was my pleasure meeting you tonight. I look forward to seeing you around."

Liam wasted no time with getting up and returning to the small group of people he had been with. I took a moment to assess the group, and I'm not going to lie, they were all some good-looking people, Liam included. Yet, I couldn't help but notice that the alarm bells going off in my head got louder the longer I stared. I tore my eyes away from them and moved to get up to follow Conor back to the bar, "I don't know that I've ever been more appreciative of someone interrupting a conversation."

"Don't thank me yet, they're not gone," Conor said in a hushed tone. "Try to keep your distance from that lot."

"You don't need to tell me twice."

Conor and I settled back into going through the closing routine. I kept my eye on the group Liam was a part of, willing them to leave. When it was clear they weren't making their way to the door any time soon, Conor shouted at them, "Any day now! Some of us like to get sleep."

There were a couple of crude replies, but Liam's group finally left the pub. Liam looked over his shoulder, throwing me a little finger wave as he walked out the door. Conor wasted no time with getting the place locked up, and as he turned around to me, he said, "Like I said, keep your distance from them. They can tear your life apart if you let them. See you tomorrow, Val. Way to tough it out tonight."

He didn't offer any more details as he walked towards his small desk in the back to review the paperwork I just completed.

I glanced at Lou who was looking in the direction Conor just went. I gathered my stuff I kept hidden under the bar and placed my hand on Lou's shoulder, "What do you say we get out of here and enjoy some greasy food at home?"

I got a lopsided grin in return. Lou got up silently and draped his arm around my shoulder. I know it was probably his way of keeping me close so nothing happens, but there was a part of me hoping this also had something to do with the relationship we're test running.

Once on the road in the comfort of Lou's car, he glanced over at me, "Want to tell me what that was all about?"

I closed my eyes, laying my head on the headrest, "Where do you want me to start?"

"Hmm," Lou said, thinking while he drummed his fingers on the steering wheel. "How about we start from the top when I got there."

I didn't have to be psychic to know he was talking about the interactions with Liam. I absentmindedly rubbed a hand over my arm as I started, "Well, remember that nightmare I had and mentioned there was guy with blood all over his face?"

"Yeah. Have a run-in with your ex, too?"

I cut Lou a glare, "Not funny."

"Sorry, continue," he said, trying not to let a laugh escape.

"My nightmare turned into a little bit of a reality. That same guy was at the pub tonight. His name is Liam, and *man,* was he trying to hit on me. Every instinct was telling me to run, but of course I couldn't do that. I just had to keep serving him if Conor wasn't around. Anyway, there was a point where he basically death gripped my arm and wouldn't let go until I joined him and his friends."

I started rubbing my arm where Liam had gripped earlier, noticing there was a little ache every time I ran over that spot. I was starting to zone out when Lou said, "Yeah, I saw that. Anyone else would've thought he was just being friendly."

There was a low growl in his voice bringing me back to reality. *So, he picked up on that. Guess he's not one to hide his jealousy.* I glanced over to him seeing his grip tightening on the steering wheel.

"I didn't realize you were the jealous type," I said, nudging him in the ribs.

My quick remark only got him to further tighten his grip on the steering wheel. He let out a breath through clenched teeth, "I'm *not* jealous."

Got it, this is not the time to make a joke.

The only sounds filling the space were Lou's tense breathing. There was no way I was going to be the one to speak next. If I did, I would probably erase all the work Lou just did to calm down. Some more seconds passed with more breaths until I saw his grip loosen and his shoulders relax. There was one last sigh before Lou glanced over at me, "The entire time I was in that pub, I kept an eye on that guy. I got nothing but bad vibes from him, so call it a crime for me to care about your safety." Lou paused then let out a scoff, "I know that asshole has no chance with you."

"Oh yeah?" I playfully asked, jabbing an elbow into his side.

He looked annoyed as he glanced at me from the corner of his eye, "Out of what I just told you, you're picking up on the last part?"

I lifted my chin in pride, more as a joke than being serious, "It's not very often I get a compliment like that out of you."

We went back and forth with more banter for the rest of the ride home, which wasn't too long.

The minute we stepped in the house, a wave of tiredness washed over me. I let out a big yawn and started making my way upstairs, "I'm wiped. I didn't think I would be this tired from one day, but I'm calling it a night."

Lou didn't say anything. Instead, he followed me upstairs and headed to the bathroom next to the room he was staying in. Realizing he wasn't following me to my room, I turned around and planted a soft peck on his cheek, "Goodnight."

"Goodnight," Lou said, wrapping me gently in his arms before kissing my forehead.

I rolled over in bed slowly blinking myself awake, glancing towards the balcony doors admiring the morning light filtering in the room. I guess I didn't realize I had fallen asleep as fast as I did, but thankfully, it also meant no nightmares to occupy my mind.

I laid in bed a little while longer trying to shake the remaining sleep away and get my bearings when I started smelling food. It didn't take too long to get moving with that kind of motivation. I came downstairs to Lou whipping up a breakfast of pancakes, fruit, and bacon. I skipped over to him, leaning my head against his shoulder, "My favorite!"

Lou softly chuckled, "Good morning to you, too."

I planted a kiss on his cheek, mostly to distract him from me swiping a piece of bacon. I checked my phone to see a message from Conor telling me when to be there. I looked back up at Lou who was serving us both up, "You good if I take the car since I'll be working later?"

Something that looked like anger flickered over Lou's face for a brief second while he thought about his response. I didn't press him, but I could tell he wasn't liking this idea. The silence stretched on and it was almost as if I could see all the ideas funneling into his head then exiting through his ears as he discarded them. He finally brought his gaze back to me, "Yeah, just let me know if you run into any issues."

I gave him a thumb's up while I shoveled pancakes into my mouth.

After breakfast, we spent the rest of my free time tinkering in the lab with the device to see if we could make any further progress on seeing if there's a recharge time. We finally gave up and decided the only way to see if there was a recharge time would be to test it by going back to Lou's world.

"I was hoping it was going to be something easy," I wiped my hands on my shorts.

"I was with you, but that would've been way too obvious," Lou murmured in agreement, tucking the device back into its hiding spot. "It's about time for you to head out, right?"

I took a quick look at the time, "Shoot, I guess I better get ready. I'll let you know when I make it there."

I parked in the same garage we used on our date then made my way into the pub. Looking at the clock, I knew I was cutting it close with it only being minutes until opening. Conor made his way out from the back, "Everything's ready for you. I didn't want to be too mean with this being your second day and all. Plus, we're probably going to be here a little longer than yesterday, so buckle up."

I flipped the sign to open and people wasted no time filling up the space. From the minute customers could walk through the door, it was nonstop. I don't think I had ever filled as many beers as I had today. When I finally got a chance to take a break, I was already seven hours into my shift and had Conor coming up to me. He jerked his thumb in the direction of the breakroom, "Get off your feet and get something to eat. We still have a while yet before the night is over."

I nodded my head then made my way back to the kitchen, thankful the crew had already made me a sandwich to chow down on. I looked out the window before closing myself in the breakroom to see the sun had already set. *Geez, I lost all track of time.* Shaking my head, I got myself comfortable, shot Lou a quick text to let him know it's crazy busy but I'm still standing, and took a couple of bites of my sandwich. I had only finished a few more bites when Conor burst through the door, "You gotta get back out here. I can't keep up with these orders on my own."

"No worries," I mumbled with a mouthful of food. "I'll be there in a second."

I brought the sandwich back to the kitchen asking if they could keep it for me for later, then rejoined Conor. The line was at least three people deep all the way around the bar with no room between shoulders. These people were packed in here like sardines. We were flying to get through all the orders when I asked, "Is this normal for even this holiday?"

"Sort of," Conor started, not missing a beat with what he was doing. "It's a little busier than last year, but at least the money's good."

"That's one way of looking at it," I said, passing a beer to the next person in line. I felt an ice-cold touch on my hand jarring the steady rhythm I had going to a halt. I looked up to meet the eyes of Liam. Surprisingly, he didn't say anything, just disappeared back in the crowd. I didn't like how he wanted to make sure I was aware of him being there. While still staring out into the sea of people trying to bring myself back to reality, I caught a glimpse of familiar blond hair inching through the crowd. *No way ...*

"Conor, I'm going to grab some of the empty glasses, you got it here?" I called over my shoulder already making my way out from behind the bar.

"No choice, we're running low on glasses," he answered, not even looking my way.

I started making my way around the tables hoping I could get a better glimpse of the person the blond hair belonged to before just blindly assuming I knew who they were. I kept inching my way closer and positioning myself so I can see this woman's face while keeping my distance. She finally angled her face so I could get a good look, making me almost drop the two tall stacks of glasses I was carrying when realization dawned on me. *Jennie's here! I can't believe I found someone this quick.* I stood there a little while longer feeling the excitement get taken over by confusion when I saw the group she's with – Liam and his crew. *What the hell is she doing with him?*

Not wanting to stand there too much longer, I made my way back to the bar. I passed the glasses through the window dodging an annoyed look from Conor, "Sorry, it's packed out there. Didn't mean to take so long."

"Don't worry about it."

We got back into our rhythm as soon as the now clean glasses got passed back to us. Conor did a couple of rounds of gathering more dishes and cleaning off the tables while I continued working through the lines of thirsty customers. At least a couple more hours passed before the symphony of laughter and voices died down to a more reasonable volume, signaling people starting to leave. Conor returned to the bar placing my sandwich in front of me, "Sorry for keeping your food away from you so long. Eat up! Where's your fella tonight?"

Not realizing how hungry I was until I took a giant bite out of my sandwich, I answered with my mouth full of food, "I took the car tonight, so he's most likely at home doing whatever."

"You know? You're not the most lady like."

I laughed, "I never said I was."

I finished the bite in my mouth when Jennie made her way up to the bar still talking over her shoulder to someone. I put my sandwich down hastily and pasted a smile on my face. When she turned around ready to order, her mouth dropped open, eyes widening to the size of saucers.

"Hey," I said, giving a little finger wave. "Bet you didn't think you'd see me here."

"No kidding! Is it really you?!"

"It's really me."

Jennie let out a squeal doing a little dance before making her way over to the end of the bar with her arms stretched out for a hug. I walked over, letting the warmth and familiarity of her hug consume me. I didn't realize how much I had missed her until now.

"I can't believe you're here, Val," she said into my hair not quite letting me go yet.

I smiled, "We have a lot to catch up on."

We finally let go of each other when she said, "We really do! How are you even here right now? Do you work here? Is it just you?"

"Slow your roll there," I said, now understanding how Lou feels when I drown him in questions. "It's a pretty long and crazy story that I'll have to tell you when I have more time, but I do work here. Give me your number so we can catch up. If I don't hurry back, boss-man over there is going to lose it."

We both turned to look at Conor who had his signature scowl firmly in place. Laughing, we exchanged numbers and Jennie went back into the crowd forgetting her drinks. I walked back over to my sandwich just as Conor rang the last call bell. There was another quick wave of orders, but after that, it calmed down enough for me to finish my food.

Conor finished wiping down the bar top and leaned against it, "I'm assuming that lass was a long-lost friend or something?"

I smiled at him, "Yeah, we haven't seen each other in a while and weren't sure if we were ever going to see each other again."

It was Conor's turn to smile, "Well, I'm glad I'm the one who facilitated that."

"Yeah, right. That was all a chance meeting and you know it," I joked with him.

"We'll agree to disagree. Help me start closing up."

I filled the rest of my shift with the same closeout tasks as the night before. When I wrapped everything up, I said goodnight to Conor and made my way into the cool evening air. The streets were filled with the sounds of happy people, a rare occurrence here since Lou and I arrived. I wonder what holiday was coming up making people feel confident enough to break the norm to leave the safety of buildings. I started walking back to the parking garage, shooting a quick text to Lou to let him know I have exciting news to tell him when I'm grabbed from behind and pushed into the alley, almost dropping my phone because of how aggressive I was being handled.

"I don't have anything of value on me!"

Instead of a response, I got slammed into the wall, hitting my head hard enough to make me see double. *There was no one around me when I left the pub – who would want to mug me?*

"You know you're such a tease? I've been watching you all night just wondering what you would taste like."

Those words confirmed I wasn't going to get mugged, sending a new shot of fear through my body. I had no idea what was about to happen when my attacker continued, "The thing I don't get is why the *hell* I'm so drawn to you."

I must've hit my head harder than I thought because there's no way this could be Warrick. I tried to work my way out of the hold I was in with no luck. My mind kept trying to search the file cabinets for who this voice could belong to because it was familiar, yet I couldn't place it.

"Is it because I'm attracted to you?" he asked, pushing me harder against the wall while brushing my hair aside with his free hand to expose my neck. "Or is it because your new which means you're *fresh*?"

I tried to open my mouth to protest, to ask for my freedom back, to say anything only to find I couldn't get any sound out. My body was starting to feel weaker from hitting my head, the edges of my vision a little blurry.

"You're not getting away from me this time," he whispered, lips brushing against my ear.

I shivered, but it was in that moment I placed the voice. *Liam.* I struggled more against his grip trying to push back against his hand holding me hostage, but to no avail.

Liam's breath suddenly felt hot on my neck. He was moving closer to me the longer we were here. I struggled some more only to get pushed harder against the wall. This time, it was his body holding me down while he still held my hands behind my back. His breath was back and I started feeling something sharp putting pressure against my neck.

"Liam!"

Liam let out a small growl of frustration at being summoned while not moving an inch.

"Get your arse over here and leave the poor lass alone," the same heavily accented voice said.

There was a moment where I wasn't sure if I was going to be let go, but the weight of Liam finally lifted. I stayed where I was, frozen in place by shock, as well as pain.

Liam didn't say anything else to me as he worked his way out of the alley. I glanced over in the direction the voice came from to see a man standing there in a leather jacket, white shirt, torn jeans and combat boots. He was looking right at me the entire time with no emotion. More alarm bells started ringing in my head sending shivers of warning down my back.

Once Liam joined up with the rest of the group, the man turned and started to walk away. I kept watching them make their slow exit so I knew when I'd be safe to move again, noticing he had his arm draped around a woman. She glanced over her shoulder at me with a face filled with concern. When I took a long look at her, I couldn't help but recognize similarities between her and the reflection I see every day: the caramel-colored hair, the slightly tanned skin, the way her facial features were defined yet still soft.

"Shit," I mumbled to myself now alone in the alley.

Chapter 3

The drive home was slow and arduous. The pounding in my head was worse and the dizziness was enough to make staying in my lane difficult. By the time I pulled in the garage and stumbled into the house, I felt like I was going to collapse.

"Val?" Lou called out.

"Here," I squeaked.

It was that moment my knees gave out. I started falling to the floor only to be caught by Lou before adding more bumps to my head.

"What the hell happened?"

I opened my eyes to see his grey ones searching me frantically for any indication as to what was going on.

"Did you get in an accident?" he asked.

"Sort of," I said, sitting up on my own.

"I let you drive yourself one night and you wind up getting hurt," Lou started only stopping when I put a finger to his lips.

"I didn't crash your fancy car if that's what you're thinking. I got cornered by Liam. I'm fine, just a little dizzy. Nothing sleep can't fix. No, you don't need to worry about doing anything right now. I think we have bigger problems. Did I answer all your questions?"

Lou's mouth opened and closed a couple of times before he finally mumbled, "Yes."

I tried to stand up again, using Lou as support only to see he had set up a romantic evening for us. There were candles illuminating a table covered in rose petals accompanied with plates of pasta and glasses of wine. I glanced back at Lou who was looking the other way, "What's this?"

He turned his gaze back to me, adding a soft smile as he did, "I wanted to do something special for you."

"I don't want to keep letting it get cold, let's go eat."

We slowly made our way over to the table, and by the time we got there, I was finally able to hold myself up. *Making progress already.* We settled in, starting to enjoy the meal when Lou asked, "You were saying you think we have bigger problems?"

I nodded my head, "Yeah."

"You also mentioned you had exciting news, too. You must've had a night."

"You're not wrong," I said with a small laugh. "What do you want first? Good or bad news?"

Lou raises his eyebrows, "Let's start with the good. I think I need to recover from anything related to bad news with you stumbling into the house."

I took another bite of pasta before answering, "Well, I think we landed in a good spot. I found one of my friends today."

The fork paused on its way to Lou's mouth. He lifted his head to look at me, "Really? You found someone? Who? How? Where?"

A laugh escaped me, "Now it's your turn for the questions. The pub was so packed today that I was just on autopilot, as much as I could be with it only being my second day and all. I glanced up and happened to see someone who looked familiar to me, but I didn't want to get too hopeful in case it wasn't one of my friends. I decided to play it safe to avoid the risk of embarrassing myself so I kept my distance for a while until she came up to the bar to order a drink. That's when we recognized each other. I've known her for about the same amount of time I knew Daryl."

I trailed off, a wave of sadness crashing into me at the memory of Daryl. Now I'll have to tell Jennie about what happened, and given how we left things before we got transported, she might completely blame everything on me. Especially since it's my dad who is behind the bombs ...

Lou reached across the table, placing a comforting hand on mine. His thumb started rubbing my hand, "Hey, I'm happy you found someone who's so important to you without having to think too much about where to start looking. Do I get to meet her?"

I did my best to brush off the sadness and forced a weak smile, "I hope you get to meet her soon. Although, I wonder if Chris came with her ... I think he was in the same room. If Daryl ended up getting transported with me just by sharing my room, maybe that applies to them, too."

"I think there's a good chance."

Before we could say anything else, my phone lit up with a text from Jennie like she could tell I was talking about her.

Val! I still can't get over the fact that we're both in the same place!! EEEEEEEE!!! Can we get together to catch up? Soon?

I typed out a response in no time: *How about in a couple of days? I think I'll get a break from work. You can come over and we'll catch up over s'mores or something.* ☺

She sent back three thumbs up. I looked back up at Lou and said, "Sounds like you'll get to meet her sooner rather than later."

"Yeah?"

"Probably in the next couple of days. Depending on whether or not I can get a couple days off, so I'll check with Conor tomorrow when I go in."

Lou just nodded his head as he continued shoveling spaghetti in his mouth. He gave me the chance to take a couple more bites before asking, "So, what about the bad news? And will you tell me what the hell happened to your face?"

"My face? What's wrong with it?"

"Go take a look."

I hurried my way over to the bathroom. In my reflection, there was a decent sized strawberry shaped road rash spreading across my left cheek where my face had kissed the wall. I gingerly touched it, wincing as it burned. *Well, I'm going to have to find some way to cover that up tomorrow.*

I made my way back out to join Lou at the table, "I'll tell you about that in a second. The bad news is more important."

"I'm on the edge of my seat, Val," Lou said, words dripping in sarcasm. "You're not doing the best at just getting on with it."

I waved him off, "Whatever. Anyways, I think Warrick does have a way to jump worlds."

"You sound confident about that. What makes you so sure?" Lou asked, his face hardening.

"I saw a person tonight that looks exactly like someone he described to me. I can't remember her name, but I'm almost certain. If she's here from your world, then that means she got transported. The only other person I know of that was trying to figure out how to do that was Warrick. It also means that it could be any day before he shows up here."

"Her? I wonder who it is ..."

I waited for him to continue processing everything I just said in silence. I knew exactly who it was I saw tonight, but the jealous, immature side of me didn't want to say her name out loud especially considering the feelings he may still have for her. *Melody, the woman who shares some of my looks. The woman who stole Lou's heart.* I'm finally taking a relationship at a slower pace, and it's been about the best thing that's happened to me since Gabriel (minus all the crazy shit that's happened). I also couldn't help but wonder if Warrick knew Melody was alive and he just sent her somewhere else considering he was pretty convinced she had died by his hand. *Did he transport her here? If that's the case, then he did a damn good job at convincing everyone of her death ...*

"You know?" Lou started again, snapping me back to reality. "You're probably right. Warrick could show his ugly mug here any day now. He has the sequence for this place, and I know that if he has a device that works, then he's going to keep trying until he can be the one transported. I just wonder how it happened."

"I was thinking that, too. On top of that, does he even know his device works?"

"He's got to. You can't just plug in a sequence without anything happening. He would see some sort of portal open regardless of whether or not he chose to go through it. But ... I don't know why he wouldn't jump through it at that moment since he's been so hungry to be successful with this."

I shrugged, "Maybe he was preoccupied with something else going on at the same time? Maybe he was blinded by the rage and fury that seems to consume him at every waking moment?"

"Maybe," Lou mumbled. "Either way, we need to keep our heads on a swivel. He'll go after you. I'm thinking I need to start driving you back and forth from the pub that way I can keep a better eye on you and not let this happen again."

He pointed at me with his fork, making me roll my eyes, "I can take care of myself, you know."

"The number of times I've heard that and seen the opposite happen doesn't really convince me."

"Fine, but at least give me the chance to handle things on my own before you intervene. Deal?"

I stuck out my hand so we could shake on it. Lou reluctantly reached out, but he still agreed.

Lou wiped his face with his napkin then asked, "Now do I get to hear about what happened tonight or are you going to make me wait another 5 years to get that answer?"

I let out a sigh and shot him a look full of daggers to show him my annoyance, "Not if you ask like that."

He held up his hands in defense trying to hold a smile back. *This asshole's just messing with me.*

"Fine," I said. "Like I said, I got cornered by Liam as I was heading to the car. He pushed me against the wall and was spouting all this crazy talk about tasting me and wanting me. I had no idea what he was going to try to do, but it seemed like he was going to bite me until the group he was with caught up to him. That got him to leave, but he didn't hold back with manhandling me, no pun intended."

"I could kill him for you," Lou calmly suggested. For him to be this calm when he said that scared me.

"Let's not worry about him for now. He's a small fish in the pond. We have bigger fish to worry about in the moment."

Still keeping his calm demeanor, Lou said, "Just say the word."

"You know?" I asked, desperately wanting to change the topic. "We're not really good at this whole dating thing. I mean the last date we went on, things took a serious turn, too."

Lou cocked an eyebrow, "You saying I'm not romantic?"

"I mean," I started, drawing out the words. Lou didn't give me a chance to come up with an answer before he scooped me out of his chair and hurried us upstairs. He set me down gently on the bed, which ended the trail of rose petals. I heard the bath water start in the bathroom. My curiosity got the best of me, leading me into the bathroom to find Lou prepping a bubble bath.

"You've had a tough day, so you're going to relax first," he said, moving towards me.

"You really don't have to do this."

Lou was standing in front of me now, his face inches away from mine, our breaths entangling, his woodsy scent filling my nose. His fingers grazed the skin covered by the hem of my shirt as they curled over the fabric, "Who said I have to do anything? I promised I would take care of you, didn't I?"

Being so close to him like this reminded me of how wildly attracted I was to him. Honestly, with everything going on, it was hard to have any time set aside to be romantic with each other. Getting settled in a new place does that.

Lou leaned in, letting his lips graze mine. He waited a moment to see if I would kiss him back. The instant I did, Lou was all over me. There was something different about the way he was kissing me tonight, almost as if he was hungry and my kiss was the only thing that could satisfy that hunger. Nothing was holding me back from getting lost this time. When his hand returned to my waist after turning off the water, he gently pushed me against the wall. We stayed entangled for a few moments longer, our lips pushing and pulling to meet each other's desires.

Lou pulled away, resting his forehead against mine and braced himself by leaning against his arm just above my head. He closed his eyes, "I can't tell you how bad I've needed this."

I reached up to cradle his face in my hands, "Then don't stop. Let me fill your every need and want you've been holding on to."

A quiet growl escaped his lips before they met mine again. He started tracing small circles on my stomach under my shirt, barely touching me but giving just enough to send electric tingles to every part of me. A soft moan broke free from me only encouraging Lou more. He moved his lips from mine to my neck, kissing the tender spot while he inched my shirt up. My hands reached forward to do the same only lingering when I could feel his muscles flexing underneath me. We were both shirtless in an instant when Lou continued trailing his tender kisses across my breasts as he removed my bra. He teased my nipples with his fingers causing me to moan again, this time full of want. I felt him smile against my stomach while he got to work removing my pants. It wasn't long before I was completely naked, Lou bringing his mouth back to mine.

I started to reach for his pants, but he stopped me by grabbing both of my legs and wrapping them around him. His grey eyes were showing hints of the glowing silver I've grown accustomed to seeing with his wolf. I traced his jawline as he said, "Not yet, Val. I want to enjoy every second of you first."

I kissed his nose, "Won't that be torture for you?"

"Not in the slightest."

Lou whisked us out of the bathroom and laid me on the bed getting back to planting sweet kisses all over my body while letting his fingers dance along my skin, sending my senses into overdrive. I tangled my hands in his soft, dark blond hair and traced my hand along his back only hoping I was making him feel the same way he was making me feel.

His fingers continued their dance moving closer and closer to my core until they finally teased me.

"Lou, this is torture," I whispered in a husky voice.

"I wouldn't have it any other way," he said, brushing his lips against my neck. "You're so wet for me, Val."

Before I could say anything in response, his fingers slid into me. He moved them in a steady rhythm while he moved his hips against my leg, letting me feel his attraction. Words were nonexistent for me, with the only sounds leaving my lips being moans. Lou went back to trailing kisses down my body with the occasional nibble until he reached my core. His tongue teased my clit making me squirm then entered me. I have never had someone eat me with such ferocity, but with such gentleness.

My back arched as I started feeling the first signs of an orgasm building. Not wanting this to be over quite yet, I lifted Lou's head, "At least let me return the favor."

Lou smiled at me, gave my clit another tease with his tongue, then stood up holding a hand out to help me get on my feet. I followed his lead and got down on my knees. I worked him out of his pants, pausing to revel how big he was.

I kissed his hips before teasing his tip with my tongue. I heard a sharp intake of breath the moment I put his shaft in my mouth. It was my turn to move in a steady rhythm taking a few moments to adjust to his size. While I was working Lou, I reached down to tease myself only making Lou enjoy this more.

"Shit, Val," he said, fisting my hair. "It's taking everything I have to not come right now."

I stopped, looking up at him, "Want me to continue or?"

He picked me up again to move us to the bed. Lou was back on top of me, his fingers exploring. I could feel my desire for him mounting based on how wet I was getting even before he touched me again.

"You want this, don't you?"

I nodded my head, "*Please.*"

That was all he needed to hear to put on a condom and slide into me. He growled again as I took a breath in. He picked up my signal to wait before pumping his hips, "Are you okay?"

"Give me a second. You're so *big.*"

"And you're so tight. It's like you were made for me," he whispered in my ear.

Lou started moving in and out of me, slowly at first then picking up in rhythm. I let him set the pace before I moved my body with his, both of us completely in sync. He was back to kissing me, moving between my lips and my neck. One of his hands was palming my breast while he brushed the other over my hard nipple. I ran my hands over his body, feeling his hard muscles contract with every thrust, admiring how strong he felt.

I couldn't hold back my moans any longer, letting them ring out into the night. Lou growled his approval, "That's it, scream for me."

And I did just that. The closer I got to my climax, the more I moaned.

"I need this, I need you."

He paused, sensing I was getting close. Lou brought his lips to my ear and whispered, "And I need you."

Lou resumed his rhythm, and combined with those words, it was all it took. My orgasm enveloped me, rocking my body with waves of pleasure. Lou collapsed on me following his orgasm, both of us breathing hard. He lifted himself off me just enough for me to scoot next to him, Lou wrapping an arm around me to tuck me in close. I pressed my body against his and we laid there for a while before he got up to clean things up. He climbed back into the bed, pulling me back into him. We laid there, savoring what had just happened. Lou occasionally pressed a gentle kiss on my head, but neither of us felt the need to say anything.

After a while of just lying there, I rolled over to face Lou, bringing my hand up to trace his jawline. Those grey eyes of his closed as he leaned into my touch. I gave him a soft kiss, keeping my voice low as I pulled away, "Can time stop? I don't want this to end."

Lou chuckled, "I wish I could do that for you. Since that's not something in my wheelhouse, though, let's just enjoy this night. Don't think of anything else right now."

I gave him a soft smile before going in for another kiss. It didn't take long for us to get tangled up with one another, Lou's hands roaming my body as his tongue traced my lips. He rolled on top of me, his knees nudging my thighs apart. I reached down, guiding him into me. A quiet gasp escaped my lips before being replaced with moans as Lou set the pace.

We spent the rest of the night like that – working each other to a climax before collapsing into the other's arms to catch our breath. I knew I'd be exhausted the next day, but I'd take this kind of exhaustion any time.

By the time morning rolled around, I was tired and refreshed all at the same time. If this is how it felt taking things slow, I should've done this more often. Lou was probably the most respectful guy I had ever been with and had given me about the best night I could've asked for. Feeling blissful and energized, I rolled over to find the space next to me empty. I looked around the room to see if there was any sign of him only to be met with nothing.

"Lou?" I called out. I waited a few more moments for a response met with silence in return. There wasn't even any sounds of movement. *Odd.*

I glanced over at the clock to see it was mid-morning and checked my phone to see if there were any messages. There was one from Conor letting me know he'll need me there in a couple of hours, but nothing else. I got out of bed quickly, throwing on clothes then started my search.

"Lou?" I tried again. Still nothing. I poked my head in every room still coming up empty. I was just about to call him when the garage door opened and he came in with some pastries and coffees.

"Where were you?" I asked.

"Sorry, I was trying to get back before you were up. I wanted to get you breakfast," he said with a sheepish grin.

I went over to kiss him on the cheek and grab my food, "It's all good. Thank you for getting us this. It smells delicious!"

"Anytime," he said giving me a quick kiss on the top of my head. "How are you feeling today?"

A smile slowly inched its way across my face, "A little sore, but good. Really good."

Lou let out a bark of laughter, "Wasn't quite what I was asking about, but I'm glad. How's your cheek and head?"

"Ohhh, my head feels fine, maybe a little bit of a headache going on. My cheek burns, but doesn't feel too bad. How does it look?"

"A little swollen, still red and irritated," he inspected the left side of my face. "You should go take a look."

I put everything down and once again went into the bathroom to inspect my face. He was right – there was some swelling and the strawberry mark was still there. Nothing much I can do about it now, so I guess I'll go into work like this. I went back out there and shrugged, "It is what it is. The only thing I can do is let it heal. I was wondering, though, what should we do about our device and figuring out the recharge time?"

"Always jumping back into business talk," Lou sighed. "I was actually thinking about that on my trip this morning. Let's take a look through your dad's notes and specs to see if there's a formula or anything like that referencing how long it'll take for the device to recharge and be used again. I'm also thinking we should test ours to get some data behind it. We've been here long enough now that we should be able to use it again."

"I have a couple hours before work. We could start looking into this now?"

"Let's do it."

We brought our breakfast with us to my dad's office. I got settled in at the desk to use the computer while Lou started looking through the handwritten files. As I kept coming up empty for any data around recharge time, my mind started wandering. If Melody was miraculously alive, maybe Gabriel would be too, I just have no way of confirming this. I decided to take a break from checking the files related to the transportation device and went on a search for any military personnel files my dad may have hidden.

I came across a folder with the letter "G" as the label. I clicked in there only to be stopped by a password protected folder. *Great, time to shake off my oh-so-fantastic hacking skills again.* I kept trying different password combinations, each time coming up with an error. I felt myself starting to get frustrated when I typed in the last possible thing I could think of, watching the wheel spin until it finally let me into the folder.

There were only a few files in there that were vaguely named, not giving me any indication of where to begin, so I clicked into the first one. It was Gabriel's service records containing everything from his first day to his last. All the missions he went on, his performance evaluations, everything. I wasn't surprised to see all positive comments about how much of a team player he was, how he stepped up when he needed to, and how everyone loved him. His warm personality was infectious which made it hard to be anything but happy around him.

I moved on to the next file which contained his autopsy report, complete with pictures. Scrolling through it, I felt every ounce of hope leave my body. It was so hard to see him pictured that way. A body once full of life and love only a shell. A shell that was badly mangled from the blast he had been caught in with singed skin, bruising, and evidence of some of his bones not being where they needed to be. *Oh, Gabriel.* There was no way he could have been transported to another world. The crushing weight of sadness started to creep its way in, and as it did so, I closed the folder. *I don't know why I would get as lucky to have the love of my life here with me.*

"Val?" I heard Lou ask while tapping the desk in front of me. "Earth to Val? Anyone home?"

"Yeah, sorry, I must have zoned out there," I said still lost in what I had just confirmed.

"You okay? I've been trying to get your attention for the last couple of minutes."

I brought my attention up to Lou to see his brow etched with concern. I tried to do my best to put on a happy face as I replied, "Yeah, I'm good. Just a lot to look through that's all. Did you find anything?"

"No," he said, looking at me skeptically, but ultimately decided to change the topic. "Also, your shift starts soon. Ready to head out?"

I glanced down at the clock, "Shit, I lost all track of time!" I hastily stood up and started running around the house gathering my things. I had 15 minutes to get to the pub and the drive alone was about that amount of time.

"I can drive myself," I called out to Lou as I made my way into the garage.

I heard Lou running through the house to catch up to me, "Val, wait!"

I was getting on my bike, putting on my helmet when he ran up. I recognize I did this to myself, but I needed a few moments alone to process my emotions after confirming Gabriel's death, especially after getting my hopes up with seeing Melody here. It was going to be a long shot if he was somehow alive.

Lou put his hand on my shoulder, "Let me drive you in."

I lifted the visor up so I could try my best to convince him that I'll be fine, "Remember our deal? Where you'll try to let me handle things on my own first? Let this be one of those times. Plus, you'll have the car to do anything you need to."

I did my best to smile, making sure my eyes showed the motion, even though most of it was covered by my helmet. Lou stood there still not entirely convinced I was okay and clearly thinking of everything that could go wrong again with me going out on my own.

I put my hand over his, "Lou, I won't hesitate or call you the minute something doesn't sit right with me, okay? I promise."

"You've said that before," he said, not fully trusting my word. I don't blame him, considering how well I did with following through on what I said I would do, or rather, not following through.

"I know I have, and I know I don't have the best track record, but I'm working on changing that. The only way you're going to see that progress is if you let me have a chance."

Lou only nodded his head and stepped back giving me the go ahead. I blew him a kiss then started my bike giving the engine an extra rev. The next thing I knew, I was going on autopilot, zipping through the streets, and reveling in the feeling of freedom my bike gives me. It felt so good to have fresh air whipping against me to bring me back to earth. I knew there was a high probability of Gabriel being dead and I just needed to accept that. I had to let go of the worries that Lou would leave me the moment he saw Melody. He's given me no reason not to trust him. Plus, Melody very much looks taken by the shady guy who came to my rescue.

I parked my bike on the street in front of the pub to minimize how much walking I had to do when my shift was over, or more accurately, minimize the chances of another Liam run in. I set my shoulders and gave myself a little pep talk to keep the ache in my heart at bay. When I walked into the pub, Conor wasted no time calling me out, "Cuttin' it a little close, are we?"

"Hey, I know I'm not as early as I have been, but I still made it in time," I shot back jokingly.

"Well, you get to take care of all the closing stuff tonight," he said finally looking at me as I rounded the corner of the bar. "What the hell happened to you?"

"What are you talking about?" I asked.

He gestured to my cheek and I mirrored his actions wincing as I contacted the scrape from the night before. I let out a little chuckle, "Oh, that. My face made some contact with the ground. You'll find I'm pretty clumsy."

"And you rode in on that thing?" Conor asked, pointing to my bike.

"Eh, what can I say? I live dangerously," I shrugged.

He had questions written all over his face, not quite believing my story, "Whatever you say, but if you run into any problems, let me know."

Time flew by again with the pub being a little busier than last night. *Only a couple more days with this kind of crowd, thank goodness.* I was moving faster tonight than I had before on previous shifts so that I was distracted, and I wanted to give no reason for Conor to continue eyeing me suspiciously. I didn't need anyone to know I was falling apart on the inside between being so vulnerable when Liam attacked me and having any hopes of a surprise reunion with Gabriel dashed.

I was ready to move to the next customer, dropping the beer in front of the person who ordered it when I stopped.

"Val, got a second? I think I have a plan."

"Lou, when did you sneak in here?" I asked, taking a moment to wipe my hands, leaning closer towards him so I could hear over the noise from the crowd.

"Not too long ago, but this place is packed! No wonder I hadn't heard anything from you," he said looking around at the people filling almost every available space in the pub.

"Yeah," I laughed. "Conor wasn't kidding when he said it was going to be busier the closer we got to the holiday. So, what's your plan?"

"I couldn't find anything on the recharge time for the device, so I want to go through with testing it. I'll head out in a couple of days and drive to a quiet place with no one around, then transport myself back to my world, taking my car with me. I'll keep trying the sequence to get back here as often as I can, and as soon as I get back, that'll tell us the recharge time. I figured that would give me time to meet Jennie and be social at least, before I jump back to my world."

I gave a thumb's up, "That sounds good to me! You'll like Jennie, she's super nice."

Lou reached out to my hand, "You good with that? You'll be on your own."

"Lou, I'll be fine. I can take care of myself. I don't have too many enemies here."

He took a sip of beer then said, "Then we're all set. I'll also have a chance to catch up with Raf and see how things are going with the pack and the pizza place."

The mention of my new favorite doctor brought a smile to my face, "I wish he could've joined us here."

"Me too," Lou nodded. "But someone needs to keep the place running, and there's no one better suited for that than Raf."

I got the hint he wanted to end the conversation, so I returned my focus back to work before Conor had another chance to get after me for slowing down. Lou stayed there the rest of the evening leaving only when Conor rang the last call bell. I gave him a quick kiss then got to work on the mountain of things I needed to do for closing. It sure takes a lot longer when you don't have the help from someone else.

Chapter 4

A couple days later Lou and I found ourselves getting ready for Jennie to come over. I finally had a day off to recoup from the hectic first week and what better way to spend it than catching up with someone who I hadn't been sure I'd ever see again. We decided to keep it simple and make some pasta that way there was plenty of food, but we weren't slaving away in the kitchen all day.

"Any pointers for meeting one of your friends for the first time?" Lou asked as he finished drying the last of the dishes.

I thought for a second, playfully tapping my finger against my chin, "Hmm, well? She's pretty tough. You'll want to watch what you say around her or you'll set her off."

I waited to see Lou's reaction hoping to get a rise out of him. He turned to me, squinting his eyes, "Unless she's another alpha, I think I can handle her."

"I'm totally messing with you," I grabbed the towel, whipping it at him. "She's probably the easiest of my friends to get along with. Super bubbly, outgoing so the conversation isn't going to be awkward. Just a happy, go-lucky kind of gal."

"You aren't that sneaky, you know that? And don't whip me with that towel unless you're ready to face the consequences," he said, lunging towards me with a grin. I squealed, running to the opposite side of the island, but his alpha speed was too fast for me. When he caught me, he sat me on the counter and kissed me hard.

We were getting caught up with one another when the doorbell interrupted us. We giggled as I hopped off the counter and straightened myself up, shooing Lou off to hide out until I gave him the signal we agreed on.

I opened the door to find Jennie smiling ear-to-ear, holding up a bottle of wine, "I hope you didn't mind me bringing company!"

As if on cue, Chris materialized from behind her also sporting a huge smile, "It's nice to see another familiar face around here."

"Chris, what a surprise! Of course I don't mind you bringing company, Jennie. At least, not Chris," I said, enveloping them both in a hug.

We all moved into the house and got comfortable at the dining room table. There was a little bit of silence while we took the first couple of bites, but no surprise, Jennie was the first one to talk.

"This is delicious! Did you change your recipe?" Jennie asked.

"I might have made a few adjustments."

Jennie pointed her fork at me, "Well whatever you did, keep it. It sure beats what you would make before."

We all laughed in that moment before Jennie continued, "Enough about the food. Tell us how you wound up here. You mentioned it was a long story. And, tell us what happened to your face because no amount of makeup is covering up that scrape."

I blushed a little bit at her calling me out. I was hoping I wouldn't have to dive into throwing one of her new "friends" under the bus quite yet, but oh well.

"Oh man," I sighed. "Where do I even begin?"

"How about when you woke up?" Chris piped in.

"I guess that qualifies as the beginning," I chuckled. "Well, I woke up in this house, obviously, just outside of a sleek, modern city that looked completely different than where we were. No one else was there and I honestly thought you all were pulling a prank on me, but I figured out pretty quickly I was on my own. I went exploring the city and stumbled into a pizza place to meet one of the locals. He was pretty grizzly at first, but he warmed up to me. Can't say no to this charm, right?"

Chris nodded his head in agreement, "It's the Val effect."

Quiet laughter filled the space acknowledging the term Mark coined, but also missing having his goofy presence around. Lou took this opportunity to ignore the signal, coming out and grabbing a plate. Jennie about dropped her fork at the same time her mouth dropped open, "Hold on, *who* is this?"

"Meet the grizzly pizza shop owner," I gestured for Lou to come join us.

"Name's Lou," he said, sticking out his hand.

"Val, you *never* mentioned this guy," Jennie acted like I had kept her from a major secret.

"I just mentioned him. Plus, we only reconnected a couple of days ago, what do you expect?" I responded.

Jennie and I went back and forth a couple more times while Lou and Chris introduced themselves, carrying on some small talk.

"Anyways," I continued. "Lou basically took me under his wing to help me out. I wanted to figure out what was going on and how to get us all back together, but I had no idea where to start. We discovered there are different worlds and that the bombs hitting us were what transported us all to different places."

"How did you find that out?" Jennie asked.

"Let me back up a couple of steps. Something that caught me off-guard was the fact that there were werewolves in this new world, so I had to watch my back."

Chris was the one to interject this time, "You said werewolves, right? Am I hearing you correctly?"

"I had the same reaction," I cast a glance towards Lou.

He picked up on my signal, "She really did. It took some convincing, but she came around."

"Are you a werewolf?" Chris wasted no time asking Lou.

Lou set down his fork, "Yeah, I'm an alpha of one of the packs in my world."

"How many packs are there?"

"Only two. I'll let Val take it from here."

I looked at Chris and Jennie who were completely sucked in to the story now, "Yeah, so I had a run-in with the alpha of the other pack. Come to find out, he had been in communication with the person behind the bombs, who it turns out, is my dad."

Before I could continue, Jennie dropped her fork on her plate in shock, "Wait, hold on. You mean your dad is partnering with the enemy and dropping these bombs on people?!"

"Pretty wild ... I'm still processing it myself."

"How are you holding up?" Chris asked.

"It's been tough. I have no idea why he would do this, but we've figured out that the bomb is a cover for some sort of teleporter."

Jennie tapped her fingers on the table in thought before saying, "Maybe your dad is working on something bigger. Or maybe he got in too deep with the enemies and this is his way of avoiding adding to the body count."

"You know, you might be on to something there," I said, the gears in my head starting to work in overdrive. "He might have been trying to find a way to avoid killing too many civilians. Instead, he found a way to transport them to different places. I would've been surprised if he was just killing them. That's so far from who he is, but I could be wrong, too."

"So, what else happened on this journey?" Chris asked, bringing the conversation back to where it started.

"Yeah, was Daryl with you?" Jennie asked a little too excited. Chris cut a quick look towards her telling me everything I needed to know with how he felt about where things were left off before we all got thrust into new lives.

I looked down at my plate letting out a sigh. Lou reached over to squeeze my hand. When I brought my gaze back up, Jennie and Chris were going back and forth between Lou and I trying to figure out our reaction.

"He was there, but things went south pretty quick. The other alpha ran a major company which Daryl got a high-ranking job at. This alpha is a bit of a loose cannon, though, and Daryl ended up crossing him which resulted in his head being delivered to me."

Jennie gasped, bringing her hands up to her mouth. Tears started forming in her eyes and Chris reached over to offer comfort. Chris looked over at me with concern, "I'm so sorry, Val. I know how much he meant to you. To both of you."

Jennie had finally gathered herself to speak, "Val, I can't even imagine."

We both knew there were unspoken words hanging in the air. *First Gabriel and now Daryl.* We all sat there giving an unofficial moment of silence, grief filling the space.

After letting a reasonable amount of time pass, I picked the conversation back up, "It was devastating, but I thankfully had Lou who helped me in more ways than I could count. Enough about us, though. Tell us how things have been going for you here."

I was happy to be done talking about all the insanity Lou and I had gone through to get here. *Just add this new layer of grief to everything I've been processing today.* Not to mention, I was thankful to be able to take a large gulp of wine and get to eating my food.

"Chris and I actually ended up in the same place, so we didn't have to try to find each other," Jennie started. "Before I get too far, Val, I want to apologize for how I acted before this all happened. I let jealousy take over and put one of the best friendships I had at risk."

It was my turn to squeeze her hand, "It's okay, Jennie, really. I'm just happy we managed to find each other here."

"Oh, me too!"

Chris jumped in, "When she came back from the pub saying she had seen you, I couldn't believe it! She was the happiest she's been since we've been here."

"Val was pretty excited, too," Lou added.

"Anyways, getting used to this new place wasn't too bad. We were able to find jobs, get an apartment, and find people to hang out with. Everyone has been super nice and welcoming here and we couldn't have asked for a better experience."

They looked at each other and I could tell something else was going on. I didn't want to press too much, so I sat waiting for Jennie to continue. When she didn't, I asked, "Is there something I'm missing here?"

Chris broke his eye contact with Jennie and looked back at me, "This time we've had has brought us closer than ever, so we decided to give a relationship a shot."

"That's so exciting! I'm so happy for you two," I said, reaching for Lou under the table. "You guys make a great couple, I don't know why you didn't do this sooner."

Jennie waived me off, "Enough about that. Something you said earlier stood out to me. You mentioned the bomb was a teleporter, so did the bombs somehow hit in Lou's world for you to get transported here?"

I looked at Lou for some support with this because we had both decided to keep the knowledge of the device limited. He turned back over to Jennie and answered, "We didn't have to deal with the war, but we don't really remember how we got here. It was one of those things where we woke up in a new place."

I nodded my head in agreement saving this story for later in case anyone else asks.

The night continued on with us getting into more light-hearted conversation. We were asking Jennie and Chris about how their relationship was going and broke the news that we were together in case they didn't figure that out already. They were telling us about all the places to go check out while we were here, us writing some of them down for a future date.

As we finished another bottle of wine, Jennie and Chris started making their way out. I pulled Jennie in for another hug, and as I stepped back, I saw a couple of marks on Jennie's arm. Pointing at them, I asked, "How did you get those?"

Jennie looked down to where I was pointing and shrugged, "Good question. They just kind of appeared."

I leaned in to get a closer look, "They almost look like bite marks."

"It's probably nothing. I'll put some bandages or something on them when we get home. They honestly don't hurt. I didn't even know they were there until you pointed them out," Jennie nervously chuckled tucking her arm behind her back.

I glanced over at Chris who was inspecting his own arms covered in these bite marks, "These weren't there a week ago."

"I think they showed up after one of our game nights," Jennie said.

As they were talking to each other, realization dawned on me. The other night when Liam had me pinned, it felt like he was about to bite me. *No, there's no way.*

"Jennie, is one of your new friends named Liam?" I asked.

She snapped her head back to me, "Yeah, you should come meet him!"

"I think I already have. This mark on my face," I said pointing to the remainder of the strawberry mark. "That was caused by Liam."

"No, that's not possible," Jennie shook her head. "He can be a little intense and horny, but he's not violent."

"Jennie, I'm not messing with you when I say it was Liam. He slammed me against a wall and tried biting me."

"That sounds ridiculous, Val. Why would someone want to bite you?" Jennie asked genuinely confused.

"Great question, but I think you should keep your distance when it comes to Liam."

"I think we'll be fine," Jennie said, patting Chris' arm. "It was really good seeing you again! We're going to head out. The wine is starting to set in, but let's get together again soon."

I nodded, but was caught up in what I just figured out. I needed them to get out of here so I could bring Lou up to speed with what's running through my head.

"It was great meeting you two," Lou said, opening the door for them.

"Drive safe!" I added.

We closed the door and watched their car pull out of the driveway. We made our way back to the kitchen to finish cleaning up when Lou looked at me, "What was that all about?"

"There's fucking vampires here," I stared out the window watching their headlights fade into the night.

"What are you talking about?"

"Do you not know about vampires?" I asked.

Lou shook his head and pulled me over to the couch, "Never heard of them."

"They're other creatures of the night who feed on blood. They can't come out during the day, avoid garlic and anything holy, and apparently have ways of making people forget they're snacks," I explained, anger starting to creep into my voice. "That explains what Liam was saying when he was talking about tasting me. I thought he meant that in a sexual way."

"I feel so out of the loop," Lou said.

I left him at the couch and made my way up to the office. When I was a kid, I was fascinated with fantastical characters, so my dad had gotten me a book on all things vampires, werewolves, and anything else mystical. I was hoping he kept that book as I ran my fingers along all the spines studying the titles. About to give up, my head whipped back to the bookshelf finding what I was looking for. I ran back downstairs with the book and shoved it into Lou's lap.

"What's this?" he asked not sure if he should touch it.

I flipped it open to the section covering vampires, "I completely forgot I had this book until now. It's made for kids, but still gets the main points across."

He was skimming through the words taking in whatever information they had to offer him, "Now I see why you were so skeptical about werewolves."

"Forget about that," I said, waving him off. "We have bigger problems on our hands. Liam's a vampire and I am willing to bet he's not alone. On top of that, Jennie and Chris are a buffet and they don't even know it. I knew something weird was going on here, I just *knew* it."

"Okay," Lou started, closing the book and placing it on the coffee table. "What are we going to do about it?"

"We're going to take these mosquitos down," I said, slamming my fist into my other hand. "I can't let my friends get sucked dry and I feel like vampires will be a lot easier to beat than wolves."

"You're probably right," Lou said slightly puffing his chest out.

"We need to start making weapons," I said with my mind going a million miles an minute. I got back up to grab a piece of paper and pen to start writing down everything we need.

"It makes so much sense now. Conor was being so weird about going out after the sun set. Liam and his crew wouldn't show up until it was dark. All of Conor's warnings. Here I thought he was just being weird," I mumbled.

Lou grabbed my hands shaking me out of whatever trance I was in, "Val, you're sounding like a mad woman. Let's get a plan in place. One step at a time, okay? I need to see it to believe it because the concept of vampires just sounds crazy to me."

"Imagine how I felt when you were trying to tell me werewolves are real. Come with me to the pub tomorrow, but don't make it obvious. I'm going to try a couple of things and I want you to observe."

"Well, when you're going off of what's in this crap," Lou rolled his eyes while pointing to the book. He shook his head to move past the kid's book on his lap, "I think I can handle following your plan."

I looked him in his grey eyes, now fully confident I knew the answer to my next question, but still wanting to hear him say it, "Do you trust me, Lou?"

He furrowed his brow a little bit, "Of course I do. Why would you ask that?"

"I'm going to put myself at risk, but I won't let anything happen."

"Val, I don't think that's a good idea," Lou shook his head.

I grabbed Lou's hands as I said, "I won't be caught off-guard this time. I'll have you with me and I'll be prepared to kill whoever I get. I just need you to be there."

His mouth opened and closed a few times as he worked to form the words. "I guess I can go through with this," he finally said reluctantly.

"Good, I'll need you to hide out in the alley next to the parking garage."

Lou nodded his head. I felt better knowing we had a plan to start tackling this because I was going to lose my mind if Jennie and Chris were put at risk any more than they already were. If I was this mad now, I can't imagine what I would be like if anything more drastic were to happen.

I got up and made my way into the kitchen looking for anything made of wood. Lou stayed on the couch watching me in silence. When I found a wooden spoon, I held it up, "The perfect weapon."

"Val, I know you're processing a lot right now, but that's a spoon," he said slowly.

I rolled my eyes, "Obviously, but when I sharpen the end of it, I have the perfect weapon for killing a vampire."

"If you say so."

I moved over to the sink and looked out into the yard before I started whittling the spoon into a stake. I was taking in the peaceful calm, looking up at the moon and the stars, and yet, I felt like I was being watched. *What is my life now?*

"You know, the moon is almost full," I said. I made a note that either tomorrow night or the next would probably be it.

Lou made his way over to me, wrapping his arms around my waist and resting his chin on my head, "It looks like it."

"What are you going to do for the change?"

He tightened his grip on me as he said, "Just run around like a puppy, I guess. This will be the first time in a long time when I can just run without a care in the world. I might wait a little bit to do our test just so I can have this time."

I looked back over my shoulder to find him staring out into the yard with a dream-like expression. It was like he was excited for this change, and I can see why. He doesn't have to look over his shoulder for Warrick and his wolves, doesn't have to worry about protecting people. He can just be a wolf.

I turned myself around dropping the spoon in the sink, drawing his attention from the outside world to here and now. I pulled his face to mine and before we knew it, we were wrapped up making love in the kitchen.

We found ourselves at the pub the next evening ready to execute phase zero of our plan – confirm if vampires are here or not. Lou was sitting at the far end of the bar conversing with Conor while I was taking care of the line of new people who just wandered in. When I had a moment to take a break, I snacked on my garlic fries, making sure I ordered them with extra garlic that way I can see Liam's reaction to it if he decided to show his face tonight.

It was like a sixth sense because I finished my last fry as he sauntered up to the bar. He flashed me a cocky grin, "I see your face is looking better."

"Yeah, no thanks to you," I replied cooly. I braced myself on the bar staring him down, "What'll it be?"

I drew out each word adding extra breath so he could get a good whiff. When I finished the question, he scrunched up his nose, "A breath mint. For you. Your breath is making me nauseous. What the hell did you eat?"

"Just a few garlic fries. Want some? I can get the order going for you."

He threw up his hands, "Not at all. I'm allergic. Just give me a pint."

"Sure thing."

As I turned around to fill up a glass, I flicked my gaze in Lou's direction to see if he heard the interaction. He gave me a slight nod indicating he had and went back to his conversation. So far that was one confirmation, or coincidence, depending on how you look at it. I have to say, though, it gave me some satisfaction knowing I rubbed Liam the wrong way.

The rest of the shift continued with me chewing on some mint gum and Conor looking over at me suspiciously almost as if waiting for me to call him over for help.

I was ready to make my way out of the restaurant, hoping I was able to frustrate Liam enough that he would try to attack me again, but this time I was ready for it. I quickly glanced over to Liam who was glowering at me over the rim of his near-empty glass. *Yup, he's pissed.* Lou was hiding in the shadows of the alley near the parking garage and I was armed with my makeshift stake. Everything was lining up.

It was another eerily quiet night as I said my goodbyes to Conor, heading towards the parking garage. My senses on alert, I tried to listen for any footsteps or other sounds only to be met with nothing. I had started walking past the alley, a frown starting to take residence on my face. While seemingly mad, it seems as though Liam wasn't provoked enough.

The moment I let out a sigh ready to give up I was yanked into the alley. Expecting it to be Lou to point out I was wrong about vampires, I yelled out, "Hey! There's better ways to handle me. You should k – "

My protest trailed off when my eyes met the chocolate brown eyes of Liam. His lip was curled, revealing an elongated canine tooth, "Is there now? Please, enlighten me."

He may have been trying to joke, but his tone was anything but. *Bingo*. I opened my mouth to speak trying my best to sound scared, "L-Liam! I wasn't expecting you here. Wh-what can I do for you?"

I cringed internally, convinced I oversold my performance. But, it must have done the trick because the anger was starting to mix with something that looked like satisfaction. Liam wet his lips with his tongue before saying, "For one thing, I didn't like that little stunt you pulled with the garlic. Secondly, you can expose that pretty little throat of yours and let me get a taste."

He gave me no chance to respond or move. I hadn't realized one of his hands in my hair until he yanked my head to the side giving him an easy target as he pushed me up against the wall again. Thankfully, my hands were free allowing me to reach into my bag to bring out my stake. Given that Liam was pressed up against my body, I didn't have the best vantage point to drive the stake into his heart, so I went with my next best option: wedging it between his ribs hoping I did some sort of damage.

As soon as the stake entered his body, he let out a scream right into my ear, "What the *hell* did you do to me, bitch?!"

I pushed him off, taking my stake with me while I stepped out of the alley as quickly as I could. Liam was standing there holding a hand over his new wound, panting. Satisfied I had all the evidence I needed, I said, "That'll teach you to play with your food. Don't fuck with me, Liam."

I headed towards the parking garage not looking back to acknowledge the slew of curses Liam was throwing in my direction. When I knew I was out of sight, I quickened my pace jumping into Lou's car the minute he turned it on. I took a moment to catch my breath before looking over at him, "So, believe me now?"

Lou let out a low whistle, "You know you're crazy, right? You see danger and head straight for it instead of turning around and running."

"You still didn't answer my question," I said, cocking an eyebrow.

"Yeah, I believe you now. Happy?"

"Yup," I settled into my seat as we left the city behind us. I felt proud of myself standing up to yet another villain in my life without needing to be rescued by Lou.

We got back to the house making ourselves comfortable on the couch in the living room. I was resting my head against Lou's chest as I looked up at him, "So, I think it's fair to say we should probably figure something out for handling the vampire problem here."

Lou was drawing slow circles on my arm as he said, "That wouldn't be the worst idea. I think we should start with getting weapons and building our strength. I should probably help you with your fighting, too."

"As much as I want to throw a jab back at that comment, I agree. I'm not the weakest person, though. I'm not gonna lie, Liam almost had me back there."

"I know. I think it's safe to say that us supernatural creatures tend to have more strength than the average human," he said with a lazy grin on his face.

I sat up and started moving towards the stairs to get ready to sleep, "It's settled then. We train for a little bit then go out for our first round of hunting."

Lou stood up, meeting my gaze, "First things first, I need to get through the change and test our theory about the device, but you could get a head-start on the training. Just promise me you won't get yourself in any danger while I'm away?"

I flashed him a grin, "I don't like to make promises I may not be able to keep."

Chapter 5

I woke up to a text the next morning from Conor letting me know to not worry about coming in. We passed the holiday which meant the pub was going to be nearly empty for the next couple of days. I put my phone back on my nightstand rolling over to cuddle into Lou. He threw his arm over, pulling me into him while he mumbled, "Don't you have to worry about work today?"

"Nope, I have the next few days off."

"Maybe from the pub, but not from becoming a vampire hunter," he said with sleep still present in his voice.

I let out a quick laugh, "I believe the term you were looking for is vampire slayer."

"I don't care what it is, you need to get up."

I propped myself up on my elbow, earning a one-eyed look from Lou. I poked him in his bare chest, "You don't get to tell me what I *need* to do."

Lou moved so fast I had no time to react, pinning me under him as he smiled, "Until you're no longer caught off-guard by me doing this, you'll need to start training."

He gave me a quick forehead kiss before releasing me and heading towards the bathroom. I stared up at the ceiling letting out a sigh. He was right – I needed to start training, and the sooner I did so, the better.

I got out of bed and dressed in workout clothes. Lou followed me out of the room downstairs to get some breakfast. As we ate, he debriefed me on what my training plan was going to look like in these beginning stages, and let me tell you, there was a lot of everything: cardio, strength, fighting, and stretching. Not wanting to miss a beat, because I was honestly feeling a little overwhelmed thinking about the list he just gave me, we made our way out to the backyard to start on the stretching portion of the day. While Lou was over me stretching one of my legs, he said, "Tonight I'll be changing, so that'll mean tomorrow I'll run our test."

"How is it that you're planning on doing a lot tomorrow when you would normally take a couple of days off back in your world after your change?"

"Believe it or not, I feel stronger here. Something about not having silver in the water will do that to a wolf. Plus, I won't be having to fight off Warrick or his pack, so with not being wounded, I should be able to recover quickly," he said, switching my legs. "You know, you're pretty flexible already."

"I did gymnastics at one point in my life and decided I liked my flexibility."

"You won't hear me complain," Lou winked.

We finished getting limber then moved on to a run. I did my best to keep up with Lou's pace, but ended up falling behind after a couple of miles earning me one of Lou's infamous looks of disapproval. *Just wait until we get to the strength training portion.* I had no idea how much we had just run, but my muscles were complaining. Bent over with my hands on my knees, I said, "Lou, please tell me that's all we're doing today."

"Calling it quits already?" he asked not sounding out of breath *at all*. "We're just getting started."

I groaned but got myself to stand straight up. I put my hands on my hips, "What's next?"

"Good answer," Lou said. "Have any weights around here?"

"Just dumbbells and resistance bands in the basement."

Lou jerked his head toward the house, "Let's get to it."

Even though the weights my parents had weren't that much, Lou was able to make my muscles burn in a way they hadn't for years. Unlike the running, though, I was able to keep up with him which earned me some praise as we moved into the fighting portion. I will admit, this was completely out of my arena. As Lou was coming at me, I had no idea what to do. Every time he swung at me, I would move right into the movement rather than dodge. I had no way of knowing how to anticipate the next move, so when he would go for my legs, I was easily dropped. It was like we were out of sync in all ways possible which is something I haven't felt with Lou before. He was trying to help with plenty of corrections until he finally sighed, dropping his shoulders, "Let's stop here for now. This is the one area you could use the most work."

I nodded trying to catch my breath, feeling the sweat drip down every inch of my body.

He put a hand on my shoulder, "I'm going to whip up something for dinner before I head out for the night. You good with focusing on the strength, cardio, and stretching while I'm away?"

"Yeah," I said, feeling frustrated.

Lou tilted my head up so I had no choice but to meet his grey eyes, "Hey, you haven't had to truly fight yet which is a good thing. We'll get you there. All I want you to know is the basics so you can understand where to throw your weight to get out of situations and turn the fight around to your advantage. Nothing crazy."

I held his gaze for a few beats before letting out a breath, "I know I'll get there. I just didn't think I was going to be this bad."

He grinned, "If only you fight as well as you dance."

I shoved myself away, making him laugh. I let the sound envelop me, washing away the frustration.

When we got back upstairs, the sun was already low in the sky causing Lou to fly around the kitchen. While I took my time eating, he shoveled the food in his mouth so fast you would've thought he hadn't eaten in days. I stopped, the fork halfway to my mouth to see he had already finished his food, "What's the rush? You have plenty of time."

"I need a good amount of time to digest before I change. It's not the best feeling when everything shifts on a full stomach," Lou answered with a voice already getting gravely.

"I guess I never thought of that."

"Most people wouldn't," Lou started. "Trust me when I say I've learned the hard way that you don't want a full stomach. It wasn't a pretty sight."

I grimaced visualizing a wolf with an upset stomach.

Lou leaned in for a kiss, "I'm going to head outside. Stay safe tonight."

I returned the kiss and watched him go. At least I didn't have to worry about any other wolves wandering around, and as far as I knew, the vampires prowled the city.

I wouldn't make Lou angry this time by accidentally getting myself in danger, so the night went on with me staying locked up in the house watching movies and enjoying snacks. Occasionally, I would hear a howl off in the distance that would make me smile. It made me happy knowing Lou was probably having one of the best nights as a wolf without having a care in the world.

The day finally caught up to me, my eyelids no longer able to stay open as I made my way up to my room. I hadn't realized I drifted off until I was clearly in a dream.

I was walking towards the cathedral as the sun was starting to set. I passed a woman rushing past me in the other direction, accidentally bumping shoulders with her. She whipped her head up, looking at me with wild eyes, "You'll only seal your fate stepping into that building."

"What?" I asked confused. I took in the sight in front of me. This woman had matted black hair that looked like it hadn't been washed for weeks. Her clothes in dirty tatters hanging off her tiny body. There was blood dripping from various parts of her body coming from wounds matching what Jennie and Chris had.

She raised a shaky finger, pointing at the cathedral, "There's nothing but misery and death in there."

I looked at the cathedral then turned back around to respond to her only to find the woman gone. While still looking for her, my body continued forward as if it had no other option but to head into the cathedral. The closer I got to its doors, the more I felt like I was in a trance. I started reaching for the handle when I heard a loud bang followed by some knocking.

I shot up in bed clutching my chest as I felt my heart racing. The knocking noise was still present and I was starting to feel like it was never going to leave my head when I heard my name being called out. *Shit, I forgot I locked all the doors!*

I ran downstairs trying to figure out if I would find Lou at the front door or the sliding doors leading out to the backyard. My question was answered when I saw the outline of a man leaning against the back door. I rushed over there and opened the door, surprised when I had to catch him, "You scared the crap out of me, Lou."

I started pulling him over to the couch as he replied, "I don't know why you locked the door."

"Oh, *now* you don't know why?" I asked sarcastically. "You've been harping on me the entire time we've known each other about how I have to lock myself up like some damn princess in a tower."

"You finally decided to listen to me?" he asked, eyes dancing with humor.

I stepped back putting my hands on my hips, "You sure are in good spirits. Maybe I should let you run freely more often."

Lou was smiling up at me, "It was amazing, you have no idea what it was like to run without a care in the world. I didn't have to constantly look over my shoulder, listen for any screams, deal with *anything.* Val, it was liberating."

My expression softened, "I'm happy you were able to get that. Now, what do you want for breakfast?"

"Anything and everything, including you," Lou said, jumping up from the couch and pulling me back down with him. I let out a squeal of surprise before his mouth crashed into mine, kissing me with such passion that I felt it ripple throughout my body. Savoring every moment, we lost all track of time as we laid there tangled up in one another. By the time we were done, we were on the floor breathing hard.

Lou looked over at me, brushing a strand of hair from my face, "You said something about food earlier?"

"You're on your own now that you wore me out. My muscles were already spent from yesterday," I said doing my best to keep a straight face.

He nuzzled his face in my neck brushing my sensitive spots with his lips, "Would this motivate you?"

I pretended to think, "Hmm, I don't know."

Lou moved himself so he was more on top of me, letting his hands explore my body some more. "How about this?" he asked in a low growl.

"I guess that could do the trick," I said.

"If you keep this up, we're never getting off this floor."

"Who said I wanted to?"

Lou nipped at my neck before standing up. He reached a hand towards me to help me up. I headed to the kitchen to start making breakfast, "You recovered fast for someone who couldn't stand not too long ago."

Lou sat at the island, "It's amazing what your body can do when it's not hindered."

"I guess that's true."

We continued talking about what it was like for him to have this completely new experience of being just a wolf while I whipped up a hearty breakfast. Despite the light-hearted joking back and forth, I couldn't escape the dread pooling in my stomach that had been there since I woke from yet another nightmare. I don't know what it is about this place, but I've never had nightmares like this. They're so realistic and I'm left with the worry that what I dream is going to happen considering I met Liam the day after seeing him.

"Everything okay, Val? Your brows keep inching together with every second that ticks by," Lou said in between bites.

Jumping a little, I threw on a half-smile as I looked over at Lou, "Yeah! Just thinking about how I'm going to keep this training up while you're away."

There was no way I was going to tell Lou about the nightmare. Not when he's had such a great change and is planning on leaving for an indefinite amount of time. The last thing I needed was for him to worry about my safety and potentially delay this test. We needed to figure out this piece of information sooner rather than later so we could try to get ahead of a possible Warrick appearance.

He gave me a skeptical look before finishing off his meal. I watched him as he dropped his dirty dishes in the sink before he looped around to give me a kiss on the forehead, "I'm going to pack stuff up real quick then I'll probably head out."

"So soon?"

"The sooner I leave, the sooner I can get back. Hopefully ..." he trailed off, and in that moment, I could tell we were both feeling and thinking the same thing. We had no idea how long it would take for Lou to get back to me so that we could move our vampire hunting plan in motion.

It wasn't long before Lou and I found ourselves in the driveway, him in the driver's seat of his car and me leaning on the cool metal. His grey eyes were filled with sadness, "You sure you'll be okay on your own? You've been a little off today."

I placed a reassuring hand on his arm while giving him a soft smile, "Of course. I'm just a little sad to see you go, that's all. Besides, you don't need to worry about me. I'll keep a low profile and won't invite any strangers in."

That got a little chuckle out of him, "Whatever you say, Val. Try not to throw too many parties without me, okay?"

I leaned in placing a soft kiss on his lips. As I pulled away, I said, "No promises."

I backed away from the car and watched as Lou made his way out of the driveway in the opposite direction of the city. I felt a pang of sadness build in my heart, but I did my best to ignore it as I turned around to go back into the house.

I woke up the next day, thankful I wasn't sweating from another nightmare. I laid there taking in the quiet of the house. No Lou making a quick breakfast, no one knocking on the door. Just silence. *I wonder if Lou made it back okay.* Thinking through what Lou could be up to, I found myself missing him even more.

I sighed as I took in the sight staring back at me in the mirror: hair matted on one side and knotted on the other, puffy eyes that looked like I had been crying, swollen face still trying to shake off sleep.

"Val, you gotta do something about this," I said to myself, shaking my head as I started working through my morning routine.

I dived in the pool, wearing a swimsuit this time to avoid another Warrick-incident, running through my training plan for the day. I figured once I was done with the weights and the cardio, I'd go see what I can dig up to use for boxing practice. Content with what I'd be filling my morning with, my thoughts shifted to my most recent nightmare. Everything ends up pointing to that cathedral, and despite all the warnings, there was a small part of me wanting to visit it. Maybe that would give me the opportunity to start scoping out some of the other vampires running around instead of going straight for Liam. The pub would also give me that opportunity if I decided to pay more attention to the group Liam always surrounds himself with.

I stopped to catch my breath after finishing one of my laps. I rested my head on my arms looking out over the rolling hills that now occupied the space behind my house. I had a plan I needed to write down so I could review it with Lou when he got back, but I knew for sure I would be staking out (no pun intended, yet) who were the low hanging fruit in the vampire group. That way we shouldn't get noticed and there would be a few less blood suckers running around to torment the locals and tourists. As Lou and I get better at taking the vampires down, we'd eventually work our way up the chain until they were completely eradicated.

I sighed, turning around to do a few more laps. After a couple of strokes, I turned my head to get some air, noticing the silhouette of a man standing at the opposite edge of the pool. I took a few more strokes before stopping, my heart starting to beat out of my chest as realization settled in and fear started taking over. Looking wildly around, I couldn't find any sign of the man who was watching me. My gaze shifted over to the back doors. *Shit, shit, shit!*

I clambered out of the pool, getting ready to grab the towel when I noticed a manilla envelope sitting there on the same chair. I took one more glance around the yard, not completely sure if I was alone or not. Tentatively grabbing the envelope then ripping the towel from the chair, I bolted into the house, slamming the door closed behind me and clicking the lock in place. I stood there taking in the silence not fully trusting I was alone in the house. When I didn't hear any unusual sounds, I placed the envelope on the island then started checking every corner of the house for any intruders, making sure every lock was set in place and every curtain was drawn as I moved from room to room.

As soon as I finished my patrol, I hunkered down at the island texting Jennie to see if she and Chris could come over later so I could have some sort of company. While I waited for a response, I opened the envelope carefully removing the contents. Quickly scanning over the papers, it looked like they were articles about my dad.

"What the hell?" I asked, brow furrowing. Jennie responded letting me know they would be there in ten minutes. I shifted my focus back to the papers in front of me. They were numerous news stories of my dad, a high-ranking military official, being captured as a POW. There were details about the ransom the enemy was demanding for the military to get him back, on top of what they would do if their timeline wasn't met. It was gruesome to say the least. In the middle of all the articles, there were pictures showing not only my dad battered and bruised, but also my mom sitting there with her head hanging limply, clearly unconscious.

My hand found its way up to my mouth as more and more words kept popping out at me. From everything I could gather, he and my mom were kidnapped when he was on a mission in another country. It was a routine mission to look into an ally's defenses since there was concern of potential attacks. I couldn't read anymore, the breakfast from this morning now threatening to come up as the room started to spin.

I had no idea what to make of everything I was seeing. Was it real? Was it fabricated? Who the hell was the man I saw while swimming? It can't be anyone here. There's no one who knows where I live except for Jennie and Chris. Who would know about my dad? There's no way it could be either of them, could it? Or ...

Dread started washing over me as realization started dawning with that last question but was quickly interrupted by the doorbell ringing. I rushed over to the door, ushering Jennie and Chris inside before slamming and locking the door behind them.

With her face full of concern, Jennie put her hand on my shoulder, "Val, what's going on? Are you okay?"

I shrugged off her shoulder heading back to the island, "Not really. Do you know about any of this?"

I held up the papers for her to see. She started looking more concerned with the more she saw. Chris came up behind her looking shocked. Jennie looked back at me, "What is this?"

"Shit," I mumbled under my breath as I slumped into the chair behind me.

Chris shifted his gaze from Jennie to me, "Val, are you in some sort of trouble? How did you get all of these?"

I was rubbing my face crafting my words to figure out where I wanted to start. I sighed, looking down at my feet, "Can you guys stay a while? Like a couple of days?"

"Sure, Val," Jennie said softly while getting comfortable in a chair. Chris pulled one up next to her before settling in and placing an arm around her shoulders. "Anything you need. Just tell us what's going on."

"I don't even know if these are real ... I was hoping you two knew something about them."

"Why?" Chris asked. "Why would we know anything about these let alone try to mess with you like this?"

He had a point. I shrugged, "I have no idea. It's the easiest explanation? The one that I can handle? These caught me completely off-guard. I know these are most likely something someone made up, but there's a small part of me that wonders if everything in front of me is true. I just don't know what to think, to feel."

I stopped before the tears had a chance of taking over. I felt Jennie place her hand over mine to offer reassurance, "I can't imagine what must be going through your head right now, especially since you're in a world far away from him, but who do you think would do something like this?"

I let out a small laugh, "That's the thing. I know exactly who did this and the thought makes me want to crawl out of my skin."

"Want to fill us in?" Chris asked.

I brought my gaze back up to theirs to see Jennie shooting him a look. She looked back over at me giving an apologetic shrug. I shook my head to let her know it's okay. Taking a deep breath to steady myself, I closed my eyes, "You remember the other alpha I mentioned?"

"The one who killed Daryl?" Jennie asked. "Yeah, what about him?"

"Well, I'm 99.9% sure that's who did this," I started opening my eyes again. Before they could say anything, I continued, "His name is Warrick and he's not going to stop tormenting me until

I'm dead because I decided at the wrong time to be bold, and of course, this would happen after Lou has already left."

Jennie cocked her head to the side, "What do you mean?"

"I'll start at the beginning and fill in the details I left out before," I said, taking another deep breath before diving into the twists and turns. "I met Warrick the same day I met Lou. Warrick took an immediate interest in me, but don't worry, everything was telling me to run from him until I learned he had information on the bombs. Lou and I hatched up this plan for me to get closer to Warrick because that was the only way I'd be getting any information out of him, so I did the only thing I knew: date him. I finally got to the point where I could gain more access to Warrick's computer which is how we found all the information on my dad. Fast forward a little bit to when he killed Daryl and I lost my mind. I marched right up to Warrick, stabbed him with a venomous knife and got the hell out. He wasn't too happy about that and now he's going on a rampage trying to take revenge on me."

Jennie and Chris were staring at me in shock, mouths gaping open. I just shrugged and continued, "Did I mention that Warrick also supposedly killed his previous girlfriend because she went running to Lou? Well, the other day I saw her here, so that instantly confirmed Warrick has the ability to teleport. Given the details on my dad combined with an unhinged alpha on a mission, I am 100% certain it's Warrick behind all of this."

A few beats passed before Chris broke the silence, "How did he know where to find you to drop this stuff off?"

"Great question," I said. "When I was swimming earlier, I saw someone standing at the edge of the pool. At first, I thought it was Liam."

"Why would it be Liam?" Jennie asked confusion etching her face.

I let out some more laughter, "Let's just say he's not too happy with me right now. I might have tried killing him to prove a point to Lou."

"You did what?!"

I winced at Jennie's question, "I had a hunch that he was a vampire and I had to show Lou what I was talking about, so I stabbed Liam with a makeshift stake."

"You've got to be kidding me, Val. You're attacking our friends now? Since when do you go around stabbing people?"

"J, I think you're missing the point here," Chris said, holding up a hand to quiet Jennie. He turned to me, "Val, I've had my suspicions about our new friend group ever since you pointed out the bite marks on us. It didn't sit right with me, and the more I thought about it, the more I realized I was missing from my memory. I never remembered specifics around our game nights with them and they were always quick to tell us about stuff that happened. Jennie and I went along with it, but now I think they were just telling us what we wanted to hear to cover up their feedings."

Jennie shot him an incredulous look before returning her attention back to me. I gestured to the inside of her arm where the edges of fresh bite marks were hiding. She looked down at them for a while. Shaking her head, she looked back up at me, "It makes no sense. They brought us in like we were one of their own."

"They were probably wanting to see if you could handle being one of them," I said cautiously. I may be going through all the emotions, but finding out my new friends were using me as a food source then lying about it wouldn't be the easiest thing to process either. "Jennie, I wasn't pointing that out to you just because I was jealous or holding on to ill-will from what you pulled with Daryl. I was pointing it out to you because I don't want see you two fall to the same fate as Daryl. I can't lose anyone else."

"Speaking of losing people," Chris interjected. "Where's Lou? You mentioned he left."

"He's back in his world for the moment. We wanted to see how long it takes for the device to recharge and it gave him a good opportunity to check on things there."

"Wait," Jennie held up her hand. "What device are you talking about?"

Shit, there goes trying to keep details to ourselves. I took a steadying breath then started, "You can't speak about this to anyone, especially when we don't know who to trust here, okay?"

They both nodded their heads in agreement as I continued, "We didn't just randomly end up here. Lou and I found enough information to be able to build a device similar to what my dad is using in the bombs. We essentially have a way to jump to different worlds without causing mass chaos."

Jennie started shaking her head, a slow smile forming, "This is something out of a movie, you know that? I can't believe this is real. How are you keeping everything together?"

All I could do was shrug, "I'm just taking it one step at a time."

"Any idea when he'll be back?" Chris asked.

I shook my head, "Nope, and I have no way to contact him, so of course things would start to go haywire."

"I don't think it's coincidental timing," Chris said.

"I don't think it is either ..." I agreed.

"Do you have any plans for dinner?" Jennie randomly asked.

"Wh – no, I hadn't even thought of that," I said.

She stood up, grabbed her things, and headed toward the door. Chris and I looked at each other then back at Jennie who was waving for us to join her. I rolled my eyes then held up a finger to tell her to give me a second. I was still in my bikini with wet hair – there was no way I was going out like this.

We were in the car, me in fresh clothes and wet hair in a bun on the top of my head. I had no idea where we were going and Jennie wasn't giving anything away. In fact, none of us were really in the mood to talk. My mind was still reeling with the fact that Warrick was here and most likely messing with me, and I'm sure Jennie and Chris have a lot on their minds too.

To my relief, we passed the pub. I wasn't feeling up to going into a crowded bar tonight to potentially have run-ins with anyone who could hurt me. We were heading up the main street, my stomach started feeling the usual uneasiness associated with the cathedral as the building loomed over us. I was chewing on my lip, starting to feel some relief when we turned and put it in our review mirror. That was another thing I wasn't ready to face right now either.

We pulled into the parking lot belonging to a small restaurant on the outskirts of the city. There weren't too many other cars there which meant it was going to be a quieter evening. I let out a sigh of relief feeling the tension fall from my shoulders.

Walking into the restaurant, Chris took care of getting us a table while I took in my surroundings. This place looked like it had once been a house with cozy furnishings, simple wall decorations that included pictures of the owners and their regulars hanging over light green walls. Where the ceilings met the walls, there was dark brown crown molding. It was lit by old oil lamps hanging on the walls and sitting on the tables. The entire area was filled with smells belonging to comfort food making my stomach growl and mouth water. There was a piano being played in the corner playing soft tunes, slightly out of key. When we made it to our table, I gave Chris and Jennie a small smile, "This place is cute. How did you find it?"

"We stumbled in here one day and felt at peace. The piano is a new addition, though, but you won't hear me complain," Jennie explained as she settled in. She looked back up at me, "Sorry about my reaction earlier. It's weird, but I can't really remember a lot either, like Chris. It's hard."

"It's okay, Jennie," I said reaching across the table to give her hand a squeeze. "Do you think you guys would be okay staying at my place for a while?"

"I think we can do that," Jennie answered as she looked at Chris. He gave a quick nod of agreement. "We'll stop by our place when we're done to grab some stuff, but we'll at least stay until Lou gets back."

"Thank you, both of you," I said gratefully.

We dived into our food, my mac-and-cheese filling my body with much-needed warmth. Our conversation went back to laughter and joking like we hadn't missed a beat. The other customers started to filter out until us three were the only ones left. We picked up on the hint that it was almost closing time, Jennie and Chris both heading to the restrooms while I held down the table. I continued to look around until my eyes settled on the piano, drawn by the familiar melody now being played. I closed my eyes, swaying to the notes until my eyes immediately snapped open as soon as I recognized the music. I flicked my gaze over to the person playing only able to see his back until he turned his head. I caught a glimpse of one familiar, ice-blue eye. He gave a little finger wave before turning his focus back to the keys in front of him.

Goosebumps erupted all over from head to toe while my dinner danced in my stomach. Thankfully, Chris and Jennie were making their way back over talking to our waiter. I stood up as they reached the table, "Are we all set?"

"Yup!"

"Good, let's get out of here."

I turned on my heels and rushed out of the restaurant not wanting to spend any longer in the same room as Warrick. When we settled in the car, Jennie looked at me, "What's the rush, Val?"

"Just ready to get back home, that's all."

I didn't need to add to Jennie's worries, not when she just treated me to dinner and is offering to stay with me as an added security blanket while Lou is away. I turned my attention out the window to meet the sinister gaze of Warrick watching the car drive away, causing the air around me to crackle with the electric energy I hadn't felt in a while.

Chapter 6

It had been a week at least since Jennie and Chris took me to dinner. We had been enjoying each other's company, filling the house with laughter and happiness, but that still didn't do anything to shake the feeling of dread after confirming Warrick is here and Lou was still gone. Jennie would catch me feeling down every now and then, and when she would, she would go out of her way to do something funny. I played along, but as soon as I was alone, I would go back to moping.

I had started my shifts back up at the pub with no incidents to report. No Warrick either, so I was hoping that meant he had no idea where I would spend my days even though I knew he was watching every move I made. Jennie and Chris would come hang out every now and then to show face with Liam and their other friends while also keeping an eye on me.

There was one night where the crowd in the pub slowed down so Conor sent me home early. Jennie and Chris were still hanging out which meant I had the house to myself for a little while. I hopped on my bike, taking the long way home, letting the wind whip my hair around and take the breath from my lungs to help lift the heavy weight that's been resting on my shoulders. When I got back to the house, I poured myself a glass of wine sitting on the couch. I let out a breath, letting my head rest on the back of the couch, enjoying the silence. The doorbell rang, sounding a lot louder than I had remembered, shattering my moment of peace.

I slowly made my way over, worried about who was going to be standing on the other side. My hand hesitated over the door handle – if this was Warrick, I was screwed. Leaning forward, I checked the peephole. I couldn't see anything, but that didn't mean he wasn't there. When I opened the door, no one was standing on the other side. Confused, I poked my head out looking in every direction. Nothing. I was about to close the door when I looked down finding another manilla envelope. *Can't I have a moment of peace?*

I wasted no time heading back into the house locking the door behind me. I could feel the anger start pooling in my stomach. *Why was I letting Warrick have such a hold over me when I haven't even really talked to him?* I shook my head to clear away all the thoughts and emotions starting to build, to re-focus on what I was holding in my hands. I pulled out a few sheets of photos topped with a note. The photos were of Jennie, Chris, and I out at dinner, hanging out in the house, and just generally out and about. Brow furrowing, I moved the one piece of paper to the top to read Warrick's handwriting: *It would be a shame if you were to lose more people you loved, but a fair price to pay in return for what you did to me. See you around, love.*

I ran up to my room since I had no idea when to expect Jennie and Chris to return. I didn't want to take a chance on them finding yet another "present" Warrick dropped off, especially since it was a threat to them. As I was setting the papers on my nightstand, I noticed my hands were shaking. From anger or fear, I don't know, but I did know that Warrick was effortlessly clawing himself back into my mind. No matter how I tried to shake him, he was there giving me that little finger wave.

I started pacing my room, chewing on my fingers, a habit I thought I had dropped years ago. There were so many things running through my mind I had no idea where to even begin with processing what I was feeling. Taking a deep breath, I paused my death march back and forth to pinch the bridge of my nose trying to bring any sense of clarity back into my life. Of the things I knew for certain, I knew I was angry and scared. Angry at him having such a hold over me. Scared because I didn't know what would be happening next. Hard to predict someone who's such a loose cannon.

Letting out a groan, I headed back downstairs to leave Jennie and Chris a note that I made it home and turned in for the night. That would at least give me some peace before having to shove all my emotions back in their boxes so those two didn't worry something was up.

Settling into my bed, it surprisingly didn't take long for me to drift off to dreamland considering how much is occupying my mind.

Riding my bike, I sped around the turns in the rolling hills here. It was a quiet night with clouds starting to drift in, threatening rain at any moment. I knew it would be risky, but I didn't care if I got caught out in a storm. Like Lou, I was having my moment of feeling free. I found myself at the end of the road overlooking the ocean. The sound of the waves relentlessly beating the cliffs in their never-ending battle provided a sense of calm. I stood there still straddling my bike when I heard gravel crunching behind me.

There were no headlights to signal the approach which immediately raised my guard I had been working so hard to let go of. I made no move to turn my head, but was keeping an eye on my mirrors to watch the black car pull up. By the time the engine turned off and the door closed, every muscle in my body was tense. I had no idea who to expect, but I wasn't getting my hopes up for Lou.

"Fancy meeting you here at my favorite spot, love," the familiar British accent washed over me.

"Didn't know we were claiming spots now," I said still not turning to him or removing my helmet. When I didn't hear footsteps approaching, I looked over my shoulder.

There was Warrick, leaning against his car with his arms crossed. He was looking out towards the ocean with his face showing a hint of a soft smile. Instead of his usual C-suite wardrobe, he was wearing a white v-neck shirt that hugged every muscle in his torso combined with leather pants that left nothing to the imagination. Oh boy ...

He brought his gaze lazily over to me, "Miss me?"

My mouth was dry from being caught off-guard by how attracted I was to him so I just shook my head.

He pushed himself off his car raising his eyebrows in surprise, "No?"

It didn't take long for him to close the distance between us making every nerve in my body tingle with desire. He reached to lift my visor so he could see my eyes. As soon as he had a better view, he knew he had me. Warrick placed both of his hands on each side of my head, hooking his fingers underneath the edge of my helmet to lift it off my head.

"*You sure?*" *Warrick asked with a voice filled with lust.*

I couldn't protest as I felt the pressure from the helmet being removed. Every part of me was throbbing with a desire I knew only Warrick could fulfill. A little voice had managed to break through, reminding me I had Lou to go home to. He knew how to fulfill those desires. What I was feeling was just from the tension building up in this moment. Nothing more.

I heard my helmet drop to the ground as his lips crashed into mine. I hated that I wasn't doing anything to stop this. It was as if I was no longer in control of my body. He maneuvered us over to his car so my back was pressed against the back passenger door while he moved his lips to the sensitive spot on my neck. My skin erupted in pleasureful goosebumps.

"This conversation has been very one-sided, love. I can stop if you want me to, just say the word," Warrick said with his lips gently brushing against my skin sending shivers down my spine.

Courage filled me, leading one of my hands to cup his chin bringing his molten icy blue gaze on me, "Don't."

I was caught off-guard by my response. It was very much the opposite of what I wanted to say, right? It had to be.

"Don't what?" he growled at me.

"Don't stop."

Warrick was once again pressed against me being rough, yet gentle. It wasn't long before we were in the car, skin against skin, hips grinding in a synchronous rhythm. Warrick knew all the right spots to elicit moans from my lips that only drove him mad. When we collided like this, everything else melted away.

I found myself tightening my grip as pressure built between my legs signaling I was about to come. I arched my back into him not able to get close enough as I let out a breathy sigh, "Please, Warrick. I need this."

"*Need what, love?*"

"*I need – *"

"Val?" I heard Jennie call up the stairs. "You home?" My sex dream was interrupted by the loud volume of her voice calling from downstairs. I sat upright patting my hands all over to make sure that was just a dream and that I wasn't really naked with Warrick, trying to catch my breath.

"Val?" Jennie called again starting to sound more worried.

Feeling the tingling sensation slipping away, I took a steadying breath as I got out of bed. I shook my head muttering to myself, "At least it wasn't a nightmare this time."

I rubbed my neck then set my shoulders, forcing a smile on my face. There was no way I was about to let them know what I was just dreaming about. I headed towards the stairs, "Yeah, I'm coming!"

There was the unmistakable sound of rain pitter-pattering against the windows. Looking outside, it seemed to be daytime which confused me. Shouldn't Jennie have seen my note from last night? I started jogging down the stairs and stopped staring at the scene in front of me in disbelief. Standing next to Jennie was Lou who was smiling from ear to ear.

I ran down to him, jumping in his arms and wrapping my legs around his waist, "You're back!"

Lou buried his face in my neck taking a deep breath, "I missed you so much, Val. Apparently, you were starting to miss me?"

I pulled back so I could look at him, "Of course I missed you, but what do you mean?"

He leaned in so only I could hear him, "I can smell your arousal."

I blushed. I couldn't tell him I just had a dream about Warrick satisfying me. Instead, I gave him a quick nibble on his ear then whispered, "Are you just going to stand there, or are you going to do something about it?"

Jennie interjected with a nervous laugh, "I'll just go now. I'm sure you two have a *lot* of catching up to do."

Lou and I didn't say anything. He tightened his grip on my thighs as we made our way back up to my room. It's safe to say we locked ourselves away for hours, our activity of choice not involving sharing too many words.

My head was on his chest, my fingers drawing circles on his stomach, "How was the pizza place and your pack?"

Lou was gently rubbing my head as he said, "It's still standing. Profitable, too, which means Raf is working magic. Everyone's good and surprisingly haven't run into any trouble."

"Any sign of Warrick?" I asked, feeling a twinge of guilt.

Lou paused then answered, "Surprisingly no. That makes me worry he's already found his way here. Have you had any signs?"

Sighing, I propped myself up. This conversation was going to happen sooner or later, so might as well rip the band-aid off even though I didn't want to push aside the bliss we were both in.

I reached over to my nightstand to retrieve both envelopes Warrick had delivered, still without saying anything. Lou sat himself up a little more, brows furrowing in concern. He examined the envelopes and their contents briefly then looked back up at me, "Val, what happened?"

"The first envelope is the bottom one which was left next to my towel as I was swimming. He watched me swim for a little bit before magically disappearing in the way he does. The top one was left on the porch last night with no trace of him. I saw him at a restaurant Jennie and Chris took me to. He hasn't made any direct contact yet, but he's definitely messing with my head."

"That explains why Jennie and Chris are staying here. I just thought you finally convinced them to move in, but I guess it didn't take much work from your end," he said while reading through the articles. "Do you know if these are real?"

"I don't think they are, but I have no way of confirming," I said, fighting back tears.

Lou picked up on the slight change in my voice and reached out to pull me in tighter, "Hey, shh. It's okay, Val. The important thing is that you're safe. I can't imagine what you must've gone through and I left you alone."

"It's not on you, Lou. Just poor timing."

"Or good timing if you're Warrick. He's been here longer than we thought if he knew I was gone."

I turned my head so I was speaking directly into Lou, "I'm just happy you're back. I filled Jennie and Chris in on everything that had happened before we got here, but I couldn't bring myself to tell them he's here and tormenting me more, especially since he threatened them. I have no idea when he's going to strike or how he's going to do it."

Lou gave me a gentle squeeze, "That's how he plays his game. We won't let him get you right where he wants you. I promise you that."

We laid there for a while longer mostly to help my emotions calm down then made our way into the lab to go over what Lou had figured out. He set the device on the lab bench in between us, "We know it's a little longer than a week before this bad boy can be used again. I think when we go to our next place, it should be easier to divide and conquer to look for your other friends now that we should have Jennie and Chris on our side. I'm assuming you were able to convince them to stop letting their 'friends' enjoy the human buffet?"

I nodded my head gesturing for Lou to continue, "Good. We should try to minimize the amount of time we spend in one world unless absolutely necessary to try to keep Warrick on his toes."

"That's a good plan," I agreed. "While we're doing this, we need to capture notes about each place we visit. That way, we don't have to worry about forgetting whether or not we tried a code and what was there."

"Exactly," Lou started, but his attention quickly turned to the live security feed to see Jennie and Chris pulling up on the street. They got out of the car and unloaded a few boxes which I assumed were the rest of their stuff. It made me happy they came to this decision without requiring me to ask. But, that meant the conversation Lou and I were having was over – we'd have to come back to the device later. We locked it up then made our way out of the lab to offer them both help.

Chris came through the door first, looking at Lou, "It's great to see you made it back, man."

"Let me grab that for you," Lou said, relieving Chris of the heavy, wet box in his arms.

"Thanks," Chris said.

Jennie rushed into the house slightly out of breath, "We decided it was time to pull the plug and move in. We're assuming you'll need us at some point when you decide to leave this place, and considering we don't want to hang around too much longer, we figured this would make it easier."

"Well, you're saving me from having to chase you down in the future when it's time to bounce out of here," I said on my way out to help unload the rest of their stuff. Thankfully, they didn't have a lot.

When I set down the last box in their room, my phone buzzed with a reminder from Conor that my shift started in about an hour.

I rushed to get ready, grabbing Lou by his shirt sleeve on my way out, "You're coming with me tonight. We'll have a pint to celebrate you being back."

"Yes, ma'am," he said not resisting.

"We got another busy one ahead, Val. Ready yourself," Conor said while busying himself with getting the place ready for the onslaught of people already lining up outside.

"Great," I rolled my eyes.

The minute the doors opened, I was flying. It was like when that holiday rolled around except there was no excuse for the crowd this time. Just a lot of thirsty people. I was beginning to think this was the norm around here. I felt like my arms never stopped moving: grab glass, pour, serve, repeat.

I was passing a beer to a customer getting ready to move on to the next order when I heard, "Thanks, love."

I froze – hearing the voice that haunted my dream just the night before was not what I was expecting today. I studied the sea of faces in front of me to see if any of them were familiar to no avail. I moved to the side of the bar where Lou was sitting. When he laid eyes on me, he went into instant protector mode, "Val, everything okay? What's going on?"

"Warrick's here," I said in a calm, monotone voice.

"What?" He growled.

I could only repeat what I had just said. Lou started wildly whipping his head around in every direction trying to lay eyes on our mutual enemy. When he turned his attention back to me, he said, "I'll go look for him. You just focus on work."

Before I could respond, Lou was out of his chair working his way around the pub. The angry tapping of an empty beer mug snapped me out of whatever la-la land I was in.

What felt like only minutes later turned out to be hours. I felt a tapping on my shoulder, "Start taking care of some cleanup, will ya? I'll hold it down here."

I gave Conor a quick smile, still feeling unsettled. I hadn't seen Lou return to his spot at the bar which must mean he hadn't had any luck with locating Warrick. I made my way out to the tables collecting glasses and plates while catching up with a few regulars, trying not to constantly look over my shoulder. As I moved throughout the space, I wound up taking care of an empty table against a wall with my back turned, making it impossible to know if anyone was coming up behind me. I was leaving myself exposed which only made my nerves worse.

I found myself being pushed towards the wall. Thinking it was Liam again, I started to spit out a slur of insults. I was whipped around to be face-to-face with the man who haunted my dreams as of late, Warrick.

He was pressed up so close to my body I almost couldn't breathe. He took a deep breath in then said, "I've missed having your body pressed against mine, love."

"Get *off* of me, Warrick," I whispered, struggling to get enough air in my lungs to breathe.

"Now that's not the greeting I was expecting," he said, trying not to clench his teeth. He followed up his response by digging something sharp into my ribs, bringing a twinge of pain. "Let's try this again, shall we? I wasn't sure if I was ever going to see you again."

Warrick placed a soft peck on my cheek making my stomach flip, "What do you want from me?"

"I want to cause you *pain*. You have no idea how much that would just make my day, love," he chuckled lowly in my ear. "But I can't get you out of my head and it drives me *crazy*."

"I have that effect on people, but you're awfully bold doing this in a public space," I was trying to stall while I worked on figuring a way to get out of this. I started to shift my weight on the leg that had more space until Warrick pushed harder against me, inching a leg in between mine to take away any advantage I had.

I froze now knowing I had no way of getting out of this, and while I was terrified, I was also weirdly attracted to him thanks to the dream last night. Heat was spreading throughout my body despite everything in my head saying not to. It was very conflicting to want someone so bad and remembering they would do whatever they wanted to torture and kill you.

"Cat got your tongue, love?" Warrick pressed another peck to my neck.

Shivering, I finally found words, "I'll repeat my question, what do you want from me, Warrick? You've been playing games, leaving folders of shit just to psych me out. You've been popping up in places so I could get a glimpse and now you've finally decided to grow a pair and show your face."

"Now, that's not the way to greet an old lover, is it? The least you could do is thank me for the gifts."

"That's the last thing I'd do," I spit out.

He curled his lip as I felt a fresh twinge of pain in my side, "Be careful, love, your end might be sooner than you think."

"If you don't watch it, the people around here are going to notice you holding me hostage, including Lou. What are you going to do then?"

Warrick barked out some laughter throwing his head back before looking at me again, "You think that's going to stop me? First off, the way I'm holding you makes it look like a couple of people sharing an intimate moment. Second off, I don't think Lou is going to be a problem."

He jerked his head in the direction of the bar, a menacing smile crawling on his face. I followed the direction he moved his head in to feel the breath get sucked out of me. There was Lou taking a sip of his beer completely captivated by Melody who was standing so close to him there was no space. It was like they hadn't missed a beat.

The low chuckle rumbling from Warrick's chest tore my attention away from them, "He probably forgot all about you. Even if he did see me here, it's not like I'd let him win."

Doing everything in my power to hold back tears, "You'd be surprised at how strong he's gotten since he's no longer being poisoned."

Warrick's smugness dropped for a moment signaling I had a way to get the upper-hand on this situation. "You didn't think we knew about that did you? Well, it didn't take long for us to figure that out when Lou changed his primary water source. You're so insecure, no, *fragile* that you had to poison someone so they wouldn't take your power from you."

I was on a role at this point watching as his face contorted with anger and I didn't want to stop. Continuing my confrontation, I said, "You can't stand if someone is stronger or smarter than you, so you find a way to tear them down. Instead of pulling the trigger, though, you do it slowly because your sick, twisted mind gets off on seeing others in pain. Just look what you're doing now – "

Warrick cut me off before I could say anything further, "You're right. I can't stand when people are better than me. You're also right about me taking my time with my prey."

This time he showed me a knife covered in a small amount of blood. Realization dawned on me – the pain I was feeling earlier was him digging the knife into me. Seeing the fear come back in my eyes, he grinned again, "Not so tough now, are we, love? Don't worry, this one isn't coated in anything that will hurt you."

He reached forward and gave my cheek a little slash. A small driblet of blood started snaking its way down my face. Before I could say anything or try to move, Warrick placed another small slash on my neck, "If you want to call out people's insecurities, you have to be ready to hear your own. You think you're hot shit, but you're scared to lose everything you fought so hard to get in your life. Your family, friends, lovers. Tell me something, Val, are you in love with Lou like you loved Gabriel?"

I looked back over at Lou losing the ability to keep the tears at bay when he whispered something in Melody's ear making her throw her head back in laughter. Her hands were on his chest, his hands resting on his knees close to her hips looking like he wanted to pull her in. Lou's eyes filled with love, displaying his true feelings, didn't dare leave her as if he was soaking in every moment he missed after she disappeared.

"Ah," Warrick started again, placing quick, fresh cuts on my arms and legs. "There it is. The moment you realize you never had Lou to begin with. He's just thought of her the entire time he's been with you. Hard not to when you look so damn similar. I mean, look at her. She's so full of pure innocence that Lou can't get enough of it. But you? You're anything but innocent, love, and that's where the biggest difference lies. I can just tell you prefer this over Lou's gentleness in bed. When he's making love to you, are you satisfied or are you left with wanting more? You like it a little rougher than what he gives out, don't you?"

Every word he said dripped with poison slowly eroding away at the walls around my heart. I was still looking over at Melody and Lou, knowing a part of what Warrick was saying was true while hating him at the same time for being the one to speak my insecurities out loud.

"How is she not driving you crazy?" I choked out not wanting to hear any more of this. "You apparently loved her. Why aren't you trying to kill Lou to get her back?"

He slammed his arm against my neck cutting off any air, "I've moved on, love, but the woman who captured my heart decided to use me. I don't take too kindly to that. I never believed in that love-at-first-sight bullshit, but then you had to waltz into my life full of a ferocity that fueled me like a drug. When you stabbed me, I was mad at first, but I was also wildly attracted because here was someone who could keep up with me. It wasn't until I discovered you two decided to hack me that I lost it."

He watched me for a moment before continuing, "You must be wondering how I figured that out so quickly. Well, I had a hunch something was up and decided to run diagnostics on my computer when you barged into my office. While I was fighting to get that cursed knife out of me, the results came back noting a flash drive had been plugged into my computer the day we had sex the first time. I couldn't let you get away with that, now could I?"

Warrick finished in a calm tone while brushing some of my hair back with the hand holding the knife. I felt the bite of the knife on my ear as he brough his hand back down to place some more painful cuts on my stomach. I was pulling at his arm still choking me at this point not caring about the knife anymore. All I wanted was air, and to get that, I needed out of this pub. Away from Warrick. Away from Lou and Melody.

He leaned in, voice barely audible, "Think next time before you fuck with me. I'll give you one more chance, love. Screw that up and you'll be counting your days."

Warrick was gone before I fully processed what he just said to me. Taking deep breaths thankful to have air coming back into my lungs, I hung my head hastily making my way back to the breakroom to minimize the chances of anyone seeing me. I faintly heard Conor barking orders at me confused why I wasn't picking things up, but I couldn't bring myself to stop and talk to him.

I slumped down in a chair, both hands covering my face as my body was racked with silent sobs. The cuts Warrick so graciously left burned with every movement I took, but that was nowhere near the pain of my heart after seeing Lou and Melody like that.

The door slammed open, "What the *hell* are you doing, Val? I need you to get your arse back out there to clean this place – "

Conor's angry tirade dropped off the moment he saw me crying. I heard the sounds of his feet shuffling over followed by the soft close of the door. He pulled a chair up to me and started rubbing my arm to bring some sense of comfort, "Hey, Val, what's going on?"

He took his hand off me when he realized he was coating his hand in my blood, "What is this? What happened? It wasn't Liam and his crew, was it? I swear if they harmed you, I'll kill them myself."

I finally lifted my head to meet his concerned face, "What happened was that a demon from my past came back to haunt me while pointing out that my boyfriend is getting cozy with the love of his life he thought was dead." My voice was hoarse from Warrick pressing so hard against my throat.

"Whoa ..."

"That's not even half of it."

Conor got up to grab some paper towels to wipe up some of the blood, "Let me get you cleaned up a little bit so we don't have certain people start drooling, then we'll head out of here.

I'll ask one of the guys in the back to hold down the fort while I'm gone."

He paused realizing what he just said then sat in front of me, "Do you know about the vampires?"

"Yes," I nodded. "Liam recently showed me all his cards."

Conor gave a quick nod, "Saves me from having to explain all that to you."

He started to help with the cleanup. I didn't even think about the fact that I was bleeding and surrounded by vampires. If Melody was there, so was the rest of the crew. Conor finished cleaning what he could then left to talk to the rest of his guys about what they needed to do. I looked down finally taking in the damage Warrick had done. The cuts weren't very big, but he knew how to draw out a lot of blood.

"Come on, Val. We'll go out the back so no one can see you," Conor helped me up.

"Thank you," I muttered quietly.

In Conor's car, we were silent except for when I gave him directions. I knew all of this would hit me later, but for now, I was numb. I didn't want to talk to anyone else for fear of losing the last shreds of composure I had.

"Can you drop me off here?" I asked when we were about a block from the house.

"Sure," Conor said, throwing the car in park. "Val, take the week off. Recover. Keep yourself tucked away. I don't know who did this to you or why they felt the need to try to carve you up, but it's not right. Especially when there were people there who would rather have a pint of blood than beer."

I smiled a little bit at that last part, "Thanks, Conor. I appreciate you driving me home tonight."

"Just text me if you need anything," he replied.

I started to close the car door, "Thanks."

It was a little colder this evening which made me regret my decision of walking back to the house, but only a little bit. The fresh air was doing wonders for me. I'm not surprised Warrick was trying to get the vampires to attack me. He seems to have everything figured out to stay one step ahead. That's what he does. I sighed, trying to find something positive to keep me from spiraling. The only thing I could think of was how lucky I am to have Conor there and that it was still just crowded enough no one would try anything else. Hell, I don't even know if anyone in that pub saw me rushing off to the back besides Conor.

I got to the house heading straight for the first-aid kit to start cleaning myself up before bundling up in my coziest pajamas to sit outside wrapped in my favorite blanket with a cup of steaming tea next to me. I looked up to the stars whispering since that's all I could comfortably do, "What am I doing here? I'm so far out of my league and it shows. Why did I get entangled with someone so crazy?"

I put my head back in my hands, "Gabriel, I need you right now. So much more than you know."

I wrapped my arms around myself picturing Gabriel here behind me, pulling me back into his warm embrace. I let myself imagine he was back, something I never do because it wrecks me every time, but when I feel like I'm shattering, it's the only thing I can do to bring me any sort of comfort.

I looked back up towards the stars, "Am I doing the right thing? How can I trust someone who will jump ship so fast or who will try to kill me? Maybe that's the way to go ... maybe then I can be back in your arms forever this time."

I let the tears flow freely. The downside of getting closer to Warrick was him learning what makes me tick. That gave him an easy opening to do what he does best. Not only that, but I watched Lou truly drop his guard to show his emotions. That was what love looked like on him, and it was no where near the look he gives me.

It had been a few more hours of me laying outside working through everything running through my head. I had no more tears left to cry at this point, fully feeling numb. The chill in the air wasn't even getting to me.

One of the lights inside the house snapped on. *Great, show time.* I was really hoping it was Jennie and Chris walking through those doors, but my hopes were dashed when I heard a voice call out in a panic, "Val? Are you here?"

It got quiet again for a moment until the back door slid open, "Val, you out here?"

I didn't move wishing he would look right over me and go back into the house. He called my name again, this time closer. I felt his hand gently put pressure on my shoulder while he spoke in a calm tone, "Val, you okay?"

"No," I said not bothering to turn my head.

"What happened to you tonight?" he asked, taking a seat in the chair next to me. "You disappeared on me. With Warrick here, I thought – "

I sat up bolt right filled with fury, "You thought what exactly?"

"What happened to your face?" he reached out towards me.

I jerked back from his outstretched hand scrunching my face to fight back the few tears that were threatening to roll down my face, "You really want to know what happened to my face? How about what happened to my neck? My arms? My stomach? My legs?"

I had ripped off the blanket at this point along with my shirt to show him the full scope of what Warrick did to me. His eyes widened at first in fear then narrowed in anger. His cold, grey eyes looked at each individual bandage until they made their way back up to me, asking in a low voice, "He did this, didn't he?"

"You're damn right he did. You want to know when he attacked me?" I spit out.

Lou reluctantly nodded his head.

I held his gaze, curling my lip, "He did this while you were having the time of your life reconnecting with your lost lover."

"Val, there wasn't anything going on there, I promise," Lou said a little too quickly, holding his hands up defensively.

"Cut the bullshit, Lou," the tears started coming at this point, but I kept talking. "Explain to me what you were doing with your face all nuzzled up in her neck whispering sweet nothings into her ear just to hear that laugh you missed so much. Or why she was so close to you there wasn't room to fit a piece of paper. How about why you were looking at her like she was the only one in the room? You know how easy that made it for Warrick to pin me against the wall to play psychological warfare? I had no way of defending myself, so I had to endure all the nicks and scratches he gave me while he wormed his way into my mind."

"I'm sorry, Val. I should've done better," Lou hung his head in his hands. He rubbed his face looking so pained by the time he looked back at me.

"You're sorry?" I asked incredulously. "That's all you have to say? Unbelievable, Lou. I know you're going to keep saying nothing happened, but that's not what I saw."

I got up taking my tea and blanket with me to head back into the house. I paused when I got to the door, "I'm going to sleep. Don't bother checking on me tonight. And one more thing, I'm happy you were able to reconnect with your true love. Hardly anyone gets that chance when they thought their partner in crime was dead."

I left him in the backyard, staring at the door looking defeated. There was a part of me feeling bad for tearing into him like that, but I really wasn't ready to hear all about Melody when I was in so much mental and physical pain.

I tucked myself in after placing the necklace holding my engagement ring back around my neck. Despite not wanting to, I set an alarm on low volume to make sure I was up before anyone in the house to tend to my wounds. I had popped a pain pill to help me sleep hoping I could avoid any dreams like the ones I've been having as of late while taking some of the edge from tonight's encounter off.

The sound of the alarm rang out making me stir. I woke up still groggy from the effects of the pills but managed to get myself out of bed. *That's a win at least.* I made my way to the kitchen grabbing the first aid kit on the way. My throat felt raw from Warrick holding me there and I was sure it was bruised again. Each cut burned, but I knew that would go away with time. And, as long as I took care of them, there wouldn't be any scars. I started getting to work on cleaning my wounds when I heard steps coming down the stairs. Pausing, I glanced to where the sound was coming from to find Lou stopped dead in his tracks. I didn't say anything as I went back to work noticing it taking him a while to get moving again.

"Val, I know the words aren't cutting it, but I am *truly* sorry. I shouldn't have let myself get distracted when Warrick was so close to you. I let my excitement get the best of me. I just couldn't believe she's alive and here and I could talk to her."

"I get it," I said quietly because that was still all I could muster with the current condition of my throat.

"You do?" he raised his eyebrows in surprise.

I was still working as I answered, "Yeah. It must have been a lot to process seeing your past love alive when you thought she was dead. If I were in your shoes, I'd have a hard time not wanting to run back to Gabriel and catch him up on all the things he missed."

"I don't know how many times I can say I'm sorry, Val, but I really am," he pleaded with me.

I whipped my head up letting him get a better view of the damage done. There were no bandages this time and each cut was an angry red mark slashed across my slightly tanned skin. He winced when he got to my neck where I assumed it was covered in bruises. "There's no Raf here to tend to me," I spat out.

All Lou did was shut his eyes. I started covering each cut with a bandage ignoring the hurt on his face, "I need some space right now."

Chapter 7

I walked out of the house without giving him the chance to say anything in return. I got on my bike taking a moment to do some breathing exercises so I didn't go out there recklessly. When I was ready, I headed out to grab breakfast going to the one place I knew: the pub. I knocked on the door and was met with a surprised Conor, "Didn't I tell you to take the week off?"

"I'm not here to work. This is the only place I could think of to get breakfast and get out of the house," I croaked out.

"Jiminy, you sound awful. Look awful, too. Get in here and I'll whip up some breakfast for you."

He moved out of the doorway to let me in. I nodded my thanks then headed to a booth away from the windows. Conor took no time at all with putting together a breakfast of eggs, bacon, and fruit. He sat across from me with his cup of coffee, "So, I take it things are rough at home?"

"Doesn't take a genius to figure that one out," I said, filling my mouth with food. I had every intention of making a breakfast at home, but when Lou came down, I couldn't bring myself to be around him without hurting more.

Conor tapped the table to get my attention, "I know you're angry right now, but I don't need you taking it out on me. Hell, I'd be angry too after seeing Lou nuzzled up with Melody. He's just lucky Cian didn't see that."

"Sorry, Conor. Everything that happened last night tripped up some pretty painful memories for me," I said sincerely. I waved that off and moved to my question, "Who's Cian and what does he have to do with Melody?"

Conor looked towards the windows to make sure no one was around before leaning in closer so I could hear his quiet tone, "He's the guy that runs the show here. Ever wonder why there's no cops? That's because Cian and his group killed them. Drank them dry. Since then, he's run this area with fear."

I nodded, recognizing the similarities between here and Lou's world with how Warrick ran things.

Continuing, Conor looked at me intently, "He's a pretty calm guy until you cross him. Then, he'll rip you to shreds. Liam's the one you really gotta watch out for. He'll go after your arse without warning. Hence why Cian doesn't feel the need to make his presence known – his henchmen do that plenty well for him."

"Makes sense, but I still don't see where Melody comes into the story."

"That's Cian's girl. If there's one thing you don't do, it's make a move on his lass. Lucky he wasn't here last night or Lou would've had a world of hurt coming his way. More than what he already did," Conor finished by pointing in my direction.

"You're going to think I'm crazy," I started.

"I already do, but go on."

I rolled my eyes, "I think it's time someone started taking these vampires down and I think that someone is going to be me."

Conor laughed, "You're out of your feckin' mind if you think you're going to get away with that."

I shot him a look that could kill, "You have no idea how much rage is in me right now. They're an easy target to take it out on and I'll be doing the people around here a favor."

"I'm not arguing with you on this one, Val. You have an uphill battle ahead of you, that's all."

"Oh, I know this won't be easy. Nothing good ever is," I trailed off letting my mind wander back to Lou for a moment before shaking myself out of it. "I'm telling you because I have no one else I can mention this to right now. I'm heading into that cathedral today to start learning the faces of who I'm going to take out. Then, I'm going out tonight to start putting this plan into motion. Oh, and one more thing, can you let me know if Lou's in here getting cozy with Melody again?"

"As long as you have everything you need," Conor said holding his hands up in defense. He got up from the table taking my empty plate away and mumbling under his breath, "She's absolutely insane. Who goes straight into the lion's den like that with fresh blood on the surface?"

Not wanting to get a lecture from him anymore, I headed towards the door, "Thank you for the breakfast! I left some money on the table."

"Wait!"

I didn't hang around to hear what Conor wanted to say to me. I hopped back on my bike, heading straight to the cathedral as people were starting to wake up and wander the streets while the sun inching across the sky. I got into the parking lot, stopping to take a deep breath while basking in the growing heat of the day. *Time to get this taken care of, Val. Stop dilly dallying.*

I set my shoulders after waiting a few hours, following a small group of tourists headed in. I looked at the ground to do my best to blend in at least until I got inside and could break away.

The large wooden doors opened to reveal a grand sanctuary while the tour guide started rambling on about the history of the place. There were stained glass windows at the end of the room displaying ornate designs of the landscape surrounding the outside of the city. The pews were neatly lined up in rows clearly well taken care of. There wasn't a speck of dust in sight and there was hardly any sunlight shining through. *Perfect place for vampires to set up camp.*

The tour guide handed the group over to one of the guys who did the tours of this space. I shifted so I was hidden behind one of the tour group members to try to get a good look at him. The guy was pale, no doubt about that. His style was very similar to that of Liam's, but what cemented my hunch of him being one of Cian's crew was the way he looked at the tour group like a fresh meal he couldn't wait to get his hands on.

As the group was herded further into the cathedral, I peeled off and took a seat in one of the pews. With a slight groan from the seat, I settled in, suddenly feeling the need to bow my head. It wasn't long before someone sat next to me, "I'd hate to see you get separated from the group. A lot of things have been rumored to happen in here."

I looked over at the person who was speaking at me. Another guy with a grin plastered on his face. I stared at him for a moment, memorizing his face to keep in mind for later with the other guy now guiding the tourists. Recognition dawned on him as we sat there, "Hey, you're the new lass Conor's got working at the pub."

"Sure am. I just needed a moment of peace. I'll let myself out."

I didn't want to waste time with small talk and really didn't want to be in here longer than necessary. I remembered the nightmare I had with the woman warning me of death living in these walls, making every part of me scream to get out of here. The dreadful feeling I had when I first laid my eyes on this place was back in full force, something I had shove aside until now.

I started walking towards the door when the man who was sitting next to me was suddenly in front of me. Startled, I clutched my heart, "Nice party trick you got there."

"Now, I wasn't saying you could leave. Let's get you back with the tour group you snuck in here with," he said, opening his arms to try to herd me back to the flock.

I shook my head, "It wouldn't be fair. I didn't pay to be a part of that group. If you'll excuse me."

I tried to skirt around him only to be blocked. I ran right into his chest, noting he didn't move an inch. His hands gripped both of my arms, hard, "Don't think so."

I shook myself out of his grip, finally getting around him, "Touch me like that again and that'll be the end of you."

I left him standing there while I exited the cathedral. Turns out it isn't as hard as I thought to start picking targets.

The day was still young, so I headed back to the house to clean my wounds and see if Jennie was there so I could fill her in. I made my way into the house stopping to listen for signs of life. Sounds of pool balls being hit were floating up from the basement accompanied by voices.

"I really didn't do anything with Melody, Jennie, but Val isn't seeing past that right now. She's torn up about it," Lou said.

"Val hasn't had the easiest time in the trust and relationship department. You have to remember she just learned she can't trust her dad which I'm sure has her questioning everything about her life. She lost Daryl and is being hunted by a maniac, which you let get his hands on her. During her whole dating escapade, which you pushed her into, I'm sure she developed some sort of feelings for him which is probably making her confused right now. On top of that, she lost her fiancé to the war that sent her away from the place she grew up in. Add in her sketchy relationship history and you have someone who's chalk full of trust issues."

As Jennie listed everything out, I stood there nodding my head. She had that 100% accurate, and in the grand scheme of things, Lou hasn't been around me long enough to understand my full history like that.

Lou sighed, "You have a point."

Chris chimed in at this point, "She's just got a lot going on now, and I'm sure you do too, but she was really counting on you to have her back."

"Shit," Lou groaned. "I did promise I wouldn't let anything happen to her."

The conversation paused and the game resumed. The hint of a smile I had on my face from Jennie and Chris defending me was quickly replaced with a scowl caused by Lou's realization.

I slammed the door behind me which made the activity stop downstairs. There was some whispering, no doubt them debating about who was going to greet me. I didn't wait around to see who drew the short stick as I made my way up to my room. I needed to grab some things to prep for tonight and some more money since I wasn't making any plans to hang around here for the day. *Maybe it's time to finally go sight-seeing.*

"Val?" Jennie cautiously asked from my doorway.

"What's up, Jennie?" I said still throwing things in a backpack to avoid looking up at her.

"Are you okay?"

My shoulders dropped and I paused what I was doing, "I'm not. I take it Lou filled you in on what happened?"

Her eyes widened, taking in the damage that was visible, "He did, but I wasn't expecting to see this."

Laughing, I said, "This isn't even half of it." I lifted up my shirt to expose more of the cuts, "Nothing like getting sliced up to bring some excitement into life."

"Now I see why you're so upset with Lou," she walked into my room, sitting on my bed. "He feels absolutely terrible, though."

I shot her a look full of anger. Jennie raised her hands defensively, "I know, I know. Let me guess ... the way he feels doesn't even compare to the hell you're going through. Did I get that right?"

I went back to packing things up, "You know me too well, Jennie."

"Where are you going?"

"I need to take care of some things tonight, so I'll be out late."

"Shouldn't you rest?" she asked, tone full of concern.

I shrugged, "Probably, but I'll be fine. Look, I'll be coming back here tonight, okay? I just need some air today."

"I get it. I'll look after Lou to make sure he doesn't do anything stupid, but that means you have to promise me you're not going to do anything stupid either," Jennie pointed a perfectly manicured nail at me.

I hiked my bag on my shoulder, "I can't make promises I know I won't keep."

I left Jennie stammering as I headed back out towards the city. This time, I just drove around taking in the sights, enjoying some new food, and shoving all my thoughts aside. No more letting Lou consume me and dictate how I feel. Instead, it's time to put together a plan for how I'm going to tackle this first night of vampire hunting. I started letting my thoughts drift back to the tourist group from earlier wondering if they ever made it out of the cathedral which made me determine my starting point.

The sun was getting ready to set, so I hopped back on my bike to head in the direction of the cathedral. As I was getting parked, I breathed a sigh of relief when I saw the tourists checking more landmarks out in their group. I once again snuck my way to the back of the group. I figured there would be some vampires waiting in the shadows to get their hands on some of these people when the sun went down, so I'll play hero for a little bit and take a couple of vampires down.

My hunch was right. The tour guide ended his speech for the day in front of the hotel I was assuming they were all staying at. He made a warning about staying out here at night, but only half the group was listening because they were the ones who wandered into the hotel after the guide was done talking. The rest dispersed with a few walking across the street to go to the pub. Another handful decided to go check out some shops. Those were the people I stuck close to.

When we walked past an alley, all my internal alarm bells started ringing like they had when I walked into the cathedral.

I reached for my bag to grab a stake I had hidden but could easily reach. We were starting to walk past another alley when I watched as a woman was yanked away with a hand over her mouth. None of the other tourists seemed to notice since they continued walking on, but I stopped and started to watch the scene unfolding in front of me.

The man who so rudely tried to stop me earlier was talking to the woman in hushed tones stroking the hair around her face to calm her down. Her eyes were darting frantically like a baby animal caught in a trap. After a few moments of this, she finally calmed down and seemed almost in a daze. The vampire turned her head, exposing her throat with ease, making my skin crawl. To no surprise, it seemed like he had done this a few times. I inched forward making sure to keep my movements nearly silent so as to not spoil the rude awakening this guy was about to get. I stood behind him with the stake poised right where his heart was, "The closer you get to her, the closer this stake gets to your heart."

He started to look over his shoulder, "Well, this is cute."

He licked his lips in anticipation, looking back at his prey standing there docilely in front of him before returning his attention back to me. He smiled, revealing his long, pointed canines primed to bite. In a predatory tone, he said, "Go ahead and try, sweets."

Glad he was underestimating me, I put all my body weight into my movement as I shoved the stake towards his heart using the little bit of knowledge Lou had taught me in our first training session. His eyes widened in surprise as he tried to jerk his body away from me. The vampire was too slow, his body starting to turn grey the moment the stake contacted his heart.

I gave one more shove for good measure, "Like my party trick? Personally, I think it's a little better than yours from earlier."

Those were the last words he heard before crumbling to ash. The woman snapped out of whatever spell he put her under, "Where am I?"

"I think you should head back to your hotel for the night. It's not safe out here," I put my hand on her shoulder. She nodded, remembering what had almost happened then turned towards the hotel.

I popped back out of the alley and caught up with the other tourists still wandering around. There were two more attempted feedings I was thankfully able to stop. It was surprisingly easy despite how my body was starting to feel, but I know that was only because I was catching these guys off-guard. After tonight, the difficulty would increase. I was sure of it.

Having enough excitement for one day, I headed back to my bike feeling sore and tired, pausing when I heard someone clear their throat. I looked towards the direction of the sound to be greeted with another alley. *What is it with these damn alleys?*

Ready to attack if needed, I cautiously approached where the sound came from knowing full well I was being stupid for not just driving away. My eyes had adjusted to the darkness at this point, but it was hard to make out any details of the person standing in front of me. I stopped so I had enough distance between us to make a quick getaway if needed, "Hello?"

"Glad to see you're still standing on two feet, love. You can take more abuse than I thought," said the familiar voice of Warrick.

"You don't know half of what I'm capable of," I said defiantly.

"Oh, but I'd like to see all of what you can take," he took a step towards me. I instinctively took a step back to keep the distance between us which earned me a chuckle. "I'm not here to cause you more harm, love. I can see I've done enough. How are things going with lover boy?"

It took everything I had not to wince at that question. He may have asked, but I'm sure he already knew the answer, "I don't have time for your games."

Another step forward, but I stood my ground this time, cursing the part of me believing he wasn't going to hurt me anymore, "I wouldn't have played you the way he did. Once I have my eyes set on someone, that's the only person I want to be with."

"Yeah? Wouldn't have played me? That's a load of crap and we both know it."

By this point, Warrick was directly in front me. He reached up to trace the cut on my cheek with his thumb, tsking as he did so. When he was done marveling at his work, he tilted my chin up so we were looking directly at each other, "Please, fill me in on what you're referring to, love."

"All the pictures, news articles, emails, the bullshit stories about my dad being captured. You've been toying with me so you can break me down and make me an easy target," I growled.

"You know? I like when you're feisty," he laughed. "You've been great for getting me more of the information I need."

That was enough. I hated being reminded I was just being used. I spit in his face and turned to get away, but was too slow. Warrick grabbed my arm yanking me back, causing something to pop in my shoulder and pain to radiate. I wanted to scream and was met with a hand covering my mouth before any sound could come out, "I don't think so, love."

I bit his hand, getting him to tear it away from my face. He slammed his head into mine causing stars to dance in my vision. I felt myself try to faint and Warrick catching me, "Bold move."

I out of it, trying to get my bearings. I knew I needed to get away, but I couldn't figure out which way was up. I felt Warrick wrap his arms around me, tossing me over his shoulder to start carrying me away. I tried to fight back, but my attempts were weak and not going to get me anywhere. I dropped any fight I had in me, starting to accept my fate, when I heard some shouting. He muttered under his breath and placed me on the ground just in time to take a punch that knocked him back a few steps.

Lou's voice came rumbling out, "Stay the fuck away from her!"

Hearing him shout snapped me out of the fog. I stood up feeling weak while clutching my now-pounding head. My arm was on fire, hanging limply at my side confirming I dislocated it. I dragged my eyes off my arm, though, and directed my focus to the scene unfolding in front of me so I could leave if things got too heated.

Warrick was standing back holding his nose while Lou was standing in between us breathing hard, "I find it interesting I'm suddenly feeling stronger, Warrick. You wouldn't happen to know what that's all about would you?"

"You broke my fucking nose," Warrick said completely ignoring Lou's question. He moved to head out the alley knocking shoulders with Lou on his way out, not putting up anymore of a fight.

When Lou felt confident the coast was clear, he came over to me, "I know I'm the last person you want to see right now, but are you okay?"

"I'm fine," I said, avoiding eye contact.

I saw him point to my arm, "That was more of a rhetorical question. Can I help get this back into place?"

"Be my guest," I grumbled. I braced myself for the next wave of pain as Lou jerked my shoulder back into place. I let out a whimper, knees buckling to have him catch me. He leaned me back up against the wall and took a step back, "Let me drive you home. You're in no condition to get on your bike."

I reluctantly nodded my head, but as soon as he made a motion like he was going to scoop me up, I held my hand out to stop him, "I can walk."

He backed off a little bit, "Okay."

We walked towards his car and I settled in, waiting for the onslaught of questions. Instead, Lou started driving in silence. We pulled into the garage and this time I accepted help from Lou. Today's events were starting to take a toll making it hard to carry myself. He settled me on the couch before pulling up a chair to sit across from me, "Val, please talk to me. I'm breaking right now and you won't even give me a chance to state my side of the story."

I sighed, "I'm tired. I just killed 3 vampires and got jumped by Warrick again while you screwed around."

"I didn't know what you were up to otherwise I would've been there to take some of the load off."

"Then why were you in the pub?" I snapped.

"I was asking Conor if he knew where to find you since you had been gone all day. He wouldn't answer my questions so I just left hoping I would come home to find you magically on the couch," he said with sadness laced in his voice. Hearing him like that made another piece of my heart break, but I did everything to maintain my composure on the outside.

"And how lucky I am you were there in that moment otherwise I would've been taken by Warrick to never see sunlight again," I shot back sarcastically.

Lou was getting agitated at this point, "Will you just give me a chance to explain? I know I fucked up by not being there to get Warrick off you last night, but I was there tonight. I wasn't cheating on you. That's one thing I won't do."

Tears started forming in my eyes, "I think we need to take a break from us. I don't know what happened, but I do know my trust was broken last night. I need some time to clear my head so we can have a rational conversation and I can't do that while still trying to be something I don't have the energy for right now."

I was bracing myself for protests, but was only met with defeat and a nodding head, "I understand."

Lou stood up to leave not saying anything else. I didn't want him to feel like he was being kicked out, I knew Jennie would take care of him, so I called out, "Stay in the house, though."

He stopped, nodded his head again, then made his way upstairs. I stayed on the couch for a little while longer before grabbing some medicine to help with my head. I probably would have a nice knot on my forehead to join the cuts and bruising on my neck. The price you pay, I guess.

The next morning, I was starting to head downstairs happy my head wasn't splitting open when I stopped, overhearing another conversation between Jennie, Chris, and Lou.

"I don't know what to do anymore, Jennie," Lou started with the same defeated tone from last night. "I've tried and nothing is working. My heart is shattering in a way I didn't know was possible, but I can't keep trying to force her to talk to me. All that's doing is pushing her further and further away. I just don't want to lose her any more than I already have."

Jennie jumped in trying to sound as comforting as possible, "Oh, Lou. The amount of love you have for her is incredible. She'll come around, I know it. You just have to give her time and space, I guess. We talked about this before, but you know her history with relationships. She has thick walls built up. Very thick. I can see she's in love with you, too, and you were able to break through that barrier once so I know you can do it again."

This time I shifted so I could see them. Lou looked up at Jennie gratefully, "Thanks. I can see why Val is so close to you."

I felt myself getting caught up in this tender moment, appreciative Jennie was there to support him the same way she would support me. Tucking the smile away for another time, I made my way out to the kitchen pretending I hadn't heard anything they had just been talking about.

"Morning," I said as nonchalantly as I could.

Lou didn't turn in my direction as Jennie pasted on her typical bubbly smile, "Good morning! You're looking better today."

"Thanks," I mumbled, grabbing a breakfast bar from the cabinets. "I'm feeling better. I think I'm going to head out for a swim and do some other workouts, then I'll be heading out for the night."

"More vampire hunting?" Lou asked tentatively.

Still not directly regarding him, I answered, "Taking a break from that. I just need some air."

I headed outside almost done with my quick breakfast. I kept the screen door open hoping they thought I just forgot to grab the main door when the real reason is so I can hear what they say. It didn't take long until their voices drifted out.

"This isn't good," Jennie said concerned.

"What do you mean?" Lou asked.

"I haven't seen her act this way in years. I know you said her head got hit pretty hard last night, but this is how she starts when she goes into one of her reckless phases."

"What happens when she's like this?"

"She'll start by shutting everyone out, just like we're seeing now. Then she'll start doing stupid shit to fill the voids which usually means she'll find someone to sleep around with for a while. She'll start drinking more, riding her bike more, refusing any sort of help. I'm telling you now, don't take things too personally during this time. Val will come around, she always does, but she needs to work this rebellion out of her system."

"Sounds like she almost tests everyone."

"That's exactly what she's doing, and just like a kid seeking attention, if you ignore her long enough, she'll stop," Jennie said bitterly.

That was the end of their conversation. I almost wish I hadn't heard Jennie say all those things, feeling hurt knowing that's how she looked at me, but I also knew she was right. I just needed to get this out of my system. On the bright side, I knew they would be giving me space which is what I've been craving. I let myself sink to the bottom of the pool for a moment. Time to shut out the hurt and frustration and just live the way I want to without feeling the need to suppress anything anymore. Tonight would be the start of a new version of myself.

Chapter 8

I pushed my bike harder not entirely sure where I'd be going. Jennie, Chris, and Lou all left me alone after I was done with my swim, sticking to their word which meant I needed to stick to mine. I had a backpack loaded with everything I needed to stay out of the house for a while, including my vampire hunting materials. Before too long, I parked my bike at the edge of a vaguely familiar-looking cliff. And I sat there. I had no idea what I was going to be doing next. I only knew it was freeing to have distance between myself and the house of judgmental people.

A sleek, black car pulled up next to me jogging my memory loose. *This was my dream where Warrick and I hooked up.* However, instead of Warrick hopping out of the car, I was met with who I could only assume was Cian. The man before me was wearing the same leather jacket I had seen him in the night I discovered Melody was still alive, but that was the only part of his outfit that stayed the same. His black hair was slicked back accentuating his lean, angular face. His body mirrored his face in that he was lean all over, the outlines of some muscles showing through his tight, white v-neck shirt and torn up black jeans.

I took off my helmet so as to not be rude as he stuck his hand out to me, "We haven't met before, but I've seen you around. Cian."

I shook his hand, regarding him with suspicion, "Val."

If this man was introducing himself to me instead of sending out his goons, I was certainly on his radar. To think I got his attention this fast was not a good thing.

"I'm going to cut to the chase here because I don't have a lot of time. You're the last person I would've expected to kill any vampires, but here we are with three of my lads out of commission by your hand. Kill any more of them and I will personally see to it that every drop of your blood is drained."

I didn't have a chance to respond before he got back in his car and sped off towards the city. I had no idea what was driving his time constraint and I was equally confused as to how he knew it was me last night. Regardless, the target on my back became much larger much faster than I anticipated. I had to come up with a new plan to not give myself away now. No more killing more than one of them per night I guess, and I needed to make sure I wasn't going out every night. I needed to make things sporadic.

My train of thought was interrupted by another set of car tires. The car door opened and closed. Without turning my head, I said, "Got your message loud and clear. I thought you had somewhere else to be."

The smoothness of Warrick's voice caught me off-guard, "I'm sure you did and I don't have anywhere else to be but here, love."

I whipped my head around ready to put up a fight for another one of his attacks, but my fight-or-flight response tampered down immediately upon seeing him leaning against his SUV wearing the same clothes as I saw in my dream. He was nudging some of the gravel with his toe looking out at the ocean. *What is it with the men here wearing white and leather?*

When I didn't say anything or move, he brought his gaze over to me, "Trouble in paradise, love?"

I narrowed my eyes, "You should know." I turned my attention back to the waves crashing against the rocks as I continued, "What are you doing out here, Warrick? Come to throw me off a cliff and end everything once and for all?"

It was his turn to not respond. Curiosity got the better of me, making me turn my head so I could look at him. When our eyes met, he held up his hands in defense, "Believe it or not, I'm just here to clear my head. Just a coincidence we both ended up here at the same time."

The niceties and change in tone threw me off. It reminded me of when we had dinner by the ocean when he let his guard down. I regarded him for a little longer to make sure he wasn't trying to lead me down a path before killing me. When I could trust he wasn't going to do anything, I looked back over the ocean. I heard his footsteps cautiously approach, "You and Lou?"

"Are you really trying to get with me right now?" I scoffed.

He laughs a little, "This wasn't how it played out in my dream, love."

Warrick turned to walk away, mumbling under his breath while I sat there caught off-guard by what he just said. He was almost back to his car when the words caught up to me, "Wait, what did you just say?"

Warrick stopped turning his head to talk over his shoulder, "Val, I didn't come here to pick a fight. I came here to clear my mind."

He must've been having a hard time to have actually used my name in a sentence over his chosen name for me. I took him in for a moment studying how he was carrying himself.

Warrick, who usually holds himself with an air of confidence, was slumped over looking more tired than ever. Seeing this, I told myself to drop the edge in my tone.

"That's not what I'm trying to do. Did you have a dream about this place?" I asked sincerely.

Warrick sighed, "Yeah, love, what about it?"

My chest warmed at the one word he added back in the sentence. *What is wrong with me?*

He sighed when I didn't answer, "What are you getting at?"

"Did I happen to be in this dream?" I asked, getting off my bike slowly making my way over like some invisible force was pulling me towards him.

Warrick turned around with impatience written all over his face, "I don't care to play 20 questions with you right now. Get to the point."

I stiffened at the anger creeping into his voice, but said, "My point is that I had a dream about us meeting up here, too. You and I were wearing the exact same things we are now."

The memory of his dream flickered across his face, replacing the anger with something softer. He took a couple steps towards me, "Did we end up in my car?"

Taking one more step to close the distance between us, I nodded my head placing my hand on his warm chest, "Oh yeah."

Warrick's pupils dilated when I uttered those words. His tongue darted out to wet his lips. In a low, husky voice, he asked, "So, I repeat my earlier question. You and Lou?"

My body was heating in anticipation as the air around us cackled with the familiar electricity I've come to associate with Warrick, "On a break."

A half grin slowly spread on his lips while he pressed himself against me, "Then I guess you're not off-limits, love."

He wrapped his fingers in my hair pulling me to closer to him while he kissed with such intensity to show how much he missed the taste of me. Warrick ran his hands down my body, sending shivers in the wake of his touch, until he grabbed my thighs so I could wrap my legs around him. He moved us to his car laying me down in the back seat, familiar music still softly playing in the background. I put my hand on his chest, "How do you have music from my world playing right now?"

When he realized I wasn't stopping him, Warrick started placed tender kisses on the sensitive spot on my neck, "I downloaded songs on my phone a while ago, love. Now, stop talking and let me make up for lost time."

The music kept playing as Warrick worked me out of my clothes discarding his at the same time. I was starting to shake in anticipation like a drug addict anticipating my next hit. He ground his hips into me showing me how much he was needing this, too. A soft moan escaped my lips giving Warrick the encouragement he needed to pick up the pace, matching the rhythm of the music. My hands alternated from tracing his muscular body to digging my nails in as the mind-numbing pressure built in between my legs.

Warrick could sense I was getting close to my climax and slowed down eliciting a disappointed moan from me. He playfully nipped at my ear in response, a low growl rumbling in his chest. His thrusts became more rough, hungrier. I thought this would be too much for me, but this was just what the doctor ordered. My back arched, moving in sync with Warrick, my eyes rolling back in my head. Instead of pulling away to keep me from finishing, he let the orgasm wash over me while he reached his climax.

We lay there panting before Warrick checked out the window to make sure the coast was clear. He got out of the car gesturing for me to follow. We put the back seat down giving us more room to work and went for another round moving into different positions this time.

After we finished for the third time, I was laying with my head on his chest while he traced light circles on my back.

"Warrick?"

"Hmm?"

"You mentioned earlier that you had a dream about this. Is that the only dream you've had about this place?" I asked curious to see if he was experiencing the same thing I was.

"No. I've had other dreams that have ended up playing out since I've been here."

I propped myself up so I could look at him, "Me too. Weird that we're sharing these prophetic dreams with one another."

He flipped me on my back again pinning my arms, "Must mean we're tied together somehow."

He didn't let the conversation continue, his lips finding his way back to mine. We had more sex, this time rougher than the last, both of us seeming to fill a void that has been growing since we arrived here. I certainly wasn't complaining because even though Lou got the job done, Warrick felt like he was made for me. As much as that thought would've normally scared me, I embraced it this time no longer holding back.

Warrick finished and collapsed on me, "Love, you have no idea how good you feel right now."

"I'm surprised I've been able to keep up with you," I said breathlessly.

"I'm not planning on being done until the sun comes up," he said sitting up. His fingers started tracing the cuts that were still there. Warrick's features darkened while he did so. I placed my hand on his thigh, "Hey, everything okay?"

"It doesn't look like these will scar. I'm happy I didn't do that much damage," he said with a distant tone. He moved his fingers so he was tracing the bruise on my forehead and the bruises on my neck, "You heal quick for a human."

"Why did you go after me like that?" I asked, curiosity getting the best of me.

Warrick moved so he was next to me, "I was acting out of rage. It's no excuse, I know. I just lost it when I saw Melody here with her new guy. Then seeing her flirt with Lou, knowing Lou was with you and him being so completely unaware of what was going on. I saw red, then saw you and couldn't control myself. The first thing that came to my mind was I wanted revenge for you stabbing me, but looking back on it, I do regret this."

I winced remembering the pain he inflicted on me and how I just came running into his arms the minute he expressed interest in me. I regained my composure in time to straddle him, "What made you change your mind about going after me?"

He gave a small laugh, "Believe it or not, love, you match my level of crazy. You're the only one who can keep up with me. You just feel so *damn* good. You're strong. You're the only woman who hasn't backed down without a fight and I realized I couldn't let that go."

Warrick was sitting up at this point bringing my lips to his. I have to give him one thing – he's smooth as hell. We sat there moving synchronously again, gentler this time to savor the moment both knowing the sun was coming up and we'd be going our separate ways the minute we finished.

When I was back on my bike delirious and sore, I looked over at Warrick who rolled down the window, "Let's do this again."

"Follow me, love."

I did as I was told, pulling up to a small cabin tangled in lush, green vines a few miles down the coastline. There wasn't another house in sight making it the quiet and lonely house on the top of a hill. Warrick got out of his car coming to meet me in the driveway as I was taking in the white stoned building.

I moved next to where he was standing, turning off my bike and pulling off my helmet. I didn't say anything as he took my hand, guiding me into the house. All I could think was how different this was compared to his high-rise penthouse overlooking the city. The furnishings inside were sparse, but cozy with a thick, soft throw blanket draped lazily over the back of the couch. My eyes wandered to the kitchen where there was a small island with a few barstools bordered by simple appliances, cooking surfaces, and countertops. There was nothing cold or modern here which was the exact opposite of what I'd come to expect from him.

"Welcome to my humble abode," Warrick took my helmet from me.

I slowly drew my gaze back to him after taking in a little bit more of my surroundings, "Not at all what I expected."

A lazy grin etched itself onto his face, "Have to keep you on your toes, love."

I only nodded, observing more of what was around me. I stepped further into the house exploring the one hallway that led to a simple bedroom while passing the only bathroom. I finished my exploring, leaning against the wall that started the hallway, "Why'd you bring me here, Warrick?"

"Thought it might be good for you to have a place to stay what with all the turmoil you'd have to go back home to."

"Just casually asking me to move in?" I asked, raising an eyebrow. "I might have to take you up on that offer."

He closed the distance between us, leaning against the wall with one arm while tracing my bottom lip with his thumb, "Good answer, love."

A rush of heat ran through me as my lips parted. Warrick chuckled pushing away. I stood there a little longer in disbelief at how easily he reads me, shoving aside the slight disappointment in not getting a kiss. *This'll be an adventure.*

I headed back towards the front door and as I started to open it, I looked over my shoulder meeting Warrick's ice blue eyes, "I'll be back in a bit."

Fresh air rushed into my lungs cooling me off, the feeling of electricity leaving my body. It wasn't long before the fatigue crept up, making me sit on my bike a little longer contemplating if I had the energy to deal with Lou and Jennie. If I was lucky, they'd be out somewhere and I'd have the house to myself.

Shaking my head trying to clear the tiredness, I revved my bike and shot out on the road. With each twist and turn bringing me closer to my house, the ache in my chest grew. It was easy to forget about that pain when every part of me was consumed with Warrick or eradicating vampires, but knowing I was going to have to face the music took away whatever was distracting me.

It didn't help, either, to be hearing a small voice in the back of my head calling me out for being so dramatic. It's not like Lou and I had been together that long for me to love him that hard. He wasn't ripped away from me, like Gabriel, yet the pain was still there making me question every action I was now taking.

I gave my head one last shake as my house came into view. *I really needed to get some sleep if I'm this deep in my thoughts.*

I walked into the house, pausing as my feet made it across the threshold. My ears were met with the sweet sound of nothing – just pure silence. I let out a sigh of relief as I headed upstairs to throw some clothes and essentials in a duffel bag before heading back to Warrick's place. The last thing I needed was any sort of confrontation with Lou, let alone Jennie and I didn't think I was anywhere near being ready to explain where I'd be staying for a while.

I sat on my bike for a moment, staring at the house letting the sadness have its moment. There was a part of me that wanted to believe Lou, but another part of me just wanted space. It may not be the mature move, but I'm human, too.

I shot back out on the main road after failing to see if I could move past this right now. *Maybe another time.* Thankfully on the ride back, there wasn't another car on the road giving me all the time I needed to zone out and relish in the wind whipping past my face. By the time I got back to Warrick's, any of those lingering negative feelings were tucked back away in their safe so they couldn't bother me any more today.

I closed the door behind me, dropping my duffel bag on the floor fully aware of the delicious aromas dancing to me from the kitchen. I finished getting out of my riding gear, "I can't wait to try whatever you're cooking."

The only response I got was a low laugh. I walked over to sit on the opposite side of the island to try to see what he was stirring in the pot. Resting my head on my hands, "What is it?"

Without pausing or bothering to look at me, Warrick answered, "Chicken noodle soup, one of my favorite comfort foods from when I grew up. Figured you might need that today given everything that must be running through your head."

"Chicken noodle soup. Really? I wouldn't have pegged you for someone who would like that too much."

He turned around, cocking an eyebrow at me with a bowl of soup in each hand, "Believe it or not, I wasn't always rich. Eat."

I watched him as he took the seat next to me, tempted to ask him more about his childhood, but also getting the sense he wasn't wanting to relive his past too much. So, we sat there not exchanging any more words, letting the soft slurps fill the space instead.

Warrick was the one to break the silence first, "What's the deal with the bike, love? Not something you see a woman riding every day."

I rotated so I was facing him, "It was right after I met Gabriel my freshman year of college. I was completely enamored with him at this point and just found out he liked to ride, so for one of our dates, he asked if I wanted to go out with him. I wasn't going to miss out on the opportunity to spend more time with him. When the time came, we went out with a bunch of his friends just riding around town, finding the back roads so we could fly. Let me tell you, there was nothing more freeing than the feeling of adrenaline in that moment you lean in and watch your speed get faster and faster. It didn't take much convincing for me to get my own."

"A lot of things about you go back to Gabriel," Warrick said casually.

I looked down at my hands, "He was a big part of my life, Warrick."

I brought my gaze back up to meet his seeing a combination of fire, lust, and sadness. He gave a slight nod encouraging me to continue. I looked back down letting out a small laugh as I relived the memories, "Everyone hated it. My mom thought I was trying to kill myself. My dad wasn't quite at the same spot as my mom, but he wasn't too happy. Daryl and Jennie both thought I was being reckless, and yet, I didn't have a care in the world. All I wanted was to have a little escape."

"That still the same bike out there?"

"Yup," I gazed longingly in the direction of where I parked it. "If anything happened and I couldn't repair it, I would be devastated. That bike feels like the last thing I have connecting me to Gabriel."

When I looked back at Warrick, I saw something flash across his face before he returned to his neutral expression, "Impressive you've been able to keep it running, love. I would imagine it's been you doing the maintenance on it."

Even though it wasn't a question, I felt compelled to answer, "Yeah, it wasn't easy at first either, but now it's second nature."

Warrick got up to clean the kitchen, "I'm glad you're staying here even if it's not permanently. It'll be nice to have someone around."

I was caught off guard by the change in conversation so much that any words I had escaped me. Instead, I found myself staring at him effortlessly moving around the kitchen. When he saw me staring, he slowly smiled, "What? Can't I be appreciative of something that isn't sex with you?"

"Just surprised me with how out-of-the-blue that was considering you've barely said anything since I got back."

He ran his hand through his hair still grinning, "I'm tired, love. That's all."

I nodded then looked over to where I dropped my stuff, "Me too thanks to someone not letting me sleep."

Warrick closed the distance between us in no time, scooping me up in his arms then taking me back to his room. He sat me on the bed helping me get out of my clothes then he did the same. I blinked at him a few times before realizing he was laying down to sleep and not to continue our activities from the night before. I followed in his footsteps making myself comfortable, pulling the soft comforter over me and settling into this new space. For a brief moment, I started to get caught up in how weird this is sleeping in his bed when I had only done that once before, but it didn't take long for my eyes to close.

I was making my way through the maze of hallways in the cathedral trying to find the exit. An eerie silence blanketed the space putting all my senses on alert. I patted my body searching for anything I could use as a weapon in case I came across one of Cian's vampires. Nothing except for a dress. Pausing, I looked down to see myself dressed in a form fitting satin black gown with black stilettos and jewelry to match. I shook my head. There was no way I could do anything dressed like this. I kept myself moving forward not wanting to linger anymore when I started feeling the hairs on the *back of my neck stand up. I turned another corner only to stop dead in my tracks. Liam was standing there almost as if he was waiting for me. Saying nothing, he disappeared only to reappear directly in front me, his face inches from mine.*

"I've been waiting a long time for this," his words dripping with desire.

I tried to take a step around him, move any of my muscles only to find I was frozen in place. I opened my mouth to speak unable to even do that.

He laughed, "Cat got your tongue?"

Liam reached up, placing both hands on either side of my face, "You made a mistake coming here."

He yanked my head to the side breaking my neck and everything went black.

My eyes popped open, my heart racing, sweat dripping from my face. It took me a moment to realize where I was, but when my senses came about, I remembered I was staying with Warrick, who was drawing lazy circles on my back, "Morning, love."

I turned to face him, finding him laying so he was facing me, head propped up on his hand. I took a deep breath, getting rid of any fear that may still be around, "What time is it?"

"It's seven in the morning."

"There's no way," I said in disbelief. "You're telling me I slept for more than twelve hours?"

"If you call what you were doing sleeping," he snorted. "Another nightmare?"

"Yeah, this time Liam broke my neck. You?"

Warrick pulled me in so our bodies were pressed up against each other's, "I watched as he did that to you."

There was something dangerous about the way he said that, making me want to scramble away. Alarm bells were ringing in the back of my head telling me to not trust him, but they weren't loud enough to drown out everything telling me to give in.

I melted into Warrick, lips passionately searching his. I rolled him onto his back pinning his arms above his head. He let out a low growl of approval. I slowly started grinding my hips against his, doing my best to drive him crazy. It didn't take long for him to pin me on my back so he could take control. *Mission accomplished.* Warrick's hands inched their way down until he slipped his fingers inside of me, earning him a moan filled with want and need. Just like I was moving slowly to drive him crazy, he was doing the same, letting the pressure build between my legs. When he realized I was about to climax, he paused trying to get some sort of reaction out of me, but was met with a smirk and a quick movement of my hips to send me over the edge.

"You may be stronger than me, Warrick," I panted out. "But you won't always have the upper hand."

He nipped at my neck, "I'll let you have this one, love. Only because I have to take care of some things today."

Warrick placed a passionate kiss on my lips before lifting himself off me to get ready. I laid there a few moments longer, testing out how my body felt, deciding what I was going to do today since I didn't have to go to work and I really didn't want to risk being seen by anyone I knew.

The shower started, shaking me out of whatever daydream I was being sucked into. I grabbed one of his shirts as I made my way out to the living room. I stood there a moment before deciding to sit at the small desk in the corner of the room. I ran my hands over the smooth, cherry colored wood, noticing Warrick's laptop was setup with some files next to it. I glanced back towards the hallway to see if there was any indication of him being done. The water was still running, so I let curiosity get the better of me and started looking through what he had on his desk.

The first folder contained nothing but financials from his company. I don't know how he was getting the data, but everything was from last week when he was most definitely here. When I looked closer at the numbers, my jaw dropped. There were more zeros than I had ever seen on anything outside of a math class. *No wonder he's living so comfortably in his world.* I moved to the next folder not wanting to spend too much time learning about his company. That's not what I was really looking for anyways.

The second folder started off looking a lot like the first one, a bunch of numbers and dollar signs. I was getting ready to give up and move on to the next one until I came across an email between Cian and Warrick talking about a timeline. I read it over and over, hoping more details would become apparent but quickly becoming frustrated with how vague they kept the discussion. Sighing, I moved to the next page finding another copy of an email chain, except this one was between my dad and Warrick. There was more of the vague language that eventually ended as I got closer to the end of the conversation where Warrick was pressing my dad for more information around the codes and where they led only to get directed to me. *He didn't care if I was dead or alive and now he's telling Warrick I know where all the codes lead?*

I shook my head moving to the next few pages within the folder. A couple of them were schematics for Warrick's device with circles and questions all around trying to figure out what will make it so he can bounce from world to world with little to no recharging time. I put those pages in the stack of the ones I had already looked at with my attention fully focused on pictures now laying in front of me. They were clearly focused on a man with black hair kept in a messy style. He looked like he was on the taller side, but it was hard to tell since the pictures seemed to be captured from a security camera. His face had some scruff to the point where it wasn't fully a beard, but it wasn't the beginnings of one either. In all the pictures, he was wearing a flannel shirt with a black V-neck t-shirt and faded jeans. His sleeves were rolled up to the elbow revealing a tattoo of a pack of wolves in a forest. His body art drew me in. The longer I looked at his tattoo the more I couldn't shake the feeling of him being familiar.

"Having fun, love?"

I jumped, realizing I had completely stopped paying attention to any sounds coming from the bathroom or bedroom. I quickly glanced down at the clock while tucking the contents of the folder back away to see that just over an hour had passed. I smiled up at Warrick who was leaning on the island, "Sure takes you a long time to get ready."

He pushed himself up to start making his way over to me, "I like to dress to impress although your outfit of choice isn't half bad."

I gave a quick gesture up and down my body, "Oh this old thing? I haven't worn it yet, so I figured I'd give it a shot today."

Warrick was now bracing himself on both hands either side of the laptop, giving me a dark look. To say I was feeling nervous would be a massive understatement. My hands started to tremble, forcing me to keep them under the desk, yet I didn't break Warrick's gaze.

He traced my jaw with his thumb, examining the places where I had been bruised by him, "That sleep worked wonders on healing the rest of your bumps and bruises. There's hardly anything there."

I kept still and quiet worried any movement would set him off. He kept running his fingers along my jaw then down my neck. My heart rate picked up when he started tsking and dropped his hand. Warrick rounded the desk throwing me and the chair against the wall, rattling the few decorations he had. In a calm voice, he asked, "Do you enjoy when people go through your things?"

Knowing how to play the game, I jutted my chin out defiantly, "No."

"Then why were you going through mine?"

"Curiosity got the better of me."

Warrick chuckled, "Don't you know curiosity killed the cat, love?"

"Good thing I'm not a cat," I said thankful for my voice not betraying how I really felt.

"Don't let me find you snooping again, Val, or this little living arrangement we have will be over," he barely whispered, his lips brushing against my ear.

Chapter 9

I left Warrick to work at his desk and run whatever errands he needed to while I hid in bed. Feeling alone with my thoughts left me emotional and isolated, but I didn't want to risk the fury of Warrick again, especially when I felt this way. Whenever I heard him leave, I ventured out to the living room to grab water and food or just have a quick change of scenery. A few of the times I went to the bathroom, I examined the remainder of my bruises to see they were almost completely gone, validating Warrick's assessment. Any soreness I had been feeling from his attack had also left my body, thankfully.

The sun was starting to set and my stomach was starting to growl. Knowing it's the start of the night, I had a hunch Warrick would be staying in and I still hadn't worked up the courage to head out there. My internal fight of sucking it up and going out there versus just staying hidden consumed me so much I didn't hear the knock on the door. I was standing near the window looking out over the ocean when Warrick's voice rang out making me jump, "Love, you don't need to hide out like a damn damsel in distress."

A heavy pause settled between us when I didn't respond. I stood rooted in my spot slowly crossing my arms across my stomach. After waiting for what felt like an hour, Warrick asked, "Can I at least come in?"

"Sure," I croaked. I shot a glare towards my empty water glass cursing myself for not refilling it since I had lunch.

The door gently opened revealing Warrick with his mouth set in a hard line. Where I was expecting anger, I was only met with a touch of sadness, "I didn't mean to keep you trapped in here all day."

I just stood there in silence, not entirely sure of what I should say and not quite trusting my voice either. He pinched the bridge of his nose trying to compose himself, "Look, love, my reaction earlier was unhinged. I didn't mean to make you feel that way and I'm sure you're asking yourself whether or not you should believe me based on the history we have. Quite frankly, I don't have the energy to deal with that right now. Know I would love for you to join me tonight for dinner. You'll need food sometime."

Warrick turned to leave pausing for a brief moment in doorway before continuing out to the main part of the house. I let out a small grunt of frustration with how well he was able to read everything going through my head.

It wasn't long before smells of tasty food came wafting in from the kitchen instantly made my mouth water and my stomach grumble so loudly the birds outside could hear it. Setting my shoulders, I convinced myself to shove my fear aside, rounding the corner to find plates of steak, perfectly roasted green beans, and jasmine rice complete with a full glass of red wine. Warrick was leaning on his hands on the island with a towel thrown over his shoulder holding back a laugh from hearing how hungry I was. I stopped in my tracks crossing my arms over my chest, "Is something funny to you?"

He gave a slight shrug as he made his way to his seat, "Just glad to see you join me. I knew you'd be hungry sooner or later. Turns out I should've placed my bet on sooner."

Rolling my eyes, I took up my seat next to him, "Yeah, yeah. Sorry for snooping earlier."

Warrick placed a hand on my knee, "It was going to happen either way, love, especially when I leave everything out in the open and you're not going anywhere. Tell me something, though. Where'd that Val go who wasn't afraid of a little old wolf? I don't know who this person is that cowers away all day. You know you can stand up to me, so just do it."

"You only ask that because you didn't see that side of me. Lou did," I said with a phantom of a grin. "Warrick, you really got this whole Jekyll and Hyde thing going on and it's a little unnerving. I don't know if I should run or join in."

He put his fork down slowly turning towards me, tilting my chin up towards him, "You already know my preference."

Shivers ran down my spine sending heat with them. I felt my pulse quicken earning a low chuckle, "See, love? You know what you want so why not go after it? You might just be surprised at how everything plays out."

I didn't get a chance to respond before he was kissing me, softly at first then full of hunger. My hand had barely touched his face when he pulled away, "Eat up."

It was like I was caught in a trance or something because I didn't realize I had followed his command until half my plate was empty. I glanced over to find Warrick watching me like I was some sort of prey. Inhaling slowly before taking another gulp of wine to work up the courage to ask him something that had been on my mind since this morning. I lightly tapped my fingers on the counter, giving my energy some place to go as I asked, "I'm going to cut to the chase here. Did you only offer for me to stay because my dad said I was the key to getting the answers you're looking for?"

I must have asked the wrong question because the minute I finished it, the muscle in his jaw started twitching. He took his icy gaze away from me as he answered, "Despite what you think, I'm not using you. I do actually see you as something more than a means to an end." It was Warrick's turn to down the rest of his wine before continuing, "Any information you give me is merely a bonus, love. I just want someone to share a life with."

His last sentence nearly knocked the wind out of me. Here he goes again being all sentimental and I have no idea what to think. I didn't think he had this side in him. I'd be lying if I didn't say my confused heart felt something towards him, especially when I get glimpses of him letting his guard down.

Not wanting to leave him waiting for long, I took a swig from the bottle not bothering to refill my glass before sitting in his lap, "I don't know if I can promise you a lifetime, but I can at least promise you love in this moment."

We were intertwined both running our hands along the other's body. Our breathing quickly became heavy with lust as we tried our best to take our time and savor this moment. Warrick's hand worked his way up to my hair, fingers getting entangled before he gently pulled my head back to expose my neck. He started with tender kisses, moving from my collar bone up to my jawline before teasing me with his teeth. I let out a soft moan starting to set the pace. I soon felt the thumb of his free hand tracing the bottom of my breast, sending sparks of electricity down my body. Warrick couldn't resist keeping both hands away with the reaction he got out of me, now palming both of my breasts freeing me to bring my lips back to his.

I nibbled the bottom of his lip, met with a groan of satisfaction and a brief tightening of his grip. My hand fell to his crotch putting slight pressure to tease him and enjoy how aroused he was. I went to move my hand away only to have Warrick keep my hand in place using me to stroke at a slow pace. While he took control, I took my turn at nibbling at the sensitive spots on his neck, switching between that and soft kisses.

He stood up, grabbing my thighs to lay me down on the island, "Enough of this game, love."

Warrick joined me undoing his pants while I worked at his shirt. I started fumbling with the buttons the moment his fingers worked their way under the hem of his shirt, stroking my thong to see how wet I was. He grinned when he got his answer. With a husky voice, he asked, "What are you waiting for?"

I let out a growl ripping off his shirt, buttons flying. I sat up yanking my shirt over my head, leaving me in my bra and thong. I moved to remove my bra and thong when Warrick grabbed my hands, "Not yet."

He laid me back down, his hands pinning mine while his lips found their way back to mine. His tongue traced my bottom lip while he started moving his hips in a slow, steady rhythm only making me want him more. He started kissing all over my body, his fingers barely touching me as he lightly traced his fingers along my skin sending shivers of want in their wake.

Warrick pushed my thong aside still teasing me and driving me wild. "Please," I begged, catching myself off-guard.

"Please what, love?"

"Please," my voice barely above a whisper. "Please don't make me wait any longer."

That was the green light he was waiting for. My thong was ripped to shreds and he was in me faster than I could form the words to beg him again. We were moving in a synchronous rhythm as if we had been with each other for years. He knew everything that drove me crazy and I knew everything to return the favor. I raked my nails down his back earning me a loud groan. "Not yet," he ground out.

"I'm tired of hearing you say that tonight," I said in a breathy voice.

Beads of sweat started forming on his forehead showing me how much he was trying to hold back. Warrick looked at me with hints of his wolf starting to show in his eyes, "Trying to correct me?"

"What are you going to do about it?"

"You'll find out soon enough," he said with gritted teeth more from concentrating than anger. He pulled out, went back to his room, then returned and flipped me over. He leaned over me so his lips were barely touching my ear, "I'll teach you what happens to women who think they can correct me."

"Punish me, Warrick," I said encouragingly while he tied me down like he did in his office.

"Fuck," he moaned while caressing my ass. The warmth of his hand was soon replaced with the sting of his belt. I let out a yelp in surprise which brought his hand back to rub the spot he just smacked. "Too much?"

I let out the breath I had been holding in those few moments, relieved in knowing he wasn't going to be too aggressive. I looked at him from over my shoulder, "Just right."

He repeated that sequence of actions for a little longer, a smack from the belt followed by his hand soothing the sting. Warrick lifted my hips, "Take it like the good girl I know you are."

He was back in me, this time rougher than before. Each thrust brought me closer to the edge making me tighten more around him. His groans became louder dancing with mine in the air until pleasure was coursing through me, my limbs limp. We lay there panting for a moment until Warrick moved to untie me. He lifted my chin up kissing my forehead, "You have no idea what you do to me, love."

We finished another bottle of wine leading to another round of rough sex eventually collapsing on the bed catching our breaths. Warrick tucked a strand of hair behind my ears then pulled me in. The warmth from his body was all I needed to drift off into a sleep so deep even the nightmares couldn't surface.

I opened my eyes in the morning to be greeted with a plate of pancakes, eggs, and bacon. Warrick wasn't anywhere in the room and as I moved to get up to find him, he came through the doorway with a couple glasses of orange juice. Seeing me awake, his smile lit up the room brighter than the sun, "Good morning, love."

I accepted the glass looking at him skeptically, "I don't think I've ever seen you smile like that." My face relaxed letting a smile take over, "You look good happy. And thank you for the food."

"I haven't felt this happy in a long time, love. This is the least I could do for you," he said, gesturing to the plates in front of us. "Enjoy."

We ate for a while talking about completely normal things for once. No past relationships, nothing dark, no scheming or plotting. It was weird to feel like everything was right in the world when at any moment it could be ripped away.

My phone interrupted our bliss with several text messages flying in. I looked over at it, hesitating to check what was going on.

"You going to get that?" Warrick asked clearing his throat.

"Oh, I guess," I answered, void of any emotion. I picked up the phone to see a few texts from Conor and a single message from Jennie. "Shit," I mumbled under my breath.

Ripping the bandage off, I opened hers first to be met with a guilt-trip interwoven with a ton of questions. I rolled my eyes moving to Conor's messages which were just checking in to see if I was okay. *Those* were the messages I decided to respond to.

Warrick placed a hand on my knee, "Everything okay, love?"

"Yeah," I nodded. "Just Jennie trying to mother me and Conor checking in."

"Need to go to work?"

"Not yet. He said to take a couple more days, but then he'll need me because some sort of big event is coming up that brings in a lot of people."

He nodded his head, thinking carefully of his next response, "Well, we better make the most of these couple of days."

I let out a small laugh, "It's not like I'm leaving you."

"True, but we wouldn't have the whole day to be with each other either."

It was like I had awakened a whole new side of Warrick. One who was cheery and full of love rather than violence and anger. We went back to the light-hearted conversation occasionally giving each other bites of the other's food. When we were done, Warrick chased me outside around the house acting like we were in high school in love for the first time, both of us cackling in between quick kisses.

The rest of the day was like the beginning, filled with what seemed like never-ending happiness and chasing away any doubt I had about staying here. I was cooking dinner for us with Warrick hugging me from behind when I felt him stiffen. I paused, "What's wrong?"

He moved away from me, his attention focused on the front door. He flicked his gaze back at me, "Spray yourself with my cologne and throw yourself under my clothes in our room."

I turned the burner off not wasting any time listening to his commands. Warrick ran out of the house for a second before I heard the door close signaling he was back inside. There was nothing but silence for minutes until the familiar sound of the gravel crunching under the weight of a car broke it. *Who the hell is coming here?*

Two car doors slammed shut and a knock sounded on the door. Warrick started talking and when the person answered him, I immediately recognized the voice. I didn't dare move a muscle, didn't breathe out of fear his visitors would want to investigate.

"How are things coming along?" Warrick asked.

"We're ready for next week," Cian responded. "Are you planning on being there?"

"My answer has remained the same. You remember the deal, right?"

"Don't talk to us like we've never worked with someone before," Liam spat. "There are things we *have* to do to be ready. We won't go beyond that."

"You normally let your second talk that way?" Warrick cooly asked.

"Enjoy your dinner, Warrick. We'll be seeing you soon," Cian responded avoiding Warrick's question.

They left as quick as they got here. I remained still until I could no longer hear their car. When I came back out to the kitchen, Warrick had resumed cooking. You wouldn't have been able to tell anything had just happened unless you looked at his now-twitching jaw. I put my hand on his back, "What was that all about?"

"Nothing you need to worry about, love. Even if he isn't a wolf, alphas don't like when others are on their territory."

I knew to say nothing more and to resume cooking our meal, but the flashes of Warrick's emails with Cian stood out to me. They were clearly working together whether they liked it or not and they were moving right along with their timeline. *Timeline for what? Were they plotting for some sort of mass destruction? Is Warrick bringing Cian and Liam along with whatever journey he's going on with the device?*

"Everything okay, love?" Warrick asked bringing me back to reality. I blinked a couple of times getting my bearings before giving him a soft grin.

I placed a hand on his arm, "Yeah, why?"

His brow furrowed slightly, "I've been asking you some questions and when I looked over at you, you were venturing in some far away land."

"Sorry, just hungry that's all. What were you asking me?"

"Do you know when you have to go back into work? And, this one might be a stretch, but do you think you could help me with some things?"

My curiosity completely piqued at this point, I turned around to start serving our dinner hoping I was playing it cool, "Conor gave me a couple more days, so I can help you depending on what it is."

He picked up on my humor giving me a little chuckle. Warrick grabbed me at my waist pulling me in closer to him, "Since you rummaged through my things, you obviously saw that I was trying to get more information about the device and where it can take me."

I searched his face for any sign of lingering anger that was there when he caught me in the act, but there was nothing. He had clearly moved on from that incident.

Warrick continued, "Instead of just beating around the bush, love, I'm outright asking you for your help."

"I don't know how much help I'll be, but sure."

He gave me a kiss on the cheek before setting the food out. Conflicting feelings started stirring with Lou's voice in the back of my head warning me about helping Warrick. Those feelings, however, were quickly overshadowed by frustration at the thought of Lou still having some sort of influence over me.

We had spent the rest of the evening enjoying each other's company. I found myself slowly getting obsessed with Warrick's laughter. The sweet, rich sound ringing out and filling the space with nothing but light, taking away anything dark with it.

In the morning, I woke up alone. There was no sign of Warrick around the house outside of the note he left me informing me he'd be back in a couple of hours. Sighing, I sat at his desk munching on the quick breakfast I'd thrown together while looking through the information he had on his device and the codes. There wasn't much there except for all his questions scribbled in the margins of the papers. I began digging through his drawers and looking under papers for his device to see if there was anything that stood out to me, being careful to put things back as I found them.

I was about to give up on my search when I found a hidden compartment at the bottom of the last drawer I looked in. Reaching in, I grabbed the device and started turning it over in my hands. His was similar in shape and size with the one Lou and I had made, but the major difference is the number pad in the middle where we had a couple of buttons.

"Smart," I mumbled still examining every inch of the device.

It was like something smacked me. I went back to Warrick's notes wondering about recharge times when I remembered that Lou and I were able to open a portal again after opening one the day before when we were originally testing it out. Ours didn't have a recharge time meaning Lou lied to me when he went back to his world. He could've come back here any time, but instead chose to stay away, letting Warrick have more time to play his mind games.

I threw Warrick's device on his desk, "Asshole!"

"I hope you're not talking about me like that, love."

I jumped up pushing away from the desk clutching my chest, "Jeez, Warrick! You need to stop sneaking up on me like that."

He came over to where I was standing and gestured for me to sit in the chair. I followed his silent order not fully trusting he wouldn't try to hurt me again despite asking for my help the night before.

"Have you been able to sort anything out?"

I looked back at the device in front of me and the folder of his notes next to it, shaking my head, "All I've been able to figure out is that the device Lou and I made never needed a recharge time. You can use it to open a portal at least 24 hours after you've already done one, if not sooner. As for the codes, I have absolutely no idea how I'm supposed to know what any of these number combinations me –"

I trailed off as realization started dawning on me. I looked at Warrick who was confused at this point, "These aren't just random numbers, Warrick. They're combinations. Each are eight numbers, and knowing how my dad liked symmetry, it's either two sets of four numbers or four sets of two numbers. I don't know where my dad pulled these numbers from, but I know they'll have some sort of significance."

I went back to looking at the pages to see if there were any patterns jumping out at me. Nothing. I let out a groan of frustration, dropping the paper and putting my head in my hands. Warrick reached across the desk, placing a comforting hand on my arm, "Let's take a break. You've at least started figuring out the trail we need to be on, but we don't need to solve the whole mystery in one day. Scooby Doo and his crew didn't solve everything overnight."

I grinned at the reference, "Sure, okay. I think I'm going to head out for a little bit of a ride to get some fresh air."

What I didn't tell him was that I was going to grab the device at my house to see what differences there were between the wiring and components within Warrick's device and mine.

I pulled into the driveway after a quick ride missing the comfort of my space. *Get ahold of yourself, Val.* Squaring my shoulders, I made my way inside once again listening for any signs of life. I heard some laughing coming from the basement, so I made sure to keep my movements as quiet as possible. Heading into the lab, I went straight to the cabinet we locked the device in then moved to grab as many of the components I could think of while in a rush.

I closed the lab behind me smiling at the thought of *Young Frankenstein* being the inspiration behind my dad's secret lab and the memories I had with my dad. I paused before heading back downstairs to make sure the coast was clear while taking in the space one more time. Once I heard the smacking of pool balls hitting each other, I made my escape. I started my bike and once I started pulling away from the house, I heard my name. I looked over my shoulder to see Jennie standing there with a mix of confusion and hurt in her eyes. I felt a twinge of sadness, but shook that away, speeding down the road. I couldn't let this brief interaction take away from the happiness I've been experiencing lately.

I opened the door of Warrick's house, my journey back here quicker than when I left, making him snap his head up, "Got some presents for you."

"I thought you were going to be gone longer than that, love," he leaned back in his desk chair.

I sat across from him putting my device and components on the table, "I may be no help with the codes right now, but we can at least get your device working faster. Have tools?"

Warrick looked at me with amazement for a few moments then grabbed his toolbox to start opening both devices up. Every time we removed a layer, we examined everything from the wiring to the boards and other components he used to see if there were any differences. There were a few spots where the wiring was placed in different areas that we corrected, but there wasn't much beyond that.

We finished putting everything back together when Warrick muttered, "We'll have to see if that did the trick." He punched in the combination associated with his world to see a portal open up in the living room, his icy eyes glowing with excitement as he glanced back over at me, "I would say it did. I've been trying this thing every day for a while now and got nothing. You haven't even been here a full week and you've managed to solve one of my problems, love."

I stared at the portal a while longer. In a detached voice, I said, "Guess I'm useful after all."

Warrick closed down the portal and moved to stand in front of me. Tilting my chin up so I was looking him in the eyes, he asked, "What do you mean, love?"

"Don't worry about it," I tried to look away. Instead, he moved my chin so that no matter what direction I looked in, I was always looking at those hypnotic blue eyes. Warrick said, "I'm not using you, Val. I want to be perfectly clear on that. You don't have to help me if you don't want to and I certainly didn't ask you to go into the lion's den to grab your device. I appreciate you keeping true to your word, but don't feel like you have to sacrifice yourself for the sake of making me happy."

"Sorry," I said finally able to pull away from him. "I've been putting a lot of pressure on myself here to try to make things right only to keep making things worse."

"Look, love, I don't want to dive too much into this right now. The only other thing I'm going to say on this topic is that you're doing so much more than you think, so give yourself more credit."

I nodded my head grateful for this conversation to be done. I don't know what caused me to be so in my head like that. It was probably going back to my house, not wanting to hang around because I wasn't going to be welcome. I shook my head to clear the last of the pity party out before looking back at Warrick with a smile, "Thank you."

He was about to ask a question when I closed the distance placing a tender kiss on his lips. Warrick pulled away, looking at his watch, "As much as I want to stay here caught up in you, I have to run real quick, love."

"That's okay, I was planning on heading over to the pub. There's a couple hours before opening and I want to surprise Conor."

"Are you up to that?" Warrick asked.

"I think I can handle a shift. It'll feel good to get back into a little bit of a routine. Plus, it might spur some ideas," I gave him a little wink.

He laughed softly, "I'll stop by the pub later to check on how you're doing, but text me if you need me there."

I quickly nodded and we went our separate ways.

I made my way back to the house sneaking back in to put the device where I found it, praying Jennie wouldn't catch me on my exit again. When she didn't, I shot out towards the city, pulling up to the pub a little while later, giving my usual knock on the locked door. Conor poked his head around the corner ready to yell the hours of the pub until he saw me standing there. I gave a finger wave then pointed to the handle. He unlocked the door, "What in the hell are you doing here? Didn't I tell you to take a few more days off?"

I stepped around him, breathing in the comforting smell of wood and beer, "Is that any way to treat your favorite employee? I'm feeling a lot better, thanks for asking."

"Just caught me off-guard is all," he locked the door behind me. "Go sit over there, I'll bring you a plate of something."

I settled in only waiting for a couple of minutes for Conor to join me in the booth. He dropped a plate of freshly baked soft pretzels, "You look a hell of a lot better than the last time I saw you."

"Thanks," I said in between bites. "Took some time to rest and recover. How has business been?"

"Hopefully resting far from the lad who did that to you," Conor said skeptically. "The usual, thankfully. Lou and your friends have been in here quite a bit, though. Sometimes with Melody, sometimes steering clear of that bunch."

I was thankful he had picked up on what I was really asking even though I hadn't necessarily wanted to hear the answer. I took a steadying breath, pushing down the anger trying to rise to the surface before responding, "Believe it or not, the guy who attacked me is the one I'm staying with, but we've made amends."

"Christ, Val," Conor started rubbing his face in his hands. "Are you out of your damn mind? Why would you stay with someone who tried killing you?"

"Where else was I going to go?"

"You could've stayed with me," Conor jabbed a finger into his chest. "I would've left you alone and given you all the rest you needed."

"I know I sometimes don't make the best decisions. Hell, I don't make any good decisions, but that was something I needed to do," I held up my hand signaling I wasn't done. "Conor, I don't want to analyze my actions right now. All I ask is that you don't tell anyone where I'm staying, and I mean it. The man I'm staying with, Warrick, is most likely going to be popping in here while I'm working. Please don't confront him. Just let him be. And before you ask, I won't get all emotional if Lou comes sauntering in to hang out with Melody. All I need is for you to not intervene and let me take care of the customers. Deal?"

"Deal," he grumbled. I could see his mouth twitching, the questions not wanting to stay tucked away any more than they already have, but he kept true to his word. Instead, we went on catching up on some of the funnier details I missed while I was out and covering what he needed the most help with now that I was back.

We got up to start tackling our lists to get ready for opening. I was giving the bar top a final wipe down when he came around the corner carrying a box full of clean pint glasses, "What's this event you messaged me about?"

"We have a few big things close to each other that really draw in a crowd. We had the holiday that happened not too long after you started and now we'll be having this next event. You'll be finding out about it soon enough, so I'll spare you the details, but it's another thing that draws in a big crowd. Lots of tourists come in to partake in the festivities," he explained, nodding his head toward the door.

I looked out to see the longest line ahead of opening since I've started here. I turned back to Conor, "I guess I came back at the right time."

Conor scoffed, "You sure did. Ready?"

I gave a quick nod and set my shoulders. He moved towards the door, unlocking it and signaling to the eager line the pub was open for business. A wave of people headed straight to the bar, shouting their orders over the volume of conversation filling the space. It took me a few beers before I started picking up my pace and getting into my steady rhythm of pouring and serving.

The hours flew by as fast as the beers were being handed over to the thirsty customers. There was a break in the crowd, giving me the chance to replace the now dry kegs. I was hooking everything back up when I heard someone approach the bar. Not pausing what I was doing, I shouted, "What can I get you?"

"Two pints, please."

I dumped the first glass I poured which consisted of all foam then went to complete the order. I slid the beers across the bar top stopping when I realized who was in front me.

"You're looking good, Val," Lou said, a soft smile taking residence on his face. "I'm glad to see the bruises are gone."

I narrowed my eyes, "Thanks, Lou." I nodded towards the two beers, "Got a date or something?"

"You could say it's something. Just grabbing a couple of beers for my friends. Can I actually get one more?"

"Sure," I mumbled annoyed with myself. Conor was watching me like a hawk and I wanted to prove to him that I could push my personal stuff out of the way to focus on doing a good job. I handed the last beer over, "There you are."

"Thanks," Lou said. He looked at me like he was going to say something else when he visibly bristled.

"Well, that's a mug I haven't seen in a while. Lou, how have you been?" Warrick asked, clapping a hand on his shoulder hard enough to make Lou stumble a little bit.

I took a step back from the bar moving closer to Conor. I leaned over whispering, "Better to just let this one play out."

"I wasn't planning on getting involved anyways," he whispered back.

We returned our focus toward the two alphas who were doing everything in their power to not try to rip each other's throats out.

"Fuck off, Warrick," Lou grumbled. "You've done enough."

Warrick, not phased one bit, kept pushing Lou's buttons, "I really don't think I have, though." He looked between Lou and me. "Don't tell me there's trouble in paradise. That would be a shame."

Lou set the beers down before turning back to Warrick, "Don't patronize me. I think you know full well what's going on here. And don't even think about laying a hand on her."

Warrick chuckled taking a step closer to Lou, "Too late, Lou. I did more than lay a hand on her after you chased her away trying to rekindle that old flame between you and Melody. As a matter of fact, I wouldn't mind hearing the sound of her screaming my name again."

The sharp intake of breath next to me reminded me that it wasn't just Warrick, Lou, and I in the room. I looked over at Conor to see him staring at me with raised eyebrows. I shook my head keeping my voice low, "Moment of weakness?"

"You really are crazy," was all Conor could say.

I let out a breath thankful he was playing along with the act Warrick and I were putting on.

Lou looked between Warrick and I, "You've got to be kidding me."

Warrick responded to keep Lou's attention from me, "Don't get wrapped around the axel, Lou. From what I understand, you two were, and still are, on a break. She's a grown woman and can make her own choices just like you can make your own. And speaking of making your own choices, the smart one would be to walk away from the conversation and pretend nothing ever happened."

Lou lurched forward ready to attack, but Warrick knew what was coming. He grabbed Lou by the back of his neck and slammed his face onto the bar making both Conor and I jump. Seeing Lou like this instantly reminded me of the summer solstice ball and I wondered if he would put up more of a fight this time now that he should have more of his strength back. Lou struggled for a second then gave up. Warrick curled his lip, "That's it. Now take your precious beers to the other side of this pub and don't let me see you up here again."

He let Lou go, who casually grabbed his drinks, doing his best to play off what just happened. Warrick straightened his shirt then slicked his hair back. When Lou was far enough away, Warrick motioned for me to come over, "Sorry about that, love."

"It's okay, thank you for not causing too much of a scene."

Warrick gestured for Conor to join us and when he was standing next me, Warrick said, "I take it you're in on what's going on?"

Conor looked at me with panic in his eyes. I gave a gentle nod encouraging him to speak, "With what's going on between you two? Yeah. Val caught me up with all I needed to know this morning. Name's Conor."

Warrick glanced at me then back to Conor, "Nice to formally meet you, Conor. I'm sure you know who I am. Like I said, I'm not trying to cause a scene, so sorry if that disturbed any of your customers. Just wanted to come in, grab a drink, and hang out until close."

"Make yourself comfortable," Conor said. He put a pint in front of Warrick, "Let me know if there's anything else I can get you."

Conor vanished into the crowd giving me some time alone with Warrick. I glanced around the bar to make sure no one was waiting to be served then stood in front of him. He started to reach for my hand then stopped, looking around to see if anyone was watching us, "I'm doing my best to keep my space from you, love, but damn it's hard. Don't want to set Lou off by letting him know you're staying with me."

"Appreciate it."

"I have something for you," he said, changing topics and reaching into his back pocket. He slid a blood red envelope over to me

"What's this?" I asked, picking it up. When he lifted his glass to his lips to take a long drink, I knew he wasn't going to answer my question, so I worked the envelope open pulling out a thick piece of cardstock. Neat, cursive handwriting covered the paper inviting me to a ball. I let out a quick laugh, "So many balls with you creatures of the night."

Warrick let a faint smile grace his lips clearly holding back laughter of his own, "We like to go all out with having an excuse to get dressed up for an evening. Care to be my date?"

Trying my best to keep the joy hidden in case anyone was watching, I said, "Sure."

"Good answer, love. Don't worry about a dress, I'll get that taken care of."

Any chance of me responding was interrupted by a group of drunk customers coming back up to order another round. I slid the invitation back to Warrick who took it before getting up to find a secluded seat with a view of the bar.

I finished out the night without any more run-ins with Lou which probably had something to do with Conor. We chased the lingering customers out and closed down the pub for the night. I threw a towel over my shoulder and put my hands on my hips, "You could've at least given me a head's up that this big event is a ball."

Conor didn't look at me, "It's not something us locals like to talk about very much."

I dropped my arms feeling any ounce of humor I had me leave, "What do you mean?"

He let out a sigh, dropping into a chair, "It's something Cian and his crew put together every year. They use it as a way to feed on people, no strings attached. I know you didn't look at that invite too closely, but there's fine print on there basically saying to enter at your own risk. The reason they rely on a big tourist population for this ball is because the locals all know what they're up to. That's why we hide at night and steer clear of them, but we have to go because Cian claims he's doing this as a way of saying thanks. We all know he just wants it to look crowded in there otherwise the tourists would get suspicious. I would tell you to watch your back, but with Warrick, I think you'll be more than fine as long as you stick with him."

I was fighting off shivers as I said, "So, this is basically one big buffet disguised as a fun time."

He only nodded in return.

Chapter 10

About a week had passed since my first night back at the pub. Warrick and I kept up the façade that he was still trying to chase after me to keep people off our trail. Our whole charade was working since Lou, Jennie, and Chris had no idea where I was staying or that Warrick and I were having the time of our lives being wrapped up in one another when we weren't trying to decode the numbers representing different worlds.

Letting the water wash over me, I rested my head against the cool tile of the shower. The day of the ball had finally approached and I still had no idea what I was going to wear since Warrick hadn't let me even think of looking at dresses. *Am I just going to this naked? I wouldn't be surprised if Warrick was trying to play a game.*

Lost in my thoughts, I hadn't realized Warrick walked into the bathroom until the shower curtain started moving back. I let out a scream causing Warrick to rip back the curtain, "Really, love? I even announced myself this time. First with a knock and then letting you know I was coming in."

"Sorry, Warrick, just wondering when I'm going to see this dress you promised."

He smiled clearly checking me out, "I wish I could enjoy this view all day."

I laughed, playfully shoving him back, "Shut up."

"Anyways, love, I came in here to tell you your dress is waiting for you on the bed. I have someone coming by to help get you ready since I don't have any makeup or anything to do your hair with outside of the blow dryer."

"Thank you," I blushed. He was going all out for this by hiring someone to do my hair and makeup for me. I don't think I had ever been that spoiled, but my mind had to ruin the moment by reminding me I hated the fact that feelings I had for Warrick were growing. That was quickly replaced, however, by that warm fuzzy feeling hitting my heart again.

I finished my shower in peace and started to blow dry my hair when Warrick ran back into the bathroom. His eyes were wild, "I need you to hide again."

"Cian making another impromptu visit?" I asked.

"No. No time to explain."

This time he threw me over his shoulders taking me into our room. He sat me on the bed next to a giant white box I only assumed was my dress. Holding my shoulders, he urgently said, "Take your dress and go into the closet. There's a hidden door in there. I need to you stay behind that."

Warrick left as quickly as he had run into the room. I felt like I was moving in slow motion, but I was able to get myself and my dress tucked away like he instructed. I was surprised when I realized I could still hear everything like I was sitting in the middle of the bedroom still recovering from the confusion of why he didn't instruct me to hide here when Cian and Liam stopped by not too long ago.

When a knock on the front door rang out, I held my breath, my thoughts stopping in their tracks.

"To what pleasure do I owe this surprise visit, Louis?" Warrick asked distastefully.

What the hell is Lou doing here and how did he know where Warrick was?

I heard Lou step in, "I wanted to stop by to call a truce for this evening."

"Wasn't even thinking about trying anything, but now it's on the forefront of my mind. I'm going to ask again," Warrick paused, trying to keep his anger in check. "Why are you here?"

"Is Val with you?"

My body went rigid in the closet. Warrick had gotten me my own toiletries so I wasn't stuck using his stuff all the time, but I didn't know if Lou could smell that or not.

"Why the hell would she be with me?" Warrick spat.

"I've been looking all over for her and have been coming up empty. Thought this would be the last place I'd find her, but I've been surprised before. Smells like you have a woman here, Warrick."

"Have you ever thought she may not want to be found? You played a dirty trick on her with Melody."

Lou took more steps further in the house, "I just need to talk to her. Her friends are also concerned, and she isn't responding to anything. When she's at the pub, she's unapproachable. There's more we need Val for besides her companionship."

"That's far enough Louis," Warrick growled.

"Hiding something, Warrick?"

I tucked myself as far back in the closet as I could. Lou continued, "I'm not as afraid of you as I used to be. Who are you hiding?"

I heard a slam and only assumed Warrick had gone after Lou. There were more sounds of a struggle followed by Warrick snarling, "Why do you have to be in everyone's business, Lou? If you really want to know, I have a date tonight. I have no idea where Val is. If you would drop your rose-colored glasses for two seconds, you would realize she wants nothing to do with you because you have done nothing to alleviate her concerns about you and Melody." There was another slam before he continued, "She's not someone who can just be toyed with, so stop chasing after Val! And another thing, I have my own mission. You're not the only one with important *shit* to do. Next time you cross me, I won't be as nice. You have five seconds to get out my house before I rip your damn throat out and put an end to all this!"

I heard them scuffle for a little while longer until the front door slammed shut. I waited for a few breaths before easing my way out of my hiding space to find Warrick bracing himself against the wall breathing hard. I put a hand on his back, "Hey, you okay?"

He whipped his head towards me, eyes ablaze with anger and his wolf, "If it weren't for you, he'd already be dead."

My stomach dropped, but I didn't move an inch, "How did he know where you were?"

Warrick sighed closing his eyes, "He figured out where I was living a while ago. Why do you think it took me a while before making myself known to you here?"

"You don't think he's been staking this place out?" I asked while adding one more tally to what Lou had lied to me about. It was hard not to worry about Lou watching my every movement when everything I'm doing is already under a magnifying glass with Cian and his crew.

"I would've sensed him," he dropped his tension, relaxing his muscles as he turned towards me. Warrick caressed my face, "Keep getting ready, love. I want to have a good time with you tonight."

I went back to drying my hair. By the time I had finished, Warrick let in the woman who was in charge of my hair and makeup. She was incredibly friendly, going on and on about how beautiful I already was and how lucky Warrick is to have me. She also wouldn't stop talking about how wonderful the ball is, making me wonder if she was the only local to be excited.

She finished in record time, showcasing her experience. Warrick escorted her out while I sat there gaping at myself in the mirror. My caramel-colored hair hung in perfect loose waves with half of it pinned back. She had executed a flawless smokey eye with gold eyeshadow that sparkled when the lights hit it just right. Combined with the false lashes, my eye makeup made my green eyes vibrant. Everything else on my face was done in a way the accentuated my best features and hid the ones I was most self-conscious about. To top off the look was a bold red lipstick instantly building my confidence while making me feel sexy at the same time.

Warrick came behind me putting a hand on my shoulder, "I think you're seeing yourself as beautiful as I always see you, love."

I looked up at him, "Thank you. For this and everything lately."

He gave my shoulder a squeeze and tilted his head towards the room, "I think it's time to get dressed. We should be leaving soon."

I followed him back into the room ready to find out whatever this white box was hiding. I pulled the ribbon, carefully removing the lid. I lifted up the fabric letting it drop to the floor cocking my eyebrow at Warrick, "Why always black with you?"

Warrick looked away, but not before I caught the slight reddening of his cheeks. When he figured out what he wanted to say, he brought his gaze back to mine, "Because there's no light left in me, love."

Any light heartedness vanished and was replaced with a subtle ache in my chest. An earlier conversation of ours floated through my head reminding me that despite his success, he's lived a hard life.

I dropped my towel holding out the dress to him with the hopes of alleviating whatever was trying to hang over us, "Help me?"

He slowly bent down to start working the dress over my body, our brief conversation already fading away. I reveled in the smooth, satiny fabric hugging my body in all the right places. The dress was a simple one, with its shine coming from the finish of the fabric. It was held up by two thin straps with a neckline plunging midway down my stomach. Warrick brought me over to a mirror, turning me so I could see the back of the dress. It went dangerously low, so much so that I felt if I moved the wrong way, people would be getting more of a view than they thought. I turned back around, examining the rest of the dress, "I don't know how you get something to fit my body so perfectly every time."

"I don't forget something that's mine," he purred. He grabbed the rest of the items from the box to finish the look. Warrick gently reached around me to drape a simple, but stunning, diamond necklace around my neck, clasping it into place while I did the stereotypical action of reaching for it to see if it was real. He followed that with a matching tennis bracelet then held out my shoes – sheer pumps with carefully placed diamonds.

"Warrick," I gasped. "This is too much."

"This is nothing, love. Please, allow me."

I was getting the royal treatment. He knelt down putting my shoes on for me. As he moved to stand up, he hiked my dress up enough so he could lightly kiss the inside of my thigh before moving to get dressed in his suit. I watched him, the butterflies in my stomach had taken full flight as I stared at him in awe.

We were in the car on our way to the ball not too long after Warrick finished getting dressed. I glanced over at him, laughing earning a confused Warrick, "What's so funny?"

"I just couldn't help but think we're like Selina Kyle and Bruce Wayne. Passionate lovers dressed to the nines."

He shook his head laughing, too, "Glad you picked up on my theme, love. What's on the menu for you to steal tonight?"

"If I told you, I'd have to kill you," I said sensually.

The jokes went on a little while longer until we pulled up to the cathedral which made my heart rate creep up. The usual dread was back, but Warrick sensed my increasing anxiety, placing a warm hand on my thigh, "Stick with me, love. You'll be fine."

He reached into the backseat pulling out two masks, mine sticking with the diamond theme and covered in sparkling crystals where his was a plain black mask. Our doors opened and he handed the keys over to the eager looking valet driver while making our way inside. The ball was in full swing, the dance floor packed with a ton of people and even more standing on the perimeter enjoying drinks and hors d'oeuvres. I scanned the crowd to see if I could spot Conor or even Lou, Jennie, or Chris with no luck. I let out a breath. I'd be able to focus on enjoying this evening a little more without having to worry about constant judgement from them.

Warrick squeezed my hand, bringing me back to the present. He led us down the stairs, people parting for us to make our way on the dance floor, the conversations quieting as we walked past. The live band switched to something slow, leading Warrick to pull me in close to him as we swayed to the rhythm of the music. Others started following suit thankfully taking the attention away from us. I brought my focus back the handsome man in front of me, earning a smile while he slid his hand lower, "Thank you for accompanying me tonight, love."

"I couldn't have turned down a chance to be dancing with the most handsome guy in here."

Warrick chuckled, "Very cliché, but I'll let it slide this time."

His other hand caressed my face while his moved closer to mine stopping inches from my lips. He let out a sigh resting his forehead against mine, "We have company."

We were pulled out of whatever bubble we were in. I turned my head left then right spotting Jennie, Chris, and Lou standing against one of the walls. Jennie shook her head, pursing her lips together while Chris was looking around avoiding any eye contact. Lou was casually leaning against the wall, one hand in a pocket, the other holding a glass of what looked like whiskey. When our eyes met, his were filled with a mix of sadness and anger.

I returned my attention to Warrick, "Fuck them." I leaned back in for the kiss that was interrupted, Warrick not hesitating, returning the action with full force.

After a few more dances, we exited the dance floor heading in the opposite direction from where Lou and the others were standing. Warrick grabbed me a drink and said, "I'll be back, love. Have to run to the restroom."

He was gone before I could say anything. I tapped the side of my glass taking in more of my surroundings – we were in the sanctuary with all the pews removed. Several of who looked like Cian's men were stationed around doorways leading to places they didn't want others to see. I made a mental note of what they were wearing with the intention of taking some out later. *If I can kill at least one vampire tonight, it would be one less to torture the innocent people they drug in here.* Putting that plan in place, I started to see if there was anything I could use as a weapon against these guys when someone new came to stand next to me.

"If you're looking for something to use against these vampires, I hid something in the plant next the stage."

Without looking at him, I responded coolly, "Lou, I don't need your help."

"Not trying to help. Simply informing you. Dance with me?"

I glanced at him out of the side of my eye. He was in a simple suit wearing a plain grey mask holding his hand out for me to take. Rolling my eyes, I set my glass down then placed my hand in his, "Only one."

We maneuvered out on the floor joining the other couples in another slow dance. We said nothing to each other for moments, avoiding the other's gaze. To keep myself busy, I scanned the room looking for any signs of Warrick only to come up empty. Besides, I couldn't bring myself to look at Lou – it would only confuse things more for me than they already were and I just wanted to have a good time tonight.

"Why are you here with Warrick?" Lou asked being the first to break the silence between us.

"I can make my own decisions," I dragged my eyes to finally meet his. "I wanted to have fun tonight, not stay hidden in my lair."

"Look, I know what you saw looked bad. I wasn't flirting with Melody or trying to get with her. I wouldn't shut up about you."

I put a hand on his chest to stop him, "It clearly looked like you were talking about me especially with how she threw her head back and laughed. That sure makes me feel *great*."

"You're not listening to me, Val."

I couldn't keep my frustration in check any longer, "And you're not giving me the space I need to clear my head. I'm hearing you loud and clear, but what you're saying isn't matching up with what I saw. If you were talking about me, why were you so close? If you were bragging about me and telling her the feelings you have, why was she laughing like that?"

"How are you going to be clearing your head when Warrick's filling it with manipulative crap?" he asked frustration creeping into his voice now.

I scoffed, "You have no idea what's been going on. Warrick and I are just having sex, and in case you were wondering, we don't spend a lot of time talking about you when he's in between my legs."

The song finished and the band was starting up a new one. I looked in that direction then back to Lou taking a step back, "Your dance is up."

"Val," he pleaded. "Don't."

"I think it's time for the lass to have a new dance partner," Liam said behind me. His voice was sandpaper going down my back, but I couldn't let Lou see that. I turned to face him, "And you think that's going to be you?"

Liam curled his lip, "Better than the alternative." Brushing his suit and shaking the look on his face, he started, "Considering you're the most beautiful woman here tonight, it would be a shame if I missed a dance with –"

His face contorted with pain as a hand clamped down on his shoulder, squeezing hard enough to break his collar bone, "I don't think so." Warrick's face was stone as he said that to Liam in the calm, scary voice of his.

"Cian isn't going to like this," Liam whimpered.

"I don't give a damn what Cian will or won't like. She doesn't want your slimy hands touching her and you need to respect that. Ask Lou, I'm not above killing someone for crossing a line."

He squirmed out of Warrick's grip walking off the dance floor in defeat. Warrick slung an arm across my shoulders, turning me to face Lou, "Are you done here?"

"You sure are protective of her, Warrick. I haven't seen you act that way since Melody."

Warrick stiffened, "Stop playing, Lou. Get out with it."

"Seems odd to me when all you two claim you've been doing is each other," Lou said, not caring to hide his suspicion.

"Think whatever you want, but that's all we're doing. I would hate to lose someone who knows just what I like," Warrick leaned down to kiss the sensitive spot on my neck. I let a small moan escape just for show, making Lou look away.

Warrick kept kissing me, starting to let his hands roam over my body when Lou finally walked away after seeing enough. I turned around to Warrick my skin flushed, "Excuse me for a moment while I go cool off in the restroom."

I walked away, fanning myself while hearing Warrick's chuckles behind me. Once in the restroom, I let out a big breath. Being surrounded by too much tension was starting to weigh on me. I pinched the bridge of my nose using a few more seconds to collect myself when someone approached me. *Jennie.*

"Val," she said barely putting her hand on my arm. "Can we talk?"

"If you're going to give me the same interrogation as Lou, then no. I don't need to explain myself and why I'm here with Warrick."

Jennie retracted her hand, hurt etched in her voice, "I just want to make sure you're making smart choices. I can only assume you're staying with him and since he was the man who almost killed you, I don't want to see you get hurt. You can be reckless when this kind of stuff happens."

I whipped my head around to her, "Stay out of this, Jennie."

I stormed back out to where everyone else was. I did a quick scan not seeing Warrick anywhere, so I headed over to the plant Lou mentioned earlier. *Time to blow off some steam.* I started searching the plant, reaching for anything that might feel like a wooden stake. Believing Lou only pointed me in this direction to see if I would still trust him, I was about to give up when I finally felt the familiar texture of wood. I pulled it out of the plant doing my best to press it against my side since there was nowhere for me to hide it. I made my way over to one of the doorways that surprisingly had no one guarding it. I gave one last look over my shoulder before moving forward with exploring.

The sound my heels were making echoed off the walls. If I didn't take these off now, I would have no element of surprise. Holding my shoes in one hand and the stake in the other, I continued creeping forward. I paused at each door I approached, moving closer to the cold wooden surfaces to see if I could hear anything. I would take a moment to hide behind any of the statues or plants to make sure I wasn't being followed. I rounded a corner pressing my ear to a door when I heard familiar voices coming from behind it.

At first, I couldn't make out what was being said. Their voices were pretty muffled, but they must have turned towards the door because I was suddenly able to hear them more clearly. From what I could pick up, Cian and Warrick were talking strategy for whatever they had been scheming. *Explains why I couldn't find him.* I couldn't make sense of what they were talking about because I didn't have enough of the details, but it sounded like they were gearing up for a fight. Their voices started to become louder signaling their approach towards the door, making me hold my breath. I crept away, finding a spot to hide right as the door opened. I heard Cian's voice first, "Make sure your woman steers clear of my guys. Liam is already itching to kill her, and I know she's waiting for the right moment to take out a few more. We can't afford to lose anymore, Warrick."

They were both out of the room at this point, "You're not telling me something I don't already know."

Both men headed back towards the festivities giving me the opportunity I needed to let out the breath I had been holding. At the rate I'm going, I'll be able to hold my breath for days with how often I have to hide myself from supernatural beings. Waiting a little longer, I moved out of cover when I finally deemed the place empty, continuing my routine of pressing my ear against each door I came across. I wasn't going to stop my plans just because Cian gave a warning to Warrick. His bark was worse than his bite, anyways. It wasn't until I reached the third door from where I heard Cian and Warrick talking that I heard something else.

There was a small scream quickly cut off followed by the sounds of struggles. This was my shot. I slowly opened the door, doing my best to play the role of someone who was lost. I found a woman being held down by a couple of Cian's vampires with another one standing over her, his fangs fully bared. Recognition dawned on me as I realized this was the same woman who was in my dream warning me about the death in this place.

"Oops, sorry," I tried to plaster an innocent smile on my face. "I thought this was the way to the restroom. I'll just keep looking."

I made like I was going to leave hoping I was able to bait them enough to shift their focus off the poor woman and on to me.

The one who wasn't holding their victim down moved closer, "No need to rush out of here. I'll escort you. Can't let a pretty little lamb get lost in the maze."

He was standing inches from me now closing the door behind me. I moved my hands behind my back, urging my fear to kick in so my heart rate would climb. He noticed, running his fingers along my neck practically salivating, "No reason to be scared. You're safe here."

Yeah right.

He slowly started moving towards my neck. As soon as I felt the tips of his fangs against my skin, I yanked my arm from behind me, driving the stake up into his heart. He made gagging noises until he finally collapsed against me, all signs of life gone. I pushed him to the floor, his body slowly turning to ash, and looked at the remaining two, "Anyone else want to try to show me where to go?"

The other two looked at each other then let go of the woman. She jumped up, running towards the door I just opened. I closed it once she was clear, returning my attention to my attackers. I dropped my shoes and kicked the first one in the groin distracting him enough so I could turn on the other throwing a punch. It connected with his nose, a cracking noise filling the room. He collapsed, a whimper of pain escaping his lips as he held his freshly broken nose.

The one who had been doubled over from my kick growled then rushed at me. I ducked down and propelled myself forward so I could have the advantage. My shoulder met his diaphragm, knocking the wind out of him. I slammed him into the wall and thrust the stake into his chest before he could try to make any defensive maneuvers. When he was dead, I yanked the stake out and turned my attention on the remaining vampire.

He wasn't in the spot I left him. I looked around wildly, knowing how dangerous it is to lose sight of someone in a fight, especially someone who could drain me in moments if given the chance. *This room isn't even that big, where could he have gone?*

He dropped down from above, sending us both crashing into the ground. I let out a grunt and felt my stake leave my hand. His breath was on the back of my neck, "Not so tough now, are we?"

I growled, thrashing my body trying to throw his weight off me. I wanted to give up, but if I did, that would be the end of things.

All of my moving made him need to adjust his grip on one of my wrists. The minute the pressure lessened, I yanked my arm back, freeing it to start pushing myself up. I was able to move my body in a position to keep this guy off-center and give me an advantage. I sprang up to my feet trying to land another kick. He knew what was coming and caught my foot pulling me towards him, "That trick won't work on me."

When I was close to him, he started moving in to bite my neck. I quickly ducked and headbutted his diaphragm to knock the air out of him. While he was trying to catch his breath, he let go, giving me the chance to grab my stake. Once I had it back in my hand, I whirled around only to be kicked into the table the woman before me was on. I pushed myself back up as quick and as forcefully as I could to try to knock him back. I turned on him, stabbing blindly with the stake.

Not feeling the usual resistance that comes with hitting someone in their heart, I ripped my hand back then stabbed again, this time higher. The vampire finally stopped attacking, confirming I hit my mark. He sank to the ground motionless. I pressed my back against the wall, working on catching my breath. I straightened my dress out and used one of the vampire's jackets to wipe any blood off my skin hoping I did enough to keep anyone from smelling it on me. It was going to be hard to keep the scent down considering there was probably some on my dress, but I couldn't do anything about that at the moment.

I held my breath, leaning against the door checking for sounds one last time. When I deemed the coast was clear, I headed back towards the music with my anger sufficiently worked out of my system and tired muscles. I strode back in to see the same scene of people dancing and mingling as if nothing was going on in the depths of this building. It made me sick to think about it. I slinked along the wall towards where the restrooms were then made it look like I had just come out of them.

The spot where my face had hit the table was starting to throb, but not enough to make me worry about it being seen. I grabbed a drink, gulping it down when Warrick approached me, "That good of a night, love?"

"You don't even know," I said turning to face him. "Jennie cornered me trying to play the good cop after Lou came in as bad cop. Please don't leave me again."

Warrick brushed my hair behind my shoulder, "I don't plan on it."

"Where'd you run off to anyways? There was no way you needed to use the restroom again that quickly after going the first time," my voice full of suspicion.

"I should be asking the same thing about you," he stepped towards me. He lowered his voice, "You reek of blood that isn't yours, love. If you did what I think you did, we need to go now. You'll learn soon enough how stupid that was."

I grabbed another glass of wine, chugging it down like I did the one before. Warrick raised his eyebrows at me only to be met with a quick shake of my head, "Let's go."

He placed a guiding hand on my lower back navigating us through the crowd to leave. We didn't exchange another word until we were in his car, far enough away from any listening ears as we headed back to his house.

"I wish you didn't put yourself in danger like that. Why are you trying to take them out?"

"They attack innocent people," I mumbled.

Warrick placed a hand on my knee, "I'm not mad at you, love. They choose their targets carefully. Tonight's the one night they get to let loose and they only drink enough to get their fill, not to kill."

"How do you know so much about them?" I asked, untying the mask.

He sighed, "Because I've questioned Cian about this. All I'm saying is you need to pick and choose your battles, and this is one you should walk away from."

I clamped my mouth shut knowing he was right. We pulled into his driveway and headed into the house. The wine chose this moment to hit me all at once, causing me to catch myself. Warrick threw his jacket on the couch rolling his sleeves up. He watched me, "You okay, love?"

"Just feeling the wine a little, that's all. Care to resume what we were doing on the dance floor?"

"You mean this?"

He started kissing me along my neck as he reached up to let my hair down. Warrick guided us to a wall pressing my back against it, causing me to hiss at the feeling of the cold against my bare skin. The cold stopped getting to me, though, his fingers inching closer to my inner thighs and making me tremble in anticipation.

"That's it," I whispered. "Keep going."

Warrick's laugh rumbled deep in his chest, "Have you been this wet for me since the ball?"

I let out a breathy, "Yes."

He continued exploring me, moving his fingers in a way that made me want to scream out in pure ecstasy. He ripped my dress off tossing the pieces of fabric aside and got back to work. I was reveling in the feeling of mounting pressure in my core when there was a quick knock on the door.

Warrick stopped, growling towards the door. He looked back at me, "Go put my jacket on and sit at the island."

I did as I was told, confident in whatever plan he had. He tossed my dress further down the hall before answering the door, Cian standing there, expression blank. The only indication he was feeling anything was how abruptly he walked into the house. He looked at me then turned to Warrick.

"By all means, come on in," Warrick's voice dripping with sarcasm. "I wasn't busy or anything."

"I wanted to see if you knew anything about three of my guys being stabbed," Cian said getting right to the point.

Warrick moved behind me, his hands palming my breasts and pulling me back into him. I closed my eyes arching my back. If there's one thing I've learned with Warrick, it's that every action is intentional, so even if it meant exposing a little bit of my body, I leaned into it.

Cian looked at us starting to show his anger, "I don't care what I've interrupted." He pointed his finger at me, "*She* has been known to kill my men. *You* showed up with her tonight. I might as well start with the first person on my suspect list."

Warrick continued to play with me, "The only time I took my eyes off her was when she was in the restroom. I'm surprised your guys weren't doing more thorough checks. You think she was able to hide anything in that dress she was wearing? And you know I wouldn't bring anything to put our deal at risk."

"I'll drop this for now since you clearly can't keep it in your pants when you have an audience, but if I find out she was the one behind this, I will kill her."

Cian turned, slamming the door behind him.

Chapter 11

W arrick started pacing the room, but I couldn't focus on anything except for how attracted I was to him. *Damn wine.* I stepped in front of his path, tracing the hard outlines of muscle under his vest and shirt. When he tried to move around me, I stepped in front of him, dropping his jacket on the floor, "I know I'm an idiot, but we can deal with that later."

His pupils dilated, letting me know he liked what he saw. Warrick tossed me over his shoulder and took us back into his room where the rest of our night consisted of me being on top of him and him being on top of me.

W e spent most of the next day trying to come up with a plan to pin the vampire killings on someone else. The best we could do was come up with a story that led Cian to Lou, but we weren't entirely convinced that would work. Needing a break from a moody Warrick, I headed out on my bike back to my house to grab some more clothes, hopefully ones that would help lighten his mood a little bit.

I quietly ran up to my room, not caring to be as sneaky as I had been before, and started rummaging through my drawers. I tossed the lingerie I wanted on my bed along with the other clothing items I wanted. I started to turn around when I heard Jennie clear her throat. I groaned, turning to face her, "Yes?"

She looked at the bed seeing what I had grabbed. "No, no, no," Jennie said shaking her head, pinching the bridge of her nose. "We're not doing this again, Val."

I narrowed my eyes, putting my hands on my hips, "Not doing what, exactly?"

Jennie stood up straight, "I'm not standing by you while you act reckless. You're throwing yourself at the one person you really shouldn't be while letting a perfectly good man's heart break and you're holding the hammer."

I cross my arms, "I don't need you to babysit me, Jennie. I'm perfectly capable of taking care of myself and if I need a good lay, then so be it."

"You're kidding me, right? You're the one making us out to be the bad guys! We've been waiting for you to come back so we can have a reasonable conversation about this."

I jammed my finger in my chest, starting to raise my voice, "*I'm* the only one doing something around here. *I'm* the one setting out to do what I promised I would while Lou hasn't done anything except for cry and run to Melody."

Jennie rolled her eyes, "Let me bow down to the almighty Val. The hero we didn't know we needed. And yes, I'm aware of the Lou and Melody situation. In fact, the other night, the four of us had dinner and I can confirm there is absolutely zero things happening between them. He comes back here moping, wondering what he can do to get back into your good graces. That's why he isn't out there helping you with the vampire problem. He doesn't want to distract you."

She paused, taking a steadying breath, "Let me ask you this. Is there something Warrick is getting out of this besides a good time? He sure put on a show last night, but I couldn't help but wonder if he has ulterior motives. Has he been asking questions to get info about your dad, the device you made, and anything else that could add to his power?"

I stopped momentarily before snapping out of it. Hefting my bag over my shoulder and grabbing my helmet, I glanced over my shoulder, "Don't let me keep you up at night, Jennie."

Those last questions were tumbling around in my head as I got back on my bike to head to Warrick's place. I hated to think she was on to something, but she was probably right. I didn't know who to believe and couldn't trust my gut to steer me in the right direction. All I knew was to head back to what was bringing me the most comfort right now, and that was Warrick.

I looked down at my speedometer to see it reading over 100 miles per hour. I shifted to the next gear, pushing it faster only wanting to see the number increase. The higher the number, the faster I could escape my problems. A car suddenly flashed its headlights on right in front of me. We were too close for me to brake, so I tried swerving only to be met with a car door. I flew off my bike, getting a nice view of the clear night before slamming onto the road, tumbling in the grass, rolling a couple of times before finally coming to a stop.

Every part of me hurt. I laid myself on my back, fighting to retain consciousness, the outer parts of my vision starting to turn black. I let out a groan before being yanked off the ground.

"You *bitch*! You sat there last night letting Warrick fondle you while you both denied killing more of my men," Cian spat, slamming me against his car.

I screamed out as pain exploded in me. There was no holding back the sobs as I tried to shake my head, "We never outright denied anything. You only assumed. Warrick had nothing to do with it."

"So you admit you drove that blasted stake through them?" he asked, slamming me against his car again.

"Yes," I forced out in between sobs. "I'll stop. Please. You've already caused me enough pain."

He threw his head back laughing, "You think this is pain?" He ripped my helmet off, causing another scream to shatter the quiet of the night. "I haven't even begun to show you pain."

He threw a punch making a few of my ribs crack in response. He slammed me against the car one more time making me nearly black out with pain. He kneed me a few times breaking more ribs. He leaned in, eyes wild, mumbling something to me I couldn't hear over the throbbing in my ears. When I didn't answer, Cian broke my nose sending my pain level well beyond my threshold. I was delirious at this point, my head rolling back and my eyesight starting to fail me.

Cian yanked my chin forcing me to look at him. There were multiples of his sneering face floating around my vision. When I could focus on the real one, I spit blood in his face. "Had enough fun yet?" I slurred.

He laughed again, a cruel cackling sound. "You taste delicious. I can't wait to drain every last drop of blood out of you. That way I'll finally get you to stop interfering with my plan. There's more at play here, but you couldn't see past your own *foolish* agenda."

Cian suddenly dropped me without any warning. I crumpled to the ground unable to hold myself up without excruciating pain. There was snarling and hissing, but I couldn't keep track of what was going on. I was fighting to keep myself from passing out in case I was still in danger, but I couldn't keep that up for long. Before everything faded to black, though, I heard a howl ripping through the quiet night followed by a car speeding away.

S teady beeping pulled me from sleep, my eyelids weighing a thousand pounds as I tried to pry them open. My mouth was so dry I'm convinced I'm giving the Sahara Desert a run for its money. Yet, the one thing I noticed that took the cake over everything else was the pain throbbing throughout every inch of my body.

After a strenuous fight, my eyes were finally able to stay open allowing me to take in my new surroundings. Sterile, white walls greeted me from every side. The beeping coming from a machine on my left showed my current heart rate and other numbers I couldn't even guess what they meant. Light was streaming in through a window on the opposite side of the room where Warrick sat holding his head in his hands. I looked over myself shocked at being the person in the hospital bed and even more shocked by how battered my body appeared. Taking a deep breath, I turned my attention back to Warrick.

"You're acting like someone died around here," I croaked out, my voice showing signs of how desperately I need water.

He whipped his head up, the once clear, icy blue eyes now bloodshot and framed by dark circles underneath. A mixture of worry, relief, and anger crossed his features in moments, finally settling on relief. Warrick approached me from where he sat, "Val, love, you have no idea what a relief it is to see you awake."

"You're being dramatic. I haven't been asleep that long," I said, trying to keep the confusion from creeping in.

He held a cup of water to me, "It may feel that way for you, but you've been out for three days. Drink this."

I gratefully accepted the cup, downing it in no time. Before I could respond, though, a doctor followed by an army of nurses rushed in pushing Warrick away from me. They started running through their checks, thrusting a bright light into my eyes, prodding me with needles, and doing who knows what else since panic wasted no time setting in. My eyes darted around wildly. "Warrick?" I called out.

I felt a gentle hand land on my leg, "I'm right here, love. They're just running some tests to finish their assessment of the damage done. I'm not going anywhere."

I took a deep steadying breath trying to calm down while also trying to follow the doctor's orders to move this and that limb, rate my pain on a scale, and if I have any memory of what happened.

The last questions left me stammering. I had no recollection of what had caused me to wake up in this bed and not in the coziness of Warrick's house. All I could remember was getting in a fight with Jennie after going to grab some things at my house. I kept trying and each time I failed to recall what happened, the doctor's concern grew. He finally gave up, signaling to Warrick he wanted to talk out in the hall about whatever he was able to figure out about my condition. Warrick gave my leg a reassuring squeeze before following the doctor and his nurses outside of my room, dashing any hopes of hearing them.

Looking down at my hands, I couldn't keep the worry at bay any longer. If Warrick was this concerned, then I must be in rough shape from bad circumstances. I fiddled my fingers a few more moments before deciding it was time to get up. I angled myself to get out of the bed, starting to swing my legs over when pain shot through me and I yelped. Warrick hastily made his way back in the room, "Let me help you, love. What are you trying to do?"

"I need to use the bathroom," I paused, choking down the emotion welling up in my throat. "But it hurts too much."

"Here," he slid a bedpan under me. "Use this."

I turned my head away not wanting him to know how embarrassed I was at him helping me or the fact that there was no holding back any tears now. I finished and he called a nurse in to take care of cleaning up, returning to my side when the nurse left. He pulled one of his chairs next to the bed, stroking my hair and face. Warrick wiped away a tear with a touch that was light as a feather only making more tears follow the one he chased away. He let out a quiet chuckle, "You're going to be okay now."

"What happened?" I whispered.

His brows furrowed together, "You really don't remember?"

I shook my head looking down at my lap again. I was scared to hear what had happened if this was how everyone was acting.

One of Warrick's hands covered mine as he kept stroking my hair, doing everything he could to bring me an ounce of comfort. He waited a few beats longer before diving in, "It's safe to say you're the first motorcycle incident this place has ever seen, but that wasn't the only thing that landed you in here. Cian is pissed, love. He figured out who killed three of his men at the ball, nicely done I might add, and wasn't going to sleep until he found you especially after we lied to him. About 20 minutes after you left my place, he showed up on my doorstep practically shaking with rage trying to find you. Cian tore my place apart looking for you, but after determining you weren't there, he went around driving. It wasn't until he saw you speeding towards him on your bike that he smacked you with his door then took to beating the crap out of you. It was a full moon that night, so I was already in wolf form just wandering around the fields when I smelt your blood and your pain. I heard your screams, confirming my worst nightmare. By the time I had gotten there, the damage was done, but I was able to chase him away hoping he hadn't killed you. Then, I brought you here and have been with you since."

Guilt washed over me. Warrick had warned me about any more attacks against Cian's vampires, but I hadn't listened and look where it got me. I glanced down at my lap again, signaling for Warrick to continue. He moved closer to me, lowering his voice to provide more comfort, "Love, the doctors are surprised you weren't worse off. Yeah, you were in a coma for a few days, have some broken bones and bruises, but that's it. They're going to run some more scans and tests to make sure you didn't sustain any damage to your brain, but they aren't too worried. Take that as a good thing to come out of this."

"But I'm in so much pain, Warrick."

"You will be. They said you'll be in here for at least a few more days, but are hoping you'll make significant progress during that time."

"Why are you staying here with me?" I asked, bringing my gaze to his. I didn't ask in a malicious way, but in a genuinely curious one because this was the last thing I suspected from him.

If anything, I thought his alliance with Cian would've kept him busy and far enough away from me.

"Because as ironic as this is going to sound, I couldn't bear the thought of you being in this much pain on your own, waking up in a hospital with no one here to advocate for you or to give you any comfort. Because, love, the thought of you not being here to mess with or to share laughter or love with nearly broke me. I don't care if we don't end up together in the end, or if this is the moment you've decided you've had enough, I just want you to be okay. I haven't done the best in the past, but I'll be there for you. I'll protect you; I'll fight with you; I'll do whatever you want. I told you before you've captured my heart, and I meant what I said with every muscle in my body."

I was dragged back to that night in the pub when he finally made his presence known. The wild-eyed, out-for-revenge Warrick had been replaced with someone who just wanted to share his life with me. Every word was filled with a sincerity sending thousands of butterflies in flight within me. I reached up, cupping his cheek, him leaning into the touch with closed eyes. I opened my mouth to say something in return when we were interrupted by a slow, light knock on the door.

Warrick's head whipped towards the door, my gaze following his to find Lou standing there with a monstrous bouquet of flowers. Clearing his throat, he said, "Hey, am I interrupting something?"

I squeezed Warrick's hand, signaling him to keep quiet, "No, come on in."

Relief visibly took over as he came into the room, grabbing the other chair and sitting opposite of Warrick. Silence filled the space for what felt like hours while Warrick and Lou stared each other down. I kept looking between the two wondering who would be the first to try to attack the other given the rising tension between them.

I started fidgeting with my hospital gown, looking down at my lap for what felt like the millionth time, "Thanks for coming by, Lou."

He didn't break his gaze from Warrick's as he replied, "I'm just glad to see you're awake. Last I heard, you were in a coma and not doing well."

"And just how did you hear about that, Louis?" Warrick asked with hostility laced in every word.

"Conor, who seems to be the only one who can see past the bullshit," Lou spat back.

"You want to say what's really on your mind?"

I looked between the two again dreading how this was going. The last thing I wanted to see was them going at each other when Lou was trying to make a nice gesture. I opened my mouth to say something, hoping I could keep the fire from growing when Lou abruptly stood up, Warrick doing the same. Lou leaned in to be closer to Warrick, "Wanna know what's really on my mind, Warrick? When Conor told me she was in the hospital, it took everything in me to not just run down here to make sure she wasn't being wheeled out in a damn body bag. The first thing that ran through my mind was that you finally did it, you finally killed her and any chance I had of setting things right was gone."

Lou turned his attention to me, "I know what you think of me, Val. I just wanted to make sure you were okay."

Warrick grabbed Lou's shirt, "You're an *ass* if that's all you think of me. *I* was the one who saved her. *I* was the one who got her here before it was too late. You want to accuse me of trying to kill her? Get your facts straight before you come waltzing in here trying to play Prince Charming."

"What happened, then? What did so much damage to her if it wasn't you?" Lou asked calmly removing Warrick's hands and looking at me.

I took a deep breath, "I was in an accident on my bike. Flew off after going too fast."

"Who put the bruises on your face? It wasn't from flying off your bike since you religiously wear your gear," Lou's brow furrowed with doubt.

My gaze drifted back down again prompting Lou to run his hands through his hair, "Well, if neither of you are going to say something, then I'll figure it out on my own."

Lou started making his exit as Warrick called out to him, "Lou, drop it. We don't need you doing something stupid."

He didn't give any sign of acknowledging Warrick by the time he was out of the room.

I reached over and squeezed Warrick's hand, "Hey, if he's going to do something stupid, let him."

Warrick was still focused on the door, "Not if the consequences get taken out on you, love." He brought his gaze back to mine, continuing, "I have to go take care of some things, but I'll be back in a couple of hours with some decent food now that you're awake. It'll make it easier, too, if you have anyone stopping by and I'm not here."

He leaned down, placing a soft kiss on my forehead before heading out. When the coast was clear, I sighed, dropping my head back on my pillow, closing my eyes, succumbing to a quick nap. I didn't realize how much energy that interaction zapped from me until now.

A knock jolted me awake bringing my full attention to the door to find Conor waiting to be invited in. I waved him over, "Hi, stranger. Don't you have a pub or something to run?"

"The guys are taking over for a second while I'm here," he said getting comfortable in one of the chairs. "What mess did you get yourself into this time?"

"Are you going to run to Lou the minute I tell you?"

Conor flinched a little, "Sorry if I caused any trouble with your bodyguard. Speaking of which, where is he?"

"He'll be back in a little bit. Thank you for stopping by," I said sincerely.

"As soon as I heard you had been in a bad accident, I wanted to check in on you. You're probably the only employee I've had with this kind of luck. So, are you going to tell me what happened?"

I laughed, shaking my head a little, "Always getting down to business. Alright, but I don't need you telling Lou about any of this because he's ready to go off half-cocked to do some sort of grand gesture for me."

He only nodded prompting me to go on, "On the night of the ball, I was feeling adventurous and wandered throughout the cathedral. I ended up going into a room where some of Cian's guys were getting ready to drink a woman dry, which didn't sit well with me. I ended up attacking and killing them. Cian clearly wasn't too thrilled with what happened, especially after he found out I was the guilty party, so he tracked me down while I was riding my bike and hit me with both his car and fists."

What I kept out was that I sought out my latest victims in a fit of anger because I let Lou get under my skin. I didn't need him thinking I couldn't keep things in check when it came to Lou. *I'm just going through a phase right now.*

"Jeez, Val," Conor started. "I don't know whether to say you have balls or you're just asking for a death wish. Of course, Cian was going to come after you. That's one of the main rules you learn here: don't kill any of his men. That would explain why Liam was running his mouth."

"What was Liam saying?" I asked, snapping back from my thoughts, a picture of the half-crazed vampire flashing in my mind.

Conor shook his head, "I heard him the other night in the pub talking to a few of his friends around him. He kept going on and on about what he would do to you if he got the chance. Liam was pretty fired up and practically jumping at the opportunity to be let loose when Cian finally told him to shut it. It wasn't too long after your accident and I started to wonder if everything was related, but now I can see –"

Conor was interrupted when another knock floated into the room followed by Jennie's voice, "Can we join the party?"

Conor looked down at his watch, "Ah, I better get heading back to the pub. Glad to see you're awake, Val."

"Thanks, Conor," I gave his hand a squeeze before turning my attention to Jennie and Chris. Jennie bustled in carrying another large assortment of colorful flowers while Chris followed behind her unsure if he should be here or not. *Clearly the bromance between him and Lou has blossomed.*

"I knew that bike was going to be the death of you someday," Jennie started.

I threw her a glare, "If all you're going to do is scold me, then please leave."

Chris jumped in before any words escaped Jennie's open mouth, "We're just glad to hear you're finally awake. We were all pretty worried."

"Well, I'm glad you stopped by, then," I responded, trying to keep the annoyance from my tone.

Jennie was examining the flowers Lou had brought earlier, her hand cradling one of the blooms, "I see Lou stopped by."

"We didn't get back together if that's what you're implying."

Her shoulders dropped, Chris fidgeting behind her. They moved to sit in the chairs. Once comfortable, Jennie placed her hands over mine, "Look, things have been rough between all of us for a while. When Warrick stopped by –"

"Wait, Warrick actually went by the house and you all had a civil conversation?" I asked, the question tumbling out of my mouth before I could stop it.

Chris and Jennie both chuckled before Jennie continued, "I don't know if I would call it civil, and before you interrupt me again, yes, it was Lou who lost his temper. Anyways, Warrick stopped by letting us know you had been in a bad accident and were in a coma. It rocked us with Lou taking the news the hardest. He practically stormed out to the back yard not hearing the rest of what Warrick had to tell us. Granted it was after he had heard the news from Conor, but he didn't believe it then. Warrick was the one who got through to him and thankfully brought Chris and I up to speed."

I looked down at my lap, "Thank you for being willing to talk to Warrick. That's pretty big of you since I know you both aren't the hugest fans."

"It was big of him to not only tell us, but tell us in person especially with his guard down," Chris chimed in. "He didn't get all hot-headed when Lou tried jumping down his throat. You could tell he was torn up about what happened and wanted to make sure to do right by you. It wasn't hard to convince us that he truly cares about your well-being."

I could feel the tears brimming, "I'm happy you could see that side of him."

Jennie shot a look towards Chris, "Despite that, we're still not completely sold, but it meant a lot that he came to us."

I gave her a soft grin, watching as she reached into a bag to pull out some of my favorite pajamas, "We thought you might like these since you're probably going to be here a little while longer."

"Thank you," I said, holding the pants that felt like butter in my hands. Jennie must have seen the hesitation written all over my face. She turned towards Chris, "Can you get us some coffee?"

"Sure," Chris nodded, picking up the subliminal message.

As soon as he was out of the room, Jennie brought her attention back to me, "Here, let me help you."

We were silent as she helped work me into the clothes with the occasional grunt and whimper of pain escaping me. I got settled back in along with the awkwardness that now filled the space between us. My heart ached at the thought of losing another person I was so close to, but I had no words to try and repair what damage had happened between us by the argument we shared a few days ago.

Jennie was the first to break the silence, her voice filled with sincerity, "Val, I'm so sorry. For everything. I should have taken the time to step back and see things from your perspective and I didn't. Instead, I continued to step on your toes trying to tell you what you should be doing rather than helping you work through whatever pain you may be dealing with. I may not be the biggest fan of Warrick, but I can see he's been trying to take care of you. Even though you've been reckless, he's helped you keep it reeled in. And I'm seeing a spark in your eyes that I haven't since Gabriel has been around." She paused, letting out a small laugh, "I sure have been apologizing to you a lot lately, yet you've been nothing but a sister to me. You've been mad, sure, but you haven't been mean."

"You're going through a lot, too, Jennie. You're going to have those knee-jerk reactions because that's you, you're human. We'll make it through this together. I know I haven't been the best person to you, Chris, especially Lou. I just needed some time and space to think through things and I happened to get wrapped up in Warrick."

With a smile on her face, she squeezed my hand while she stood up, "I'm glad we're putting this behind us. I think Chris may have gotten lost on his way to grab coffee, so we'll be heading out, but we hope you get out of here soon. If you need anything else, just let me know."

"Thanks, and Jennie?" I asked. She paused in the doorway, "Can you make sure Lou doesn't do anything stupid? He seemed pretty riled up when he left here earlier and I don't want to see anything happen to him."

"We'll keep an eye on him, Val. Leave that worry to us and you just focus on what you need to do to feel better," Jennie tapped her hand on the doorframe before leaving.

Things may still be a little tense between us, but I think we're heading in the right direction.

The rest of the afternoon was filled with me being carted from room to room, shoved in this machine and that for the medical staff to get their scans in. The doctor reviewed the extent of damage in my body they knew of and shared their hopes of having me out of here in a few more days. I still had an uphill battle with recovery, but I could at least get to a point where I could stand on two feet. We went through the pain management plan where the doctor pointed out I would still need to be on a regular dosage of pain killers after I told him how much it hurt to make the slightest of movements thanks to my ribs, but we also put a plan together to slowly decrease the dosage as time went on and a tentative discharge date.

By the time the doctor left and I was alone in my room, the exhaustion took over. Between everyone stopping by, the tension between Warrick and Lou, and being shuffled around the hospital to be poked and prodded, it was hard for me to keep my eyes open. My lids drooped closed, my breathing slowing as I drifted back to sleep.

I heard the soft rustling of a bag followed by quiet footsteps approaching my bed. There was no strength in me to try to open my eyes to see who was coming up to me, but I had a hunch. A soft kiss was placed on my forehead, Warrick whispering, "Love? Are you up to eating?"

"Hmm?"

"Would you rather sleep?" he asked, thumb stroking my cheek.

"Eat," I mumbled this time putting more effort into opening my eyes. When I did, Warrick was putting everything out on a tray before sliding it over to me. I studied him, making note of how tired and worn he looked. His usually pristine, clean-cut look was disheveled and lacking any shine. A five o'clock shadow was prominent, the dark circles under his eyes exaggerated by the hospital lighting. I put a hand on his arm, stopping him momentarily, "Warrick, have you slept? Are you taking care of yourself?"

"I'll be fine, love. Focus on getting yourself healed."

I didn't push the issue any longer, but rather dove into the food he brought for me: a familiar order of mac-and-cheese with a piece of chocolate cake for us to share. He went to that place Jennie and Chris took me to the night I saw him playing piano. I mumbled my thanks, wishing I could offer more if I weren't so tired. When he got up to use the restroom, I called a nurse in asking if there was any way we could get something more comfortable for him to sleep on added to the room. Even though there wasn't much I could do, I'd at least start with the small things I could take care of. She wasn't sure, but she said she would try. As Warrick was coming back in the room, the nurse was following him with a small couch noting that this was all they could offer at the moment. We both said our thanks then turned our focus back to each other. Warrick's eyes softened as he looked at me, "Thank you, love. I would've been fine with the chairs."

"I wanted to try to make it a little more comfortable since I'm sure you're planning on staying here until I get discharged."

He nodded, "I wasn't planning on going anywhere for too long. In fact, I took too long today, but I shouldn't need to leave again. I see Jennie and Chris stopped by." Warrick gestured to my change in clothes, making me smile at the thought of how their visit ended. I only mustered a small nod. Warrick sat down again, watching me the whole time, "How is your pain today?"

I filled him in on everything the doctor went over with me today including all the scans and tests they ran. He occasionally murmured his approval until I was done walking through everything. I watched him for a moment longer until I worked up the courage to ask, "How are you holding up, Warrick?"

He rubbed his hands along his face, every movement showcasing the tiredness coursing through him, "I'm doing alright, love. Like I said earlier, focus on getting better."

"Stop dancing around this and just answer the question."

He chuckled, "You just don't give up, do you?"

I gave my head a little shake, "Nope, and I don't plan on changing that either."

"The last few days have been hard. Seeing you crumpled there on the street after what Cian had done nearly broke me. It took everything I had in every fiber of my being to not rip his throat out. I never thought I would see the sun until you came into my life. For crying out loud, I had laughed in a way I haven't in *years*. I didn't even think I had it in me anymore. I was finally feeling like I could live a little again instead of having to be the cool, calculating villain everyone paints me to be. You have no idea what kind of weight that lifted off my shoulders. Then, this happens and I could only see red. I wanted revenge. I wanted to cause Cian as much pain as he caused you, or worse."

I ran a hand through his hair, "Thank you for being honest with me, Warrick, and for staying with me."

He closed his eyes, leaning into my touch while visibly relaxing and letting his guard down. That all went away when a nurse walked in with my next dosage of pain medication,

Warrick watching her like a hawk. As soon as she was out of the room, he started cleaning things up and I drifted off into a deep sleep feeling the lightness that came with the meds they were giving me.

A soft slam startled me awake. I don't know how long I had been out, but it was dark in the room save for the lights coming from the various machines I was hooked up to. I did a quick scan trying to determine the source of the noise when my eyes finally found Warrick. He was shirtless, muscles rippling as he pinned a struggling man against the wall. I blinked a few times getting my eyes to adjust to the darkness and focus on what was going on in front of me.

The man Warrick was pinning was none other than Liam who was spitting incoherent words in a blind range. With each word that came out of his mouth, Warrick shoved him against the wall harder, "So help me, if you lay a hand on her, I will throw the deal I have with Cian out the damned window and rip every limb from your body after breaking every bone."

Liam was wildly flailing his arms in every direction trying to do something, anything, to Warrick and failing. Every now and then, the small amount of light in the room would reflect off his extended canines making me shiver. Liam caught this movement leveling his gaze on me. He slowly stopped fighting back at the same time his signature sinister grin crawled across his lips. Warrick sensing the sudden change, whipped his head around to me, eyes glowing indicating he was summoning his wolf's strength. He hissed a few curses under his breath, and in those few seconds, Liam managed to wiggle himself free and was crouched over me.

"You being awake will make this even better," he was practically salivating at the thought of whatever torture he was about to put me through. He moved to tilt my chin up to get a better look when Warrick grabbed him from behind slamming Liam into the ground.

Warrick threw his knee into Liam's chest, the sound of ribs cracking filling the space. Warrick leaned closer to his face, growling, "Did you not listen when I said don't touch her? Don't put me in this spot, Liam."

Liam's struggling resumed as he pushed against Warrick's weight to try and get him off. Every push only made Warrick press down even harder. He lowered his voice, still growling, "Has Cian not reminded you what's at stake here?"

This made Liam go wild, "You're kidding me, right? She can get off with no consequences after killing so many of our kind and we can't even take one life? No eye for an eye?"

Warrick shifted his weight to keep Liam pinned while he swept his arm back to point to me, "Does that look like no consequences?" His voice lowered even more, making it hard for me to hear him over the beeping, "Believe it or not, she's vital, too."

Liam wasn't buying it going back to hissing and spitting at Warrick to get free. There was a moment where Liam got close to biting his captor, butWarrick landed a punch knocking him out cold. While he was unconscious, Warrick snapped his leg like it was a dead tree branch before dragging him out of the room.

I sat there still in shock at the scene I witnessed after just waking up. If Warrick hadn't been there, I would have been dead.

Even after all of that and Warrick dragging Liam out of the room, no nurses or doctors came running in. In fact, the hospital was sleeping as though nothing had happened.

Everything Warrick said caught up to me, though, and my memories of the accident hit me like a ton of bricks. Cian had mentioned something about a plan, something bigger than me, and Warrick had referenced something being at stake with Liam being here tonight, as well as a deal he had with Cian. *What on earth is going on here?*

I moved to get out of bed doing everything I could not to whimper with the jolts of pain zipping through me when Warrick ran in to help me, "Love, stop. What do you need?"

I paused, giving him the opportunity he needed to lay me back in the bed. "What's going on here, Warrick?"

"What do you mean?" he asked, his brow etched with concern.

"I remember the accident and everything Cian said to me. He referenced a plan and something bigger than me. There's been multiple times I've heard you guys talk about a deal, so what's going on? Does this have anything to do with the device and the picture of the guy I saw on your desk?"

At mention of the picture, his face hardened. A muscle started twitching in his jaw almost as if he was having a hard time deciding what he was going to tell me. Releasing a breath, he said, "Cian and I have a deal worked out where he's letting me stay here to gather some things needed for my labs. The deal is that as long as I don't hurt his guys, he'll leave me alone."

He completely ignored the mention of the picture I came across as I was snooping, so I asked again, "Who was that guy in the picture?"

Warrick looked away, "Go back to sleep, love."

"But – "

Warrick cut me off, lowering his voice, "I'm tired and want to sleep, you should do the same."

I didn't argue any further, instead looking away from him not understanding what I did to strike a nerve. Eventually sleep took over again and I didn't open my eyes until it was light outside.

Chapter 12

I blinked the sleep from my eyes while a nurse tended to me. I gave her a soft smile getting ready to tell her thank you when she motioned for me to be quiet and pointed to my lap. I glanced down to find Warrick fast asleep, his head using my lap as a pillow. I pushed some of his hair out of his face, gently tracing his relaxed features. He had a protective arm draped over my legs while his other arm somehow made its way underneath me. His breathing was deep and slow indicating he was still in a deep sleep. I didn't dare move a muscle not wanting to risk waking him since he had clearly been so tired even before the incident last night.

I looked towards the door to see Conor lingering his hand poised to knock. I shook my head pointing to Warrick, but motioned for him to come in. Conor quietly made his way over and dropped a box of breakfast on the tray table next to me. He had a couple more boxes for him and Warrick that he set down before pulling out his phone to type a greeting. We communicated like this for a little while longer until it was time for Conor to head over to the pub to get things ready. I hadn't realized he had been there for a couple of hours, but I was more surprised by the fact that Warrick hadn't stirred with the smell of food in the room.

I went back to gently rubbing his back when Cian entered the room. Sensing that I stiffened, Warrick woke up immediately on guard. He took a look at Cian who signaled for Warrick to talk to him out in the hall, grabbed a shirt, then headed out of the room. I figured he did that for a couple of reasons. One, to make me feel less threatened and to make him not feel like he was stuck between a rock and a hard place. Two, he didn't want me to overhear the conversation so I wouldn't dig in to the details he's keeping from me.

I started eating the food Conor dropped off when Warrick returned alone. He looked over at me where I held out the other box of food for him that he wasted no time digging into once he sat back down.

"How is Cian able to walk in the daylight?" I asked with a mouthful of food.

Warrick paused his eating to give a small laugh at the sight of me with food stored like a chipmunk before answering, "Umbrellas, sunglasses, and basically anything else that will block the sun. Helps that today's pretty overcast, too. It does makes him a little more irritable than usual, so he only goes out during the day when absolutely necessary. Before you ask your next question, love, he was stopping by to talk about last night's incident. Everything is squared away."

"Oh, I'm glad you guys were able to stay civil about things."

"Believe it or not, we usually are. There's been some extenuating circumstances that may have made things bumpy for a little bit, but we're back on track."

I finished my food, itching to ask more questions but holding myself back since I know they would be met with more answers skirting around the truth.

We moved from eating to Warrick pulling out his laptop and the folder containing the list of codes for the different worlds.

He looked at me, asking, "Are you up to any of this today? Figuring out what these codes mean?"

"Sure," I answered.

He handed the list over to me, the numbers still as unfamiliar as they were the last time I looked at them. Something finally clicked into place. Each code consists of eight numbers with the last four digits of some of the codes resembling years. "Wait," I started. Warrick's head snapped up from the files he was working through, "Did you figure something out?"

I held my hand up not quite ready to answer that question. I looked at the two codes that were circled – one representing the werewolf world and the other the vampire world. The last four digits still looked like a year, but the first four seemed randomized.

My shoulders slumping, I shook my head, "No. I thought I did, but now it's back to square one."

"At least tell me what you've figured out, love," Warrick encouraged.

"I don't think it means anything, but the last four numbers of some of these look like years."

He moved my arm to give him a better view and stared at the page for a while, "I see it, too. Do you think these other four could be the rest of a date, like the month and day?"

"It could be, but dates representing what?"

Warrick shrugged, "Think about your dad, love. Is there something he really cared about or was passionate enough about that he could associate dates with these different worlds in a way that's logical? What date would represent this world of blood and death?"

The gears in my mind started turning thinking of anything my dad would remember the dates for that held this much significance. Nothing was immediately standing out to me, Warrick noticing my struggle. He took the list from my hand, giving me a squeeze, "Let's take a break. Do you trust me?"

I slowly nodded my head as he tentatively reached under my shoulders to lift me out of the bed. I let my feet fall to the floor, wincing a little as I did so. I couldn't put hardly any weight on my left ankle, and when Warrick noticed, he grabbed the crutches that had been hiding in the room's bathroom.

"A walk might do the trick, love," he smiled at me.

"Okay," I replied a little shakily.

I hoisted myself onto my feet putting all my weight on the crutches. Standing there, I took a moment to determine what movements caused the most pain and which ones were fine. Turns out, I was able to walk with minimal pain as long as I didn't put weight on my bad ankle. We ventured out of the room, Warrick and I talking about the possibilities of the codes in between the smiles and small talk with the nurses who were happy to see me up. Our quick lap finished, surprising me with how exhausted I felt. Warrick was helping me back into bed when a chipper voice came from behind us, "Special delivery! Am I interrupting?"

"It's nice to see you again, Jennie," Warrick answered, helping me maneuver into a comfortable position.

"What's going on?" Jennie asked, setting a large box of food down and making her way over to my bed.

Smiling up at Warrick, I took my turn to answer, "Just got back from a quick lap and it surprisingly wasn't too bad."

"Val, that's incredible! I'm happy you're strong enough for a walk. I visited at the right time. The guys will be so happy to hear that."

"What's the occasion for this visit, Jennie?" I asked. Warrick started serving us food from the box Jennie brought over from the pub, the extra serving of garlic fries not going unnoticed.

"Warrick asked if I could bring over food, mentioning he didn't want hospital food but didn't want to leave your side either. I have to get running so I'm keeping this one short. Enjoy," Jennie gave us a little wave on her way back out.

I looked over at Warrick, "Thank you, I guess, since she bustled out of here as quick as she arrived."

"Anytime, love. Now, eat."

There were only the sounds of us working through the fresh pub food while we were lost in thought around the codes. Nothing was breaking loose still and I couldn't fight the sleep washing over me thanks to the next round of pain medication.

I woke up in the middle of the night again, scanning the room to make sure I was in the clear. *Thank goodness there's no Liam this time.* Warrick was fast asleep on the couch with his computer and files on the tray table easily within my reach. I quietly pulled it closer to me to look at the codes again. Frowning, I grabbed the file with some emails from my dad searching for some sort of inspiration. I read the words for what must have been the hundredth time with no more luck than what I was having earlier. I threw my head back, a sigh escaping my lips. *How am I*

supposed to be the key to all this? Those dates must be tied to me somehow, but what dates? The years cover so much ground.

That's when it hit me. I snapped my eyes back open, searching for anything to write finally finding a pen on the other side of Warrick's computer. I immediately remembered the first day we watched *Young Frankenstein* together, the inspiration behind his lab where he crafted his device that eventually led me to Warrick and Lou. That was the date for their world. The date for the vampire world was when we finally finished the *Buffy* series. My world was dated with my birthday, but the rest of the dates escaped me.

Hope left my body as quickly as it arrived when nothing else immediately popped in my mind. I glanced over at Warrick to see he hadn't moved an inch from his sleeping spot. *Guess I'll have to wait until Sleeping Beauty wakes up to tell him the good news.*

I studied the codes a little longer, looking at each one and trying to remember what was happening that day. One date early in my life stood out to me as the day the *Scooby-Doo! And the Witches Ghost* movie was released. I smiled fondly at the memory of my dad coming home, his arms stuffed with candy, popcorn, and the movie. He was so excited to watch it with me that we wasted no time ordering pizza, building a fort, and soaking up every second. Still smiling, I made a note this code was likely associated with a witch world.

With one more figured out, I moved to the next one wishing for the same luck. Nothing immediately jumped out at me, so I continued working through the list pausing at each combination of numbers until I got to one that was familiar. It was the year we went to the Caribbean for Christmas and I wouldn't let go of my newly gifted Tinker Bell doll, which meant this code must lead to a world with fairies.

I put the pen down as a light throbbing started filling my head. I lay my head back on the pillows, closing my eyes willing sleep to take back over with no success. I was wide awake. My eyes roamed the room to see if there was anything else I could do without waking Warrick, lingering on his other file folders for a few moments. Deciding against snooping again out of fear of the wrath of Warrick, I made up my mind to take a lap around the hospital.

After what felt like hours of a fight to get on my feet by myself, I was roaming the hallways, stopping at the nurses' station to fill more time. I finished my lap to find Warrick rushing out of the room almost barreling into me.

He placed his hands on my shoulders, eyes filled with concern, "I thought they got you, love."

"All is calm tonight. I couldn't sleep, so I took a lap."

Warrick scooped me into his arms to guide me back into my hospital bed, "Are you feeling alright?"

I smiled, "Feeling a lot better than when we walked earlier."

His thumb stroked my cheek, "Try to sleep for me, love. That'll help you heal."

I opened my mouth to argue only for a yawn to take over. He chuckled a little while pulling the blanket up to cover me. He squeezed my arm before making his way back to the couch and my eyelids slowly closed.

S unlight filtering through the gaps in the hospital curtains mixed with the sounds of Warrick furiously flipping through his files, waking me up. I studied him for a moment, knowing he was aware his files had been touched by someone other than him, hesitating to say anything considering his reaction the last time I had gone through those same folders. Finally building up the courage to speak up, I smoothed out my blanket, "Good morning."

Warrick's head whipped up at the sound of my voice, "Morning, love."

"Everything okay?"

He ran his hand through his hair collapsing back into his chair as I watched his mask of calm fix itself in place before Warrick replied, "Find anything interesting in your perusal of my files again?"

"Only to find the list of codes," I said, doing everything in my will to not betray my outward confidence with the nerves rapidly building on the inside. "I promise I didn't look through anything else."

Warrick stared at me a little longer assessing what I said before looking back down at the one folder I didn't touch. Flipping through the pages, he finally pulled out the ones containing the codes and my newly written notes, "Did you have a breakthrough last night?"

I let out an internal sigh of relief, grateful in his trust, "Some of those numbers jumped out at me and I wanted to start documenting what I knew before I forgot."

I watched him reading through what I had wrote, seeing the gears turning in his mind. "This is big," he said in a faraway voice still examining what I wrote.

Before either one of us could say anything else on the matter, an army of nurses returned to start running their usual tests on me. Seemingly satisfied with the results, they wheeled me out to grab more scans to see what other progress has been made. A couple of the nurses gave me a reassuring smile after taking a preliminary glance over the scans filling me with the smallest amount of hope. I guess things were progressing the way they needed to.

We were greeted by a pacing Warrick as I was brought back into the room that had been my home for a while now, the doctor following closely behind his team. Worry etched in his features, he looked between me and the doctor, "Well?"

"You'll be happy to know she's good to go. There's still a good amount of healing that needs to take place for Val to get back on her feet without any assistance, but she can do that in the comfort of her own home," the doctor explained. He directed his attention to me, continuing, "I'll need you to start getting active again. You're going to be sore for a little while longer, but that'll go away with time as long as you keep moving. I'll also need you to use a crutch to support that leg of yours. Any questions?"

I looked to Warrick to make sure I wasn't going to cut him off before jumping in, "Any pain medication or anything I need to take when I'm at home? Anything I need to be doing?"

At this point, a nurse came in carrying a crutch and a packet of discharge papers that Warrick immediately started taking care of.

The doctor glanced from him to me, "Everything you need is in those papers."

And with that, he left. I positioned the crutch to help me stand while Warrick buzzed around gathering everything we needed to get out of here. I started to move out of the hospital bed, but stopped the moment all my confidence left my body. I knew I was still in pain and that it would hurt when I started to put more pressure on my bad leg, especially without the crutch, but I also knew I wasn't quite ready to take that step (no pun intended). I sat there for a couple of minutes until Warrick came back into the room immediately rushing over to me, "You good, love?"

"Yeah," I answered, my voice a little shaky. "Just working up the courage, that's all."

He gave me a kind smile, "You were walking all over this floor last night, use that confidence."

I gave a quick nod, sucked in a deep breath, and released the air while working myself into a standing position. The crutch was poised, ready to bear my weight despite my lack of trust. Before I knew it, I was standing with only a slight throbbing in my bad leg. Looking up at Warrick, I flashed him a smile indicating I was ready to break out of these four walls that have been my home lately. Warrick held out his arm giving me the option to use him as an additional crutch to take more weight off my leg as he guided me into a wheelchair. *Thank goodness I don't have to walk myself out of here.* I gratefully accepted the gesture, the two of us finally making our exit.

After a quick journey back to his house, Warrick told me to wait while he got everything back in the house. I sat for maybe a couple of minutes waiting for him to return, but I haven't always been the best at following orders, so I lifted myself out of the car and limped into the house.

Warrick was flying around like he had been in the hospital room putting everything back away so I didn't feel the need to help him. Taking in another deep breath filled with the relief that only comes with returning home, I slowly smiled as I noticed the "Welcome Home" banner and chocolate cake waiting on the island.

"Warrick, you didn't have to do this," I said.

He straightened up before turning to me, "You were supposed to wait, love."

All I could do was shrug. Warrick closed the distance between us, the air starting to fill with the familiar electricity that only comes with him. He tilted my chin up, whispering, "Well, welcome home."

His lips pressed against mine gently at first, but it didn't take him long to unleash the passion that had been bottled up while I was laying in the hospital bed. I returned the energy, my tongue brushing against his, eliciting a small groan. We went back and forth showing the other how much we missed this, how much we missed each other.

Warrick slowly pulled away, earning a frustrated noise from me which made him chuckle, "Don't worry, love, we'll pick up where we left off after a couple of things. I do have a surprise for you. Will you wait for me to come and get you this time?"

The corners of my mouth turned up, "No promises."

He pursed his lips for a brief second before he disappeared to his room and emerged with one of his ties. Warrick used it as a blindfold for me. "This should deter you from doing too much," he finished the knot. *He had me there.*

There I was, standing in the entryway of his house trying to listen to what he was doing to get some sort of clue. All I knew was that he ran outside, closing the door behind him so I couldn't completely make out what the sounds meant. As I was waiting, though, the throbbing in my leg started to send jolts of pain into my body as a reminder I wasn't completely ready to go yet. I shifted my weight to lean more on the crutch with the hopes of giving my leg some reprieve the moment Warrick walked back in.

"Alright, give me your hand," he said. "You okay?"

Warrick must have noticed me trying to position myself to help with the pain. From what I could tell, he was behind me, so I stuck out my hand saying, "Yeah, I think I'm just getting to my limit with my leg."

"Here," he scooped me into his arms like I weighed nothing. The crutch clattered to the ground as he turned to head out the front door. We had only taken a few steps when Warrick whispered, "I'm going to take your blindfold off, but I need you to close your eyes."

"You sure are acting like this is a grand reveal. Must be something big."

"You'll see."

I did as I was told, keeping my eyes closed tight while the tie slipped away. Warrick was still leaning in when his breath tickled my ear, "Open your eyes."

The minute my eyes fluttered open, I let out a gasp bringing both of my hands to my mouth. Tears started welling in my eyes as I glanced up at Warrick who was beaming down at me, "You didn't have to do this."

"I wanted to, love."

I looked back in front of me taking in the sight of my bike, completely repaired and looking brand new. There were moments while I was lying in the hospital bed convincing myself I would have to move away from this bike because it was probably trashed. That realization was harder than I thought it would be since it felt like the one thing truly still connecting me to Gabriel. The tears were falling now as I said, "You have no idea how much this means to me. How did you do it? I was sure the bike would've been totaled."

I wiggled enough to convince Warrick to set me down. He tried to hold me up, replacing the crutch, but I couldn't stand here anymore. I limped over to the bike not thinking of the pain at all. I was filled with shock, wonder, love, and fear – grateful it was fixed, but worried about getting back on it. I ran my hands over the seat glancing back at Warrick who was standing there with his hands in his pockets and a smile still on his face, "It took a lot of searching since motorcycles aren't the most popular around here, but I found the one guy on the opposite end of the city who had what I needed and he helped me with getting everything back to the way it was. There was no way I would let you say goodbye to something that holds this much value in your life."

"You have a real soft side when you want to, you know?"

He shrugged, "Only the people who mean a lot to me get to see this side."

"Did Melody?" I asked before I could stop the words from flying out of my mouth.

"No, not like this," he responded, smile faltering momentarily.

I started limping back to him, and once I was within reach, he scooped me back up to take me into the house and set me on the couch.

"I'm sorry. That question just slipped out," I said. "I didn't mean to ruin a good moment."

Warrick was in the kitchen grabbing us some plates and cutting the cake, his back turned to me the whole time. I could tell my question had ruined the moment despite him trying to brush it off.

The couch dipped as he sat down, me leaning on him as a result. He handed me the plate, "You have every right to ask whatever question you want, love. Just caught me off-guard."

Our night started to wrap up when I could no longer keep my eyes open. I had maybe two bites left of the slice of cake Warrick brought over to me that he took out of my hands. When he stood up, I lost what I had been leaning on instantly falling over, grunting as I hit the couch.

My eyes were still closed when Warrick laid me down in the bed. I felt his lips brush against my forehead before I was lost to sleep for the rest of the night.

Chapter 13

The next few weeks were spent going through the same routine everyday: wake up to a delicious meal cooked by Warrick, him helping me work through the pain in my leg to start building my strength up and being able to sort of walk on my own (I still definitely had a limp), and us working on decoding the list of numbers I started on in the hospital. A full moon came and went where Warrick changed, but instead of running around the hillside like I expected him to, I opened the front door to find him sitting there on high alert. He had mentioned he wasn't going to leave me alone even though I was healed enough to hold my own if it came down to it, but I wasn't expecting this.

When I woke up this morning to a bowl of oatmeal, fresh fruit, and orange juice, I couldn't help but groan making Warrick rush back in the room, "What's wrong?"

"I don't want you to take this the wrong way because I do truly appreciate everything you've done for me," I started. "It's felt a little like *Groundhog Day* for a while now and I think I'm ready to change it up a little. Maybe when I finish eating, we can go into town for a little while to get a change in scenery?"

Relief flooded through me when his face softened, "Sure, love. Let's eat and we'll head out."

I was practically bouncing with excitement when we were driving towards the city not caring about where our destination might be. Warrick and I were talking about whatever came to our minds and it was nice to feel normal for once. We pulled up to the pub, Warrick giving my hand a squeeze, "Someone's been missing you, love."

I didn't have to guess who when Conor burst through the door not even giving me a chance to get out of the car. He yanked open the door, earning a laugh from me, "The damsel is finally allowed out of the castle."

"It's nice to see you, too, Conor," I started to get out of the car. I watched as Conor's eyes widened when he realized I no longer needed anything to support my weight. I returned his surprise with a smile, "Not bad, huh?"

"You know, Warrick has been keeping me updated, but it's good to see you on your own feet in person. When I visited you in that damn hospital, I wondered how you were ever going to recover especially knowing that Cian got his hands on you. Come inside and let's have a beer."

It made me happy to see Conor again, and even though I still had a slight limp, his reaction reminded me how much progress I've made. Warrick placed his hand on the small of my back more out of protection than guidance. Despite the happy reunion, we were both aware I was fully in Cian's territory and there was no telling what would happen.

Once we were seated in a booth by the front window, Conor brought us a few pints and matching glasses of water. He looked at Warrick, starting the conversation, "When you first came around, I thought you were nothing but trouble. Now I see I was wrong about that."

Warrick shrugged taking a sip of his water. When he set it down, "Considering we didn't start off on the best foot, I'm not surprised. Circumstances have changed." Warrick looked over at me, giving my leg a gentle squeeze.

"I know what she's doing here," Conor continued. "But what made you come here? I was convinced it was to hunt Val down even though I don't have the full story. Now, I'm not so sure."

Warrick turned his attention back to Conor, "I'd be lying if that wasn't part of the reason, but the other part is business. You can ask all the questions you want about what I mean by that, but I'll just clear the air now – I'm not going into a lot of specifics on the latter. Just know that I'm not here to cause harm."

"Well, if you're going to be close-lipped about your business, why were you hunting Val?"

"How much has she told you?"

Conor shrugged, "Hardly anything at all."

Warrick looked at me for permission to bring Conor up to speed and I gave a nod. He ran his fingers through his hair before he opened his mouth, "I'll give you the quick version. Val popped up in our world the same day one of my new employees did. I came across her with Lou in his pizza shop he runs across the street from my company. See, she caught me off-guard because she looks almost identical to Melody who I thought I had just gotten rid of. We started dating, or at least I thought we did, until one day she waltzes into my office, stabs me, then runs to Lou to keep her safe. That set something off in me and I wanted nothing but revenge. When I discovered they had left my world, I started jumping from world to world to try and catch up with them. It happened to work out perfectly that I needed to make a stop here and I discovered Val working at the pub. At first, I thought this was my chance to take her out, but I wanted to torture her a bit. Then, circumstances changed and here we are."

The way Warrick had casually talked about the rough parts in our past unsettled me a bit. He can definitely play the whole calm-villain character no problem.

Conor nodded his head, "I see." Turning his attention to me, he said, "What's your side to this tale?"

"Warrick had information I wanted, so I thought the best way to get that would be to get close to him. Little did I know I was playing with fire."

Conor and Warrick both let out a bark of laughter with that before Conor chimed in, "You weren't wrong. When I saw you get all cut up that night, I knew you had messed with the wrong person, but I wasn't sure if it was Cian's boys or someone else. Remind me to never get on your bad side, Warrick."

"I don't think you'll ever have to worry about that," he tipped his glass toward Conor.

"And I take it you and Lou are enemies?" Conor asked.

"You could say that," Warrick said, taking a long swig on his beer.

"Conor, you sure are wanting to know all the details," I cut in to the conversation.

"What? This is my first opportunity to really get to know the people sitting across from me where I'm not having to run around pouring drinks. We still have a couple of hours before that happens," he said defensively.

I narrowed my eyes a little, "What has Lou told you about us?"

"Well," he started then took a swig of his drink. "Lou has had nothing but good things to say about you, Val. Warrick, on the other hand, he's painted you in a pretty harsh light. You didn't exactly treat him the best."

Warrick sighed, "Let me guess, I'm a power-hungry monster who isn't afraid to kill to get what he wants. Does that sound about right?"

"You guessed it," Conor chuckled.

"He's not wrong," Warrick said nonchalantly, not breaking eye contact with Conor. "I've done it before, and I'll probably do it again."

Conor looked out the window clearly feeling uncomfortable, "At least you're honest."

Awkward silence filled the space between us, Conor sorting through the quick exchange between him and Warrick. I glanced at Warrick who was carefully studying Conor, plastering his familiar mask of calm on his face. I had been around him and Lou enough to know when they kicked in the power that comes with being alpha which is exactly why Conor looked away.

"What's on your mind, Conor?" I asked, daring to break the silence.

He still wouldn't look our direction, "Warrick's ruthless for sure, but I don't have the same fear Lou has for him. From the stories Lou has told me and what I saw from Val, you don't hold back, Warrick, but I've seen worse here with the monsters living around me. Liam may be constantly chomping at the bit to cause damage and wreak havoc, but Cian is the only one I've seen take that kind of pleasure in dishing out pain. Val, you don't know how lucky you are to have survived that kind of interaction with him."

I nudged Warrick under the table hoping he would pick up on the signal to quit intimidating Conor before answering, "That's why I'm stopping my crusade of eradicating the vampires."

"Good," Conor finally turned his focus back to the two of us. "I do have to say, though," he looked at Warrick. "You're a hell of a lot better than Lou in my book."

"How so?" Warrick asked, cocking an eyebrow.

"First of all, you didn't let Val get killed. Second of all, you're not running around here nuzzling up on other women while your lass is in trouble. I also take it that you've owned up to the crazy shit you did to her?"

Warrick turned to me, "I would say so."

I gave Warrick's leg another squeeze before turning back to Conor, "Has Lou been in here getting close to Melody again?"

"Not like that first day, but they've been in here with another couple just chatting until Melody goes back to Cian's group."

"Asshole," I muttered under my breath.

Both Conor and Warrick clinked their glasses together in agreement to my statement, making us all burst out in a fit of laughter. I was still getting used to the golden hue of Warrick's genuine laugh, letting the sound of it warm me. He looked at me with light dancing in his eyes and a million-dollar smile drawing me in to give him a kiss.

"Aww, cut it out you two. I can't handle the affection," Conor joked getting up from the table.

When he was out of earshot, Warrick leaned in to me, "I like him."

I gave him a nudge with my elbow, "You only like him because he likes you more than Lou."

"He has good judgement."

"What was with the whole display of dominance earlier?" I asked, changing the subject.

Warrick shrugged, "I wasn't sure where he was going when he was making his judgement of me. I didn't want him to think I had gone soft."

"Why does that matter?"

Warrick opened his mouth to respond, but quickly shut it when Conor came back with his hands full of food. As he sat down, he asked, "What did I miss?"

"Nothing," I replied, giving Conor a smile. "Warrick was telling me how he liked you."

"Don't let it go to his head, love," Warrick jumped in.

It felt good to be joking around with people I wanted to be spending time with. This hasn't really happened since the first night Jennie and Chris came over. I can't even begin to describe how refreshing it is considering everything that's happened while in this new world.

I finally enjoyed a sip of my beer smiling at the jokes flying between Warrick and Conor. When there was a pause in the conversation, I spoke up, "It's good to see you this relaxed, Conor. I don't think I've seen this side of you."

"To be honest, Val, I think of you as a sister and this is the first time I've been able to not worry about you since you first walked through my door," he said, pointing to the front door.

"I'm glad I haven't rubbed you the wrong way," I responded.

Conor glanced down at his watch, "Ah, I need to get things ready for opening. You two get comfy and stay as long as you want."

"Thanks, Conor," Warrick said. He turned to me, throwing an arm around my shoulders, "Let me know when you want to leave, but this is all about what you need."

"Appreciate it," I gave him a quick kiss on the cheek.

We spent more time talking each other up, going back and forth enjoying each other's company. To be able to feel like we were on a relaxed date in our own little bubble was energizing. As each minute passed by, Warrick leaned in closer to me alternating between pushing my hair behind my ear or stroking my jawline with his thumb.

Our bubble was burst when Warrick let out a small growl, his attention shifting to whatever was happening through the windows behind us. Not daring to look, I pushed Warrick's face toward me, "Look at me. What's going on?"

"Not a fan of who's walking in," he ground out.

Still not taking my attention off him, I asked, "Who is it?"

"Lou, Melody, and your friends," Warrick answered in a low, flat tone. This time he was focused on me, not daring to break eye contact. I looked between his eyes taking in the laser focus etched within the icy blue eyes that have become so familiar to me.

I ran my thumb over his cheekbone, "They'll probably come over here and try to sit with us, but don't let them get into your head. We'll be fine. Don't even think about a scuffle and walk away if Lou tries to start something."

"You got it, love," Warrick gave me a kind smile. "You're incredible."

There was no hesitation as he moved to kiss me with such ferocity that I wasn't sure if he was doing this to make a statement to the group approaching our table, if this is what he felt in the moment, or a combination of both.

A throat cleared, a familiar voice following the sound, "Don't you have someone waiting for you at home, Warrick?"

Warrick slowly pulled away from me, once again sporting a mask I had grown accustomed to seeing: a knowing, smug grin. He kept his body in a position where our audience couldn't quite get a view of me, "What are you trying to accuse me of, Louis?"

"The same thing you managed to convince her I was doing, yet the difference between us is that I didn't actually do anything and you're here shoving your tongue down someone's throat."

"Choose your next words wisely," Warrick said with a subtle undertone laced with threat. He then changed the focus of the conversation, "How are you, Melody?"

"I've been well. Thank you, Warrick. You look like you're doing well, too," Melody said kindly. I didn't shift to see if she had a smile to match her words simply for not wanting to step on Warrick's toes, but I could only picture how the smile amplified her beauty.

"That I am," Warrick dropped the threat.

I heard Jennie scoff and mumble something to Chris, probably for them to go find somewhere to sit. When the silence took over, Warrick shifted to give Lou and Melody a clear view of who exactly he was kissing before they interrupted, "Care to say hello to my date, Lou?"

I gave a little finger wave and watched the color drain from Lou's face. Not only had he been wrong, but he was standing there knowing he had been caught red-handed with the person

I accused him of cheating on me with. I plastered a smile on my face fully knowing it was a fake one while extending my hand, "It's nice finally meet you, Melody. I've heard so much about you."

"Likewise," she responded with what I was assuming was the same smile she gave Warrick when they were making small talk. "Lou, I'm going to find a seat."

She walked away after letting her hand linger on his shoulder a little longer than normal. I wasn't sure if it was to offer him reassurance or if it was a play in this game going on between the two alphas. I shifted my eyes to Lou, who still had no color. "It's not what it looks like," he croaked.

"Sure," I replied calmly. "But this," I gestured between Warrick and I. "This is exactly what it looks like."

Lou didn't even attempt to hide the hurt, giving me the slightest feeling of guilt. He dropped his head, glanced over to where the rest of his group was sitting, then back at us, "See you around."

He moved to sit with Jennie, Chris, and Melody without waiting for us to respond. Warrick turned his attention back to me, "Nicely done, love."

I just shrugged, downing the rest of my beer. I glanced towards their table to see Lou still staring at me, hurt written all over his face and Jennie with an expression full of shock. I couldn't help but feel bad for playing into Warrick's game. It was conflicting to be feeling this way, yet that tells me I'm ready to have an honest conversation with Lou to try to put this in the past which is more to say than how I've been feeling for a while now.

"Would you like another beer, love, or anything else?" Warrick asked, bringing me back to reality.

I offered a quick grin, "Please. Thank you."

I felt some relief when he walked away to dance through the crowd that had now filled the space of the pub. I glanced out the window for only a second until Jennie sat across from me, "Val, it's really good to see you!"

"Is it, Jennie?" I asked not able to keep the words contained.

She let out some nervous laughter, "I guess I deserve that for my reaction earlier. I'm serious, though, I'm happy to see you out and about after your accident. How are you feeling?"

"A lot better even though I still have a bit of a limp, but I could've walked away from that way worse than I did."

"You could've died, Val. When Warrick explained everything that happened," she trailed off shaking her head. When Jennie started talking again, her voice was shaky and there were tears in her eyes, "I'm just happy I didn't lose someone else in this crazy adventure. I don't know if I could have done nearly everything you've done so far to get to this point."

I reached across the table to grab her hand, giving her a reassuring squeeze, "Don't think about that, Jennie. I'm right here, I'm still alive, and I don't plan on going anywhere. You may not like him, but I owe a lot to Warrick for what he did. Speaking of not liking him, how's Lou doing?"

Jennie sighed, looking at their table before bringing her gaze back at me. In a lowered voice, she said, "Not well, Val. The guy is barely eating. I know it upsets you to see him here with Melody, but she's just trying to help lift his spirits. All he does is talk about you, and when he's not doing that, he's trying to figure out how to make your device better or where we should be headed next. I think it would be good if you guys had an open, honest conversation. Not one where either of you are hostile to each other, but one that can actually help you both move forward if it's true you'd rather be with Warrick."

"I'm starting to agree that would probably be better at this point than keeping my distance. I've had a lot of time to sort through things even if you think I've been distracted."

"Now that you bring that up, are you absolutely sure Warrick isn't just using you? Before you go and get all defensive, there's just something not sitting right with me when I watch how he acts around you. I mean, that whole kissing thing when we showed up definitely seemed like a power move over Lou."

I looked out the window, "There's a dynamic between those two you haven't quite seen yet, Jennie. As twisted as it can be, Warrick likes to toy with Lou to remind him who's on top. But, don't think I haven't kept that in the back of my mind when it comes to what Warrick and I have right now. He's not telling me everything, and when I ask, he gets tight-lipped."

"Speak of the devil," Jennie said before I could keep going. *This is the first time in a long time I've been appreciative of her.* I turned my head as Warrick got back into the booth, a pitcher of beer sloshing as he set it down.

"Hi Jennie, glad to see you've perked up in the short time you've been here," Warrick joked.

"You know, if you hadn't taken such good care of Val, I'd probably shoot something back at that remark," she said light-heartedly with a slightly serious undertone.

"What'd I miss?" he asked.

"I was just telling Val how happy it makes me to see her out and not stuck in a hospital bed," Jennie answered.

Warrick gave me a soft smile, "You're not the only one who shares that sentiment."

"You guys melt my heart, in a weird way," Jennie said. She mumbled, "So the monster does have a soul."

Warrick stilled, "What was that?"

Jennie's famous cover-her-ass smile took over, "Nothing. I'd better be getting back before Chris thinks I ran off. See ya!"

I had never seen her move so quickly, but she knew she was getting in the danger zone with that last remark.

Warrick watched her, his jaw twitching and I knew she got under his skin by saying that. I've lost count the number of times he's been called a monster, and I could only imagine how it was probably starting to wear on him.

To give him a distraction, I turned his chin toward me and pulled him in for a deep, longing kiss. Each time our lips met, I was reminded of how long it had been since we slept with each other, the desire growing with each kiss.

He cupped my cheek with one hand, the one others could see if anyone decided to watch what was going on in this booth, while the other hand started inching its way up my shirt. Goosebumps formed a trail of where his hand had been, my back starting to arch in anticipation of where he was going.

"Alright kids, break it up. You are in a public place, you know," Conor interrupted. "Thought I would bring some more apps by since you're still here."

Warrick and I quickly pulled apart, my face as red as the tomato sitting on the salads he brought out. Another plate filled with nachos followed. Warrick pulled everything closer muttering his thanks. When Conor walked away, I took a closer look at Warrick's face to see a slight blush, "I'd never thought I'd see the day when Warrick got embarrassed."

"We might have to do something about this when we get home, love. It's getting harder and harder to not jump you here and now," he said, cheeks still red.

"Hmm," I leaned in closing the space between us so I could whisper in his ear. I reached down letting my hand rest on his upper thigh, "Who's saying we can't have a little fun in the meantime?"

Warrick angled himself so his back was to the rest of the dining room, "What did you have in mind?"

My hand inched higher up his thigh, "We could stay here and let the thrill of potentially being caught fuel us, or there is a single stall bathroom you could meet me in."

"You don't have to tell me twice. Lead the way," he stood up to let me out of my seat. "I'll be there in a few minutes."

I took a deep breath to regain some composure in order to make the trek to the restrooms on the opposite side of the pub. It was a slow walk with the limp I still had, but I was thankful to make it over there and find the single stall bathroom empty. I slipped in, locking the door behind me as I moved to lean against the sink and check my appearance. I wasn't entirely sure if he would give me a few minutes once he knew I made it back here, or if he had meant that he would follow me after a few minutes even if I hadn't gotten in here. I checked my phone making a mental note of the time then moved to lean by the door in case he was quiet.

While waiting, I was doing my best to not let Jennie's words repeat on an endless loop to feed into the doubt starting to make a home within a corner of my mind. Surely this had to be as real for him as it was for me and he wasn't just using me to get what he wants. Not with all the new sides of him I've seen during this time.

I shook my head pulling out my phone to check the time again. At least five minutes had gone by and he still hadn't come back here. *What the hell?*

I exited the bathroom to make the slow walk back to the table where he was sitting and chewing on some of the nachos. Warrick was focused on something that made him unsettled judging by the look on his face.

"Hey, decided against following me?" I asked, nudging his shoulder so he would let me get back into my seat.

"Sorry, love, I didn't mean to leave you hanging, but I think it's time to go," he said still staring at something I couldn't make out.

"Why? Conor just brought us some more food," I trailed off. "Ohhhh, you're just jumping to the point and want to have your way with me where there's no risk of anyone hearing."

"I've already asked for to-go boxes. I'll tell you more in the car, but that's part of it," Warrick responded finally looking at me. He gestured to the spot across from him, "At least take a seat there until we can get things packed up."

Whatever had Warrick's attention before had it again, so I knew there was no use in trying to talk to him. I started fidgeting while people watching until I found myself drawn back to Lou. He was still staring at me, more confused than hurt this time, but didn't have Melody by his side. I mouthed *everything okay* to him earning a surprised look then him mouthing *what's going on* in return. I shrugged my shoulders to which Lou scanned the room and responded with the same gesture.

Conor finally made it back, blocking my view of Lou and handing us a couple of empty boxes with a couple of already packed up ones, "Thought I'd treat you two to dinner as well since you're headed out. It was good to see you here, Val, and thanks for the surprise, Warrick."

"Anytime, Conor. Thank you for the food," Warrick wasted no time with packing everything up.

When Warrick was ready to go, he offered his arm to me as extra support and guided us to the door at a hurried pace. I took one glance back to see if there was anything amiss when my eyes eventually landed on Liam who had his usual sinister smile plastered on his face, giving me a little wave.

Chapter 14

Once in the safety of his car, I turned to him and asked, "How the hell is he able to be out right now?"

"I was hoping you weren't going to see him, love," Warrick said putting distance between us and the pub. "To answer your question, I have no idea. I sensed him before I saw him, and the minute I did, I wanted to get you out of there so he didn't have a chance to have an afternoon snack. I know what it's like to see weakened prey, to know how easy it is to take them out."

"I don't know if I'd call that an answer," I retorted.

"I haven't been able to figure out what Cian and his core group are capable of yet, but they clearly can hide out in a building as long as direct sunlight doesn't hit them."

"That's comforting," I scoffed. Between the shock of seeing Liam and the annoyance of Warrick standing me up, I didn't care to continue the conversation.

Warrick, however, didn't pick up on the hint. He reached over to give my thigh a little squeeze, "I truly am sorry I couldn't join you. Believe me, I'd have much rather been intimate with you instead of keeping an eye on someone."

I patted his hand, "Don't worry about it."

We finished the rest of the drive in silence. I eventually let go of the negative emotions now feeling more tired than anything. Warrick put the car in park, wasting no time with leaning over the center console to kiss me. When he pulled away, he asked, "Still up for continuing what we started in the pub?"

"Give me a couple of minutes to freshen up," I gave him a wink.

"Don't have to tell me twice, love," he said, running a hand through his hair. "You have until I get the food put away."

I hurried as much as I could with this damn limp to get back into the bedroom and in a lingerie set. I chose one that was mostly straps before laying on the bed in time for Warrick to grab the top of the door jam and lean, exposing the skin just above his pants. The sight of him standing there like that made the butterflies take flight again. He let out a low chuckle, "You wasted no time I see."

"I wanted to give you a picture of what you were missing out on earlier."

"Now that's no fair, love," he said slowly making his way into the room. "You see, I knew exactly what I was missing which made me even more annoyed with what was going on back there. I don't take kindly to others interrupting, in case you don't remember."

"Oh, I remember," I said, doing my best to maintain this confidence while pushing away the memory of Daryl barging in on Warrick and I in his office.

At this point, Warrick was on top of me, moving my arms above my head as his lips found mine. There was such a need that had been building to this point I was almost convinced I wouldn't be able to take what was coming my way. Sensing the little bit of hesitation, Warrick paused, "Let me know if anything I do causes you pain. I may get carried away, but I don't want to hurt you, love."

I nodded, prompting him to go back to leaving a trail of kisses down my body. As he was doing so, he ground his hips into me, allowing me to feel his arousal. His teeth teased my nipple forcing a gasp to escape my lips. Warrick groaned in approval, "This. I have been missing this."

"You're telling me you didn't do anything that entire time I was laid up in the hospital bed or here gathering my strength back?" I asked a little breathier than I intended.

He looked up from in between my legs, "There's no one I'd rather be with than you, and I mean that in more than just a physical sense. If that means I have to wait, then I'll do it. Whatever I have to do to share this life with you, love, tell me."

Warrick kept his speech simple, but something exploded within me that I haven't felt for an incredibly long time. Any doubt I had was pushed away. There was no one and nowhere I'd rather be than in this moment with the man in front of me bearing all his heart.

"Warrick," was all I could muster. I grabbed his shirt pulling him closer to me so I could convey how I feel through a kiss. I may not have been able to say the words, but I was hoping he understood how much he means to me.

He slowly pulled away from the kiss, looking first at my lips then bringing those icy blue eyes to meet mine. He started gently stroking my lips with his thumb, "I'm sure you'll think this is cliché, love, but seeing you that first day in the pizza place made something snap into place I've never felt before. All I could think about, all I could want was you. Don't feel like you have to say anything in return. I couldn't hold it back any longer and wanted to make sure you knew how I felt, especially when I was so close to losing you."

His lips were back on mine within seconds, and as his tongue traced them sending electricity down my body. My heart swelled with emotions that weren't quite love, but weren't far off. Yet, something in the back of my mind was not on the same page as everything else in this moment. Jennie's question from the pub flashed behind my closed eyes. *Is Warrick just using me? Is he saying all these things right now to get laid?*

I put my hand on his chest slightly pushing while I pulled my head back. Confusion knit his brows, "Everything okay, love?"

"Warrick, you're not just saying these things to have a good time are you?"

He quickly propped himself up to give us more space, "Haven't you learned anything about living here? I don't have to bear my heart to have sex with you, love. Almost losing you made me realize I wouldn't be able to live with myself if you died and I kept my feelings to myself."

I paused to let his words soak in. Placing my hand on his, I looked in his eyes, "Thank you for being so honest and vulnerable with me."

"Anytime," he said as I leaned back in.

It didn't take long before he was naked on top of me, thrusting his hips in a steady rhythm, my body wanting to be closer to his each time he buried himself deeper. Instead of our usual frenzied lovemaking, we were patient, giving in to each other's wants and desires. Warrick was showing a new side where he was leaving everything on the table, but the seed of doubt was still there threatening to grow into something devastating.

Warrick traveled down my body again and was starting to tease my clit with his tongue. The movements were driving me wild, letting me push that doubt aside to enjoy the moment.

His fingers started sliding in and out letting the pressure build between my legs until it was all I had in me to focus on keeping the orgasm at bay.

A moan, louder this time, escaped my lips, causing Warrick to pull back and chuckle, "You drive me mad when you do that, love."

I reached towards his head guiding him back in between my legs. He sucked slightly, encouraging another moan to fill the room. When the pressure started becoming too much, I pulled him back up to me then flipped him on his back. We didn't need to say anything to each other in this moment, seemingly communicating through our touch.

It was give and take, Warrick and I taking turns on who was leading the rest of the night. Finally reaching our climaxes, we collapsed on each other in a tangle of limbs, feeling satiated. Warrick tucked a strand of loose hair behind my ear following the motion with a tender kiss on my forehead. Resting his forehead against mine, he whispered, "You are incredible, Val. Know that I love you."

Words were still struggling to form, so I tilted my chin to give him a long, deep kiss as a way to communicate the feelings I have for him. Only this time, I had a guess as to why I couldn't say those three words back and I had a bone to pick with Jennie.

M*y eyes felt heavy as I tried to open them. I tried to move my arm only to find they were both restrained. As my eyes adjusted and brought things into focus, I realized I was hanging upside down, slightly swaying back and forth. The room I was in*

was dark, the only sound a steady dripping. I could make out that the walls were made of the same stone as the cathedral, the door a solid piece of wood. There were no windows, bars, or anything that would give me a glimpse as to what's on the outside of this room. I lifted my head up to see I was being held and bound by chains. When I looked to the floor, I discovered the source of the dripping.

"Shit," I muttered.

The buckets were slowly filling with blood coming from the dozens of cuts on my body. The one thing immediately standing out to me, though, was the lack of pain. There was no stinging, aching, or anything to tell me something was wrong. I tried wiggling myself to test the strength of my restraints only to find I wasn't going anywhere unless someone got me out of here.

I heard the sound of a lock sliding, bringing my full focus to the only exit. My body stilled, the chains faintly clinking. Fear took over the minute Liam stepped in his face breaking out in a wide smile. He sauntered over, circling me like a shark until he crouched down in front of my face. He took my chin in between his thumb and forefinger, letting out a low laugh, "How the mighty have fallen. You have no idea how long I've been waiting for this day."

I couldn't say anything before he moved, digging his teeth into my throat. There was only a pinch until everything became numb. While I knew what he was doing would only drain me of my life, I did little to resist (not like there was much I could do in the first place). One of his hands moved to palm my breast as images of him and I having sex started replacing the dark, empty room. I somehow knew this was a vision being projected, but it was hard not being able to lose myself to the sensations I was seeing and feeling.

As soon as the vision started taking over my senses, it was gone as Liam was ripped away from me. My vision was now almost gone *reminding me of how much blood Liam had taken, so I couldn't see who was coming to my aid.*

A growl ripped through the room followed by a thud and snaping bones.

I sat up trying to catch my breath while looking around. I was back in Warrick's bed, the lights off and stars filling the sky outside the window. I ran my hands all over my body checking for any of the cuts from my nightmare while looking at the space next to me. My body was fine, but Warrick wasn't there. That's when I heard the muted sounds of a scuffle outside.

I jumped up, throwing one of Warrick's shirts over my head before rushing to the front door. I threw it open trying to locate the source of the sounds I was hearing.

"Get back inside, love," Warrick shouted over his shoulder. I looked from him to the person in front of him getting ready to throw himself at Warrick again. *Liam.*

I stood rooted where I was, unable to offer any help to Warrick. Liam slammed into the wall that was Warrick trying to get to me. Warrick had no problem throwing Liam back on the ground where he lifted his head up, sending me the same smile he did in my dream, "Good morning sleeping beauty."

"You don't get to talk to her," Warrick said through gritted teeth, landing a kick to Liam's ribs. He grabbed Liam's hair, yanking his head back, "Why the hell are you here anyways?"

Liam started laughing, not breaking eye contact with me, "Haven't you heard?"

Warrick picked Liam up by his shirt and snarled. "What is he talking about?" I asked Warrick, panic creeping into my voice.

Neither of them said anything for a moment. Warrick stood there holding Liam not bothering to acknowledge the question. Liam was the first to break the tense silence, hysterical laughter ripping through the night air, "Don't tell me you don't know about the ashes on Cian's doorstep?"

Warrick shook Liam, "Clearly we don't."

"If he doesn't elaborate, I can always drive a stake through his heart," I said, sounding more confident than I felt.

Liam's smile faltered as he nervously looked between Warrick and myself before holding his hands up in defense, "Cian sent me to check things out after getting a little message earlier today."

"So you assumed it was Val," Warrick said in more of a statement rather than a question.

"She does have a track record," Liam said, keeping a conversational tone.

Warrick slammed him down, hitting him against the ground a couple of times before finally pinning him there, "Stop *fucking* around, Liam. Start talking."

"I don't know what else there is to say, *Warrick*. Ashes representing the fallen ended up on our leader's doorstep. More of our group was murdered which hasn't happened until *she* got here," Liam jerked his head in my direction. "I was ordered to take care of the problem, and as a leader, I would assume you would understand what that means."

"Stop assuming you know what it means to be in my head," Warrick delivered a blow that would knock a normal person out cold. Blood spurted from Liam's nose as Warrick continued,

"She's been cooped up in this house until we went to the pub today. You want proof? Check her limp she still has because Cian decided it was a good idea to try and take her out."

"As a second, I'm just doing my job," Liam said, more nervousness creeping into his voice with every word.

"Despite being a second, you should be able to think for yourself. You could ask anyone in this damned city and know that we haven't been out before today. Val has been with me all day, and you think I'm going to let her out of my sight with everything that's happened? There's no *fucking* way," Warrick said, his tone filled with unbridled anger.

This isn't good. There was nothing I could do as I watched Warrick start going at it with Liam. His fists connecting with Liam's face making more blood splatter out to make it look like a murder scene. Warrick then picked Liam up to throw him against a tree on the edge of the property, the sound of more bones cracking filling the air.

"Please," Liam begged. "Please, stop. Remember the deal, Warrick."

Warrick paused momentarily before throwing one more punch, "You can tell Cian we're even now."

He let Liam go who collapsed, clearly trying to hang on to consciousness. Liam looked back up at Warrick giving a single nod before vanishing from the area completely.

Still on the doorstep, I stood there with my mouth hanging open waiting for Warrick to look at me. He slowly turned, rage still contained in his posture. I took a deep breath to steady my voice, "Warrick, I'm tired of hearing about this deal and not knowing a damn thing about it. Please, tell me what's going on."

"Don't worry about it, love." Warrick replied shaking his head. "Let's go back to bed."

"That doesn't help me," I said still not wanting to move from where I was.

He held my face in his hands, "I'm tired. Please, let's go back to sleep."

Warrick walked past me barely making contact. I knew better than to argue considering how he was still feeling in this moment, but I wasn't happy with the fact he didn't care share any more information. Sighing, I followed Warrick and settled into bed wanting to press the issue, but knowing that would get me nowhere at this hour.

I didn't remember falling asleep as I woke up. I turned over expecting Warrick to still be there only to find the bed empty again. I grumbled while throwing off the blankets to head out to the kitchen to find Warrick casually cooking breakfast. He was completely different than the man I had seen hours ago.

"Warrick, you never explained what's going on," I said not willing to drop the issue I brought up last night.

He flicked his gaze in my direction before returning back to his task at hand. He put some pancakes on my plate, "It's not something you need to worry about, love. Eat."

I dropped the issue for now, but I wasn't ready to completely let things go. Warrick was clearly keeping things from me, and despite everything he confessed last night, the seed of doubt had plenty to feed on to grow into something more today.

We ended up back in our usual routine of him pouring himself into the other files he keeps under lock and key while I stared at what seemed to be the endless list of numbers still having no luck outside the eight codes I figured out a while ago.

I let out a groan, "There's no way my dad knew about this many worlds."

Warrick took a break from what he was working on to look at me, "Maybe he has some unknown worlds listed there, or maybe he has filler codes to try and throw people off."

"If I'm the key, how am I supposed to know that? He made it seem like I should know what every string of numbers means on this page, but I just don't."

He leaned back in his chair, "Don't be so hard on yourself, love. You've started figuring out some of these, and in my opinion, you've figured out enough of them to start crossing places off your list when it comes to finding your friends."

"You've got a point," I looked back at the list in front of me. I didn't continue the conversation, instead turning my focus back to trying to figure out at least one more code. Every now and then, I stole glances at Warrick, admiring the ruthless man sitting in front of me who had no problem letting down his walls last night. Yet, Jennie's words kept replaying in my mind adding to my frustration.

I jumped up, making my way towards the door. Warrick jerked his head up, "Where are you going?"

"I need some air," I mumbled as I took a step outside. I was hoping he wouldn't follow me so I could have some time to sort through everything running through my head without risking saying anything stupid. Pausing at the closed front door, I waited a few moments listening for any sounds of movement that would tell me if he's joining me. When I was confident the coast was clear, I began walking towards the cliffs to sit and take in the sounds of the ocean crashing against the rocks.

My slight limp was keeping me from walking at my full speed and made it even more challenging to sit on the edge of the cliffs. When I finally got comfortable, I leaned back on my hands letting my head fall back. Eyes closed, I took in a deep breath to release everything that had been building up since I had arrived in this world. I had accomplished everything I wanted since arriving: found Jennie and Chris, kept them safe, and smoothed things over with Warrick. *Why the hell am I still here?* I brought my gaze back to the ocean in front of me pondering that question. There's nothing left to do here and the only way to keep myself from causing any more trouble, and hardships for Warrick, is to move on to the next place to see if I can continue finding my displaced friends before anything happens to them.

"Val!" Warrick shouted.

I looked over my shoulder to see a panicked Warrick running towards me, his face as white as a ghost. Confused, I asked, "What's wrong?"

"What are you doing out here, love?" he asked, crouching down to hold my face between his hands.

"I told you I needed to get some air. Did I do something wrong?" I asked, searching his eyes for any indication as to why he was acting so worried. "Did you think I was going to jump?"

Placing a quick kiss on my forehead, he said, "You seemed really upset, and after last night, I had no idea what was running through your mind. I come out here and find you sitting on the edge of a cliff. All I could see was you looking at me then falling."

I put a reassuring hand on his, "I appreciate the concern, but there's nothing you need to worry about."

He moved closer to me so I could rest my head on his shoulder. We sat there quietly for a few moments until I broke the silence, "Did you have a nightmare last night?"

"Yeah, I did. You?"

"Yeah. What was yours about?"

"I saw you in the cathedral bleeding out and I was just trapped there unable to do anything about it until I thought you were dead," he said in a faraway voice.

"I had the same one," I trailed off. I lifted my head so I could look at Warrick, "Have you had any of these nightmares recently before last night?"

"Not for a while," he paused. "Why so many questions about these dreams, love?"

I looked back out to the ocean in front of me trying to piece together the next question, "Do you – do you think vampires have any magic?"

"I haven't been able to definitively answer that, but I have my theories. I know they can drink from people and make it a pleasant experience, which I'm sure you were able to figure out, too. What I don't know for sure is what else they can do."

"I'm surprised your best friend Cian hasn't said anything to you."

He raised an eyebrow at me, "It hasn't come up."

"Anyways," I said, trying to focus back on the topic at hand. "I'm beginning to wonder if Liam is behind the nightmares. Most of mine has had something to do with him, from when I first met him to now. Plus, I've never had this many vivid nightmares that have had some part come true."

"You have a point," Warrick started. "It's been a very long time in my life since I've had any sort of nightmares, but I come here, and they start happening on a regular cadence. In fact, they started happening after I began working with Cian."

I could see the gears turning in his mind as he worked through this idea. He moved to get up, dusting off his pants before offering me a hand. We made our way back to the house, Warrick's jaw muscles twitching. He closed the door behind us as I asked, "Why did you start working with Cian?"

He whipped around pinning me to the wall. With his faces inches from mine, he said, "This isn't something you need to worry about."

"But – ," I started.

Cutting me off, Warrick got closer to me, "I don't know how many times I need to tell you it's not something that concerns you before you get it in your head."

Fear was starting to creep into me. I wasn't confident that Warrick would go back to trying to torture me. *The next words out of his mouth better not be him admitting he used me.* I raised my chin, hoping I could fool him into thinking I wasn't worried, "*I* don't know why this is such a hard conversation for you."

He blinked a couple of times, his icy eyes somehow getting colder each time they opened. "I think it's time you to head back to your house now. You've healed up well, your bike is fixed. I clearly can't keep you safe anymore," he responded, letting go and walking away from me.

Chapter 15

It was like he grabbed my heart and crushed it. My world started spinning and I had no idea what to say next. I watched Warrick head back to his room, listening to him gathering what I assumed to be my belongings. I stormed in there as best I could, "What do you mean?"

Warrick watched me, pain in his eyes, "I don't want this any more than you do, love."

"You sure have a fucked-up way of showing it," I gestured at my bag he was filling on his bed. "You're practically throwing me out for asking a couple of questions."

"You're telling me it's not obvious?" he asked in disbelief. "I don't care that you asked questions. Did I get annoyed? Yes, but I'm not throwing you out because of that."

"Then why?" I asked, my voice becoming shaky with emotion.

He finally stopped packing and came over to me. Warrick tucked a strand of hair behind my ears, "I can't keep you safe anymore. Liam almost got you last night. When I realized I was in a nightmare, I woke myself up. You want to know what I saw? I saw him standing over you salivating. I can't even begin to describe what emotions went through me in that moment. I threw myself at him and finally wrestled him outside before you found us. I knew if he got his hands on you, that would be the end of it. I couldn't face the thought of losing you again in such a short amount of time, love."

I watched him a few moments, checking for any signs of a lie before finally letting out a breath. I hung my head still fighting to hold the tears back, "Fine, but I can't drive my bike yet. I don't trust my leg."

"That's fine. Do you believe me when I say I hate this, too?"

"Yeah," I nodded. "I do."

We finished packing everything in silence before I got into the driver's seat of his car. He threw his leg over my bike, started it, then looked over his shoulder at me to see if I was ready. I threw him a thumb's up and we set off. While I understood his reasoning, I couldn't deny the ache in my chest that grew stronger every time I thought of being away from him. It didn't help that little seed of doubt Jennie planted either.

It wasn't a long drive, so when we pulled up to my house, I wiped my eyes checking my face in the mirror. The last thing I wanted with this surprise move was for Jennie, Chris, and Lou to see I was crying. Warrick tapped the window on my door telling me to open it.

"You okay, love?"

I got myself out of his car before I looked up to him, "No, but I will be."

"This isn't goodbye," he pulled me into a hug.

I buried my face into his chest inhaling the fresh, ocean-like scent I've grown accustomed to. Keeping my face where it was, I said, "It sure feels like it."

He tipped my head up so our lips could meet. We were locked in a long, deep kiss that sent goosebumps down my entire body. Warrick pulled away, stroking my bottom lip with his thumb, "Let's go."

Warrick led me to the front door, standing in front of me while we waited for someone to answer the knock. I heard the door open and Jennie take in a breath. Her voice laced with sarcasm, and a hint of worry, she said, "Warrick, what a surprise. To what do I owe this pleasure?"

"Nice to see you, too," Warrick started. "I'm returning Belle to her home."

"What are you talking about? I don't know anyone named –"

Her eyes widened when I stepped up to Warrick's side. I grabbed his hand giving him a quick glance. Jennie came out of the house to embrace me in a warm hug, "You have no idea how happy this makes me."

I gave a small smile in return, not quite ready to say anything in case my emotions betrayed me.

"Who's at the door, J?" Chris called from the house.

"Val's moving back in," she called over her shoulder.

"What?"

There was a bunch of clanking dishes, a couple of chairs scraping against the floor, and heavy footsteps heading our way. Warrick rolled his eyes then put on his usual mask of calm when the other two guys filled the doorway. Lou looked between Warrick and I, making me look off in the distance. "Does this mean?" he asked.

"Cut the crap, Lou," Warrick started pushing his way into the house. "We're only doing this because she'll be safe here."

"What are you talking about, Warrick?" Jennie asked.

We made our way around the kitchen island, me being the only one who took a seat because my leg was starting to throb. Warrick helped himself to a beer chugging half of it before answering Jennie's question with one of his own, "None of Cian's crew have been invited in, have they?"

"No," Chris said slowly, clearly on guard.

"Good," Warrick said between sips. "While we were sleeping, Liam decided to show up and exact his revenge for some more dead vampires. You wouldn't happen to know anything about that, would you, Louis?"

I sucked in a breath. Even though we all know I'm not capable of taking out any more vampires right now, I wasn't expecting Warrick to waltz in here immediately accusing Lou of doing the job. And yet, I have no idea who else would've been that crazy to kill more of Cian's vampires when he was already pissed.

"Cut the bullshit, Warrick. Stop playing your games and come out with it," Lou clenched his fists.

Warrick calmly set down his now empty beer can, "When we were in the hospital, I told you not to do something stupid. Now you've put Val at risk because your anger once again got the best of you. She doesn't need a knight in shining armor."

Lou moved to attack Warrick, but he saw it coming and grabbed one of Lou's arms, throwing him on the ground. Lou was face down while Warrick held his arm in a way he could dislocate his shoulder at a moment's notice. Lou let out a growl more out of frustration than a threat before tapping the ground giving me a glimpse into what their fighting sessions must have been like when Lou worked for him.

"Good choice," Warrick snarled. He let Lou up while he ran a hand through his hair. "Don't let anything happen to her."

Warrick started grabbing my stuff as a tense silence fell over all of us. When he finished bringing things in, he lifted my chin up so I was looking at him again, "Let me know when you want to go on a date. I'll occasionally stop by, but it won't be every night. With that, I'm always a phone call away, love."

He gave me another kiss before leaving. A heaviness settled over me I wasn't quite prepared for. I wasn't ready to dive in to unraveling what was left behind when I stormed out of here, so I grabbed my bags to get settled back into my house.

Seeing my limp, Lou jogged over, "Let me help."

"I got it, Lou."

He pried my bags from my hands, "Seriously, Val. Let me help. You look like you're in pain."

"Fine," I huffed out. I looked at the staircase ahead of me already missing Warrick's stair-free house. I took a steadying breath then slowly made the climb up to the second floor. By the time I got up there, the throbbing had intensified to a point where I didn't want to put any weight on my leg. *Why is it bugging me so much?*

"Look, Val" Lou started in the same gruff tone he used when we first met. "Know I'm not upset with you, but it hasn't been easy."

I narrowed my eyes at him, "This isn't the time, Lou."

"When will it ever be the time?" he sighed, running his hand through his hair. "I just hope you know what you're doing being with a guy like him."

He made his way out of my room, me staring in disbelief the entire time until I heard him walk back downstairs. I sank onto my bed dropping my head in my hands thankful for the relief my leg was finally getting, but fighting back the tears. I figured I would be walking into an awkward environment especially with how I acted the other day in the pub when Warrick and I ran into Lou. What I didn't expect was the tense, angry setting I would be living in again. *What mess did I make for myself this time?*

A knock startled me. I whipped my head up to see Jennie standing in the doorway with a couple of mugs and a kind smile, "Hey, want some tea?"

I nodded. She moved into the room and sat next to me, offering the mug. I wrapped my hands around it savoring the warm, comforting feeling starting to fill my body. We sat there for a while before Jennie broke the silence, "I don't know what Lou said to you, but it is good to have you back. I'm sure this is incredibly hard separating yourself from Warrick, though."

"Yeah," I said before taking a sip. "Thank you for bringing the tea."

"Of course," she said still talking in a soft tone. "I figured you'd want some of your favorite peppermint tea to help make this transition a little easier. How's your leg feeling?"

"It started hurting once I got in here, but I'm not sure why," I said, looking down at my still-throbbing leg. "I must've been on it too much."

"We'll make sure you take it easy tonight. Did Liam really try to attack you in your sleep?"

I stared off in the distance bracing myself for the onslaught of questions that were about to come. Jennie wasn't one to beat around the bush too long with small talk. Shrugging my shoulders, I answered, "I'm not sure. I woke up because I heard something outside and Warrick wasn't next to me, so I decided to go check things out. When I got there, Warrick and Liam were going at it."

"Warrick mentioned something about Lou doing something stupid. What did he mean?"

"Lou probably killed the vampires that were delivered to Cian."

"Shit," Jennie muttered under her breath. "Now I see why Warrick wants you to stay here."

Changing the topic, I asked, "Do you still think Warrick is using me?"

"I – I shouldn't have said that," she said, voice full of regret. "I can see that he truly cares about you. I was getting caught up in all the villain-talk from Lou and let it go to my head."

"Warrick hasn't exactly done much to convince you he's not the villain, though," I said with a slight flinch at the more confrontational memories with him. "I keep going back to what you said to me in the pub. He practically kicked me out today which is after I've truly hit a brick wall with all the codes my dad left behind."

"Wait," she put a hand on my arm. "You figured out the codes?"

"Yeah, but only some of them," I turned to face her. "They're dates that hold significance between my dad and I."

"This is huge, Val. We could have an idea of where we're going next rather than taking a shot in the dark. It could help us at least prepare for what we might have to deal with."

"True. It doesn't help that Warrick has this information, too, and now he can run off with it whenever he wants to keep working on his mission for ultimate power."

"Val, don't think that. He brought you back here because none of the vampires have gotten inside this house, so Cian can't kill you. Plus, you have Lou whether you like it or not."

I gave a slight nod, looking past her out the windows to watch a storm roll in. Jennie moved to stand up, offering a hand, "Have you eaten yet?"

"No, but I'm not hungry."

"Stop. Come downstairs and eat."

I grabbed her hand using her for extra support while we slowly headed towards the kitchen. As we approached, the warm scents of pizza filled my nose, making my stomach growl despite my attempted protest. I sat next to Jennie at the island and Lou slid over a slice, "Figured you wanted something comforting, if that's still the case with my pizza."

I lifted the slice to take a bite out of it hoping I wasn't giving any signs of enjoying what I was eating. Lou shook his head chuckling, "You're one of the most stubborn people I know, Val."

I set the food down and rolled my shoulders back. I looked at the three of them who were watching me with confusion before landing my gaze on Lou's, "Look, I still don't believe the fact that you didn't do anything with Melody, but before you go get all defensive with me, let me get this off my chest. I have missed being around the three of you, but things have changed since we first got here. Lou, I'm sorry. You still need to give me time. There's a lot more playing into this then just me thinking you and Melody got all cozy together."

He held his hands up, "Then please, elaborate."

"Seeing Melody alive got my hopes up at the thought of Gabriel being alive, too. He fought in the war back home and it would make sense if he ended up getting transported somewhere else. Did I think if that were the case that he'd be with someone else? Yeah, the thought crossed my mind, but at least I wouldn't have the giant, gaping hole in my heart I've been trying to fill. Then, I saw you with her. I don't need to rehash what I saw, but it made me feel like I was just filling the same kind of hole in your heart in a twisted, ironic way. It didn't help I had Warrick playing head games with me at the same time to make everything even more confusing. So, I did what I always do. I went on a reckless streak –push my closest circle away, and try to numb the pain with either alcohol, sex, or both.

"Something happened to me during that time, though. I saw a more human side to Warrick. One who actually laughs, not snickers. One who isn't cold and calculating. One who would do anything to keep me safe. I mean, if he hadn't been there the night of the accident, I would've been dead. We all know that. I couldn't just walk away after seeing that side of him. Even if there's doubts, I know the feelings there are real. I wouldn't have been able to sort through it all if I hadn't spent that time with him. I'm sorry I'm not giving you the story you wanted to hear, Lou. I don't want to hurt you because you hold a special place in my heart, too. I just can't go back to the way things were because the trust I had in you is broken. Not only did you try to make a move on Melody, but you also lied to me about our device needing to recharge and knowing Warrick was here. Who knows what else you're keeping from me."

"I didn't think the recharge time was a big deal," Lou said as he cast his gaze down, "I also didn't want to freak you out about Warrick.

"It's not, and if you told me about Warrick, you would have saved me a lot of panic. Yet, you chose to leave me for a week *knowing* I was at risk."

"I get being upset about Warrick, but why are you bringing the device up when you're saying it's not a big deal?"

I closed my eyes, pinching the bridge of my nose, "It's not what you lied about that was the problem. It was still the fact that you lied to me at all."

"Well, I'm sorry Val," Lou started. "I see your point and I didn't mean to hurt you either. Can we move past this now and start working on getting back to where there's trust between us?"

"I think so, but I'm going to need you to be patient with me," I said. I gestured towards the pizza continuing, "Don't think that feeding me pizza and owning up to your shit is going to make me wake up in the morning completely fine. It's going to take time, which I know you're tired of hearing, but Jennie can attest to."

"I sure can, but I want to back up to something you said earlier," Jennie paused. "Could Gabriel really be alive?"

She was staring at me with wide eyes. I took a steadying breath, "No. There's pictures of his body cut up on an autopsy table and the report to go with it. He'd been caught in a blast. There's no way he's out there somewhere."

"Val, I'm so sorry," Jennie said, voice full of emotion. "I can't imagine the emotional rollercoaster you had to go through thinking there was some way he could still be alive only to find out he's truly dead."

"Can we change the topic, please? I've spilled my guts here and really don't want to keep dissecting things."

"Pizza still as good as you remembered it to be?" Lou asked with an eyebrow cocked up. He didn't miss a beat with changing topics, making us all break out into laughter. The longer we laughed, the more tension was lifted from the room. When we finished, I wiped the tears from my eyes, "Don't worry, you haven't lost your touch."

"To keep things on a lighter note," Jennie interjected. "Val's figured out some of the codes."

Lou whipped his head to me as if looking for confirmation. I gave him a nod, "Means we can sort of plan for what's next so we don't get blindsided by a new world's threats like we did here."

"It also means we might actually get a handle on things and begin to make some progress," Lou added.

"Exactly, but this is something we can dive into more later. I think I might grab myself some wine and enjoy some alone time," I said as I started moving towards the fridge. The throbbing was still there, but now my leg was incredibly stiff after sitting still for a while.

Jennie and Chris were getting lost in their own conversation while Lou was watching me the entire time as I slowly retrieved my bottle of wine from the fridge. Ignoring his stare, I tucked the bottle under my arm and braced myself for having to deal with the stairs again.

"Can I at least help you get up to your room?" Lou asked.

"I guess," I answered.

There was no hesitation as he scooped me into his arms effortlessly. He was careful with where he placed his hands to make sure he was being respectful while also keeping me secure. "Thank you," I quietly muttered.

"All you have to do is ask," Lou said, keeping his voice down. We made it into my room, Lou setting me gently on my bed then moving my bags off. I glanced outside seeing the rain splash against the door to my balcony.

"Thank you for being so honest," Lou said, bringing my attention back to him.

"You weren't going to let it die, so I figured there was no harm in laying it all out there."

"I needed to hear it. I had no idea the level of grief you were having to deal with when that happened. I'm also glad you didn't say it down there in front of Jennie and Chris, but I didn't uphold my end of the bargain by keeping you safe from Warrick."

He was kneeling in front of me now, reaching for the wine bottle to help me open it. I handed it over and watched him work the cork out, "A lot has happened in this place, Lou. The grief I had to work through was also losing you. You were making me feel things I hadn't in a long time, but doing what you did also reminded me why I don't let myself get close to others. Now I had to go and do it all over again with Warrick. I just don't have the energy to handle these emotions anymore."

"Hey," he said, handing the wine back over to me and resting a hand on my knee. "You don't need to be strong for any of us. Take the time you need to rest and work through what you're going through."

"Thanks," I said. I looked down at his hand then back into those grey eyes I hadn't seen for a long time. He started moving closer to me, my breath catching in my throat. Lou's face was inches from mine when I finally recovered my senses and patted his hand, "I think it's time for you to go."

He froze before clearing his throat and standing up, "Yeah, I think so."

Lou got to the doorway then paused, "It's good to have you back, Val."

He was gone before I could say anything. I let out the air I had been holding in, frustration quickly taking its place. I hadn't been here for a full day and he was already trying to make a move on me. *He's out of his damn mind if he thinks I get over things that quickly.*

I took a long swig from the wine bottle then limped over the door to close it. Jennie, Chris, and Lou were all laughing and having a good time. I smiled a little bit, fully closing the door to finish my bottle in peace. I checked my phone, my heart slightly aching when the screen was void of any notifications. I didn't let myself read too much into that. Instead, I wandered around as best I could searching for a book or movie to distract myself with. *Damn it, I left everything downstairs.* I drank some more while contemplating my next move. I remembered my parents kept some DVDs in their room, so I went across the hall.

It had been forever since I wandered into this space and it was kept the same way since the last time I had seen them: the bed was neatly made, nothing out of place on the shelves. I scanned the space trying to locate the cabinet that contained movies, "There it is."

I grabbed *Young Frankenstein*, running my hand over the case then made my way back into my little sanctuary. I changed into my pajamas and started the movie. I settled into bed, taking small sips from my bottle eventually losing myself in the movie. This has been about the most normal thing I've done since this whole adventure started.

I finished my bottle halfway through the movie. I was starting to feel light from the wine, thankful I could start ignoring my leg. My eyes started to close and I was almost about to fall asleep when I heard a quiet knock. My eyelids lifted again, my attention on my door thinking it was Lou coming by again. The knock came again, but not from the door. I looked over to my balcony to see the outline of someone standing there. I couldn't help but feel worried it was Liam trying to finish what he couldn't at Warrick's place, and yet, I still moved over to the door trying to get a better view.

I opened the door, letting the cool air rush over my skin, smiling from ear-to-ear, "Warrick."

"Miss me, love?" he asked with that cocky grin of his as his hair dripped into his face. He held up a bottle of wine, one of my favorites in this world, "Mind if I come in? It's a little wet out here."

"Of course. I missed you," I moved out of his way to let him in. I turned to go back to my bed while he quietly closed the door behind him, still limping pretty good. When I turned back around, his eyebrows were knit with worry, "What's going on with your leg?"

I shrugged him off, "It's nothing. Just making it work a little harder, I guess. To what do I owe this pleasure?"

"I knew today was going to be hard, so I wanted to check in to make sure you were holding up," he said doing his best to mask his concern. He glanced at the empty bottle on my nightstand, "Looks like you've already started the party without me."

I reached for the bottle in his hands, "Who said it needs to stop?"

I got the bottle open, taking a sip from it then handing it over to Warrick who did the same. He set the bottle down and picked me up wrapping my legs around his waist. He kissed me deep and slow before nestling his face into my neck, "I don't know how I'm going to sleep without you by me tonight."

"Then stay," I said, running my hands through his soft, wet hair.

"Are you sure, love?"

"Absolutely positive."

Warrick turned to lay me on the bed, drinking more wine once I was settled. He started examining my leg, carefully working it with his hands to help alleviate the stiffness. I couldn't help when little moans escaped. It was feeling so good. He was managing to find all the pain points and work them out without adding to the misery I was already feeling because of my leg.

"If you're not careful, they'll think you're having a good time up here all by yourself," Warrick chuckled.

"Let them," I said.

Warrick laughed a little at that, still keeping his volume down. I propped myself up on my elbows, watching him. This moment erased all the worry, pain, stress, and the constant need to be thinking about the next move and replaced it with the comforting glimpse into what my future could look like.

"Is that the famous *Young Frankenstein* you've told me so much about?" Warrick asked.

"Yeah, this is it."

He finished giving my leg a massage before crawling into bed with me. He handed me the bottle of wine while he stripped down to his underwear and settled under the blanket with me. I took another sip then laid my head on his shoulder. I started the movie over and let myself drift off.

I startled myself awake a couple hours later, the title screen looping on the movie and Warrick breathing softly beside me. He managed to finish the bottle of wine and set it on the other nightstand to avoid spilling anything on the comforter. He looked so innocent in this moment that I couldn't help myself with brushing the few strands of hair out of his face. His eyes fluttered open, "Hi, love."

"Hi," I whispered back.

He pulled me tightly against his body, burying his face into my neck. Mumbling, he asked, "What time is it?"

"There's a few hours before the sun comes up."

"Damn it. I was hoping it was earlier than that so I could stay longer."

I pulled back a little, "So soon?"

"Unfortunately," he said, pulling me back towards him. "But I'll be back."

Warrick kissed me then rolled out of bed quietly searching for his clothes. When he was dressed, he pushed his hair back into its usual slicked-back style before giving me another kiss, this one longer than the last. He pulled away, resting his forehead against mine and running his thumb over my cheek, "Stay strong, love."

"I'll try," I said not ready for that longing and heartache to replace the warmth and comfort he brought me.

He stood halfway out on my balcony, "I know this isn't the time, so I'm sorry. I'll be moving on to another world soon, but I'll make sure we have a way to communicate with each other."

Chapter 16

"Wait," I said, sitting up and fully awake now. "You're just going to casually drop that news on me now? And how soon is soon?"

"I know, but there was never going to be a good time to tell you, love. And I'll probably be out of here within a week"

I made my way over to him, "Will you at least tell me where you're going?"

He shook his head, "I can't. I'm sorry."

"Right," I said, feeling like I had been slapped. I took a step back, "You have some sort of mission to carry out that's too important for you to involve me in."

"Don't be like that," he pleaded.

"Are you worried that if you take me you'll get too close? Or that I'll ruin your efforts like I did here?"

He took a step towards me making me take another one back, "You can be mad at me all you want, love, but you and I have two different missions that will likely lead us to different destinations. I don't want to keep you from finding everyone and getting a normal life back."

"It's too late for that, Warrick," I said with tears streaming down my face. "My life will never go back to the way it was."

"You're acting like this is goodbye, but it's the farthest thing from it."

"Really? Because you're the one who just announced you're leaving and are pushing me away. Why can't you tell me anything?"

"The more you know, the more danger you're in. Before you get all defensive on me, I'm not being overcautious. This has something to do with the war raging in your world that could quickly spread to other worlds. I may have a solution that will put an end to all of this, but the less you know, the safer I can keep you, love. Unfortunately, the more time I spend here means I have less time I have to keep this war from spreading, and if it does, then it could mean the end of everything. There wouldn't be an us anymore nor would there be a home to return to."

Surprised he actually let me in on a little bit of what's going on, I stared at him a few moments until I was ready to talk to him, "Even though you're still being a little cryptic, I can appreciate you letting me in a little bit. Doesn't take away the hurt of you leaving, though."

I let him get close to me this time. He reached out to me, wiping my tears and pulling me close for a hug, "Please don't cry for me, love. We'll reconnect, I promise. In the meantime, let's try to enjoy the time we have here, okay?"

I nodded into his chest now savoring every moment we spend together even more than I did before. *Why does this hurt so much?*

"I have to go, love, but I'll stop by later today whether that's here or the pub."

I nodded again, feeling his lips against my forehead. In a matter of seconds, he was out the door and climbing down from my balcony leaving me alone once again. The heartache weighed down on me once more.

I knew I wasn't going to be able to sleep again, so I made my way to my dad's office. I rubbed my face trying to shake the sleep and sadness in case anyone came in while I waited for the computer to turn on. I logged in, opening the document that contained the codes. Finding the ones I was most familiar with, I started adding my notes so we were ready when it was time for us to jump. I finished typing my last note and zoned out, transporting myself to moments ago when Warrick dropped his news.

He didn't do anything to quell the doubts I had despite him sharing a little bit of what he was working on. He did, however, actually start telling me what he was working on. With the information he shared with me, I wasn't quite sure what that had to do with going to the other worlds. Maybe he was going to warn the other leaders what was coming their way, but that doesn't exactly hint at what his deal may be with Cian. *Is he giving them supplies to be ready for whatever attack may be coming? Is he sharing the tech he's researching in his labs?*

"Hey," Lou said softly from the doorway.

I nearly jumped out of my skin. I hadn't heard anyone approach and wasn't exactly expecting anyone to be up at this hour.

"Hey yourself," I snapped back. "You nearly gave me a heart attack."

"Clearly," he made his way into the office and settled in the chair across from me. "What are you doing in here this early in the morning?"

"Couldn't sleep, so I figured it would be a good idea to update the list of codes we have with what I figured out. I don't want to forget anything and screw us over later on."

"Not a bad idea. It sounded like you were talking to someone, though."

"Warrick asked you to keep me safe, not monitor my every move," I said not caring to keep the frustration out of my voice.

"All I'm doing is making sure there's nothing I have to worry about," Lou said casually.

"Well, you have nothing to worry about."

Lou shrugged, "Okay. Want to tell me what's on your mind, then?"

"It's a long one," I said, rubbing my face again in the hopes he wouldn't be able to tell I was crying not too long ago.

He leaned back in his chair, interlacing his fingers behind his head, and kicking his feet up on the desk. With a smug grin, he said, "I have time."

I scowled at him, "Can you take a hint?"

"Nope. So, what's on your mind, Val?"

I groaned, "In the time I was with Warrick, I kept hearing him and Cian talk about a deal they have in place. They're working together for some reason and I could never figure out why. Before you ask," I pointed a finger at him. "I did ask Warrick and he wouldn't tell me."

"Isn't this ironic," he said still grinning. "It seems like he doesn't fully trust you."

I shot him another scowl, "Are you going to take this seriously or are you going to just keep rubbing things in my face?"

Lou finally leaned forward in his chair to show he was engaged in our conversation, "Sorry, Val. You left that one out in the open. Do you think we should be worried about whatever Warrick is doing?"

"Thank you," I acknowledged his change in tone. "The only thing we should be worried about is if we kill any more vampires. It seems like Warrick has been keeping Cian and his crew from attacking us or I think we would have been dead a while ago."

Lou ran his hands through his hair, "The answer is no, then. Got it."

"Lou," I started then stopped. Something else was weighing on my mind and I couldn't shake it.

"Yeah?"

"Never mind."

He locked eyes with me, "Tell me, Val."

I stared at him for a moment before looking away to ask my question, "What happens when a werewolf truly falls in love?"

He shifted in his seat, bringing it as close as he could and lowered his voice, "What are you talking about?"

"I guess," I wiggled in my seat a little, trying to find the words to clarify the question. "I guess I'm asking about mating in the sense of finding someone you're supposed to spend the rest of your life with. Is that a thing with werewolves? What happens? How do you know? What happens to the other person? Is it possible with a human? Would the human know? Or is this something the legends make up?"

"Slow down," Lou said, holding his hands up telling me to pause. "What's bringing this on? Actually, I don't know if I want to know yet." He let out a sigh, "First of all, we call it fating since we don't have control over who it happens with. It's more like fate is playing a hand into who we end up with. It starts by being drawn together whether you want it to happen or not, and you both just start ending up finding each other. There's no fighting it when fating takes place, it just does, and you know there's something different about the other wolf or person, I guess. Um, from what I've heard after that, it's hard to be apart. I would compare it to what you feel when you're in love, but more intense which would answer your question of how you know. I haven't heard of anyone having a defined moment where they knew they were fated to someone. I have seen when two wolves try to avoid it, but they always ended up back together.

"I've never heard of a wolf being fated with a human, but that doesn't necessarily mean it can't happen. I don't know how it would affect you, for example, if you fated with a wolf. My guess is that you would feel the intense love and affection toward the wolf just as he would feel that way towards you. So, moral of the story, this isn't something the legends make up and you can compare it to the whole love-at-first-site thing. Does that help at all? It's hard to explain when it's a natural instinct."

"Yeah, that helps I guess," I said, absorbing everything Lou just covered.

"Have you been getting feelings for someone?" he tentatively asked.

I scrunched my nose a little bit thinking about how I wanted to answer. I let out a breath, "I'm not entirely sure what I'm feeling to be honest. It's been a little hard to focus on my feelings when everything has been so chaotic. I can't trust if what I'm feeling is real, either, or if I'm just imagining it based on what I've had to endure here."

"Either way, I hope it becomes clearer to you. Know that I'm here whenever you have questions or want to try and sort through what's going on," Lou said, reaching across the desk and placing his hand on mine.

"Thanks, Lou," I gave him a small smile. "For putting up with my twenty questions this morning when the sun is just coming up."

"Are we interrupting something?" Jennie asked hopefully from the doorway.

Lou and I pulled our hands back as we stood up. Lou was the one who answered first, "No, Jennie. Just talking through some things."

"Sure," she said, smiling like she now had a secret. "Breakfast?"

"Yeah," I cleared my throat. "That would be good."

We all filed out of the office, Lou behind me in case my leg gave out on the stairs. As I took the first step down on my bad leg, I was fully expecting the throbbing to start back up, but it didn't which reminded me to text Warrick to let him know he worked magic.

Even the thought of Warrick stirred something in me, bringing me back to the conversation Lou and I just had. *It could be possible that Warrick and I are fated. I wonder if he's thought about this too, or if he knows anything.*

"How's your leg this morning?" Lou asked, leaning down to my ear.

"Better," I said keeping my answer short. The last thing I wanted was for Lou to think my questions earlier were related to him. He may have stirred some feelings in me when we first arrived here, but they were nothing compared to how I was feeling about Warrick. I picked up my pace a little bit to put some distance between us.

Chris started whipping together food and we all gathered around the island in silence, more from being tired and awake at this hour than from tension. Jennie passed mugs of coffee all around, each of us collectively taking a sip.

Jennie turned to face me, "So, what are you thinking of doing today?"

"Um," I started, trying to think of something. "I might see if Conor can use some help at the pub, but I have no idea how I'm going to get there."

Lou launched himself into the conversation not letting a beat pass before Jennie said anything else, "I can take you."

I stared at him trying to decipher his intentions. I looked back at Jennie taking another sip of coffee, "I guess that solves that problem. I might swim if the weather holds. Try to get some strength back in me after not doing anything for so long."

"Not a bad idea, Val," Chis smiled at me. "Maybe lose at some poker later, too, if you're up for it."

Jennie rolled her eyes, "You've just been itching to play with someone who gives you a challenge, haven't you?"

"You have no idea, babe," Chris winked at her.

I shook my head at the both of them, "We'll see how the day goes first."

We fell into the easy rhythm of a chill conversation joking with each other, but every now and then, I would miss an inside joke they shared during the time I was staying with Warrick. Lou kept trying to steal glances at me and I did my best to ignore him, throwing my attention to my phone and texting Warrick: *Thank you for stopping by last night. I don't know if I could've slept alone either.*

The three dots popped up on the screen then were quickly replaced with a message: *That wasn't a one-time thing, love.*

I'm thinking of going into the pub for a quick shift, I answered back.

Warrick sent back another quick response: *Let me know when you want to head over there. I'll come grab you.*

I sent a quick kissing emoji back to him thankful I now have a reason to not have an awkward drive with Lou. I shot a note over to Conor letting him know I'm planning on working today for a few hours before it gets dark out. All I got in return was a thumb's up and him asking me to come in a little earlier than usual so we can catch up.

Chris had a classic breakfast ready: pancakes, eggs, hashbrowns, and bacon. The moment the plate slid in front me, my stomach growled and I didn't hesitate to dive in. Between bites, I thanked Chris for the food and the conversation I could participate in resumed. When things died down for a bit, I looked at Lou, "Thank you for offering to drive me into the pub. Warrick said he's going to be stopping by in a few hours to take me over there, though."

Lou momentarily let a shadow cross his face before shrugging it off, "Sounds good. I'll hang out here."

Jennie looked between the two of us then sent me a message: *Is there something going on between you two? Things are a little weird.*

Yeah, I'll have to tell you later in the pool when we're by ourselves. I think it has something to do with a conversation Lou and I had earlier. I might have made things weird …

Jennie put her phone down, giving me a slight nod while she finished her first cup of coffee.

We ended up hanging out on the couch watching whatever movies we could find quickly just to have some background noise. I hadn't realized how much time had passed until the doorbell rang and Jennie ran over to answer the door. The familiar sound of Warrick's voice carried over to me, sending the butterflies in flight. Maybe it was the conversation with Lou, but I now felt hyperaware of every feeling I had when it came to Warrick.

"Hi, love," he said, leaning over the back of the couch to kiss my head.

"You're early," I returned, looking up at him.

"Not really. It's about time to go meet with Conor."

I looked at the time on my phone, "Shit!"

I bolted upstairs as fast as one could with a limp to throw some clothes on and run back downstairs. I noticed Warrick hadn't moved an inch which was getting under Lou's skin. Not wanting to see another conflict, I rubbed Warrick's back, "I'm ready."

He grunted in return, throwing an arm over my shoulder and guided me out of the house to his car. It wasn't until we were on the road that he said something, "What's going on with Lou?"

"You're not the only one to ask me that question," I answered. "I have no idea. He's been acting weird in general. I don't know if it has something to do with him overcompensating to get me to trust him again or if he's jealous. I'm just doing my best to ignore him."

"Interesting," Warrick mumbled. "What have you two talked about?"

"I set the record straight with why I shut him out. Then we talked about the codes because he walked into the office this morning while I was updating my notes," I said. I made sure to leave out the conversation about fating because I wasn't sure if I was ready to confront Warrick about that yet. Not if I wasn't sure what I was feeling was real and I don't think I could take it if he rejected me so soon after telling me he was going to be leaving.

Warrick reached over, grabbing my hand and kissing it, "Let's not focus on him while our time is limited here. Plus, we have an overly excited barkeep to talk to."

I laughed when I looked out the window to see Conor enthusiastically waving at us. When we parked, he ran up to the car to open the door and help me out, "You have no idea how happy I am to see you again. And you're looking great!"

"Just remember Conor, I'm only here for a few hours. I can't really be out after dark anymore," I looked over my shoulder at Warrick then leaned into whisper to Conor. "Dad here is enforcing a strict curfew."

Warrick let out a loud laugh, "You are something else, love."

"Come on you two love birds," Conor threw his arms over both our shoulders and led us to the pub. "I need to hear more about this curfew."

When we got settled, Conor looked between us expectantly, "So, what's going on?"

"There's a couple reasons why I can't work more than a few hours today," I started. "The easier one to explain is that my leg can only take so much and this is about to be the most time I've spent on it."

"You can stay behind the bar today and I'll give you a chair. Next."

Warrick jumped in on explaining the curfew, "Let's just say Lou screwed Val over by killing some more of Cian's vampires as a way to get revenge for her accident."

"That fecking guy," Conor spat.

"Exactly," Warrick continued without missing a beat. "His choice has put the vampires on high-alert and Val is their number one target. Keep her where they can't get to her when it's dark out and we're good."

"Understood. We'll make sure your shift wraps up with plenty of time to get you home before the sun goes down. I'll be happy with any help I can get, as you know," Conor moved to get up.

When he was gone, Warrick leaned closer to me, "I'll be here as long as you need me, love."

"You good with the whole time?"

"Sure, makes it more of a sure thing that I'll get you home on time."

I looked past him out the window, "I'm not the biggest fan of being so locked down."

"I know, but I'm happy you're actually listening rather than agreeing and then doing whatever you want."

I flinched a little at that, "I deserve that."

"Don't worry about it, love," he said, kissing my head.

Conor came back with the familiar opening paperwork along with a few other stacks, "Can you start working on this for me? I'll run around to get everything ready."

"Sure," I said with a smile.

Diving into the paperwork, I was happy to finally be focusing my attention on something that wasn't codes or devices. Plus, it was a nice distraction from being so in-tune with every movement Warrick made and what it could possibly mean. *Damn it, I'd bet anything that we're fated. How do I even bring this up with Warrick?*

I cleared my throat, "Um, Warrick? Do werewolves mate?"

He choked on his water, scrambling for his napkin to clean up the mess he made. When he finished patting himself down, he looked at me, "We do, but why are you asking?"

"Just something Lou mentioned earlier in a conversation," I said nonchalantly hoping Warrick wouldn't read too much into that.

"Ah, well, what do you want to know?"

Phew. I straightened the papers, "I guess I'd like to know what you know about it."

He ran his hands through his hair making sure no strand was out of place, "For starters, it's fating for us. Not mating. Same concept where you're bound to your mate for the rest of your life, just a little more whimsical of an explanation: Fate lays her eyes on two souls and binds them together for eternity to share an unrivaled connection. It's rare for two people to become fated, but it does happen. Although, it's incredibly rare for it to happen between a werewolf and a human."

"But is has happened?" I asked.

"I think once before," he said.

I didn't dare ask any more questions to avoid raising suspicions. It would make sense he doesn't know the feelings since he clearly hasn't gone through this before and I did ask him to tell me what he knows.

The conversation died down between us for a moment until Warrick asked, "Why was Lou bringing this up in a conversation?"

I closed my eyes, "I might have asked him about it."

"Suddenly his behavior makes sense," Warrick said quietly chuckling.

"What do you mean?" I asked a little confused.

He cupped my cheek, "He thinks you have those feelings towards him, love."

"Ha!" I laughed. "There's no way. I don't feel anything towards him right now except for skepticism."

Warrick cocked his head to the side in a motion that reminded me his wolf shares his body with him, "Do you have any feelings towards anyone?"

Conor thankfully chose this moment to come back to the table, "Ready?"

"Yes," I answered almost a little too quickly. I walked over to the bar appreciative of the beer pouring station Conor set up for me, complete with a chair, glasses, and a bin to dump any dirty glasses that get returned.

Conor opened the pub and the few customers waiting filtered in. When there was a little more noise around us and we had a break in the orders, he leaned over to me, "Figured you could use some rescuing from that conversation."

"Yeah, thanks," I said, sounding relieved. "Wasn't ready to go down that path yet."

"I get it," he started. "I've been there before and I've also messed up by expressing my feelings sooner than I should. Not to say you shouldn't if the time is right, but you'll know when that time is."

All I could do was nod my head.

Business picked up and I spent the few hours of my shift filling up so many beers I lost track of time. Warrick came up to the bar, tapping the bar top, "Time to go, love."

"Get out of here," Conor said over his shoulder as he took food to a table. "Thanks for coming in today. Let me know if you're ready for this again tomorrow."

"Sure thing," I said, getting off my perch. Thankfully, my leg was still pain free today and I was moving a little better than what I was doing before Warrick came over.

We rode back to my house in silence. When we were parked in the driveway, Warrick leaned over to give me a kiss, "I'll be by later tonight."

"I'll see you then," I said before I got out of the car.

Chapter 17

"Jennie?" I called out when I closed the door behind me. "I'm going to head out for a swim. Want to join?"

She poked her head up from the stairs leading to the basement, "Yeah, let me grab my suit."

We both headed upstairs to change and dived into the pool. We swam over to the edge farthest from the house and hung our arms over the edge like we've done so many times before. I looked towards the door to make sure the coast was clear then turned my attention to her, "I figure we don't have long before the guys join us out here, so here it goes. I made the mistake of asking Lou about werewolves mating."

"Well, that explains some things. Why the hell would you ask a fragile guy about that kind of stuff?" Jennie asked, giving my arm a little smack.

"I was tired and wasn't thinking."

"Please dish, though."

I groaned, "I asked too many questions that might have led him to believe I was implying this kind of relationship between him and I."

"Of course you did, Val," she rolled her eyes. "That's not what I want to know."

"Apparently, it's called fating, not mating. It's a lot like love, just more intense and you can't change the course of it when you're fated with someone."

"I'm sure it was a longer conversation than that, but I get the message."

I gave her a little shove, "I don't need to give you the play-by-play. I made an even bigger mistake, though."

"Don't tell me you asked Warrick?"

"I did," I cringed waiting for her to scold me.

Jennie's jaw hit the floor, "You didn't?!"

"I really did."

"What's the deal between you and Warrick? Do you have feelings?"

I nodded my head, "I do and I'm scared of what they may be."

"You don't think?"

"Yeah, I do think."

"Shit, Val," Jennie said, checking for any signs of the guys. "Do you think he feels the same way?"

"He has admitted having feelings for me and that I'm the one for him, but I don't know if that's because he wants information or sex or what."

"Valid concerns, but you do know there's only one way to find out, right?" she asked, playfully poking my side.

I giggled, pushing her away, "I know. I'm not ready for that, though. And as a head's up, he's stopping by tonight."

"I'd be surprised if he didn't," she said.

"Why?"

Jennie tilted her head towards me, "You're not as sneaky as you think you are. I saw him running through the back yard last night."

"How did no one else see him?"

"Chris and Lou were playing one of their many games of pool and I didn't care to hang out with them."

"Fair enough," I said. "Keep it between us?"

She pushed away from the wall, "I wasn't planning on doing anything but that with this conversation."

I nodded. The door opened and Lou and Chris jumped in with us. Chris joined Jennie, pulling her to him before glancing at me, "Aren't you supposed to be swimming laps?"

"Yes, coach," I joked. I ducked under the water and started swimming the moment I noticed Lou heading my direction. *Time to avoid him for a little bit.* I could tell my muscles were weaker as I took a break after a couple of laps, panting and starting to feel the soreness ache in my body. I ended right where I began which just so happened to be next to Lou. He watched me carefully as I did a quick check on how my legs and arms were feeling.

"How was the pub?" he asked.

"It was good. Conor was a little too happy he was getting some help back today and he even set up a station for me so I didn't have to strain my leg too much," I responded, smiling at the visual of Conor waving the way he did earlier.

"Good," Lou flashed me a smile. "Look, about earlier. I'm sorry if I made you feel uncomfortable in any way. I don't want to force anything if you're not ready."

I immediately felt awkward again searching for an answer that isn't rude, "Thank you for being so considerate, Lou. Just know I'm not at that point right now."

"Got it. I'll keep my distance," he said, giving no signs of hurt. *Guess he's getting better at masking his emotions, too.*

"I'm going to knock out a few more laps before I call it a night."

"Yeah, go for it. I'll be on the lookout for anyone who shouldn't be back here," he gestured to the yard.

I dived back under the water letting it wash over me as I pushed my way through. I had missed swimming and the workout it gives. What I missed even more was the chance to truly be alone and to process what was running through my mind. *I hope Lou sticks to his word about giving me space right now.*

I finished my laps, Lou escorting me back into the house where Jennie and Chris cooked up some burgers. I headed upstairs to take a quick shower, mostly to rinse off the chlorine, and throw my pajamas on, unlocking the balcony door in case Warrick made his way back up there while I wasn't in my room. When I got back downstairs, Chris and Lou were in some heated debate over their latest pool game while Jennie zoned out. I grabbed my food to sit down next to her, "So, they seem close."

"Yeah," she giggled. "They're practically attached at the hip."

"Makes me feel better that Lou's not feeling like an outsider, although, I can't say the same about myself."

She looked at me, surprised, "What do you mean?"

I patted her leg, "Calm down, Jennie. I don't mean anything negative by it. It would be more worrisome if this weren't the case. Just means you guys really bonded while I was gone."

I could see Jennie visibly relax, "Yeah, you could say we've spent a lot of time together."

Chris didn't wait for everyone else to finish before he was back at the table with the poker set. Despite just wanting to retreat into my room for the evening, I didn't have the heart to tell him no when he was looking at me so expectantly with a smile practically taking up his entire face.

I put down what was left of my burger then glanced at Jennie who just rolled her eyes then over to Lou who was watching me very carefully. I swallowed the bite still in my mouth then asked him, "Do you know how to play?"

"Chris taught me," Lou answered not breaking my stare.

"Do you know what you're getting into?"

"He warned me."

"Alright," I said, looking over to Jennie. "You good with dealing?"

"Do I have a choice?" she asked with a light tone.

"Probably not," I laughed. Chris was watching the interaction like someone watching the ball at a tennis match; his head was on a well-oiled swivel turning to watch each person who spoke. "I'm up for a couple of rounds then I need to get some sleep."

We finished our food and moved to the table where Jennie took up her spot to shuffle and deal. Chris distributed some chips despite this being an incredibly low-stakes game. I couldn't help but feel like we were back home in our world the night before everything so drastically changed with how the scene was unfolding in front of me. The only major differences being that Lou was here, we weren't expecting our friends to be showing up, and we weren't at our true home. None of us were.

I glanced at Jennie, and judging by her facial expression, she was feeling the exact way. She looked my way and a silent communication passed between us while Chris was busy reminding Lou of how to play. There was something reassuring about her also silently mourning everything and everyone we had lost. There was also hope that none of our other friends met the same fate as Daryl.

Cards went out and we all focused in. Even though it had been a while since I had played, everything came back to me as muscle memory. I stretched my neck to loosen up to try and get in the heads of my opponents. I studied Lou for a little bit since I had never played with him to see if he was giving anything away, but his poker face was firmly in place as was Chris'. I should've known he wouldn't be an easy read if Chris was his teacher. I moved some more of my chips in, not entirely giving away that my hand was a tough one to beat, but not letting them think I had nothing either. Chris raised his eyebrows at me as he pushed more chips in to see if I would match his bet. Lou followed suit leaving me with no choice. We played like that for a while, seeing who would fall for the bait until it was finally time to reveal our hands.

"Royal flush, boys," I said smugly, laying down my cards and reaching for the pile of chips.

"Shit, I really thought I had a chance," Chris muttered.

Lou watched his chips gets added to my pile, "You warned me about this. Man, I wasn't expecting a smack down on the first hand."

"Get used to it," Chris sighed, leaning back in his chair. "Val and J have some sort of agreement worked out between the two where she gives Val the best cards."

"Really?" Lou asked.

"No, but I wouldn't be surprised."

Jennie and I once again shook our heads at the two of them, her smiling the entire time.

The next couple of rounds went the same way: Jennie dealt us all in, I tried to not oversell what I had, Chris or Lou getting confident they had a hand that could beat mine, and the two of them getting disappointed when I proved them wrong. They were almost out of chips when I yawned and stood up, "I think it's time I stop making you two feel bad about yourselves and head up to bed."

Lou looked at Chris, "You weren't kidding when you said she was a shark."

"One of these days I'll figure out how you do it," Chris added, watching me as I walked away.

"Just the luck of the cards," I said over my shoulder.

When I got back into the quiet calm of my room, I looked down at my phone to see if there was anything from Warrick. Nothing, again, so I hoped this meant he would show up like he did last night. I headed to the shower waiting for the water to warm up now feeling the soreness settle in from the pool. Thankfully, my leg was still feeling better. Not 100%, but getting there.

I took my time getting clean mostly to let the warm water help my muscles recover with a small part of me stalling so I could walk out there to Warrick waiting for me. Besides, I hadn't really cleaned up when I hopped in here earlier and my skin was starting to itch. I finished up, drying off and checking my appearance before making my way out to my room, turning off the light as I did so.

The lights in my room were turned off and the music I had playing before I went into the shower was still playing. My eyes were still adjusting from the light of my bathroom so all I could see was the outline of a man laying on my bed.

"Hi you," I called out softly.

He propped himself up on his elbows, saying nothing in return. I closed the distance between us ready to straddle his legs when I could finally make out the details of his face.

"Lou, what the hell?" I backed up, clutching my towel to my chest. "What are you doing in here?"

I didn't bother hiding the frustration in my voice. I thought he had gotten the message loud and clear earlier, but clearly he wasn't planning on giving me the space I needed. I checked my balcony door for any signs of Warrick out there to be disappointed when there was nothing.

"Clearly interrupting something you had planned," Lou responded just as annoyed as I sounded. "Expecting company tonight?"

"Are you really surprised by that?"

"I guess I shouldn't be," he shrugged.

"What are you doing in here?" I asked again, not wanting to do the whole back and forth thing Lou has been so fond of lately.

He stood up making his way over to me. With each step he took forward, I took one back eventually running into the wall and having nowhere left to go. He grazed my cheek with his hand, focused on my lips, "I wanted to talk to you."

"Really? Because I feel like you're wanting something else," I said, doing my best to hold my ground.

"We need to start thinking of where we want to go next," Lou dropped his hand and got down to business. "I think we've spent enough time here, and considering Cian is sending his vampires out to hunt you down, I don't see any better time."

"You have a point," I watched him carefully. "Is that all you wanted to tell me?"

"No," his voice dropped down to a husky whisper. "Our conversation from earlier got me thinking."

Lou didn't give me a chance to counter with anything that might have diffused the position we were in. He leaned in, kissing me with such passion you would have thought his life depended on it. One of his hands held the side of my face tilting my chin up to get a better position while the other hand was firmly planted on the wall next to my head. He shifted his weight so his body was pressed against mine, giving me an idea of how much he missed me.

I threw my hands against his chest trying to push him away except he wasn't budging. I tried to turn my face away only to be met with his hand keeping my head in place. My only other option was to knee him. As soon as my knee connected with his balls, he doubled over and ended the kiss, letting out a whimper of pain. I moved towards the door leading out into the hallway trying to contain the rage I felt.

I yanked the door open, hissing at him, "Don't you *dare* try that shit again. I don't want to see you in this room again."

Lou recovered from my attack. He squared his shoulders not giving away any emotions as he said, "Know that I have no regrets."

"I don't give a fuck about what you do or don't regret. Get *out*."

I let out a breath the moment he walked out of the doorway and I slammed the door closed. I shut my eyes, leaning my forehead against the cool surface of the wall. There was no way I would have been able to keep him off me if that didn't work, the realization making me shake.

When I got my emotions in check, I stood out on my balcony for a few minutes scanning the yard only to be disappointed when there were no signs of Warrick. I threw myself into bed trying to fall asleep, only able to toss and turn.

Morning came and so did another disappointed check of my phone when there were no messages from Warrick. I shot him a quick message letting him know I missed him and decided I didn't want to hang around to see if he responded or not. I threw my phone on my bed then made my way to the room Chris and Jennie were in.

I gave a quiet knock then waited. Jennie opened the door, eyes halfway open. Clearly, I had woken them up and immediately regretted bugging them, "I'm sorry. I was hoping you two would already be awake. I didn't mean – "

"Is everything okay, Val?" she asked, cutting me off.

I gave her a soft smile, "Yeah. Again, I'm sorry for waking you up. Go back to sleep."

She yawned, closing the door and I made my way downstairs. I was alone. A sigh of relief escaped my lips. I got to work making myself something to quickly eat before going back upstairs to get ready for my day. When I finished getting dressed, I looked at my phone only seeing a message from Conor telling me what time to be there. I responded to him with a thumb's up and told myself not to read too much into Warrick's silence. *He's probably busy getting everything ready to go when he jumps worlds.*

I sat on the edge of my bed for a few moments testing my bad leg. Deciding it was good to go, I made my way down to the garage checking for any signs of Lou along the way. I safely made it to where my bike sat parked. I stared at the machine I nearly died on, questioning if I could ride it again. *Not like I have very many options at the moment.*

Taking a deep breath, I threw on my gear, opened the garage door, and pushed the bike down the driveway. I didn't want to take any chances of anyone hearing what I was up to, so I continued to push it further away from the house only taking breaks to catch my breath and check in on my leg. Every now and then, I'd glance over my shoulder towards the house checking for signs of life. There weren't any yet.

I was far enough from the house that I felt confident I could start the bike without waking them up. Settling into the seat, I calmed my breathing down and worked on hyping myself up for finally getting back on my bike. It's crazy what an accident does to your mind, making you second-guess every movement that was once muscle memory.

Shaking my head, I finally eased into motion, taking the familiar path to Warrick's house. I wanted to see if he was there because I could really use some time with him right now. I didn't like where we left off on our conversation yesterday and I wanted to clear some of the air. Maybe there was a small part of me hoping it would be enough that he would let me join him.

His car wasn't there and his house was all closed up so even if I wanted to look in the windows, I wouldn't be able to see anything. Cursing, I continued my drive that eventually led me to the other coast that I had never visited before.

I moved stiffly from my bike and removed my gear to get a little air. I sat on the edge of the cliff staring out to the ocean again. Lou's actions last night confirmed he thought I was talking about being fated to him with all my questions I asked. The problem plaguing me now wasn't the fact I would have to tell him I don't have those kinds of feelings for him. No, it was the thought of him having those feelings for me. I was reminded of the one question I didn't ask: is it possible for only one person out of the pair to be fated?

I shook my head, the ache in my chest starting to grow stronger. I was fighting the thought of Warrick potentially not feeling the same way despite what he admitted to me. I wasn't counting out the chance of him using me to get the information he wanted so he could have an upper hand on carrying out his objectives, either. But that was a path I really didn't want to think about right now.

Instead, I cleared my mind and watched the ocean churn beneath me, the waves smacking against the stony face of the cliff in a way that made me wonder if she was angry. It was as if she was beating against his chest almost mirroring the way I was feeling.

I lost all track of time watching the ocean in her never-ending battle, jumping when I felt my phone buzz. I had been out here for hours and was risking running late judging by Conor's message conveying nothing but worry and urgency.

"Crap," I mumbled to myself as I got back on the bike. I still wasn't ready to zoom into town despite increasing my chances of running late.

When I pulled up, I had an annoyed looking Conor waiting for me. "I know," I said, following him into the pub. "I could've at least sent you a message. This one's on me for not paying attention to time."

"Your damn right it is. Lucky for you, everything is ready to go and we're having another slow start this morning."

I made my way back to the breakroom to deposit my riding gear then slowly moved back out to take up my post behind the bar. Conor was busy pouring some pints when he said, "Chair's there if you need it, although it looks like you're moving better today. It would be great if you could help me out front today while you're here, if you feel up to it."

"Got it, boss."

Not wanting to push my luck any further than I had this morning, I told myself to suck it up and pull my weight. It had only been a couple of hours into my shift when my leg started throbbing and I needed to sit behind the bar. In the middle of fulfilling an order, Conor came up to me, "It's not like you to be late, Val."

"I know. I am sorry about that," I said fully meaning it, too.

"Everything okay? I was worried something happened to you."

I finished filling the last glass then turned so I was facing him, "Just had a lot running through my mind this morning, so I went up the coast to think."

"No Warrick today?" he nodded towards the bike.

"No," I paused. "He's probably busy and I didn't want to bug him."

"No one else to bring you?"

I shook my head, "They were still asleep and I wanted out of the house. I've been cooped up in houses for longer than I wanted."

"I get it," he said, taking care of a refill for me. "I'd want to stretch my legs, too, if I had to stay shut away for as long as you have."

Our conversation was cut short by the next wave of customers. I stayed behind the bar until everyone was taken care of. The throbbing in my leg had dulled to a bearable level, so I went out and grabbed empty dishes while Conor was in the kitchen helping cook up some orders. He had been back there for a while, so when he came out wiping his hands with a towel and saw me, his eyes widened, "What are you still doing here, Val? You have to get home."

"What?" I asked.

"You really don't pay attention to time, do you?"

I glanced out the windows to see the sun going down, "Shit! I need to go."

I did my best to hurry around him, but I wasn't moving too fast at this point. I had overdone it on this shift trying to be the most help I could be after annoying Conor this morning. He followed me back into the breakroom where I was throwing on my gear, "I can take you home if you need me to."

"No," I waved him off. "I'm sure I'll be fine for one night."

"If you say so," he said doubtfully.

"See you, Conor," I said, making my way out of the pub.

He followed me and called from the door, "Stay safe out there, Val."

I threw down my visor on my helmet giving him a thumbs up. However, I turned around to find my bike missing from the spot I parked it this morning.

"No, no, no, no. This can't be happening to me."

I turned around and went back into the pub, taking my helmet off to make it easier to hear Conor. He was wiping down the bar top when I made my way over to him, "My bike's gone."

"Oh, one of the guys in the kitchen moved it to the parking garage so it didn't get damaged," he started. "We noticed a couple of cars getting too close for comfort and there were too many people looking at it."

"And you didn't tell me?"

"Sorry, Val," he winced. "I forgot. Want me to go get it for you?"

I threw my helmet back on shaking my head, "No, it's okay. Just glad to know it's not stolen."

Crisis averted. I started the familiar trek to the parking garage, glancing at the cathedral at the end of the street while also thinking it was odd they would move my bike without saying anything. The place still sent shivers down my spine and I was looking forward to the day I no longer had to look at it.

The sun was now fully set, the stars dancing their way across the night sky. I made it about halfway across the street when alarm bells started going off in my head. I slowed my pace checking my surroundings for anything that may be the cause of the unease growing in my gut. Not seeing anything out of the ordinary besides a lack of people on the street, I chalked it up to me being paranoid.

"Get it together, Val," I told myself. I took one more step and the next thing I knew, I was upside down. I wanted to scream out more from pain than from shock at having my world literally flipped, but couldn't get anything out. Instead, tears filled my eyes as I hung there whimpering. I lifted my head up to see what had snagged my bad leg, eyeing a rope strung up from the top of the parking garage. I tried to lift myself up to see if I could save myself, but there was no way I could move like that in this gear.

I had just let myself hang again, swinging back and forth in the middle of the street, when Liam walked out of the darkness of the parking garage. He sauntered up to me so he was standing directly beneath me. He reached up taking off my helmet and steadying me as his usual sinister grin crept on to his face, "Think we were just going to let this one slide?"

"I have no idea what you're talking about, Liam," I spat at him. He may be able to sense how I was feeling, but in the event he couldn't actually get an idea of what was going through my head, I did my best to portray anything but fear.

He started examining his fingernails as if he were bored, "Seems like you don't have any of your wolf friends to protect you, so what better time to bring you to Cian than now?"

"Someone's going to see you," I said through gritted teeth.

His chuckle started low at first then broke out in a full-blown laughter, "You really think that's a concern? Look around, Val. There's no one here. You're in one of my creations. No one can see us or hear us."

Anger ripped from my throat in a high-pitched scream. I tried to reach out to grab Liam, but he casually side-stepped to avoid my attempted attack.

He tsked then said, "I've had enough of this."

Liam reared back then headbutted me with full force turning my world to black and knocking me out.

Chapter 18

I slowly opened my eyes, the pain in my head raging. I couldn't tell where I was, only that I was lightheaded and my world was spinning. The edges of my vision were still fuzzy, but what I could make out was a dark room with walls of stone. There was hardly anything in this space and it was quiet except for the sound of a steady dripping.

As I came to, I realized I was once again hanging upside down, but this time, my hands were bound and hanging below my head. I lifted my head, doing my best to ignore the flood of pain as I looked at my feet which were secured by a heavy chain, same as my hands. *Crap, I've been here before.*

What I didn't remember is how my clothes became soaked with blood. I also couldn't single out a source for my pain. I knew my head was on fire, my bad leg throbbed, but my entire body was stinging. I needed more light to be able to see what was going on.

I turned my head to the left to see if I could examine my arm a little better finding numerous cuts of various sizes littering my arm. I turned my head to take in my other arm seeing the same thing. I knew in that moment the blood covering my body was mine, not someone else's as a result of a fight. Terror gripped my throat. *I'm in the worst possible situation I could have gotten myself into.*

I let my gaze trail down to the floor underneath me to see several buckets collecting the blood dripping from my body confirming the source of the only sound I could hear in this damn room. I threw my body around trying to see if there was any hope of having a way out of this only to be met with the clinking of the chains against each other.

"Damn it!" I shouted. I let out a groan closing my eyes. There had to be some way to get out of this mess. There's always a way.

My eyes snapped open, focusing on the door where Cian stood clicking his tongue, "I keep my promises unlike others."

I narrowed my eyes at the man standing before me who was calm, collected. This was all a game to him and he was going to draw this out to make me pay even though I didn't break my end of the arrangement.

His footsteps echoed in the space as he made his way closer to me. He grabbed my chin forcing me to look at him. Cian stood there examining my face for a moment before curling his lip and dragging his knife across my neck adding to the cuts already covering my body. I let out a whimper as the drips fell into the buckets below in a steadier rhythm. He licked the blood off the knife before saying, "You have no idea what you just got yourself into."

"Please," I forced out. "I didn't do anything. I didn't kill those vampires. I was with Warrick the whole time."

Cian was halfway to the door before he turned around. He waved the knife around, "You see? I don't know that I truly believe that. All signs point to you being the one behind the deaths in my family and I don't take that kindly. Remember the first time I warned you to stop? Here's the result of that."

He gestured to the buckets below me, his face unreadable. I looked beneath me again, assessing the buckets to be about five gallons each. There were at least four of them arranged in a way to make sure no drop of my blood was wasted and they were slowly filling which told me I didn't have very much time.

"Oh, don't worry, your end is not as soon as you think," Cian started as if he could read my mind. He came back over to me so we were face-to-face. "This is going to go on for days until I've had my fill. I might even share with Liam since he's been practically salivating since the very moment we got you in here. You want to know the worst part about this whole situation?"

I couldn't move as he admired the knife he was turning over in his hands. The last thing I wanted was for more cuts to speed up this whole ordeal.

"You don't even know how much of a mess you made."

"I think I have a pretty good idea at this point," I said, my voice wavering.

He let out a laugh then looked at me, glowering at the sight in front of him, "No, I don't think you do. Your actions have not only hurt the plans Warrick and I have, but they've physically hurt me. Each one of those vampires I created which ties them directly to me. They die, I get hurt, so every time you drove a stake through one of their hearts, I spent the night feeling that same pain and coughing up blood. That's why I'm taking this so personally. That's why you haven't even begun to feel the pain I want you to. The night of the ball? I was with Warrick when you landed your fatal blows. Did you ever wonder why he wanted to leave so quickly once the two of you were reunited? He knew I was going to hunt you down. The night I knocked you off that bike? I was going to kill you until Warrick showed up, so take that as a gift.

"Yet, you threw that gift in my face when my chest erupted in fire and I had to open the door to see the ashes of the fallen. There was one more thing," Cian tapped his finger on his chin. "Ah, that's right. I can't forget the fact you took away a couple of our voluntary blood bags, either. We don't like when a food source suddenly stops showing up. Needless to say, I've been nice up until this point, but I can't keep pushing things aside any longer."

Tears started forming and I couldn't hold them back any longer. "Please," I begged again. "I swear I didn't kill anyone else. I was cooped up in Warrick's house the entire time."

"Except for when you went to the pub with him. Oh, and there was that period of time before he made his presence known. Can't forget about that," Cian said matter-of-factly. "Correct me if I'm wrong, but there were a few moments where Warrick didn't have his eyes on you and that's not good enough for me. I underestimated you when you first arrived here, but I'm not doing that again. Who knows what you could have done during that time you two were separated? Even Liam said he lost sight of you for a while."

"I was in the bathroom, Cian."

He chuckled again, "You really think I'm going to believe you? The position you're in at present says otherwise."

This time he turned and made his way to the door. There was nothing left I could say or do to try to convince him of my innocence. He already had his mind made up.

Cian looked over his shoulder at me one last time before finally making his exit, "Don't think anyone is going to rescue you here. Hell, no one knows that we have you, and your so deep in this cathedral, your screams won't reach anyone."

I couldn't help but think if I had just let things go, just convinced Jennie and Chris to join me instead of seeking vengeance on their behalf, I wouldn't have been in this situation. At least I knew why I was so light-headed and dizzy. I've already lost a good amount of blood with no signs of that stopping anytime soon. My sobs took over at this point. *What good was it going to do if I kept trying to play tough when there was no hope?*

I heard more footsteps approaching thinking I would see Cian filling the doorway again. When Liam stood in the doorway instead of Cian, I knew I was in trouble. There was nothing holding him back anymore now that I made it through Cian's lecture and he knew it too.

He walked up to me, inhaling when he was inches away from my face. Liam got even closer, bringing his hand up to caress my face, "Not so tough now, are we?"

I flinched away from his touch, not wanting him to touch me in any way that would come off as romantic.

"Shh, I'm not going to hurt you. Yet, anyways," he grinned. "I wanted to get a taste of what you've been denying me for so long."

"No," I protested trying my best to swing back from him. I felt his grip tighten behind my neck, not even realizing he had his hand back there in the first place.

Liam cocked his head to the side feigning hurt, "I can't be that bad, can I? Too bad you're not going anywhere."

He yanked me close enough to him there was hardly any space left. His breath hot on my face, he smiled as he wiped his finger along one of my cuts covering it in my blood. Liam sucked the blood off, his pupils dilating as he was finally tasting what he had been wanting for so long. He shivered a little bit, still not letting the space between us grow, "You taste even better than how Cian described you."

I couldn't stop him as he leaned in kissing me. There was no way I was going to return the kiss, and he sensed that, too, eventually getting frustrated and pulling away. Liam studied me for a few moments which was long enough to let me collect my thoughts, "Why? What point is there in kissing me when I'm just going to die?"

"Ah," Liam started. "Cian got in your head. Don't you know that he sent me in here to heal you up just enough so that we can draw this torture out for a few days?"

"You?" I asked confused and alarmed. I now understood what game I was going to have to play and I had to fight to keep myself from throwing up.

He came close to me again, "Yes, me. Cian also mentioned that if I felt it was time to end it, that I can do that too. Although," Liam looked away for second contemplating the potential outcomes of different scenarios. "If I ended your life right now, we wouldn't have as much blood to sustain us which would be a pity. So, this is going to go one of two ways. The fun part is *you* get to choose how things play out. You see where this is going?"

"I figured out where this was going a while ago," I was now annoyed. Liam was playing with me, trying to get a reaction I wasn't going to give him. Not after I was practically begging Cian to let me go then watched him walk away. My only options were to die now or die in a couple of days while the vampires had their fun.

"Then I take it you know your options."

"Either I do what you tell me to, or I die. It's as simple, and cliché, as that."

"What will it be, then?" Liam said with a hunger in his eyes that made my stomach turn again.

"Do I really have a choice?" I asked, trying to stall.

"You won't if you take any longer," he said, starting to sound annoyed.

"What benefit do I get out of the first choice?"

"Some pain relief, some love before your life fades from you. I guess the latter isn't exactly what you want since it's not coming from one of your wolves. Impressive, I might add, that you have two powerful alphas wrapped around your finger."

"I'm not screwing with them, if that's what you're getting at," I snapped.

Realization dawned on his face, "Ah, so you do have feelings for one of them, but which one?"

I didn't answer his question, prompting him to start tracing my jawline. He brought his gaze back to mine once again grinning at me, "Tick tock, Val. My patience, and therefore your time, is running out."

I clenched my jaws together as I closed my eyes. I didn't have to see him to know he was moving in. I could feel his lips brushing against mine as he whispered, "Good choice."

He crushed his lips against mine one more time while his hands wandered up my body. At first, I was getting angry at him for being able to take advantage of me in a situation like this, until the level of pain dulled. Liam was keeping his word and healing me.

When he finally pulled away, Liam grinned at me, "That wasn't so bad, was it?"

"I'm not a fan," I stated. "Tell me how this works. Do you have to kiss me every time?"

"It makes it go quicker, but no, I don't. That's more for my enjoyment."

"You bring pleasure and pain," I said, trying to think through the heavy fog clouding my brain.

"It's a blessing and a curse. Take this moment in time, for example. Does this all feel familiar?" he asked.

"Unfortunately, yes."

"The nightmares I send to people are a glimmer of their future. Of course I put my own spin on things, but that's how I was able to reassure Cian the time would come for him to exact his revenge on you," Liam explained.

"If you can see a little bit of other people's future, then did you see me killing any more vampires after the accident?" I asked, hoping the answer would be one that I could use to my advantage. If he saw the truth and can somehow project that to Cian, then I would be able to get out of this mess, and I would do just about anything for that to happen.

He looked away, "No, I didn't see any of that."

A part of me knew he was lying considering he couldn't look me in the eyes, but another part of me knew if I called him out on that, any chances of me making it out of this were gone.

Liam focused his attention toward the door before studying me again, "Any other questions?"

"What else can you do?" I asked. I shifted my tactics from being reactionary to trying to get things to work in my favor. Somehow getting Liam to fall for me using the "Val effect" Mark had explained to Chris was now my light at the end of the tunnel. If I could get him on my side, then I might be able to persuade him to let me out of here.

"In terms of powers, that's about it," he said slowly smiling. "If you're curious about other things, though, I'd be happy to show you during your stay."

"I only wanted to know about the powers, Liam. Do all vampires perform the same tricks?"

He hesitated with his answer clearly debating how much he wanted to tell me, "No, our abilities are unique to us except for a few things. We can all make you feel pleasure when we're feeding and erase any memories of that experience if we need to. We can all transport from place to place, and we can all create illusions like I did when you were strung up out there."

"Interesting," I said, trying to think of my next question.

"That's enough for today," he quickly said while wiping away more of my blood on one of my arms. He sucked it off his finger again before making his way to the exit leaving me alone once more.

I couldn't keep it together anymore. The sobs returned making the chains clank together serving as a reminder I had no way out on my own.

It felt like hours passed by, but there was no way of knowing for sure when there were no windows. Considering I wasn't hearing any footsteps, I was assuming it was daytime, letting me know I was going to be getting a break from any visitors for a while.

After being upside down for so long and letting the adrenaline wear off, I slipped back into unconsciousness again. I had no idea how long I was out until I was brought back to reality by feeling someone gripping on to me. My senses kicked in, forcing me to open my eyes to see Liam back in here. I jerked my body from his touch after being startled back to consciousness.

"Calm down, Val," Liam sounded annoyed. "I just have to flip you right side up. Apparently, we can't keep you upside down for too long."

When he set me on the ground with my feet under me, I crumpled, quickly dashing any chances I had to run for the door. Liam scoffed at the sight of me, "Looks like you're not going anywhere anytime soon. Cian will be happy to hear that."

"Shut up," I was tired of him rambling on.

He whipped around to me snarling, "Remember, this is a two-way street. The minute you stop catering to me is the minute I carry out my orders to end your life."

Liam kicked me in the ribs to solidify his point. I hadn't taken advantage of the lower pain levels before now as black dots danced around my vision as a result of feeling a couple of my ribs break again.

It was effortless for him as he picked me up from the ground and reattached the chains, this time with my feet pointed to the floor. Liam lined the freshly emptied and cleaned buckets under me in the same formation again, reminding me of what's headed my way.

"Have fun," he called over his shoulder. Liam made no effort to have a more in-depth conversation today like he did yesterday making me wonder if he got scolded for doing so.

My thoughts were soon interrupted by Cian marching his way into my torture chamber, "I see you managed to play nicely with Liam."

"Just get on with it," I said more confidently than I felt. This was the man who easily broke down my shields yesterday and I knew I had only seconds before he started again.

"Get on with it?" Cian laughed. "You had the pleasure of being knocked out for the first round of cuts, but know this isn't going to be a quick experience now that you can fully enjoy what's coming to you."

With that, he gave the first slice on the top of my thigh. The blade of the knife bit, but not enough pull a scream out of me like Cian was hoping for. He tsked his tongue in disappointment bringing the blade up to his mouth for another taste. Him and I stared each other down and when it was clear I wasn't going to look away, he got in my face, "I'm getting more pleasure out of this than I had hoped."

Another slice, this time near the ribs Liam just broke.

"Hm, not hurting enough yet?" Cian asked, throwing a punch into my stomach before I had a chance to respond. He repeated the motion until I started coughing up blood, but I wasn't going to give him the satisfaction of seeing me in pain like he wanted.

"You're not as easy to break as I thought you would be," he said. Then, his knife made quick work of my arms, following those motions with a few more punches.

"What happened to the woman sobbing before me yesterday?" he spit out clearly frustrated with my lack of response.

"She's gone," I choked out, my head rolling to one side.

Cian shook his head, "No. No she's not. Nice try."

He continued alternating between slices and punches trying to get me to scream. He almost gave up until I could no longer hold it in. He slowly dragged the blade across my broken ribs, blinding me with pain smiling as a blood-curdling scream ripped through the quiet cathedral.

"There it is."

"Happy?" I asked out of breath.

"More than you know," he said, turning away. The sound of footsteps carried down the hallway to the room I was in. It must be Liam coming in clean up after Cian.

Cian turned his head, his back to me, and said, "I hope you don't mind, but I brought you a visitor."

I had no idea what he was talking about as I was once again hanging there with my blood running down my body and adding to the buckets. The footsteps stopped when they reached my doorway, but I couldn't bring myself to look. He probably sent another one of his vampires to have some fun with me.

A hand reached out to cup my cheek and I jerked back again. I was getting tired of these vampires thinking they could take advantage of me while I'm hanging here helpless.

"Val, love," a familiar voice crooned. My eyes shot open to see Warrick's face filling my vision. Relief poured through me, a sob escaping my lips.

"Hey," he said, stroking my hair and wiping my tears. "It's all right."

"Please get me out of here, Warrick," I cried. "Please. You know it was Lou. You know I didn't have anything to do with what he did."

"Sorry, love," he said, turning my blood cold. "I don't know that I can trust that."

"Wh-what do you mean?" I stammered.

"It's all about who you know in this world and what side you choose. Clearly you choose to side with Lou."

Everything stopped, "What are you talking about?"

"It's hard not to think you were just using me this entire time as a distraction so you and Lou can continue sabotaging what I'm trying to work towards. Pretty ironic considering you seemed convinced *I* was using *you*. Let me paint a picture for you, love. I'm climbing up to the balcony looking forward to a night with the woman I couldn't picture my life without, especially after she was asking me about fating. I thought I finally made it. I was even going to clue you in on my next stop so you could happen to show up in the same place I did. Yet, everything came crashing down on me when I saw Lou's tongue down your throat," he curled his lip. "Were you just playing me? Just trying to get a good lay with the big, bad wolf?"

The tears started coming again. "No, Warrick," I sobbed. "Everything between us is real."

Warrick shook me out of frustration, "Don't you lie to me, Val! Don't toy with me now just because you're desperate to get out of a situation you got yourself into."

"I'm not," I cried out. "He let himself in my room and forced himself on me. That's what you were seeing. I promise."

"But I don't know if I can believe you," Warrick said quietly while shaking his head. "When I saw you two together in the early days of being in this place, you were all over each other. Nothing was going to separate you, so it's a little hard to convince me this wasn't all just an elaborate scheme."

His eyes traveled my body before landing on my face again, "Look where that's gotten you. I spent so much of my time, effort, and let myself open my emotions just to have you slap me in the face. So, imagine my surprise when Cian approached me last night informing me that you were bleeding out in the cathedral because you walked into a trap. I was so hurt by what I had seen that I couldn't keep my mouth shut when he started questioning me for the millionth time about his damn vampires."

"You told him it was me?" I asked in disbelief. "Why would you lie like that?"

"Great question, love. Why would I lie like that when my person lied to me? Why wouldn't I protect her? I wonder what would make me say something that would get her in a situation like this. Oh, wait," he snarled at me. "She decided to make out with the one person I can't stand."

My heart was ripping into a million shreds with every word he threw at me. No matter how much I tried to fight what was going on, he was never going to believe me. Instead of trying to stand up for myself, I let the sobs take over.

"You're just going to give up like that?"

"What difference does it make, Warrick?" I asked. "All you're going to see is what you convinced yourself of. I could beg you and plead with you, but that's not going to change what you've already made your mind up about. There's no amount of torture Cian and his crew could put me through that compares to the pain I'm feeling now."

Warrick studied me for a moment before shifting his weight and bringing his hands down to my side. I winced as they grazed the spot where Liam kicked me and where there was now an open wound. He stopped his movements, looking at me with concern, "Does this hurt?"

I nodded letting out a small whimper, "Yes. Please help me. I swear I'll make it up to you."

"And how would you do that?"

"Anything, Warrick. I'd do anything for you."

His eyes hardened, turning as cold as they've always looked. Yet, there was something there holding him back from whatever he was about to do that told me everything I needed to know about the conflict raging in his head. He was contemplating what I said and I thought I might actually have a way out of here.

"I don't know if I believe that, love," he said in the calm voice I've learned leads to nothing but pain. Warrick dug his fingers into the fresh cut from Cian making the edge of my vision blur as I screamed out. He dug his fingers into the cut further making me scream louder, begging for him to stop.

Each time I pleaded with him, he dug in even more, a growl ripping through his throat.

He finally stopped, giving me a chance to catch my breath, "Cian was right when he said you would make me lose focus. I can't believe I let myself fall for that."

Warrick turned like he was leaving and I knew this was my last chance to get him back on my side, "Choose me."

Those words made him freeze, so I kept going, "Choose me, Warrick. I'll help you with whatever you're trying to accomplish. I'll stand by you. Just don't leave me here to die."

He came back to where I was hanging, reaching towards the chains binding my hands making me think I might have gotten through to him only for Warrick to grip my hands with a crushing force.

"Sorry, love. You may have chosen Lou, but I've chosen my side, too," he whispered into my ear. He pulled away, "Thanks for the fun run."

Warrick turned to leave, slowly making his way out the door. "No!" I screamed after him following that with more begging and pleading. He turned to look at me one last time, a shadow of doubt crossing his face proving to me this was just as hard for him as it was for me despite what he said moments ago.

He ducked his head then walked in the direction he came in from. I couldn't stop the screams anymore. Gone was the last shred of hope I had, and out of any forms of torture Cian could throw my way, this was by far the worst.

I finally stopped screaming when my vocal cords were done and the only sounds coming out were squeaks. My head was pounding from all the tears streaking down my face, but that was nothing compared to the giant hole Warrick left in my heart. It was like I couldn't breathe anymore and any fight I had in me left as he walked out of the room.

When Liam came in slow clapping, I didn't bother to lift my head, so he did it for me, "What a performance. I didn't know what to expect when Cian brought Warrick here. If anything, I thought he was going to try to bust you out, but what he did was so much better than anything I could have imagined."

"Go away, Liam," I croaked out.

"Aw, don't give up now," he chided. "We still have so much to do."

I raised my head to look at him, narrowing my eyes and spitting in his face. I was tired of this. Tired of the games he was trying to play, tired of trying to find a way out of here, and tired of this mess of a life.

Liam wiped the spit away from his face, nodding his head while he figured out what his next move would be, "You're going to regret that."

I didn't care to respond anymore, and when he saw just how done I was, he yanked my head to one side and sank his fangs in me, an animalistic sound coming from his throat. He drank, slowly taking my life away from me. I closed my eyes, knowing he wasn't bothering with any of his parlor tricks to make this a pleasant experience.

Suddenly Liam was ripped away from me, Cian pinning him against one of the walls, "We're not done with her yet."

"You said I could make the call when I felt the time was right," Liam protested.

Cian hissed at him, "Well, the time isn't right. Fix her so we can get more blood."

Liam shrugged Cian off, bumping shoulders as he made his way to me. If Cian's comments had bugged him, he wasn't showing it. Instead, I got a bloody smile, "Pucker up."

His lips were back on mine, Liam clearly enjoying the fact he was able to take advantage of me even though he didn't need to be kissing me to heal me. He finished, slowly pulling away and resting his forehead against mine, "There will be a day when I miss this."

I had no energy to respond to his witty remarks anymore. There wasn't even any energy for me to lift my head to look at him, so he and Cian left.

He hadn't fully healed me this time as evidenced by the dripping still ringing out in the room, but my ribs were no longer broken and I could tell most of the cuts were gone.

I looked back up to my hands wondering how everything got so sideways. I laid low, did what I was told to do, and now I ended up hanging here like a piece of meat in a slaughterhouse. I started to feel the sweet embrace of unconsciousness creeping up my spine when the door banged open and Liam walked back in.

He held a glass to my lips and growled, "Drink."

"I'm not drinking any blood," my voice still hoarse from the screaming.

"It's water," Liam sighed. "Drink."

He pushed the glass into my lips, trying to force them open. When I wasn't budging, he reached up to force my mouth to open making me jerk my head away from him. I was tired of being touched by these monsters who only wanted to make me snap.

"She can be broken," he said sarcastically. "Look, you may be done with your life, but we're not, so you need to drink."

"I get to make those decisions, not you," I said angrily, completely forgetting about my plan to use Liam as my ticket out. I couldn't fight anymore.

"Oh, so she does show signs of life."

"Fuck off, Liam."

He threw the cup of water in my face out of frustration then threw the glass against a wall, "This is ridiculous. I'm not fecking putting up with this anymore."

Liam finally stormed out slamming the door behind him. I licked some of the water dripping down my face savoring the wetness on my tongue. *I shouldn't have wasted that.* I knew it would be a matter of moments before him and Cian came back in here to put an end to things with how he carried himself out of here.

"It's been a good run, Val, but I think we've finally reached our end," I said out loud to myself. "Gabriel, I hope you're ready to be reunited. Maybe we can finally love each other without interruptions."

The door slammed open, Cian leading the way with Liam behind him just as I suspected. Cian grabbed me by the throat and stabbed me with his knife multiple times not saying a word. Liam stood off to the side with his arms crossed wearing the same grin he did as the first time I saw him. *This is it.* Another thrust of the blade followed by Cian pulling my head back by my hair, "You want to die so bad, well here you go."

I let out a quiet laugh as he slowly pulled back the blade, delirious with the lack of blood and pain running through my body.

"She's insane, Cian," Liam said in disbelief.

"Take notes, Liam," Cian started. "That's what happens when you let love guide your decisions."

Out of all the ways I pictured myself dying, vampires wasn't one of them. *At least now I know how my story ends.*

Acknowledgements

I, uh, well? I'm writing this in disbelief - the fact I now have two books published blows my mind! I keep going back to my younger self who let doubt fill her mind, let the people telling her she can't, win. Well, to have been able to push aside that doubt not only once, but twice, is a major win. That win wouldn't have happened without some key people, though ...

Kyle, my amazing, wonderful, supportive, kind, loving (there's too many adjectives to describe you!) husband - you patiently sat with me a couple of years ago, listening as I rambled on about an idea I had for a book. You told me to go for it even when I kept asking, "Are you sure?" For that, I am so grateful. You've encouraged me to open my creative side back up after it was locked away for *years*. There are not enough thanks to express how I genuinely feel. Having your support makes me feel so incredibly lucky.

Thank you again, Mom! The fact that you were excited to get your hands on this second book to edit helped boost my confidence - my confidence in knowing I could write an engaging story and my confidence in knowing you would help strengthen this next piece. And, thank you for sticking through the spicier scenes even if you kept telling yourself your daughter wrote them.

To my family who kept asking me when they can read my books - thank you for your patience! You've had to deal with me telling you, "maybe next month" way too many times.

Thank you to the team at Miblart for cranking out the cover art that has helped bring some of these characters to life! I always let out a squeal when I get a new message letting me know I have some art to review because I know it's going to be everything I imagined and then some.

For all of my readers, I appreciate each and every one of you taking the time to read my books, deal with my constant teasing and lack of concrete dates, and for sticking with me as I got started. THANK YOU! You all are the ones making this possible and helping me live out my dream, and without your support, this dream would escape me like a balloon losing all its air before it could be fully blown up (noises and all). I already said it, but thank you times a million!

Thank you again for taking the time out of your busy schedule to shove the world aside and escape into *Blink and You Miss It*! I really hope you enjoyed it, and if you did, please leave a review!

Did you know?

Indie authors are small business owners (yay for supporting small businesses!). Reviews are our bread and butter, and mean the world to us. Fun fact – it takes **50 reviews** *minimum* for exposure on Amazon. The best way to support an author (after reading their book, of course) is by leaving a review, even if it's just a few words!

Thank you sooo so much for your support!

Want even more content? Check out my website and socials to be in the know for all the latest and greatest updates:

www.toriegwriting.com

www.facebook.com/toriegwriting

www.instagram.com/toriegwriting

www.goodreads.com/torie_gaylord

About the Author

Torie is a passionate adventurer who finds inspiration in the beauty of the outdoor world, especially in her backyard of Colorado. When not hiking through the mountains or torturing herself with running, she enjoys the company of her loving husband and their two cats, who serve as her trusty sidekicks as she types away . A lover of engaging storytelling, she often loses herself in a good book, movie/tv show, or video game. Eager to create her own worlds, Torie is excited to share her adventures through writing, inviting readers to embark on journeys of their own.

Read more at toriegwriting.com.